Helen began writing novels after retirement from teaching. She has just had published her first novel in a trilogy set in Victorian England, but her focus has always been the fifteenth century. She combined this with a love of Shakespeare and achieved a PhD from The Shakespeare Institute, Birmingham University, in 2009. Research for her thesis was on Warwick the Kingmaker in the three parts of Henry VI. Later, she wrote a quartet of novels on Warwick's life—Lodestar. During research for them, she came across Thomas Malory.

Dedicated to my grandchildren: Jack, Mylo, Lewis and Daphne.

Helen Lewis

# MALORY'S GRAIL

AUSTIN MACAULEY PUBLISHERS™

LONDON • CAMBRIDGE • NEW YORK • SHARJAH

A CIP catalogue record for this title is available from the British Library.

ISBN 9781398478824 (Paperback)
ISBN 9781398478831 (ePub e-book)

www.austinmacauley.com

First Published 2023
Austin Macauley Publishers Ltd®
1 Canada Square
Canary Wharf
London
E14 5AA

I would like to thank Professor Kate McCluskie for her continuing advice, support and encouragement.

# Table of Contents

# Prologue

In the darkness of the sick room, the doctor leaned over his sleeping patient. 'Rest easy, my friend!' he whispered in the man's ear. 'Your burden will soon be lifted.' The man in the bed remained motionless and unresponsive.

The bedchamber, its shutters closed, was one of two on the top floor of a small terraced house. Inside the room, the atmosphere was stuffy and airless; neither was there a chink of light, other than two candles in wall sconces on either side of the bed. A small table was covered in coloured bottles and vials of medicine. Downstairs, the wife of the patient had been ordered to avoid the sickroom at all costs, particularly since there was a young baby in the house who would be at great risk from the infection. 'I urge you to keep away, mistress, however much you would wish to minister to your husband. The contagion is particularly dangerous to children. It is just unfortunate your husband should have picked it up now when the child is most defenceless.'

'I am very grateful to you, doctor, and to our sponsor who has been generous in sending you to us. I'm sure my husband could not have better treatment!' The doctor bowed and took up his bag.

'I'll return in two hours and the nurse will be in attendance again tonight.'

'Thank you, doctor!' And the mistress of the house turned to her baby, anticipating another long and lonely evening.

\*\*\*\*\*\*

'I have good news, mistress. Your husband is making a very good recovery; much quicker than I anticipated. These infections generally run their course for at least a fortnight. It's eight days since he was struck down and I'm pleased to say that last night the fever abated; it will now be safe for you to enter the sick room. He is feeling very tired and weak, so I prescribe bone-broth and nourishing slops to start with. I think he can be allowed out of bed in two days. There will be no need for me return, so I will wish you good day and good luck!'

'But doctor, it seems he has recovered very quickly, considering your assessment was so grave when you first arrived.'

'As I say, his constitution is such that he has fought this dreadful disease with great vigour. You should be thankful for that!'

'Indeed, I am. Thank *you* for all your invaluable attention, and your master who sent you.'

'Lord Waurin wanted this to be an anonymous arrangement, under the maxim "doing good by stealth". He wrote the letter to you so that I might gain entry; but he would wish the matter to go no further. His lordship felt it was his Christian duty to help a good friend. He would rather you didn't thank him; he was just delighted to be of assistance.'

'But it seems churlish not to acknowledge that he—you—saved my husband's life. Most people die of measles, don't they?'

'Perhaps an exaggeration, Mistress Pickle. As I said, your husband is a strong man—stronger than he looks. But, if you really insist on thanking his lordship, although I am in haste I'll wait while you write a short note and take it to him myself. I have been ordered to report Mister Pickle's progress to Lord Waurin and he will be delighted to hear of his recovery.' Mistress Pickle nodded, found quill and paper and quickly wrote an effusive letter of thanks which she sealed and gave to the doctor as he waited, drumming his fingers on her kitchen table.

'I'll see this is delivered, Mistress Pickle. Now, I must be on my way back to Lille. I wish you good fortune and goodbye!' The doctor picked up his large leather medical bag and opened the door. As he walked through, he turned and said, 'It's been an absolute pleasure, mistress. An absolute pleasure!'

# Chapter 1

We catch up with great national events;
become reacquainted with old friends; briefly meet a key
character;
and hear of further devious plotting by those who should
know better.

April 1483 and the heavy bell of St Paul's tolls out across London to inform its inhabitants that their king: the large, lusty, greedy, gregarious, but sometimes contrary, Edward IV is dead.

'Do we know what he died of neighbour?' is the question on many lips today, especially in the taverns and inns of London.

'I heard it was an apoplexy from overeating,' says a butcher still wearing his slaughterer's apron and wiping his bloody hands on it before taking a long pull from his tankard.

'That's not surprising!' grunts another citizen who has come in off the street to idle a while.

'No, it was an ague picked up in the marshes of France years ago—you know, the shivering sickness,' says another speculator, draining his pot and wiping his mouth on his cuff.

'I've heard,' and, jug in hand, the potboy speaks in lowered tones, 'he was poisoned and probably by his relations who want to get their hands on the crown through their nephew, young Prince Edward.'

'Careful what you say, boy!' says an old soldier, looking around for spies and informers.

A man emboldened by his third pint says, 'I just hope we aren't going to suffer the same fucking problems there were after Henry V died, when all the relatives started fighting among themselves over who ran the country. To my mind, that was when all the troubles started.'

'Not many of us were alive sixty years ago to remember that, my friend. Anyway, young Edward's not a baby like Henry VI. He must be about twelve surely? Old enough to hold a sword and defend his right.'

'Thereabouts, neighbour. But what we can be sure of is that those bastard nobles will be fighting like cocks on a shit-heap for power again. Whoever holds the Prince of Wales holds the country.'

'Where is the prince? Does anyone know?'

A man across the room—for this conversation is taking place in Cheapside in *The Hog's Head*—a popular London tavern and a most natural location for an exchange of uninformed and speculative opinions—leans forward conspiratorially and says, 'Ludlow.'

'Where the fuck's that?'

'No idea, but he's there and with Earl Rivers.'

'You seem to know much, friend,' observes a customer who is standing at the table waiting for his tankard to be filled. 'What is your source of information?'

'I have a chapman friend who goes up and down the country and picks these things up. Believe me—Prince Edward—or should I say King Edward V—is safely behind the walls of Ludlow Castle waiting to come to London to be crowned. Once the old king's buried, Rivers will waste no time in bringing his nephew here for a coronation. Let's hope they're generous with the ale!' And the discussion of matters of great moment are held in abeyance as the communal and pleasing thought of free liquor circulates.

\*\*\*\*\*\*

The man at the bar, or at least his chapman friend, was correct. Edward V, yet to be crowned, was in the care of his maternal uncle, Anthony Woodville, Earl Rivers, who had seen fit to keep the boy safely out of the orbit of his paternal uncle, Richard Duke of Gloucester. The machinations of the Woodvilles and Edward IV's youngest brother were set to come into play the moment the old king took his last breath and hinged on the conditions as laid down in Edward's will. He had determined that, since his son was a minor, his son's protector and that of the realm should be Richard of Gloucester, who would head and control the king's council. The Woodvilles, with the prince in their hands, felt empowered to defeat Gloucester's claims and institute a Woodville-dominated majority on the council before Gloucester reached London, the duke being in the north when his brother died.

To that end, Rivers prepared to move down to London with young Edward and two thousand armed men at his back. Gloucester and his allies, the Duke of Buckingham and the Earl of Northumberland, could not be expected to arrive in London in time for a crucial council meeting dominated by the Woodvilles.

The complexity of these stratagems and plots went completely over the heads of most of the population, whose only concern was that they knew it would be their taxes which would pay for it all. 'It's always we poor bastards who fund their schemes and ambitions,' was the consensus in the market places and taverns. And it was in the same *Hog's Head* Cheapside that we find three of our old friends, late of Bruges, but now firmly re-established within the city walls of London.

\*\*\*\*\*\*

'What do you think will happen when Duke Richard reaches London, Pom?' Jack Worms sat back in his chair and wiped his mouth with the back of his hand. 'You always have a sensible opinion on these matters!'

'Honestly, Jack, I've given up trying to second-guess the nobility. So long as I can trade freely, make a little profit and hold a glass of good Burgundy in my hand, I try not to think about anything I can't control. And I'm certainly not able to control what's happening in Westminster! What do you think, Monty?' And he turned to his friend of long-standing who was sitting opposite and sipping slowly from a pot of Master Pegge's finest ale.

'Like you, Pom, I keep out of politics. Let them fight it out among themselves. I've seen so many changes, heard of so many fights, skirmishes and squabbles that I've forgotten all but the most notable! I'm more interested in Master Caxton's second edition of *The Canterbury Tales* which came out yesterday. You've done a fine job with the binding, Jack!'

'Thank you, Monty. I was rather pleased with it myself. But Caxton's told me that's only the first of Master Chaucer's works he plans to print this year. He said, and I quote, "Master Worms, prepare the shop, bring in supplies and roll up your sleeves. It's going to be a busy year for us all!"'

Monty laughed, 'Indeed, it is. Caxton's bringing out Chaucer's poem *Troilus and Criseyde*, probably by September. I'm so busy I don't know which way to turn. We have a mass of work planned, including the same poet's *House of Fame* and a second edition of Caxton's own *Game of Chess*. The second work he printed ten years ago—do you remember Jack? After the first-ever work in English—*The History of Troy*—an enormous book—almost as enormous as—as—' and he faltered and looked down into his ale with an expression of extreme sadness.

'I'll say it for you, Monty. As enormous as *Le Morte D'Arthur*,' and Pom looked equally miserable. 'I know we try to avoid thinking about it, even after ten years, but it still haunts us. The loss of the manuscript has been a cloud over our lives since it disappeared and with no trace. We've had the conversation so many times; I've been convinced for years, Jack, that your theory as to how it was exchanged for blank sheets is correct.'

'I know it was difficult to believe at first, but it is the logical explanation. The only person who had access to your room and on his own was when you were moribund with the measles and the elusive and mysterious Doctor Varder turned up on your doorstep—and I'm sure that was a false name.'

'It still beggars belief that someone should present themselves as a respectable doctor, claiming he was sent by a nobleman as an act of generosity; at the same time duping Gisella into believing he was the real thing.'

'Who do we trust? Doctors, of course, and you had been ill and Gisella was very worried. This man turning up at your door just at the right moment must have seemed like an act of God!'

'There are still many unanswered questions, like: "Was I really ill?"'

'We've already decided you were poisoned by him to make it look as though you had a fever, although how that was done I wouldn't speculate, but he was either very clever, very lucky or both! Remember, he only allowed a nurse into the sick room—whom *he* paid; so no one could verify it was the measles. He must have fed you copious amounts of opium to keep you asleep and unaware of what he was up to. After all, he spent eight days rummaging in your bedchamber looking for the key to the cupboard; then, when he found it, substituting the blank sheets for the real thing, which he carried out with him in his doctor's bag in broad daylight. It can be the only explanation. The question is, who was he and who sent him?'

'We were never able to check whether Lord Waurin was involved—which I'm certain he wasn't. Varder said he sent him but was very reluctant to allow Gisella to write and thank his lordship—although he took her note. Undoubtedly, it was never delivered. Unfortunately, when I did get around to writing, Lord Waurin had died earlier that month.'

'The most important question is where the manuscript is now,' Pom growled and looked around him suspiciously, as if one of the other customers might have it concealed about his person.

This discussion had been an intermittent feature of evenings nursing pots of ale in London taverns. The three men were now ten years older than when we were last acquainted with them and, all things considered, had aged gracefully.

Jack Worms, at the age of forty-two, was still a reasonable-looking man; tall and long-legged, he had retained his slender build and the neat beard he sprouted when he first arrived in France in '71, imagining it would be a useful aid to disguise. The Newgate Three had all, mistakenly as it turned out, considered themselves "on the run" from regal wrath— being entered on Edward IV's long roll of traitors who had supported the Earl of Warwick. Even when Jack was told they were too insignificant for the crown to concern itself with, he had retained the facial hair which he considered gave him gravitas

He had taken to the printing and publishing trade with great enthusiasm and his background as a stationer and book binder had been invaluable when he found himself in the right place at the right time in the Burgundy port of Bruges. Master Caxton immediately recognised his value and Jack had been with him from day one when the first press had been unloaded from carts driven all the way from Cologne. He had helped build and promote the press and had made a great friend of the gruff but knowledgeable young German, Wynkyn de Worde—or "Inkin' Wynkyn" as Jack affectionately called him because of the flourish with which the lad used the ink-balls to spread the essential liquid onto the type-face.

Jack was now settled in Westminster, having acquired a shop of his own which supplied stationery not only to Caxton. However, he was exclusively employed by the Westminster printer to bind his books and, such was the volume of work generated, even though Jack now employed three apprentices and a master book binder, the profits of the business were still gratifying. They had allowed him to purchase a small house off Ludgate Hill and honourable membership of the Stationers' Guild; there was talk of him becoming an alderman. Despite Gisella's efforts, he remained stubbornly unmarried.'She'd never have me; I stink of ink and paper too much!' he laughed, when Monty's wife remonstrated at his lack of gallantry towards one of her contenders.

And what of Pom? Now a robust and hale sixty-nine, he was established as a man of probity but one who drove a hard bargain; Mister Appleby's time in Bruges had also been highly successful. Pom had taken to trading with a will and, within two years, Caxton had put him in total charge of his mercer's business. He had always had good negotiating skills—forged in the fires of Newgate, where his old master and friend, Sir Thomas Malory, insisted he must always "get fucking value for our money, Pom!" when he went for supplies in the market. Down on the quayside of Bruges he used those transferable skills to Caxton's advantage and soon exhibited a significant increase of profits in the accounts. In return, Caxton allowed him to trade in his own right in furs since, as he said, 'You can annoy the Bruges furriers all you like—it has no effect on my business as I've always avoided that commodity.' The quality of furs from the Baltic was exceptional and very profitable. Suspicious and annoyed at first, the local fur traders were hostile, but Pom soon dispelled their antipathy by seeking their advice and never undercutting them. He would also take surplus from furriers when they miscalculated their ordering, and share goods when supplies were short. Within the year, he was accepted into the furriers' brotherhood and became equally well-liked by the garrulous but unintelligible Muscovy ship-owners and crews, who sought him out when they came ashore and with whom he would take a riotous drink—or three or six. Unlike Jack, who was still hedging his bets as to marriage, Pom had been a confirmed bachelor for over fifty-five years—since he first met Sir Tom and became his life-long friend and companion. He liked women, but much preferred the company of men— rough and smooth, labourers and gentlemen—so long as they were honest, partial to a decent wine and could tell a good yarn.

Their friend Montmorency Pickle still boasted a head of thick hair, but which in ten years had turned from mid-brown to a respectable shade of grey. His face showed the normal signs of ageing for a man in his mid-fifties; retaining an open, honest expression, and those characteristics were now joined by a look of contentment with his lot, although small creases of worry stemming directly from the shock of the loss of the manuscript hovered about the corner of his mouth and eyes. He had a deeply happy marriage to a woman he adored. Gisella was equally satisfied with the outcome of that adoration—three sturdy children, the eldest Thomas, in memory of Sir Thomas Malory, now a boy of ten, and twin girls of eight, Gisella—after her mother of course, and Isolde, named after one of the beauties in *Le Morte D'Arthur*. They were not identical in looks, one favouring the father and the other the mother, and with temperaments following each parent: Gisella thoughtful and quiet; Isolde voluble and outgoing. The three children were blessed in their godparents, for Jack and Pom concentrated any natural fatherly feelings they may have had on Monty's offspring. Pom particularly adored his three Pickle godchildren and was constantly scolded by their mother for spoiling them. 'How can I ever get them to bed on time when you excite them so much with your gifts and horse-play!'

Now a successful master compositor and transcriber Monty worked exclusively for Master Caxton in his Westminster print shop. He was instrumental in helping the now famous printer set up his works in Westminster after he decided to leave Bruges in the year '76. Caxton had called the Newgate Three—as they still styled themselves, even after leaving that austere place five years before—to his chamber in his house in Bruges and shared his plans with them.

'My friends, the time has come to introduce our processes to the English market. As you all know, it has always been my intention to publish my works, or as many as are suited to printing, in vernacular English. Clearly, there's no market for that in Burgundy and, if I wish to make a decent living here I must continue to publish in French and Latin. Therefore, I have made the decision—and it is a significant one—to move to London and as soon as possible. You, no doubt, now have many questions to ask and I will forestall some of them by offering the three of you the same positions in London as you occupy here. Master Worms, you can continue to work with Master Wynkyn de Worde—who will accompany us—producing our books and pamphlets. Mister Pickle, as my chief compositor, I wish you to continue in my employment—if that is satisfactory to your wishes. Mister Appleby, you are in a different position in that you have built up a successful trading business here, which has been profitable for us both. Whether you would wish to remain in Bruges and trade under your own auspices I leave for you to decide. When I arrive in England, I will be concentrating on the printing side of my enterprises and relinquishing the mercer business altogether.

But don't be dismayed; to my mind your contacts here are transferable to England, as are your trading skills. With a little help from me financially, I feel sure you could set yourself up as a merchant and reap success from all the knowledge you have gained here. I make these offers to you all as a mark of my gratitude for your loyalty and hard-work these last five years!'

There had been a stunned silence. It was not so much the unexpected proposal to move that surprised them, it was the expression of gratitude. William Caxton had hardly ever been known to praise or show personal regard to his employees. They were struck dumb and looked back at him, mouths agape.

As usual Pom was their spokesman. 'Thank you for those words of appreciation, Master Caxton—er—er,' and he hesitated and looked from Monty to Jack for agreement. 'I for one am grateful for your offer but would like a little time to consider all the implications.'

'Quite right, Mister Appleby. I wouldn't expect anything else from a shrewd business man.'

*More praise*! thought Monty. *Where will it end? Will he offer us more money, I wonder? Probably not*! He looked back at Caxton, 'I will discuss it with Mistress Pickle and give you an answer tomorrow, sir, if that will be all right?'

'Certainly, Mister Pickle. Shall we say ten in the morning?'

Jack said, 'I accept the offer Master Caxton. It will be a pleasure to return to England and I look forward to the reception you will receive when the Caxton press is unveiled. I feel sure it will be as positive as it was here in Bruges!'

'We shall see, Master Worms, we shall see! Now, with so much information to digest, I suggest you go away and have your discussions. But I shall want answers from two of you tomorrow. Good day gentlemen!'

'Brusque as ever!' muttered Jack as they found their way out onto the street.

'I wondered how long the politeness would last!' laughed Monty.

'Well, at least we know where we stand!' said Pom and directed them to the nearest inn where they could find a decent bottle of Burgundy and seal Caxton's approbation with a few stiff drinks.

\*\*\*\*\*\*

A character who looms large for a short time in this account was, on this day April 29th 1483 travelling leisurely east from Ludlow Castle in Shropshire towards Northampton, on his way to arrange the coronation of his nephew Edward V. Anthony Woodville, Earl Rivers, had much on his mind, not least the unexpected invitation to a meeting with the new king's uncle, Richard Duke of Gloucester, together with his friend the Duke of Buckingham, at a place on the way to London "Where", as Gloucester suggested, "we can join together and escort the young king to his coronation." Young Edward lingered behind with his own men while his Uncle Woodville rode forth to settle the rest of the journey to London "with kindly Uncle Gloucester".

Rivers was an experienced and intelligent man who never underestimated anyone, especially those in the Yorkist faction like Gloucester and Buckingham, who were generally hostile to the Woodville clan. *Mostly out of envy for our status at court which gives us more power than they approve of,* was his general summing up of the sometime-fractious atmosphere around the palace of Westminster. But, as far as the earl was concerned, matters were crystal clear. Edward IV had died and his legitimate offspring, his first-born son Edward Prince of Wales must inherit. *There can be no question of the boy's right—can there*?

'Where are we captain?' Anthony Woodville asked one of his chiefs.

'Close to the Duke of Gloucester's castle at Fotheringhay, three miles out of Oundle, my lord.'

'I would expect to meet with Gloucester and Buckingham and their entourages somewhere near here; no doubt they'll give us a noble escort to his castle.' As it happened, Richard Duke of Gloucester had already arrived in the village and soon the two parties linked up—River's men setting their camp outside the castle walls. The meeting inside the great hall was a little stiff, but courteous and with joint commiserations over their mutual loss. Then the party sat down to a decent dinner, and once the wine flowed, all was "cheerful and convivial", according to later reports anyway.

*Gloucester has obviously decided not to fight us Woodvilles for the place at the top end of the perch*! Lord Rivers concluded to himself, as his servant undressed him for bed in the chilly spartan chamber he had been allocated. *Let's hope the bed's warmer than the room and that breakfast will be as plentiful as the dinner*! His lordship may have considered himself an aesthete, but he still liked his creature-comforts.

But unfortunately, Rivers was never able to judge the breakfast at Fotheringhay for, before cock-crow, a unit of castle soldiers burst into his chamber and without due ceremony ordered him to dress and then, minus his boots, marched him down the stairs to the great hall. There was no sign of either Gloucester or Buckingham. Within minutes, he was behind the stout door of the castle lock-up, out of earshot of his servants and his men.

Now, Rivers was well-known for a thick streak of religious zeal, which ran through him like yellow fat in a joint of good English beef—hence his frequent disappearances on pilgrimages to southern Spain in search of improvement to his soul—and the wearing of a hair shirt. He was certainly not given to inelegant oaths. But on this occasion, he gave way as he banged fruitlessly on the heavy door. 'Fuck it! The man's nothing but a renegade traitor! I've been duped!'

\*\*\*\*\*\*

News of this duplicity reached London in the night of 30<sup>th</sup> and the citizens awoke next day to hear that Richard of Gloucester had arrested Lord Rivers and the earl was being held "somewhere in the midlands".

One man who was particularly perturbed by this information was William Caxton. He had a great respect for Lord Rivers, not least because the earl had been one of his earliest patrons. They had met in Bruges when King Edward was in exile there in the year '70, and later, when the printer had returned to England, the bibliophile earl was the first to present a work for the master to work his magic on. Earl Rivers' own translation of the *Dictes or Sayings of the*

*Philosophers* was printed by Caxton's own hand and then beautifully bound by Jack Worms, who for many months afterwards brought it up in conversation—however irrelevant.

'I wish Jack would get over the business with Earl River's book and give our ears a rest!' was Pom's eventual sour comment.

Later this day Monty was busy in the printing shop when his master entered looking grave.

'This is a desperate business, Mister Pickle!' And Caxton, who rarely spoke of politics or matters of national moment, shook his head, 'I believe we are heading for another civil war—this time not the Lancastrians versus the Yorkists, but the Woodvilles versus the Yorkists. I take it you've heard what happened after River's arrest? No? Well, I'll tell you what *I've* just heard. The Duke of Gloucester moved onto a place close-by called Stony-Stratford and took charge of the young king, who was staying at the local inn; then he dismissed all Edward's personal attendants. After that he had the young king's half-brother Richard Grey arrested, along with his treasurer. At least, that's what's circulating.'

'If all this is true, what do you think the duke is planning, sir?'

'It's obvious! He's clearing out all the close relatives and friends of the new king and making sure he becomes protector, not only of the boy but of England. I do hope my friend Lord Rivers is being treated well, Mister Pickle, although I rather doubt it. He's a clever man and a great supporter of literature. He has a splendid library you know.'

'Indeed, Master Caxton. The Duchess of Burgundy was fulsome in her praise of the earl's collection—as one who loves books herself. After she'd read Sir Tom's manuscript, she wrote to King Edward recommending that it might be of interest to Lord Rivers—although I would never have sold it, certainly not until copies were made and I could fulfil my obligation to Sir Tom and hand the original to the monks in Winchester.'

'Yes, that was a very sad business. Just as I was seeing my way clear to looking at it for printing, it was stolen from under your nose, as I recall. Have you heard of it since? Has it come up for sale? You know, someone has it on their shelves and must be pondering what should be done with it. I wouldn't be surprised if it doesn't appear in my printing shop one day. Surely whoever has it wants to benefit from it—if only financially. Perhaps they are tampering with the text to pass it off as their own!'

Monty blenched, 'Master Caxton, that is my worst nightmare! When I think of the two years' work that went into those eight hundred pages, my heart races and my head thumps with the idea that someone would alter them and claim them for himself.'

'Well,' and Caxton frowned, 'it's strange that it has not appeared since then—ever!'

'It's been ten years next November since we discovered it was stolen and, as you know, we think it was taken in January of that year.'

'Have you still no idea who was behind the theft?'

'There is a name which occurs to me, but I think he would have stolen it to order; to gain financially, not to keep it for himself.'

'Well, looking at it logically, there are very few people with private libraries who might want it, all noblemen—Earl Rivers being the best known. You said that Duchess Margaret

29

thought he would be interested in *Le Morte D'Arthur*. Did she get as far as sending it to him?'

'No Master Caxton, she respected my obligation; but she went so far as to suggest I might take the manuscript to London and supervise it while the earl perused it. But it didn't happen.'

'But do you know if the king passed on the information? Was the earl interested? Did he actually know of it?'

'I have no idea sir.'

'Another interesting question, Mister Pickle, is what will happen to the earl's famous library if he's beheaded?'

'Beheaded sir! Surely young King Edward wouldn't sign a death warrant for his own uncle! On what grounds would he do that?'

'Don't have to be any, and it's been done many times before. I think you're being somewhat naïve; especially when you think of the state of English law and order, and even more especially among the nobility in the last thirty years. There won't be any death warrant; if the Duke of Gloucester sees fit he'll have the man executed quietly—and probably with other members of his family. That's why I fear another civil war. But I return to my question, Mister Pickle, what happens to Lord River's books in the event he's minus his head and can't read them anymore?'

\*\*\*\*\*\*

While this worried conversation is taking place, let us consider what has become of the last two of the Newgate Five. Twelve years before in the summer of the year '71 we left Sir Anthony Tanner and his lady, Margaret, viewing the English

Channel several miles from the port of Honfleur. What happened to them in the following twelve years requires a separate detailed account which is not the business of this one. It is enough to say that they did not immediately return to England, as was Meg's great wish; for Six-toed Tony was reluctant to risk his head and other treasured parts of his anatomy, not knowing if he was still on a "most wanted" list of those who had followed Lord Warwick and his treasonable actions.

'Magpie,'—he always referred to her pet name when he wished to wheedle an agreement out of her—'Magpie, we should rest in Honfleur for a few weeks while I send letters across to England and find out what my situation is. I have friends who can make discreet enquiries around the court for me. It will only mean deferring our voyage for a short time. I'd rather be safe than sorry; would you still love me if I had no head, or are other parts of me more important?'

Margaret immediately dismissed the image of a headless husband and inwardly cussed. She was very disappointed with this suggestion, for she had regarded their return to London with acute anticipation. She was tired of wandering in these damp and gloomy borderlands of northern France. She had camped out at night in singularly wet weather; had been captured by a robber, albeit a very polite and gentlemanly robber; held eight days for ransom, in which time she had found it necessary to undertake some extremely tiresome housework. This was for her own domestic comfort; the place she was held being of a poor standard of hygiene and cheer. They were then back on the road for what seemed like weeks.

However, she had to agree, their reception back in England was uncertain and Honfleur wasn't such a bad place.

After all, it was where they were married last St George's Day at St Martin's church, when they had still been "the Newgate Five" and shared adventures on road and ocean. Added to which there were tempting inducements offered by her husband.

'We'll put up in a decent place where you can enjoy the bath you've been craving. I'll also buy you the Spanish leather boots—'

'—And the gown, and the hat!'

'Indeed, everything I promised. Once I've written to England and determined my position with King Edward, we'll visit the cobbler and dressmaker together—and I don't say that lightly since I have no liking for such activities!'

Consequently, they spent a pleasant fortnight in Honfleur, where they caught up with the priest who had married them in St Martin's church and entertained him with stories of their adventures since they left the seaport in April. One thing they did not tell him was how Tony had raised the cash to pay Meg's ransom by robbing the Church. As liberal and jolly as the priest was, this, they thought, would not be well-received. 'I had to think on my feet, father!' was all Tony would say when pressed. Fortunately, the priest was shrewd enough not to enquire too deeply. He just said, 'Should there be anything you wish to confess, my son, my confessional is always open!' Tony never took advantage of the offer.

After nineteen anxious days, letters came from England via a Southampton sea-captain.

'Magpie—there's good and bad news. Which would you like to hear first?'

'Let's get the bad news out of the way and then dilute with the good!'

'I fear you're not going to like it!'

'Nevertheless, just tell me.'

'Very well. I'm afraid we must stay in France for a little while longer.'

'How little is little?'

'It might be two or three years, or even more.' There was a silence which said more than words. Then Meg said, faintly, 'And the good news?'

'I'm back in favour with King Edward. Listen Meg, he wants me to be an agent for him at Louis' court. When I wrote to him I explained what we've been doing and how in our travels I'd picked up much useful information about what is occurring here. I put some of it in a report and I think that is what swung Edward my way. His letter is most courteous, and he acknowledges as correct what I pointed out—that for years I was a loyal and faithful servant to the Yorkist cause—helped him to the throne—and that, as I was a retainer of Lord Warwick, I had sworn a sacred oath to serve him. He also agrees that my experience is "invaluable"—his word—and that, rather than waste a talent by having me hunted down and beheaded for treason, as some in the court had urged, he would take me at my word: that I'm a loyal servant of England and the crown and willing to work for my country.' He stopped to draw breath and looked quizzically at his wife. Again silence. 'Come Meg, say something—even if it's profane!'

'What do you want me to say, Anthony? You have me in the same corner as you are. The king himself has ordered you to stay and, unless I return to England alone, I have no more choice than you. But I can't say I'm happy. I miss my friends and London. How long will we really be away, and will we be able to visit England whenever we like?'

'It will be difficult for me to be seen going backwards and forwards; it would certainly generate suspicion in the French court.'

'Another thing—how will we live—where will we live? We know King Louis moves about; will we be part of his court—or on the side-lines? Will we have permanent lodgings? How will you be paid—?'

'Too many questions, Magpie! These are not insurmountable problems— I've been doing this kind of thing all my life.'

'Yes, but you weren't married—therefore able to move freely as it suited you. I will be a halter round your neck.' She fell silent, then she said with a sigh, 'I always knew this would happen one day, but I hoped it would be in England, and when you were absent on your missions I would have the comfort of friends—and—and—', she faltered.

'And what?'

'—A family.' This time Tony was silent. Like Meg, he had known this situation would arise eventually, but they had never really discussed it. Tony did not like to think about it as he had no solution and was never good at facing insoluble domestic problems. Meg, with a woman's intuition that the subject would possibly cause an argument, had been thinking it through since they were first married, but not shared her thoughts with Tony. There was no better time to do it than now.

'Anthony,' she always called him that when she wished to engage his mind on a serious matter, 'I would like children—and I'm sure you would like a son at least, to continue the Tanner line. We must talk about this and come up with a strategy which will satisfy us both. I recognise that you are now under the orders of the king and must obey them. I accept also we must stay in France. I do not accept that this means the postponement of children and, if I am to stay here with you, we must have settled lodgings where I can raise them while you pursue your quest for King Edward. Just be careful and don't get caught; you know better than most the risks of spying for one country in the court of another. I don't want to be the widow of a spy and left to languish in a foreign country.'

'Lady Tanner, the last thing I would do is take risks which jeopardised your life—or that of any children we might have. I promise you we can make this work and I will continue to do everything I can to make you happy. Of course I would like a son—and a daughter, as beautiful as her mother—and I understand that to accomplish it we must have a settled home; somewhere to which I can return.'

'I take you at your word, husband, and, if you really mean it, write to King Edward and thank him. For my part, I will take lessons in advanced French and learn to adapt to their cooking!'

*What a woman*! he thought. *There's no one like her*!

\*\*\*\*\*\*

'There's still no one like her, Pom!' Sir Anthony Tanner was of the same opinion twelve years later when he and Meg returned to England for good. It was mid-May in the year '83.

'It's good to hear that, Tony, and good to have you both back with us!' Pom sat back on the tavern settle and viewed his friend with a shake of his head. 'We're all a little older, but you seem to have weathered it better than most—still have that thick black thatch and you've kept your figure—still exercising I suppose. You must do in your business. Unlike me who spends too much time in the tavern haggling with traders!' It was true, Pom was now a portly old man, with a drinker's nose—small broken veins mapping out the self-indulgence. 'We've received many letters from you over the years, and you've made the odd visit, but, discreet as always, you gave us no idea what you have really been about in France all these years. We thought you might have been turning into a Frenchman! So, tell us, what have you really been doing— besides raising two lusty sons!' And he looked at the two young boys sitting next to their father. 'There's no doubt whose boys they are—both like you—at least, the same ears! Do Lionel and Richard have all their toes?'

'Twenty between them, Pom! But, as for my missions for King Edward, that's too long to tell and perhaps now is not the time. However, Meg and I have much to tell you all about our family, especially the boys and would rather do it over supper tomorrow, when we have settled into our lodgings. For now, I want to hear about the doings of the Newgate Three and matters in England. We've been travelling for over a month and have only had snippets. I'll be at Westminster Palace tomorrow to report to whoever's in charge, but until you tell me, I don't know who it is—Gloucester or the Woodvilles?'

\*\*\*\*\*\*

An interesting question and one to which many Englishmen and women would have liked the answer. In response to the Duke of Gloucester's seizure of her son, the young king's mother Queen Elizabeth immediately took sanctuary in Westminster Abbey with her younger son Richard Duke of York and his five sisters. Despite the assurances from her brother-in-law that his nephew was "perfectly safe with me", her grown-up sons from her previous marriage, and her remaining brothers—with others in the "Woodville group"—thought about raising an army to "liberate" the young king; but the inherent dislike and suspicion the Woodvilles had always engendered among others in England's nobility left them without sufficient support and the plot came to nothing. Indeed, certain of the group saw the writing on the wall if they would come into the clutches of Gloucester or Buckingham. Elizabeth's younger brother Sir Edward Woodville smartly boarded a ship of the English fleet, having first accessed the nation's treasure chest and plundered a third of it, and took himself off into the Channel. Others of the Woodville faction remained in the country trying to whip up enthusiasm for a gesture of opposition.

One afternoon, about the same time these momentous events were occurring around them, Meg was sitting in Gisella's parlour, having become well-acquainted with Monty's wife; they had rapidly become friends. 'The woman has great fortitude and a real love of life!' was Gisella's favourable summing up to her husband after three days in her company. Besides, they had children of similar ages to discuss and compare. Gisella's eldest child Thomas was just seven months older than Meg's eldest, Lionel—or Leo as he was known. Tony's second son Richard—Dickon—was fifteen months younger than his brother. Thomas' twin sisters were nine years old. The five children were in the early stages of finding their places in the pecking order of friendship. It was quickly established that Leo, by far the most confident was the natural leader. Both he and Dickon had a much wider experience of the world than the Pickle children; both boys could speak fluent French and had been around Louis' court and the company of soldiers since they were born. Although tall for their ages and certainly robust in action, fortunately neither were of the bullying kind, and Thomas was somewhat in thrall to Leo, lapping up the often-exaggerated experiences he shared of the Tanners' life abroad. In return, Thomas guided them through the streets and alleyways of London, pointing out the dangerous areas where it was inadvisable to walk alone, or even in pairs. Neither set of parents were aware of where exactly young Thomas roamed with his new friends and would have been extremely concerned had they realised. But the boys were all quick-witted and not incapable of defending themselves—certainly against boys of their own age who occasionally challenged these interlopers who dared to infiltrate their "patch". The Tanner boys had the advantage of a soldier for a father. But Pom had spent many hours with Thomas teaching him the rudiments of self-defence and, although of only medium height, "Young Tom" was sturdily built and, as Pom reported to Monty, 'The lad's strong for his age.' The mothers, having become firm friends, were delighted that their children seemed to be "getting along".

The talk was all about the plotting and conspiracies which swirled around Westminster like an autumn whirlwind and, as with any such excitable draught, it gathered up the dry leaves of speculation and rumour and barrelled them out into the streets, where they were idly scattered and carelessly picked over by the populace, including the two ladies sitting in Gisella's parlour on a pleasant day in early June.

'So, what's happened to the young king?' asked Meg.

'Nobody's sure. He was seen on 4th May when he entered the city with Gloucester and Buckingham and about five hundred men. Mayor Robert Billesdon and the aldermen went outside to Hornsey to greet them and escort them formally into the city. We heard afterwards that it was quite a sight!'

'What do you mean?'

'Well, the mayor and aldermen were all in their scarlet robes, and five hundred of the most important citizens turned up wearing violet—most colourful. But both dukes were wearing black and looked very sombre.'

'Was that significant?' asked Meg.

'Yes, as it turned out. It seemed that they wanted to make a serious point. They'd brought with them four cartloads of weapons which they said they'd seized from Earl Rivers and which bore his insignia.'

'Well, you said he had set out with the young king and two thousand armed men—that must have been part of their supplies, surely.'

'You would think so, but Gloucester turned it around and said it was clear proof that Rivers was planning to kill him and Buckingham.'

'Did the aldermen believe him?'

'Some did, but he made them all swear an oath of fealty to the young king—which I suppose he thought would allay any suspicions about grabbing the crown for himself.'

'I suppose it would. Tell me, Gisella, how do you know all this? You obviously take a real interest in what's going on!'

'I'm more interested than Monty. I try to get at the truth rather than the gossip, but that's almost impossible. I read what's posted up on the market cross, but no one really knows what's happening, although there was an official announcement the other day that the coronation is set for Sunday 22$^{nd}$ June and that the Duke of Gloucester is appointed Protector of England. So he got what he wanted!'

'Tony and I have spent twelve years in and around the court of King Louis. I thought that was a devious place—but it seems politics in England is as bad or worse!'

'I lived in Burgundy until seven years ago—and it was the same. These powerful men all bicker and fight to be top dog.'

'Where is Lord Rivers now?'

'Held in a fortress somewhere in the north with his nephew, Lord Grey. We never hear the full story—just gossip, so it's hard to know the truth—who's right and who's wrong.'

'It seems to me these men are just greedy—like all of them!' laughed Meg. 'I've had plenty experience of that!' Lady Tanner had been open and frank with her new-found friend. Gisella Pickle had been privately shocked at first when she heard, from Meg's own lips, the lady's history. But when she had listened to the full tale, which was not uncommon, of a woman falling on hard times and her only recourse to use her body to sustain herself, she, being a warm-hearted and emotional lady, took Meg to that sympathetic bosom and made no judgement about her, other than admiration for all she had been through.

'So, what will happen next?'

'We wait to see, Meg! If Gloucester keeps his word, then the young king will become King Edward V on 22nd June.'

'You say "if". Is there doubt?'

'There's always doubt with these so-called "gentlemen". If I could wager, which Monty has strict views about, then I wouldn't put money on a coronation!'

\*\*\*\*\*\*

'On person who won't be at the coronation is Lord Hastings!' Monty looked up from his desk, quill in hand as he struggled with transcribing a particularly poorly written script, to see Jack Worms in the doorway waving a scrap of paper. 'I found this posted up on a fence—a declaration that his lordship no longer wears his head, which has been summarily chopped off on Tower Hill—no trial. Gloucester is having it put about that the man was a traitor and plotting treason with the queen and her family. And so it begins!'

'What begins?'

'Do keep up, Monty; Gloucester's bid for the throne of course!'

'How can that be—the young king's due to be crowned in a week's time!'

'All things are possible when the king is a minor with numerous greedy uncles circling. I wouldn't give that poor boy any chance of reaching thirteen. Then there's his brother to consider.'

'Well, Richard of York's safe enough with his mother in sanctuary. No one can get at him there, surely.'

'Don't you believe it. Sanctuary's not always inviolate, whatever people believe. There have been many examples where it's been broken.'

'Tell me of one then—you seem to know about these things—although why you're so interested when we have this mountain of work to get through is a mystery to me, Jack!'

'Well, let's see, ah yes, I do know of one! In the year '71, at the same time we were settling in Bruges, after the Battle of Tewkesbury, Edward IV forced the sanctuary of the abbey there and hauled out the Duke of Somerset—promptly had him convicted of treason and executed on a scaffold in the centre of the town. You must remember that, Monty. It was Somerset who cleaved in our great friend Lord Wenlock's head at the same battle, even thought they were supposed to be on the same side. Anyway, Tony Tanner will know more than us. He's been at the council meetings recently watching what's been unfolding. He told me everyone present was taken completely by surprise when Hastings was hauled out in front of them and accused. We all thought he was Richard of Gloucester's friend. But in these times, nothing's certain, not even loyalty. I think it's all fascinating stuff!'

'You may think so, but we've seen it all before; these struggles of the nobility to put their arses on a wooden seat which is, bluntly speaking, very mundane-looking and hardly regal.'

'Edward the Confessor's Chair is sacred—it's got—er—bottom!'

'Bottoms on it—I like the joke and Pom will enjoy it too. We'll talk these so-called important matters through this evening, no doubt, when we all meet at your house. More important, I have something to bring up which I need

42

everyone's opinion about—and I don't mean who should put their arse on the throne of England!'

# Chapter 2

We are reacquainted with the whereabouts of *Le Morte
D'Arthur*;
National events begin to impact on the Newgate Five
and
Caxton has his say

And what of this manuscript, *Le Morte D'Arthur*? Sir Thomas
Malory's *magnum opus* and which, aside from his family,
means so much to Mister Montmorency Pickle—and to a
similar extent, Mister John Appleby and Master Jack Worms.
Our knowledge of its first confirmed whereabouts since it was
stolen in January '73 is in the following September, where it
sat on the magnificent oak desk of Anthony Woodville Earl
Rivers, in his London lodgings in Westminster and still
wearing his noble head.

'This was a valuable purchase, Mister Dymock!' And
Rivers carefully turned the top, rather scruffy page of a pile
of papers. 'I wish I knew where Doctor Makepeace found it
exactly and under what circumstances. How did it get from
Newgate to the continent? He was very vague about it when I
spoke to him; seemed in a hurry to get away—but I suppose
he's a busy man. Anyway, I couldn't grumble about the price.
It's well worth £20!'

'If you say so my lord,' and Andrew Dymock sighed inwardly. *Really*, he thought, *was this the time to be reading French romances when there was important works of state to be tackled? Besides, the man's very short of cash and debts are mounting.* As Rivers' attorney and administrator, anything which distracted his master from the business in hand was to be deplored. The earl had just been appointed governor and ruler of the Prince of Wales, now almost two years old, and there was a proposal that they should all decamp from the convenience of Westminster and head for that grim pile of grey stones in Shropshire—Ludlow Castle. Dymock had no love for anywhere outside the capital, considering the inhabitants beyond the city walls as barbarous and backward-looking. *Bumpkins all*! was his conclusion, and the idea of spending winters in a damp fortress in the middle of nowhere, and too close to the Welsh, was disagreeable to say the least.

However, he knew where his duty lay. 'Will we be taking the—er—manuscript with us, my lord?' Like all well-trained servants, he always used the personal pronoun plural when addressing his master with a suggestion or a question. It had a regal yet comfortingly collegiate feel about it.

'No, Andrew, I think it has travelled enough. I would like you to send it with Butside down to our property, The Mote in Maidstone. I shall give the matter some thought while I'm in Ludlow as to what I should do with it. I would really like to have it copied expertly—perhaps illuminated; the subject matter would lend itself well to colour, don't you think?'

'Indeed sir,' said Dymock noncommittally. 'I will see to the matter immediately. Then sir, can we consider the travel arrangements for yourself and the young prince. I take it we will be accompanied by appropriate nurses?'

'Certainly, the child will need the correct care. His mother, my sister, will oversee that.'

'The queen is certainly experienced in these matters, my lord!'

'Yes, six children in seven years does seem—er—er—'

'—Productive, my lord?'

'Fecund would have been my choice, Andrew! Having no children of my own, I can only wonder at the king's—er—um—'

*Spit it out, man*! thought Dymock, *don't be shy! What you mean is lechery. Anyway, it's not true you don't have a child. What about the fruit of your loins with your mistress Gwentilian—Margaret you called her. I know your paramour is married and out of the picture, but have you forgotten her*? But he did not say it; instead, emollient as ever, he suggested, '—Energy sir! I think that's the word.'

'Yes, as good as any. But we digress. Have Butside sent to me and I'll give him instructions for the manuscript to be entered in my catalogue of works and stored safely in Kent.'

Within days, his wishes had been carried out and Rivers' loyal and trusted steward, James Butside, made the journey to that splendid town of Maidstone and the queen's estate of The Mote, which she had granted to Rivers for his use. There he handed over *Le Morte D'Arthur* to the steward of the place. *I don't know what it's about—but it weighed a fucking ton*! was Butside's blunt conclusion as, with relief, he turned his horse's head back towards London.

\*\*\*\*\*\*

'*Le Morte D'Arthur* is what I wanted to talk about!'

'What more is to be said, Monty? It's gone—no trace. Nothing's been heard of it for ten years. If anyone was going to hear of it, it would be either of us. There's no one more prominent in the book trade in London!' Jack sounded exasperated. How many times had they been over this— Monty would not let it go. 'I know you took an oath to deliver it to the monks in Winchester, but it wasn't your fault it was stolen. You did everything to keep it safe. The fact that a clever caitiff—'

'—I still say it was Crosby!' growled Pom.

'Have you any evidence?' asked Tony Tanner, who was sitting at the end of Jack Worms' supper table in his lodgings in Ludgate. There were six of them: Tony and Meg, Monty and Gisella, Jack and Pom. This was the first occasion since Sir Anthony and Lady Tanner had returned that they had all been together. There had been much talk of national events and catching up with each other's doings over the past years. But Monty wanted to raise the subject of the manuscript in consideration of his conversation earlier in the week with Master Caxton.

Tony had leaned forward when he heard the name "Crosby". 'That's an interesting notion, Pom.'

'Who else could it be. We all know he chased after us out of London and tried to steal it by devious means when we were on our way to Winchester. The fact that he disappeared doesn't mean he lost interest. There's no one else I know of who might be interested, or who even knows about *Le Morte*.'

'But there is, Pom! That's why I raise it again. Caxton told me that Earl Rivers has been collecting manuscripts and

47

translating them. We all know that his works have been printed in the Westminster printing shop—'

'—And bound very expertly by me!' said Jack, examining his fingernails insouciantly.'

Pom quickly interrupted, 'So what? Everyone knows about it.'

'You remember how the Duchess of Burgundy recommended Sir Tom's work to her brother-in-law—back in the year '71, and how she wanted to send it to him?'

'But you wouldn't let it go, Monty!' said Pom approvingly.

'No, but Earl Rivers must have heard of the work and knew how highly the duchess viewed it. I'm sure he would have liked to have got his hands on it somehow.'

'Are you suggesting he put Peter Crosby up to stealing it for him?'

'It's possible.'

'But Rivers has a reputation as a very pious man. He goes on pilgrimages to the Mediterranean lands—wears a hair shirt!' said Jack, raising his eyebrows. 'Surely he would be above theft?'

'Caxton says he's an avid collector. He might do anything to get his hands on a unique document like *Le Morte*.' Monty had gone quite red in the face, and Gisella recognised it as a signal he was getting annoyed. She immediately stepped in to calm matters.

'I think Monty has a point. Some men are so determined they'll stop at nothing to get their way. Master Caxton seems to think Lord Rivers is such a man. Despite his so-called piousness, he might turn a blind eye to stolen goods if they are presented to him.'

'Yes, and there's another thing,' and Monty warmed to his theme. 'Rivers is one of a very few noblemen who has a library and is permanently in the capital. I've done a little research on the man. He has very few landed estates—surprisingly considering he's the queen's brother. Most of his money comes from his offices of state. He has interests in properties in East Anglia and a manor in Kent; otherwise his main domicile is Westminster.'

'So, why does that matter?' Jack asked.

'Putting it all together, we have a man who is a bibliophile; is in touch with literary matters in the capital; has knowledge of *Le Morte* indirectly through the Duchess of Burgundy and myself, and which other noblemen with a similar interest probably do not. Put that together with the caitiff Peter Crosby and his master Robert Stillington—who has or must have had direct contact with Lord Rivers, and I think there is the basis for further enquiry at least!' He sat back in his chair with a triumphant look on his face.

Tony said, 'Where does Stillington come in? I thought he was well out of the official picture. Wasn't he imprisoned a few years ago?'

'It gave me great pleasure when I heard that!' laughed Monty. 'After he chopped off my little finger, I had no liking for the man!'

Jack, who took note of these things said, 'He was only there for a few weeks. Something about him putting rumours around that Edward IV had been married before he met Elizabeth Woodville. If that had been the case, then the Duke of Clarence should be heir to the throne as the king's brother—Edward's children being bastards. Nothing came of it, but we all know what happened to Clarence…'

'—Drowned in a butt of wine, so they say,' sighed Pom. 'What a waste! Still—it was Malmsey and not the good stuff!'

Jack frowned at the unnecessary interruption, 'And Stillington was released and has wheedled his way back into favour. He was certainly still in touch with Rivers until a few days ago, because he worked for the earl on the young king's council. Which begs the question, if Rivers is mouldering in a midland's castle and the young King Edward is in the care of the Duke of Gloucester, what's happened to the other members of that council? Stillington must be very worried indeed now Richard of Gloucester's in charge. As Edward IV's youngest brother, Gloucester's loyal to his family and wouldn't take kindly to anyone casting vicious rumours about the king.'

'Well, as far as I remember, at the time the manuscript was stolen in January '73, if I'm right and it was the so-called Doctor Varder who was the culprit, then Stillington was still Lord Chancellor and in a powerful position at court. Crosby was still his secretary I imagine.'

'So, you think Stillington and Crosby plotted the theft because they found out Lord Rivers would pay good money for the manuscript?' Pom still looked doubtful. 'The question is, who approached whom—did Rivers ask them to do it after he heard of it from the Duchess of Burgundy, or did they do it and, knowing he was one of the most important book collectors, offer it for sale?'

'I'm not sure it matters now,' said Monty firmly. 'I just think that the manuscript is with Lord Rivers—I feel it in my waters!'

'Gut feeling's no good, Monty!' said Tony with a shake of his head. 'We need to investigate this and the first thing to do is track down Crosby, get him by the bollocks and squeeze them 'til his eyes pop—begging your pardon ladies! That'll get the truth out of him.'

'Nicely put Tony!' laughed Jack. 'But how on earth do you think we can trace him after nine years or so?'

'I think—like flies stick to shit—Crosby will stick to Stillington. Find that caitiff and we'll find his creature.'

Meg thought it time the women were heard. She knew enough about devious men and how to deal with them! 'As Jack pointed out, we don't know what's happened to him since Rivers was arrested and the boy-king brought to London. Stillington could be anywhere. The question is, is he still in favour and who does he support—the Woodvilles or Gloucester? It's difficult enough to know which side the main protagonists are on,' she continued, 'let alone a some-time civil servant. He may take some searching out!'

'I'm the man to do that!' laughed Tony. 'If anyone can nose out a rascal like Stillington, it'll be me!'

'I suppose this means you'll be off on your travels again?' sighed his wife.

'The search starts in London—and then we'll see. These are exciting times and I feel ready for an adventure.'

*I thought as much*! This time Meg sighed to herself, but smiled and nodded, as the others did likewise.

\*\*\*\*\*\*

Perhaps exciting was not the word the citizens of London would have used to describe the aftermath of the seizure of the yet uncrowned King Edward V by his uncle. "Chaos", "confusion", "havoc", were just a few descriptions which were on their lips as they crowded around notices pinned up on tavern and church doors.

'How long is Gloucester allowed to be Protector—has the Council decided?' asked one man who was particularly interested in the constitutional position—one of only a handful in the crowd it can be imagined.

'Never mind that! We want to see the young king crowned; that'll put an end to all these fucking rumours!'

'I'd like to see the young king with or without a crown. Does anyone know where the boy is?'

'In the Tower—it's no secret. Gloucester had him put there when they arrived in London.'

'I don't like the sound of that! Can we trust this man— this uncle? The Yorkists are known for their ambition. I wouldn't put it past him to take—'

'—I'd be very careful what you say, neighbour. The duke has eyes and ears everywhere—and soldiers billeted among us.'

'But you must admit, the atmosphere in the city's been very tense since he arrived. If only he would show us the new king and prove he has only good intentions towards him.'

'We all know where they lead to!' laughed a tanner who had come out of his workshop to see what was going on. 'All this rumour does business no good. We want stability— without it trade is poor and profits poorer. It's about time these magnates realised who does the real work and who provides them with the cash for their preening.'

'Am I hearing Lollardy, neighbour?'

'I don't speak against the church—only greedy magnates. We all know what I say is true. So, what happens next. I'm angry and disturbed to hear about Lord Hastings. There was a good man—generous to the poor and not one of your grasping nobility. Why did Gloucester have to have his head—and so fast?'

The man's comments were universally approved by the Londoners, who were outraged by this rapid dispatch of a "good man". They were so discomforted that once reports of it were circulating there was threat of riot in the streets. Monty came back home from Westminster in a hurry. 'We should shutter the windows and lock the doors Gisella!'

'Is that really necessary?'

'What I was hearing on my way home tells me it is. The people are vexed beyond belief and I've seen armed men roaming the streets. But it'll be the usual business—a genuine grievance gets them stirred up, then caitiffs take advantage and go on the rampage for no reason other than looting and violence. Let's take precautions and prepare for a noisy night!'

There were several incidents of cracked heads, broken shutters, street robberies and plenty of drunken noise, but no major uprising, for the simple reason that the Duke of Gloucester had some days previously sent letters to his men in the north for "their assistance against the queen, who is plotting to destroy myself and the Duke of Buckingham". These armed "savages" were reported to be heading for London, and Buckingham was already at the gates with his own army. Southerners had a violent and exaggerated fear of "the northern hordes". "Ill-bred, wicked bastards all—and they don't speak our language!" was the consensus.

Anthony Tanner, now a shadowy figure around Westminster, kept the Newgate Five informed as to the rapidly unfolding events in the Palace and Tower. His facility to merge into the background, while keeping his ears and eyes open, gave him valuable access to the key players in the political drama concerning the seizure of a crown, which was deftly completed by the end of June. His daily reports had them all on the edges of their seats.

'Yesterday we heard of the summary execution of Lord Hastings. Today Gloucester has persuaded the council that if Edward is to be properly crowned, then his young brother Richard Duke of York must be present.'

Meg shook her head, 'But he's still in sanctuary, isn't he?'

'In Westminster Abbey, with his mother and sisters.'

'Well, unless the queen agrees he can leave, there's nothing Gloucester can do. Just as well; once he has his hands on the boy, I wouldn't say much for his chances—or his brother's,' and Pom shook his head. 'It's obvious to any intelligent person—Gloucester's after the crown.'

'How can he be? All I hear in the streets is that the people don't like him; neither do they trust him or his methods. Why would the council agree to anything he asks?' asked Meg.

'Because they're scared of him—and his northerners. The way he dispatched poor Hastings has put them in a state of terror. If it can happen to him, it can happen to anyone—the noble lord was once Gloucester's friend and loyal supporter,' and Tony frowned. 'His next victims must be Shivering Rivers and his nephew Richard Grey—up in Pontefract where no one can hear them scream!'

Gisella shivered herself. 'I wish we could speak of more cheerful matters, Tony.'

'I'm afraid these things impact on us all eventually, Gisella. Even if we don't know what's going on when it happens, the consequences of official actions always come back to haunt us all. I can see no good coming of this.'

'Do you think the young king will be crowned, Anthony?' asked Meg, using his full name in appreciation of these weighty matters.

'My view is no—and once the young Duke of York comes out of sanctuary, I think that will be the death knell of both boys.' There was a long silence, as his audience absorbed his words. They had no reason to doubt he knew what he was talking about. He had direct access to some of the most senior officials in Westminster and heard first-hand of the outcome of council meetings and secret conversations in shadowy corridors. 'If I say the atmosphere in Westminster is one of terror, I do not exaggerate.'

The day after these earnest conversations among friends, Thomas Bourchier, the elderly Archbishop of Canterbury had been sent likewise to Westminster Abbey to have a "conversation among friends" with Elizabeth, the queen mother. His order was to extricate the young duke out of her clutches, on the promise that he would "be returned to your care after the coronation". The godly man possibly believed he was speaking truth—possibly not—but Elizabeth finally capitulated and walked her young son to the abbey doors and waved him farewell as he stepped out hand in hand with the kindly prelate. The fact that Gloucester had surrounded the abbey with armed men may have persuaded her that the duke would be prepared to violate the protection of sanctuary if she did not agree.

Tony was bombarded with questions when he next supped with Monty and Gisella in their rooms in Pilgrim Street, not far from Jack's house in Ludgate and close to St Pauls.

'Will the queen leave sanctuary with her daughters, so she can be close to the king?'

'There's no sign of that happening. She remains closed up behind the walls.'

'What happened to the young duke?' asked Gisella anxiously.

'He has been taken to join his brother in the Tower.' Silence. Then Monty, shrewd as ever, said, 'Tony, there's something else you're not telling us.'

'There was supposed to be a parliament today to discuss the coronation, but it was cancelled at the last minute, even though many who had received writs to attend had arrived from all over the country. Then it flashed round the corridors that the coronation had been abandoned—just like that. No explanation. Just as I said, Gloucester sent word to Pontefract Castle that Rivers and Grey were to be executed without trial—although there was some talk of a tribunal, but clearly for show. There will be a show of another kind on Sunday next; a Cambridge Doctor of Theology has been asked to preach at St Paul's Cross—to make the case why Richard Duke of Gloucester should become Richard III! I think we should all go.'

\*\*\*\*\*\*

'It as just as well we got here early. We wouldn't have seen a thing otherwise; look at this crowd. There must be two thousand people here already!' Meg hemmed in between Monty and Tony looked around, and then to the front where she had a good view of the famous pulpit. It was where Londoners gathered to listen to speeches, sermons, proclamations, edicts and declarations of war. In other words, it was the official '"parish pump" of the city. A wooden structure mounted on steps of stone, it stood in the open courtyard of St Pauls; the only nod to the weather was a lead roof. It had very recently been rebuilt by Bishop Thomas Kempe, who had generously had it made more robust for the speakers to stand in. On this day, it would be occupied by Doctor Ralph Shaw, a respected theologian, commissioned by the Duke of Gloucester to set out that man's claim to the throne. The crowd around Meg was restive as people waited in the June sunshine for the speaker to appear. It seemed they were unsure why they had been called to listen.

'Must be to tell us when this coronation will be and that we'll all be having a holiday!' said a hopeful man behind Tony.

His neighbour shook his head. 'No, it'll be something to do with Gloucester being protector for longer than parliament wants—some argument between the noble lords.' If there had been room he would have spat in derision.

Tony muttered to Meg, 'The crowd's going to have a surprise and I'm not sure how they'll take it. If things turn nasty, just hang on to me. If we get separated, make your way to the doors of the cathedral and wait for me there.'

Meg was not comforted and was just about to probe this warning when the crowd became hushed as a small man of middle-age climbed the steps and took his place in the pulpit. Dressed in the customary black of a cleric, Meg thought he looked rather lost in the space, which was large enough to hold four people. He stood, pale faced, looking down at the sea of faces beneath him and, clearing his throat, began rather nervously, 'Citizens! People of London!' Then fell silent.

The audience waited expectantly, apart from one man who called out, 'Speak up! We can't hear at the back!'

Someone else shouted, 'Get on with it! We haven't got all day!'

Shaw began to speak. 'I come before you to lay out certain facts which show conclusively that his Grace, Richard Duke of Gloucester, son of the great Richard Duke of York and sole surviving brother of King Edward IV may claim the crown of England in right of conscience and law.' There was a ripple among the crowd, and they craned forward to hear more.

'The case for this is clear. The late King Edward was a bastard—'

This time the crowd began to mutter and look one to another, shaking their heads. Shaw cleared his throat again and continued, '—was a bastard, the son of the Duchess Cecily and her paramour, an English bowman; the boy conceived and born to her in France even while her noble husband was fighting the French so courageously!'

'Prove it!' yelled someone.

'Yes, prove it!' echoed the crowd.

'Citizens, the evidence is in your own eyes! Edward was a mighty man—the tallest in England. The Duke of York was much shorter in stature—a trait which this son of York, Richard, clearly exhibits, as well as other similar features. There can be no doubt he is a true son of York; the man is a replica of his great father. Therefore, Edward's children being ignoble because of their father's low birth, Richard Duke of Gloucester, by right of inheritance, must claim the throne.'

'Something similar was put about ten years ago by another disloyal son—the Duke of Clarence. We've heard it before!' shouted a gentleman, with his hand on his sword.

People began to shake their heads, point and shout—'Not proof! Not proof!' The crowd was becoming agitated. A red-faced fishmonger looked round for support from his fellow citizens. 'Fuck it! How can Gloucester accuse his own mother? It's the worst slander a man can think of. We all know Duchess Cecily is close to sainthood—always on her knees.'

'Perhaps that's because she feels guilty!' shouted a muscular man in the crowd—confident he could make an unpopular comment without risk.

'I'll never believe that saintly lady capable of such a foul crime!' said another, and there was a general shout of agreement as they glared at the naysayer, who shrugged and decided to keep his mouth shut. The crowd continued its chant of 'Show us the evidence! Prove it!'

Shaw, clearly taken aback by this robust reception verging on the hostile, held up his hand, attempting to bring back the crowd's attention. His voice cracked as he shouted, 'My friends, I only speak the truth. But there are other proofs of illegitimacy, if you would hear me out!'

'Get on with it then!' yelled a woman, who had brought a basket of old and mouldy vegetables to throw if the opportunity arose.

'It is well known also that Edward was already contracted to marry a woman before he married the widow Grey. Therefore his union with Lady Grey was invalid and means his children are illegitimate!' He spat the word out and a shower of spittle almost reached the front row of the crowd. 'We cannot allow a precedent to be set whereby bastards may claim the throne through the duplicity and sensuousness of their parent. And, that brings me on to the greed and licentiousness of the Woodville family, who we have all known to be most ungodly in their behaviour!' More spit followed and the preacher, now desperate, fumbled in his gown, produced a small cloth and wiped his mouth.

'Ungodly?' men and women looked one to another and shook their heads. They had no liking for the Woodvilles, the general opinion being they were greedy, grasping bastards who came from poor stock, had fallen on their feet, and taken every opportunity to rob the people blind of the country's treasure. But "ungodly" was stretching matters.

'Yes, ungodly! I say to you that in England, under their rule, every good maiden and woman stood in dread to be ravished and defiled!'

'*Ravished and defiled*?' The citizens mouthed the words to each other and raised their eyebrows. A very fat tailor shouted, 'I don't believe it! Everyone knows Anthony Woodville wears a hair shirt. When he was busy defiling women, did he take it off?' And he looked round for the expected laugh and was well-rewarded.

'Probably left it on for extra pleasure!' added the man next to him. When the laughter had died down, people began to mutter and scowl again.

From the moment Shaw opened his mouth, Tony had felt the mood of the crowd changing. At first there had been genuine curiosity as to what they might hear; but the reception became increasingly hostile as the cleric struggled to pursue his points. Five minutes into his address, they were beginning to reject everything he was suggesting. It seemed to the crowd that the good doctor was scraping madly at the bottom of an old pickle-barrel, looking for any scraps he could throw to make his shaky case, and they knew as one that it was shaky.

Nearly thirty years of similar rhetoric and chest-thumping by so-called noblemen had left many disillusioned with the whole business of kingship and the incessant struggle to claim it. They had no liking for Richard of Gloucester, a tricky, uncultured northerner; events of the last two weeks had not endeared him to them. Shutting two young boys in the Tower—everyone knew how that would end. They began to boo and hiss and call out the young king's name—'Edward! Edward! We want Edward V! Bring him here! Show him to us—and his brother!'

Shaw struggled to make himself heard, feebly crying out that there was yet another good reason why Richard should be king. 'Even if you think he's legitimately born, Edward is still a boy and we know what happens to kingdoms when there is a boy in charge—remember Richard II and then the weak Henry VI who lost us France! We cannot risk instability from rule by another minor. It must lead to war again!' But his words were lost in the general mayhem which was breaking out. The mention of the young king incensed many in the crowd who were already suspicious of Gloucester's ambition. His aggressive actions immediately after the old king's death had not reassured them of his good intent towards his nephews.

The woman with the vegetables moved her hand towards the basket and prepared to make the first throw with a particularly rotten carrot. Others in the crowd had put their fingers in their mouths and were whistling derisively. People waved their fists in the air and surged forward. Had Doctor Shaw not been protected by the wooden barrier around the pulpit, they might have stormed it and dragged the cleric out to a martyr's fate.

Now very worried at this ugly mood and where it might lead, Tony grabbed Meg's hand and said to Monty, Gisella and Jack, 'Let's get out of here as fast as possible; this is going to end in a riot. We'll meet you back at Jack's house in half an hour—it's the nearest. Good luck!' And pulling Meg behind him, hand on sword and with a determined look, sharply pushed his way through bodies who cursed and shouted at each other while also trying to extricate themselves safely out of St Paul's Cross. Ralf Shaw, shaking in his academic gown, was rescued by two men-at-arms and hurried into the cool sanctuary of St Paul's crypt, where he stayed until advised it was: "All clear, Doctor Shaw!" The irony of the whole affair was that, up to that point, he had been a popular preacher; his sermons well-attended. Ever-after he was tainted with the "Cross Commission" as he thought of it, and held in contempt, to his "chagrin and remorse". He died the following year; some thought it was of grief.

\*\*\*\*\*\*

A few days later the Newgate Six had gathered in Jack's parlour. Once again, the conversation concerned the crucial events taking place in the city.

'That nasty business in St Paul's Cross tells us what the Londoners think of Richard of Gloucester.' Pom sat nursing a glass of Burgundy, stubby legs stuck out in front of him. 'Shaw narrowly missed being torn limb from limb! Sir Tom and I knew him, you know.'

'Shaw? Surely not?' said Monty surprised.

'No! Richard of Gloucester—when he was a boy of ten or so. He was a brave fighter even at that young age and despite his crooked back—which didn't seem to impede him much. He was in the care of Lord Warwick who was training him up at Middleham Castle; I met him there. He has a good record in the field—was key to Edward getting his throne back twelve years ago. You must remember—after Henry VI was put back briefly by Lord Warwick?'

'It seems he's playing a devious game now. These accusations against the morals of his mother Cecily Duchess of York—a more pious woman couldn't be found in the whole country—so they say.'

'It's a common tactic, Monty—besmirch your enemies' morals!'

'But your own mother! Hardly a chivalrous action, Pom.'

'No, I admit, it doesn't put him in a good light. But Tony, you know more of what's going on—being around Westminster. What's the latest news?'

'Firstly I can tell you it's official; by now Earl Rivers will have been executed in Pontefract Castle, with his nephew Richard Grey. No official charges were brought nor was there a proper trial, but there was talk of a sham tribunal led by the Earl of Northumberland; then they were straight to the block. Gloucester's wasting no time getting his message through! As well as that, you must have heard that he had Lord Buckingham make the same points Shaw made at St Paul's; this time to the council and a few important citizens in Westminster two days afterwards. It's being said his address was more succinct and impressive than Shaw's attempt—no spitting or hesitation!'

'Did they believe him? Fuckingham Buckingham back again—how Sir Tom would have relished all this!' said Jack.

'Malory's Buckingham was this one's grandfather. All those stories you told me of Sir Tom's hatred of Humphrey Stafford, the first duke—I never really understood where it came from—the hatred I mean,' Monty re-filled his glass and looked thoughtful. Whenever Sir Thomas Malory's name was mentioned it brought back the thought of the manuscript, it's whereabout and the possibility of recovery.

Gisella read the thoughts in her husband's head, which she knew were troublesome to him. Bringing him back, she said thoughtfully, 'Gloucester should show the young king—parade him through the streets.' Then she asked, 'Why aren't people protesting more about all this? Why is Richard of Gloucester allowed to make these accusations?'

'Fear, Gisella, and are we sure the young king is still alive? Does anyone know when he was last seen or was in contact with his family?' asked Pom.

Tony said, 'There was ominous news of that. The young Duke of York's doctor and personal attendants have been withdrawn from him according to one of my friends in Westminster. Did you know little Richard of York had an astrologer—he's gone with the doctor.'

'He should have seen that coming!' laughed Jack, but the joke fell flat and there was a silence. Then Monty said, 'Without wishing to sound unfeeling about a member of the nobility recently decapitated—now we know Rivers is dead, shouldn't we be making moves to track the manuscript down and retrieve it. Jack's mention of Fuckingham Buckingham jerked my memory back to the old days. If Rivers has bought or stolen the manuscript, it may still be among his papers or in his library.'

Pom was more cautious, 'We can't be sure he has it until we've found either Stillington or Crosby. We can hardly go about accusing the noble lord of theft—dead or not. Tony, you were going to track them down.'

'Yes, unfortunately all this upheaval in Westminster and the city has put it out of my mind, and I'm afraid I can't promise any action for a few weeks. I must stay and see what occurs. I'm fearful there will be a great upheaval, and perhaps suddenly; we saw the mood at St Paul's Cross with just a couple of thousand people. If Gloucester does take the crown, I want to make sure we're all safe. I need to be on the spot to gather information. You do understand, everyone?'

Monty nodded and said, 'Of course we do, Tony. We're lucky you're close to matters and can report to us as they unfold. Master Caxton is also grateful—Jack and I keep him up to date with all the news you bring. He was very sad to hear of Rivers' imprisonment and he'll be sorrier still when I tell him of the noble lord's execution. They shared a deep love of literature and Lord Rivers was often at the print shop. We have several of the nobleman's works currently in print.'

'Having thought hard about it, I'm coming around more and more to Monty's idea that Rivers had or has the manuscript,' observed Jack. 'But, I take Tony's point, with everything that is happening in the city, it's not the time to be going about asking the whereabouts of civil servants. People have other things on their minds—not least keeping their heads to contain them in!' And he drained his glass and regretfully stood up to leave.

Monty also took up his cloak and wondered how he would bring himself to tell William Caxton that his favourite customer was now headless and buried in a shallow grave in the grounds of a gloomy Yorkshire castle.

******

As he walked to Westminster early the next morning, despite the cheerful June sun Monty was aware of a pall of gloom hanging over the city. People were already abroad; shops were open and apprentices removing shutters and sweeping and cleaning rubbish away from the frontages. Not that it made any difference to the cleanliness of the streets— for they simply shuffled detritus from one place to another for someone else to sweep, until finally it found its way to the same places—the midden at the end of each alley or the River Thames.

It was 26th June and, if the citizens were not aware that Richard Duke of Gloucester had yesterday been "ordained king" by the council, the numbers of soldiers on the streets should have alerted them to the great changes being rapidly forced through by King Edward V's uncle. The closer Monty got to Westminster, the more armed men bearing Richard's insignia of the white boar were circulating around the palace and the abbey. Caxton's print shop was within the precincts of the abbey, where, since his arrival in London in '76, he had rented a decent-sized workshop near the Chapter House. He had been fortunate in his noble patrons to acquire such premises, but was a very reliable tenant and, in the last year, equally fortunate in renting another shop at the sign of the Red Pale in the abbey's Almonry. This was an excellent place from which to advertise his wares, being situated above the outer door and therefore in prime position to exhibit his famous monograph sign. The passage of trade over its seven years' existence had been gratifyingly profitable for everyone concerned with the Caxton Press.

Monty approached the door and prepared to inhale the smell he loved—hot metal, ink, paper, leather, glue—all the essences of the printing trade which always excited him. He had worked for Master Caxton for twelve years and had never tired of the daily routine of his work as a compositor and proof-reader. The atmosphere in the shops was business-like, but friendly. Even the gruffly spoken Master Printer Wynkyn de Worde, with his much-improved English, could now better understand and respond to the peculiar sense of humour of Englishmen in general and Londoners in particular. But this morning there was no exchange of jokes, bawdy or otherwise. Master Worms was standing in the middle of the workshop and vehemently holding forth.

'I tell you, Master Caxton, I was most put out!' Monty entered the shop to see Jack Worms, red in the face above his beard, and grinding the fist of one hand into the palm of the other—a familiar gesture of stress well-known to Monty. *Hello! Something's up*! he thought as he took down his apron and turned to them both, 'Good morning Master Caxton! Good morning Jack! Master Wynkyn! What's happened?'

'I was accosted by two loutish soldiers, that's what! I was walking here minding my own business when they stepped in front of me and asked where I was going and what my business was. I told them it was no business of theirs, and within seconds they put me up against a wall and had me pinned down for a while. I asked them on whose authority they could detain a citizen going about his lawful affairs, and they laughed and said, "The new king of England!"'

I said, 'Why would Edward V be interested in an ordinary honest Englishman?' Again, one of them laughed and said, 'King Richard III is interested in all his subjects and we have a care for the new king and look out for traitors and renegade Woodville supporters. Are you a Woodville man?' I was so taken aback I didn't know what to say. He went on, 'Better keep your mouth shut if you have any respect for your body! You could end up in the Tower!'

'So, what did they do then?'

'They lost interest since I didn't protest again, just nodded my head and they let me go after having searched my pockets, "for treasonous papers". But what is it all about?'

'Master Worms, from what I've heard, today will be a crucial one,' and Caxton slammed down a pile of papers in a rare expression of exasperation. 'The Lords are going to assemble and probably decide to accept the Duke of Gloucester as king. Everyone will be there—they were originally summoned to come to London to discuss arrangements for the coronation of young Edward, but it seems Gloucester will use the meeting to grab power by official means.'

'But why should the Lords agree, Master Caxton, knowing that Edward V is alive and the legitimate heir?'

'The oppression you experienced this morning is why, Master Worms. You were cowed by two armed men—just imagine what fear an army surrounding the city will engender among the rest of us. The summary execution of Lord Hastings, and news that my great friend Lord Rivers has probably been executed unlawfully, is enough to weaken the spine of any Londoner thinking of protesting. It will be carried through, but not for love of the man, purely out of fear!'

'So, what will happen to the young boys in the Tower?' asked Monty, but already knowing the answer, as did the others. There was silence as they contemplated the awful vision of two young children murdered by their uncle.

Caxton shook his head, 'It's an age-old theme which is threaded through the Old Testament! To keep the crown Richard must order the inevitable and dispose of his nephews. Of course, he won't dirty his hands with the heinous crime, but send a minion who will have everlasting damnation on his soul for such a foul act!'

Monty was somewhat surprised at his master's vehemence, but he knew William Caxton had a deep loyalty to the old House of York, and to Lord Rivers. While King Edward IV was not known for his literary interests, he had seen fit to visit the print shop shortly after it was established and, as others did, marvelled at the circular process of ideas turned into type, type into text, and text back into ideas. There was another aspect of Caxton's life which was rather shadowy as far as Monty and Jack were concerned, that of diplomacy. The years spent in Bruges and within the orbit of the Burgundy court had given Caxton easy access to the personalities and policies current in the ducal province. He had returned to Burgundy on a few occasions on missions for the king and had been well-rewarded for information he brought back. He was always delighted to revisit his patroness, Margaret Duchess of Burgundy with whom he had retained an enduring friendship.

Jack had calmed himself by turning to examine some fine leather, newly delivered from a tannery in Aldgate. He never failed to enjoy the soft, silky feel of the material as he fingered its quality. 'This is good stuff, Master Caxton! We should use this currier more.'

'We have plenty of manuscripts to bind this year, Master Worms. I leave all that in your capable hands!'

The name Rivers still resonating in Monty's head, he thought he would bring up the subject of the noble lord's manuscript collection. 'What will happen to Earl Rivers' property now he's dead, Master Caxton.'

'The way things are going our new so-called king will probably grab everything he can. I knew Lord Rivers very well; he shared many confidences with me when he came to discuss his latest work and how he wanted it produced. One thing I learned was that he has few landed estates—'

'—Yes, you found that out Monty; his money came from offices,' Jack interrupted his master, but Caxton continued, '—that is quite right, Master Worms and well-known.'

'So, who would inherit his property if King Richard doesn't get his hands on it first?'

'His brother Richard Woodville inherits the title of earl, but Lord Anthony left what lands he had from his marriage to Elizabeth Scales to his younger brother Edward. Anthony had no legitimate children, although he has—had a wife who survives him, Lady Mary Lewis, but she brought no lands to the marriage. I suppose she will receive something from the will.'

Monty mind was working hard. 'Master Caxton, you told me once that Lord Rivers had a substantial library—do you know where it is located?'

'I do indeed, Mister Pickle. It is down in Kent—a place called The Mote—rather a splendid building which he was restoring with a new tower. Apart from his official papers which are here in Westminster, he lodged all his books there: "Away from the damp and stink of the city", as he told me.'

'Would it be possible to access the library?'

'I wouldn't think so at this moment. It's probably crawling with Gloucester's soldiers waiting to ransack it!'

'Really, sir? Surely Lord Gloucester has other things to think about?' said Jack, who had left his table strewn with all kinds and colours of leather and was leafing through pages of Chaucer's *Troilus and Criseyde*. 'These imprints are really fine, Master Caxton!' he said approvingly. 'It will be a beautiful production. Monty—you have exceeded yourself with the layout.'

'Thank you, Jack, I worked hard on it. Just as hard as I did on *Le Morte*.'

'I see where your thoughts are leading you, Mister Pickle,' said Caxton. 'You think it was Lord Rivers who either bought or had stolen Malory's manuscript, and you wish to travel to Kent to retrieve it! Speaking for myself I'm sure that his lordship would have had no part in any criminal acts; he would never collude to steal a work or have one stolen on his behalf.'

'I'm sure you're right sir. But if there's a possibility it is in his manor in Kent—well, yes, I think I do.'

'Hm. My view is that Master Worms is correct. Even so the Mote would not be a safe place to visit at present.'

'So, what do we do, sir? Wait around for Gloucester's bullies to ransack the place—probably make a bonfire of the library out of spite—and then we'll never know if it was there or not!'

'I think you are becoming somewhat over-excited, Mister Pickle. While I agree that the Duke of Gloucester, as I still insist on calling him—he is by no means yet our king—has other things on his mind, I think it unlikely he would wish to destroy valuable property "out of spite" as you put it; most likely he will try to protect any gains he has made from Rivers' execution. My view is that you should seek out Lord Stillington, or at least his secretary and find out from them what happened to the manuscript ten years ago. If the secretary—Crosby did you say his name was?—if Crosby was involved and made money out of it, it will surely have been spent. There's no proof against him now Rivers is dead. Crosby has nothing to lose in telling you the truth, especially if you make it worth his while!'

'Pay Crosby, sir! Certainly not!' Monty was amazed at the very idea. 'The man's a rogue. He nearly burned us all in our tavern beds—besides half-poisoning me and keeping me drugged for a week.'

'You seem very certain of this man's guilt, Mr Pickle. But to my mind you are very short of hard evidence. Until you accuse him face to face and see his reaction you cannot proceed on speculation. As a lawyer you must know that!'

'Of course you're right sir. We're all acting on supposition—but I think it's reasonable to suspect him. There's no one else we can think of who was so involved all those years ago and it seems only common sense to seek him out and try to find the truth. As for approaching Lord Stillington—I have no idea where he is.'

'It's well-known that Stillington is roaming the corridors of Westminster wondering whether he should make a bolt for it. He may know of Crosby's whereabouts. Having re-invented himself as a loyal servant—after his plotting with the Duke of Clarence and a jail sentence—Stillington was appointed onto the council of the young Prince of Wales—as he was then—under Lord Rivers. His lordship told me what an oaf he thought the man was—untrustworthy and self-seeking. But King Edward had forgiven him and thought him capable of a role of responsibility on that council. Stillington has obviously made it back to London, but once Gloucester is acclaimed king today, I think he might disappear. Your friend Sir Anthony Tanner has many contacts in Westminster I believe. If anyone can track the man down, he can. I would press him to your service!'

He sat back in his chair, 'But we've spent too much time on these imponderables. Let's get back to the magic world of our next assignment: Master Chaucer's marvellous poem *House of Fame*, which is very relevant to our conversation. The poet's dream vision—a meditation on fame no less and whether we can trust "recorded renown". In other words, how much truth will there be in what is written about us in the future; extremely apt as far as Lord Gloucester's epitaphs will be! What future generations will make of that man I cannot begin to imagine!'

# Chapter 3

Tony Tanner begins his quest and flatters to deceive;
Meg has a quest of her own and shows her mettle;
Stillington reveals all in his silence

'Meg! I'm going to Westminster. I'll be back this afternoon.'
Sir Anthony Tanner, otherwise known to his friends as "Six-
toed Tanner" (for reasons too detailed to report here) called to
his wife as he took down his hat and buckled on his sword.

Coming down the stairs to the front entrance of their small
lodgings in Cornhill, Margaret Tanner gave a slight frown and
said, 'Will there be any chance that you might ask the treasury
clerk for the money that is owed you? Now it seems there's
going to be a change of sovereign, it would be a good time to
get your claim in early—before the nation's money is spent
on a grand coronation! I don't imagine King Edward IV left
much in the coffers. He wasn't known for his thrift!'

Anthony smiled and took her chin in his hand. *My God*!
he thought, *she may be nearly thirty, but she's still the most
beautiful woman I know*. 'Meg,' he said soothingly, 'I'll do
my best, but we aren't exactly short of money! The rent's not
due for another ten months; we have a secure roof over our
heads and money for sustenance—and clothes on our backs.'

'The boys are growing very fast. Both will need new boots before autumn comes.'

'And they will have them. Where are they by the way?'

'Upstairs working on their letters!'

'So you continue to try and make scholars and not soldiers of them!'

She laughed and said, 'You have your turn with them at the butts and the pell teaching them self-defence—I have no argument with that. But I'm concerned they can read and write and defend themselves adequately in a verbal argument!'

'Very well, I won't disturb them. You do know why I'm going to Westminster today?'

'To find Robert Stillington as I remember and ask him where Peter Crosby is.'

'That, and other matters which I'll discuss with you when I come home. There may be changes coming—I correct myself—there will definitely be changes coming and they will affect us all!'

'Tony, when you look serious I take you seriously and I'm not sure I'm happy with what you're hinting at—although I might take a guess.'

'No point in guessing what might not be, Magpie! Wait until I come home before you start worrying!'

'I wish I could, Anthony, I wish I could!'

\*\*\*\*\*\*

Stepping from the wherry, those small and vital craft which, for a sixpence or more ferried Londoners along and across the Thames, Tony alighted at the Westminster Wharf and, gingerly as always, made his way up the green-slimed steps to a picket-gate where two soldiers were standing, pikes in hand. This good-looking man with an air of confidence was well-known to them and they gave him a cheerful 'Good day, Sir Anthony' and let him pass. As he did so he asked, 'What news today, soldier? Am I right that the Duke of Gloucester may be declared our new king? I see you're both wearing his insignia,' and he looked meaningfully at their sleeves on which were hastily sewn cloth badges of the white boar.

One of the men shrugged and looked shifty—or perhaps scared, 'We were issued with these yesterday, but we don't get told nothing, Sir Anthony. All the captain said was to get them sewed on and check any strangers trying to get into the palace—and there are new guards in place at all the entrances.'

'Are King Edward—the old King Edward's—officials still working here?'

'I see faces I recognise and some new ones I don't!' said the second soldier shaking his head as though bewildered by the whole situation.

'I'm looking for Edward's old courtier—Lord Stillington; you remember, he was once Lord Chancellor.'

The soldiers looked one to another and shook their heads, 'Not familiar with him sir, perhaps he doesn't use this entrance.'

'Never mind. I'll ask inside. In the meantime, I appreciate what you do here, and your courtesy towards me,' and he slipped them a sixpence each. It was always useful to keep on friendly terms with gatekeepers! Bearing in mind the slippery steps, you could never be sure when you might need to make a speedy exit.

\*\*\*\*\*\*

Viscid stones can be negotiated and overcome with due care and attention. Lubricious officials require equal levels of skill in their handling, but of a different nature. If ever there was a slippery individual, it was Robert Stillington, Bishop of Bath and Wells, Dean of St Martin le Grande and one-time Lord Chancellor. He had turned his coat so often it was said it was faded on both sides. But, as befits such an oily individual, nothing of ill-repute seemed to stick to him. After every act of disloyalty, he would somehow reappear and reinvent himself. The last example had been five years previously when he embroiled himself in the plotting of George Duke of Clarence to overthrow his brother King Edward. It was said, and he denied it of course, that it was Stillington who put the story about that the king's marriage to Elizabeth Woodville was invalid because he had already been betrothed to Lady Eleanor Talbot. Clarence had seized on this rumour and pursued it. For his trouble, in the year '78, the duke had eventually been arrested and imprisoned in the Tower; meeting his end upside-down in a barrel of second-rate Malmsey, with no time to enjoy even a sip. Implicated in Clarence's plotting, Stillington spent a few weeks in that same Tower for his trouble. When he was released, he toasted his erstwhile conspirator with a decent Burgundy and, with well-practised cunning, gradually infiltrated his way back into the king's service. Sometime later he was appointed onto Anthony Woodville's prestigious council for the governance of the little Prince of Wales.

This day, Thursday 26<sup>th</sup> June '83 the bishop sat in a small chilly chamber off a narrow draughty corridor in an obscure dark area of Westminster Palace contemplating what he should do. *Those were the days—when I had a large chamber with a big desk and a fire! Things have not really gone so well for me since my term in prison. I was never able to persuade Edward to reinstate me as chancellor. The position on the Prince of Wales's council was nothing but a clerical one. They may have consulted me on matters of theology and dogma, but I was never accepted into the inner circle— Woodville kept me at arms' length; I know he didn't like me. Still, he's not in any position to hold me back now—headless in Yorkshire I'm told! And good riddance. The question is, have my plans come to fruition?*

He scratched his bald head which was exhibiting a worrying show of ringworm. More than most, and cleric or not, the man was prone to picking up invasive creatures which sought to feed off him. There was those who might have said this was simply a reversal of normal church practice—but very quietly as the opinion was pure Lollardy and a burning offence. The apothecary had sold him a little box of wormwood and garlic ointment which he told him would clear it up in a few days; but that had been a week ago and they were still there, itching and irritating. It had cost him a shilling. It was very awkward appearing in the council chamber scratching his head as though he was suffering from an outbreak of head-lice, or else permanently confused. He was sure the other courtiers and officials were staring at him. *How dare they! I've been an important public servant—I am the Bishop of Bath and Wells. I am due respect! The second question is, will I get it from this new monarch?*

He had certainly worked in the previous weeks to achieve it. He had been in the party which brought the young king down from Ludlow to London and there had been that nasty business on the way, when Woodville was arrested. The young king had naturally been very upset, and the Bishop of Bath and Wells had stepped in to try and soothe the boy, but unsuccessfully. *It was not seemly that he should use such violent language to a man of the cloth—telling me to go forth and multiply! Another who seemed not to like me; I'm sure Woodville poisoned his mind against me. Well, I'll be revenged on them all. We'll see what the Duke of Gloucester will do for me once he's king. He owes it to me for the help I've given him since we met in Stony Stratford. It's a matter of backing the right horse and I'm sure I've done so!*

******

'So, Will, which horse are you backing?' On the same day, Anthony sat in another chilly chamber in Westminster, this time with a newly-acquired friend, Will Pottinger, a humble, but busy clerk. His value to Tony was in his quick wits and sharp observation of people and events. The knight had deliberately sought someone of his type: unobtrusive, overlooked and invisible to those who ran the place. Ironic really, when those lowly beings were the very ones who really kept Westminster working and had their fingers on what was going on. Will worked in the Lord Chancellor's office and, although he didn't have access to the great man, he was constantly in and out of chambers and corridors and overheard much that he shouldn't. It was this cloak of invisibility which was so important as far as Anthony was concerned.

'The new chancellor Bishop Russell is a good man, Sir Anthony. When the previous chancellor Thomas Rotherham was arrested in May, Russell was reluctant to take the office, and who can blame him? Rotherham's still in prison, just because he gave the Great Seal to Queen Elizabeth in good faith. It's my view that Bishop Russell doesn't approve of Richard of Gloucester and the way he's doing things.'

'I suppose he has to keep his head down and do as he's told; that seems to be the general feeling about the palace.'

'Hmm, keeping one's head *on*, you might say! It's not a happy place sir, and, as usual, there are people here who are only out for themselves and what they can get once Gloucester's crowned king.'

'So, you're sure that'll come about?'

'Well, you heard what happened yesterday. The Lords have agreed it should be so. We've been told that this afternoon Mayor Billesdon, the aldermen and several leading citizens are going to petition the duke at Baynard's Castle to agree to become king.'

'What a farce that will be,' scoffed Anthony. 'I'd put money on him pretending to hesitate and then, just as they all turn away disappointed, calling them back and reluctantly agreeing!'

'You couldn't write it as a ballad could you, sir? No one would believe it!'

'No, indeed! But now we have printing someone might. But Gloucester and his ambitions are not necessarily why I'm here, Will. Have you seen Stillington on the premises?'

'Yes, he hangs about the place having audiences with Gloucester, Buckingham and others of that party. I don't know what he's been plotting—he's well known for it! He has a small room at the end of one of the west wing corridors.'

'So, what is he now? He can't be on Woodville's council—that must have been disbanded now Earl Rivers is dead and the young king's living in the Tower. As I understand it, the personal servants of both princes have been dismissed.'

'Stillington definitely works for Gloucester, but I couldn't say what he does. My master, the Lord Chancellor, keeps himself well out of the politics of this place, as much as he can anyway. Did you want to see Stillington?' Will was immediately curious. The frenzied atmosphere in Westminster had heightened his senses: the speed of change and people, one day in favour, the next executed or imprisoned.

'I do, but it's on a private matter concerning others, so I can't share it with you. If he's here, I'll seek out his chamber and try to get an audience. My knowledge of him is that he's a pompous, self-important prick; well he was twelve years ago. I don't suppose at the age of fifty he's changed!'

'He certainly hasn't Sir Anthony; you'll find he's just the same!'

\*\*\*\*\*\*

Small room, small desk and no fireplace notwithstanding, Robert Stillington, Bishop of Bath and Wells, courtier to kings and princes, ex-prisoner and all-round hypocrite and tergiversator, appraised the good-looking man opposite with an air of studied loftiness. *This senior cleric may be without specific secular status currently, but that doesn't mean I shouldn't command respect from a humble knight*, was his thought, as he stared back at the supplicant who had begged an audience "on a matter of some importance".

'I'm extremely grateful to you for sparing time to grant me this meeting, my lord!' Tony put on his most earnest expression and Stillington nodded graciously. 'My position in Westminster is a humble one and we are unlikely to have crossed paths recently.'

'You name is familiar to me, Sir Anthony. I believe you've been in foreign parts in the late king's service?'

'Yes, sir, for many years. I have only just returned to hear of his majesty's death and the imminent coronation of his brother, the Duke of Gloucester.'

'God save the duke!' And Stillington crossed himself. 'A goodly and godly man—well-deserving of the role our Lord has marked him out for.'

'Indeed, and I am anxious to serve him in any way I can.'

'Is that why you are here? To canvass my support?'

'Indeed, sir. I understand you have influence with his grace—or should I say, "his majesty-to-be"?'

Stillington examined his fingernails and looked pleased with himself, 'I do have contact with him, and he does seek my advice. But tell me, what have you been doing in these years abroad? Are you in possession of useful information from the continent which would be of interest to our new king?'

Anthony, anxious not to sell himself too successfully, spent the next few minutes describing events in France; events which anyone taking an interest in such matters would have already known. *The trick is,* Anthony told himself, *to make it seem extremely important and vital. This old fool will swallow anything I tell him and deliver it straight back to Gloucester's henchmen. They can make what they like of it—it's all out of date in any case!*

'This is all most interesting, Sir Anthony. Tell me, "Tanner" is a name I recognise from the past. Have we met previously?'

'Not exactly, my lord, although we had a mutual acquaintance—Sir Thomas Malory.' Now Anthony was taking a risk. Stillington and Malory had been long-time enemies and crossed swords metaphorically twelve years before. Tony's principle when dissembling with adversaries was to stay as close to the truth as possible. In that way, the web of deceit was a small one and he was less likely to be caught up in sticky situations later.

Stillington's reaction was violent and he leaned forward in his chair and thumped the desk, 'Malory—that caitiff in Newgate! Yes, I remember, and I remember your name from that time! You were on King Edward IV's list of wanted men!'

'I received a pardon many years ago and have been working for the crown ever since as a loyal messenger.'

'I was always convinced that Malory was behind those rumours put about concerning the Duchess of York, and her liaison with an English bowman. I tried to prove he was behind it, but the man was as slippery as an eel and I never made it stick!'

'But I gather that later the same story circulated, along with the notion that King Edward had been betrothed before he married the widow Grey.' Anthony was very careful how he worded this reply. He knew that it was Stillington who had told Richard of Gloucester these accusations against the duke's mother and brother and it was on these rumours that the duke had made his claim to the throne.

'Of course, I now know they were true and told his grace so. We can't have the son of a bastard and a dishonourable jilter on the throne!' He leaned forward again and stared at Tony through red-rimmed hooded eyes. 'So, Sir Anthony Tanner, you say you're looking to serve Richard III. But, are you sure your loyalties are with him? You've served Edward IV, but it comes back to me that you were also a retainer of that arch-scoundrel Richard Neville, Earl of Warwick. You seem to change sides when it suits you!'

*Pots and kettles, you bastard*! Tony thought, but of course did not say it. Instead he shrugged and tried to look ashamed. 'I was indentured to the earl as a boy—you know how these things work. He paid my wages for many years while we were all in the service of the House of York—the Duke of Gloucester's House. We were all instrumental in getting the throne for his brother Edward in the civil wars. I hope there will now be a period of peace and the House of York can continue to rule the country fairly.'

'Of course, that is what we all wish, Sir Anthony. Many of us have found ourselves in a same situation—serving different masters at different times. Some of us have been fortunate in having our talents recognised and avoiding the block in the process!'

'I understand you spent a few weeks in pris—'

Stillington held up his hand, saying, 'Those are matters of which we will not speak. Let us stick to the point of your request. All I can do is pass it on to those close to his maj— his grace—'

'—Not wishing to interrupt, my lord, but are we to assume the duke will be crowned?'

'Yes, and very shortly. The Lords have expressed satisfaction that it should be so. I expect to be called to the new king to assist him in his preparations for the coronation.'

'No doubt a man of your gravitas and experience will be looked upon as a great asset to his majesty.' *I can't lay it on any thicker than that*! thought Anthony.

'Indeed, I believe he will need much guidance in the coming months and I foresee my influence as being crucial.'

'I am sure you are correct, my lord. If there is any way I may serve him myself, I will be honoured to have you as a patron! A man could hope for nothing more, my lord.'

'Leave it with me, Sir Anthony. I'll see what I can do!'

As Tony closed the door behind him, Stillington thought, *Will I do anything for him? He's as much a scoundrel as any of us.* The bishop had a rare moment of self-honesty, but it quickly passed. *He could be useful in a menial way. I could get him to run errands now that I no longer have Crosby. I wonder where he is.*

\*\*\*\*\*\*

'Well, did you find out anything about Peter Crosby—like where he is?' asked Monty that evening. Tony had arranged to meet with the Newgate Fellowship and report on his visit to their old adversary Stillington. They were in Monty's house where Gisella and Meg had prepared a supper for them all.

'I didn't have the chance—'

'—But you said you would, Tony!' protested Pom. 'That was the whole point of the visit, surely?'

'Be patient, Pom. These things take time. I must ease myself into this; Stillington's no fool—though he's still as pompous and arrogant as ever! My reasons for seeking him out are to infiltrate myself into his confidence. Once I can get him talking I can raise the matter of the manuscript—but it must be done casually, as part of general conversation if you like. I know exactly how to manage matters—it's my job after all and I've been doing it long enough! Besides, this business of *Le Morte* has been going on for twelve years; it can surely wait a little longer. No one's seen it or heard of it.'

'Let's hope it hasn't been destroyed or tampered with by some ham-fisted scribe!' growled Jack. Monty shivered, 'That is always at the back of my mind. I just want to be sure it still exists and can be retrieved somehow.'

'I'm returning to Stillington a fortnight after the coronation—which has been fixed for Sunday 6th July. It's official and has been posted around the city.'

'Was there any mention of the princes? Did Stillington know if they were well—or what will happen to them?' asked Monty.

'We didn't discuss it,' said Tony.

There was silence, then Pom said, 'What do we think will happen to them? Now Gloucester's seized the throne he can't afford to have any figureheads for dissenters to rally around, even if they are locked away. Neither boy has any chance of surviving!' There was a general atmosphere of sadness around the room, then Tony said, 'We're powerless to do anything about that, but I can reassure you, Monty, that now I've forged a relationship with the bastard bishop, I'm confident I can find an opportunity to raise the subject of Malory's manuscript. He already remembers that I was connected to Sir Tom. I've been honest in everything I've told him, although it hasn't been as much as he thinks or as valuable. I don't think there's anything more I can add, but of course, I'll keep you all informed. Anything I know, you will also!'

******

'That wasn't all together true, Meg!' Anthony walked briskly beside his wife as they headed east towards Cornhill from Pilgrim Street.

'What wasn't true, husband?'

'That I'll tell them everything I know. There are other matters I am involved with, more important than finding the manuscript.'

'Your involvement with Lord Stillington—are you plotting with him?'

'Meg! I thought you knew me better than that! I hate the man. He's a hypocrite and a turncoat. I wouldn't trust him with Dickon's new hobby-horse. But let's wait until we're indoors. What I have to tell you is best kept within our own walls.' Meg said nothing but was already calculating that her husband would probably be off on his travels again. *I pray it's local and not overseas*! was her first thought.

'So, what are you mixed up in now, Tony?' And Margaret Tanner looked her husband straight in the eye; but her searching gaze was met with a gentle shrug.

'*Mixed-up* is not really a correct description. I've been asked to assist in something momentous, Meg. I can't tell you everything, but at some point, and soon, I'm going to need your help—not just support, but your involvement. I have always hesitated in taking such a step; it's dangerous work and, of course, I am concerned for your safety, but in the past, you've been more than willing to help and—'

'—But we have two boys to think of now, Tony.'

'That's the irony of it. It's two young boys I'm thinking of.'

'You mean the princes locked in the Tower?'

'That's what I like about you, Magpie, I don't have to explain too much.'

'You're not hinting that you've been asked to rescue them?'

'I would try if I thought it was possible. But I'm not sure whether they're dead or alive. They've been seen once or twice this summer, but few have access to them. My task is to find out what I can about their imprisonment and report to Queen Elizabeth. This is where I need your help; I want you to visit her. This is all part of a larger plan which I can't tell even you.'

'I see—more secrets!'

'To keep you safe, Magpie. The less you know, the more protected you are.'

'All right, if you say so. But how will I become involved with the queen? She's in sanctuary and we can hardly visit.'

'As a man it would be very difficult for me to gain an audience and would rouse suspicion. But you could easily be admitted—especially if you went disguised as a humble seamstress or laundress. You could take messages to her and receive them for me; there would be little risk—the clerics in Westminster will hardly notice you as a menial servant,' he looked at her shocked expression and said soothingly, 'I would of course. No man could fail to notice your beauty—

but the churchmen won't, especially if you're humbly disguised; they're supposed to have their minds on higher things! Anyway, what do you say?'

'The queen knows of this I suppose? It's not some kind of mad-cap scheme of your own?'

'Certainly not, I can tell you that there are many of Edward IV's councillors and courtiers who are incensed at the treatment of the young princes and are taking steps to try and have them released. I've been approached by someone I can't name to liaise with the queen.'

'Why you especially, Anthony. I know you have a sound reputation for your discretion when it comes to acting as an envoy, but you've only just returned from France. Surely there must be others whom the queen knows and trusts more?'

'It's the very fact that I've been out of the country for so long and not involved with any faction that I've been sought out. I start with a clean sheet from the last twelve years, having a proven record of loyalty to Edward IV and no other.'

'That makes sense I suppose. So, tell me exactly what it is you wish me to do—and when do I start?'

'Tomorrow!'

\*\*\*\*\*\*

'Your business, mistress?' The guard at the entrance to Broad Sanctuary was not unfriendly, but clearly had been ordered to challenge all who sought entry to the abbey. They had a famous visitor and there were many wishing to gain access for reasons good or ill.

'I have been summoned to the queen's apartments. I am a seamstress and have brought new linen for the royal family.'

89

'Let me see your basket.'

'I think the queen might think it amiss that a man had laid hands on her linen, sir!' And Meg looked shocked but obeyed his order and passed it over. The guard took off the cover and rummaged through the contents. Nodding, he said, 'Other than her husband, you mean! But he's dead and can't complain.'

'You speak disrespectfully, sir, of a great lady and the king!'

'She's only great if he's king and she's queen. As I heard it, now we have a new king we also have a new queen—his wife Queen Anne.'

Unwilling to engage in conversation on any level, especially that concerning the legitimacy of who was occupying the throne, Meg said brusquely, 'That is none of my concern, sir. I have a job to do and would be obliged if you would return the basket and let me pass!'

He handed it back and nodded her through. As she walked on towards the apartments she thought, *I hope this isn't a regular occurrence. If he were to check the basket every time, he may discover whatever it is being passed from Tony to her majesty, and back again. Since he made no attempt to search me, it would be sensible to hide anything on my person. It's as well I had nothing with me this time.*

Indeed, Tony had deliberately made this first visit a genuine one to allay such suspicions. Once the abbey authorities became used to Meg's weekly visits, they were unlikely to challenge her. She would be just one of several visiting servants necessary to the queen's comfort.

Once inside, Meg was soon seated on a bench in a draughty corridor waiting for one of the queen's ladies. *Will I speak directly to the queen, or through her waiting woman*? She had no idea of the protocols required when meeting a monarch and concerned she got it right. *I suppose I must curtsey and not look her in the face—at least someone told me that, 'Never look them in the eye—they don't like it as you may see something shifty!' they warned me. That must be nonsense. I'll curtsey and wait for her majesty to speak to me.'*

She was not kept waiting long. A middle-aged stern-faced woman, of evident breeding, came out and asked Meg to follow. They entered a large chamber which, to Meg's great surprise, was furnished regally—beautifully upholstered chairs, hanging tapestries of great magnificence. *I thought it would be austere—not a state of luxurious living*!

She approached one such well-cushioned chair on which was sitting a small woman, rather plump and with a face which reflected much worry. Meg took careful stock of Queen Elizabeth. *This will be something to tell my boys and they can tell their children. I must remember every detail.* Afterwards, when she spoke of meeting the widowed queen, all she could remember was the terrible anxiety in her voice and eyes.

'Hers was a very sad story. She once drew the eye of a handsome lusty king, who married her despite all the problems it would bring his country. She was considered one of the most beautiful women in the kingdom, but when I met her she was showing both her age and the great strain she was under. Her face was already lined at the age of forty-six and even under her coif I could see the once lustrous brown hair must be grey. Her figure was that of any woman who had given birth to twelve children in twenty years. My remembrance is she presented as a sad, desperate lady, and no wonder with her two "tender babes", as she called them, imprisoned and whose fate is still unknown.'

At this moment, the queen indicated Meg should rise from her deep curtsey and said in a low voice, 'You are the new seamstress, Mistress Limpett? I hope the quality of your work will be of the same standard we've enjoyed previously. I have some more kerchiefs and other linen to be embroidered. Leave the basket here—my ladies will find you some refreshment and bring it back to you. You understand this is a weekly arrangement?' And she lifted her still-elegant eyebrows and put her head on one side in a questioning way.

'I understand, your majesty, and I will be honoured to serve you—in any way I can,' and Meg hoped the last remark would be understood.

'Come this way, mistress,' and the stern-faced lady-in-waiting led Meg through the door to an antechamber where there was a table; on it was a small glass of wine and some sweet cakes.

'I will bring the basket back to you shortly.'

Within quarter of an hour, Meg was trudging back to Cornhill, basket over her arm. There had been no challenge at the gate as she found her way out. Indeed, the same guard, who recognised a comely woman when he saw one, waved while he was thinking, *A looker! I hope we might become better acquainted*!

\*\*\*\*\*\*

'You had no trouble getting acquainted with the queen?' Tony had been waiting anxiously since Meg left for Westminster. He was not happy about bringing his wife into

92

this circle of conspiracy, however much he would try to protect her. If she knew half of what he was involved in he was uncertain how she would react. During their years in France, on similar business, she had at times helped him in his enterprises and at no small risk to herself. But she was quick-witted and had a talent for talking her way out of awkward situations. As she once reminded him, 'It's a useful skill learned in my past life in Gropecunt Lane,' a true observation, but one which they both preferred to shut out of their minds. Meg's history was one which purse-lipped, unforgiving women and pompous, hypocritical men would deplore; but Anthony knew all the circumstances of this "fallen woman" who, granted with his help, had resurrected herself to a genteel state. *She's a natural-born lady*! was always his consoling thought.

'The queen was charming, Anthony. The guard was less so!'

'Oh? Did you have trouble getting through?'

'He wanted to look in the basket. If messages or items are to be passed in that way, it will be better if I hide them among my clothes. He made no move to search my person, although he was undressing me with his eyes!'

'The bastard! But you're right, of course. So, have you brought anything back with you? You should have a message for me.'

'I do, and I've concealed it in an inner pocket in my chemise.'

'I didn't know there were inner pockets in chemises!' said Tony. 'Would you let me explore?'

'This is no time for dallying with your hand up my kirtle!'

'There's always time for dallying—come here wench!' And he made a lunge at her.

'I thought this was important business. "Of great national concern!" you said.'

'Well, it is, but who says I can't have some fun retrieving important messages, Magpie? It's certainly an inspired idea to hide them about your person. But if I hear that the caitiff on the gate makes any moves in that direction, I'll see to it that more than his hands are chopped off!'

Meg rummaged in her undergarment and came out with a small sealed package. 'I think I'd better sew in a larger pocket. Who knows what the queen might want to send.'

'Good idea. Now let's see what she says!' And he broke the seal, read one letter and perused the names on the rest. Without saying a word, he put them away in his doublet pocket and looked thoughtful.

'Aren't you going to tell me what she says?'

'Better you don't know, but she's evidently satisfied that you are loyal and will continue with our plan for communicating. Are you still willing to participate, Magpie? There is always a risk with this type of business, but I've tried to minimise it.'

'A weekly trip to the abbey to deliver linen to the queen and bring out fresh items for sewing is perfectly innocent. There was no problem inside the Abbey. I must say, the queen lives as well in sanctuary as she does in the palace.'

'That's because after she arrived she ordered pieces of furniture from the palace to be brought in. They had to make holes in the walls to get them through! Her bed caused the most problems.'

'It sounds as though she thinks she'll be there for a long time. Perhaps she had been planning for difficulties after King Edward died.'

'That's a good point, Meg. What did she know before her husband died? Did she suspect her brother-in-law would make a bid for the crown? Perhaps having experienced Clarence's treachery, she just didn't trust Gloucester not to get up to something. Well, she was prescient. If she hadn't gone into sanctuary, no doubt she would have ended up in exile on the continent—or worse.'

'What will happen to her daughters, do you think?'

'The eldest, Elizabeth, is seventeen and a valuable political pawn. Perhaps King Richard will try and marry her off to a foreign prince. You know I heard a rumour—and it was only that—that Richard once had a plan to marry her.'

'But that's appalling! He's her uncle,' exclaimed Meg.

'The idea never took off. The pope certainly wouldn't have given a dispensation for it. No, Elizabeth is destined for another life entirely—but don't ask me what. Now, I must see these letters to the right quarters and bring back whatever is to be delivered next week.'

'Can I ask a question?'

'Not if it concerns what we've just been discussing.'

'Are we getting paid for this work? Or have we become a charitable institution in the service of monarchs?'

'I'm sure we'll receive a just reward—but, to satisfy you, I will remind our lords and masters that "Lady Margaret and Sir Anthony Tanner cannot live by honourable satisfaction alone", or something like it!'

\*\*\*\*\*\*

Over the long hot weeks of the summer, Meg made seven visits to the Abbey with letters concealed in her chemise and brought out documents carefully wrapped and easily hidden about her. To her relief, Tony was successful in his bid to receive recompense for their efforts, and a satisfying sum of gold nobles was soon mounting up in their small cash box.

'We will keep it for emergencies, Meg!' Tony said, to her disappointment. The boys still needed shoes, as she pointed out. 'Very well, take something for the boots, and anything else which is desperately needed—and I mean "desperately"—no gaudery!' Meg was rather insulted by Tony's hint that she might be profligate with their cash. Throughout their marriage it was she who had been the better at managing their income, which was sometimes irregular. But she said nothing and took what was needed to fit out their boys with decent footwear.

At the time, Meg was pondering why children's feet grow so quickly, Anthony was making yet another visit to "patron" Robert Stillington. Here was Tony's source of information, since the strategy to "flatter to deceive" had been, so far, highly successful. On this day in early August, Tony sipped at a decent glass of claret and looked attentively at the cleric who held up his own glass and said, 'What do you think, Sir Anthony, not bad, eh?'

'Indeed, it is very good sir. Where did it come from?'

'A gift from a friend—Edward Ratcliffe. Know him?'

'I've heard his name. He's close to the king I believe.'

'They're almost inseparable. Richard relies on him as much as he does on myself!'

'It's good to know his majesty has such loyal servants around him. There are so many rumours put about. It must be difficult for him to know who to trust.'

'That is so. Talking of rumours, you're about the streets—what have you been hearing?'

This was exactly the opening Anthony was hoping for. During these conversations he had long since realised the encounters were two-way streams of information. He could feed Stillington any amount of citizens' gossip; in return he would receive news confirming or countering such speculation; news which came from the monarch's inner circle. The bishop thought he was being so clever, trying casually to prise intelligence from a useful source without that source's awareness. They were both playing the same game, but Tony's moves were ahead of the fleshy rascal's sitting opposite him.

'The word on the street is that the two princes in the Tower are dead!' There, it had to come out sometime, this dreadful belief which had been swirling round the streets like a turd caught up in a whirlwind.

'Are people really saying that!'

'What else are they to believe, since the boys have not been seen since the middle of July. But, of course, you will know they are safe and well inside the Tower and being treated as young princes should! My lord?' And he left the question hanging in the air.

There was an uncomfortable silence. Stillington refilled his glass from the jug and offered it to Tony, who declined. *Keep a clear head, Tanner*! he told himself. The silence continued. *That tells me all I want to know*! thought Tony. *If it was untrue, then he would've been on his feet denying it and asking who was putting such scurrilous stories about. Instead, he can't say anything because he knows it's true.* He looked quizzically at Stillington.

'Of course, I'm sure no such harm has come to the young princes. Who could possibly imagine such a thing!' but the bishop looked shifty—avoiding Tony's gaze. Then he changed the subject entirely. 'Did you ever locate my erstwhile secretary, Peter Crosby?'

This sudden change of tack took Tony by surprise. Sometime during their encounters, he had mentioned Crosby and asked the bishop if he knew of the man's whereabouts. Stillington had been vague. 'I believe he moved to Essex— somewhere near Rom—Rom—what was it?—ah! Romford,' and he waved his hands airily, as though directing Tony some way out of the city to a land of infidels. 'He had a sister I believe and went to stay with her when I had my er—er— *Time in the Tower*? thought Tony but did not say it. '—My change in career. I haven't seen him since.'

Tony knew a diversionary tactic when he heard one but played along. 'No, my lord, but I've not taken real steps to find him, being engaged by yourself to run important errands.' For this was true. To ingratiate himself further with the crafty cleric, Tony had offered to run about the city with various messages to people of differing rank and importance. He had become a go-between for Stillington and his long-term mistress, or "housekeeper" as he euphemistically referred to her. Both now in middle-age, she had grown stout and shrewish; he had become portly and pompous and neither could stand the other, preferring to lead separate lives under the same roof. However, there had to be a measure of communication and at present Tony provided the emollient interface which enabled their domestic lives to run smoothly. Consequently, Stillington was very grateful to Tony, who he regarded as personable, young, servile—certainly no threat. He was also intelligent and could go about the town in the manner of any young buck, picking up tittle-tattle and more useful chatter which could be passed on to the right quarters.

While this work irritated Tony intensely, Stillington paid quite well and regularly. But it was the intelligence from official sources which was most valuable to him and others to whom he passed it on. Today had been a watershed. The silence emanating from Stillington told it all—the boys were dead. It was time for action.

# Chapter 4

Monty and Pom head out to Essex to find an old friend;
they search out an old enemy and secure useful
information.

'Are we sure she'll be here, Monty?' Pom pulled up his horse
and looked around him.

'The owner of The Unicorn gave me an address which he
said was the place Mistress Roberts bought after she sold him
the inn at the Stews.'

'But that was ten years ago. She may be dead or too old
to remember us!'

'It's our only chance of tracking down Crosby. Stillington
told Tony the man had gone to live with his sister in Romford.
Mistress Robert's inn is a few miles away in Barking.'

'Well, the milestone says we're three miles from there.
How far is Romford from Barking?'

'About eight miles on horseback.'

Pom looked around, 'It's awfully flat, Monty! Do you
know where it reminds me of?'

'Bruges—I thought the same—Bruges without the bustle,
the Babel of tongues and the beauty.'

'Very alliterative! Also, it stinks of fish and not wool.'

Monday August 4$^{th}$ '83. They had taken a wherry from the London Bridge wharf and landed downstream on the other side at Creekmouth, a busy Essex hamlet on the Thames estuary. At the local inn, they hired a couple of nags of uncertain age but which, they were assured by the innkeeper who'd received them in lieu of a week's lodgings, 'Were responsive to the leg and a good kick up the arse!' The horses had fortunately turned out to be more obliging than they'd been led to expect.

Scratching his mount's ears, Pom looked around the Thames tidal estuary and observed, 'It's as drearily flat as a fucking cowpat—except for the rubbish!' He was right; as the tide receded, it revealed the detritus poured and thrown into the great river by generations on both sides—every kind of animal, vegetable and mineral waste was there, lying on or protruding through the grey mud. There were the usual scruffy scavengers—human, animal, avian—picking their hopeful way through the slippery waste as keenly as a pope looking for fleas. Scattered on the banks were an array of wooden fishermen's huts of varying shapes and sizes; some newly built, others almost derelict; most mended and patched with different handy materials rescued from the mud—tree trunks, spars and other wreckage from old ships which had finally come to rest on the riverbanks. Odd pieces of planking from other distressed sheds and shelters were reclaimed to reinvigorate existing structures, giving them a curious patchwork appearance; buildings all connected to the fisheries which dominated the area, as did the piscine odour which caused Pom to wrinkle his nose.

Having given the surroundings their assessment and found them wanting, they gave their horses a "kick up the arse" as advised and moved northwards three miles to the small parish of Barking where they had been told Mistress Pauline Roberts was the owner of *The Cog Inn.* They entered the main street with small lanes and alleyways leading off into dark and dangerous places. The sign of the fishing boat painted on the front wall of a wooden shack-like building told its own story; Barking existed solely for fish and fishermen; cod, haddock, mackerel, shell-fish—every kind of creature which could be hauled from the oceans was traded here, from as far afield as Iceland on occasion. It was one of a series of small but vital fishing villages strung out on the north shores of the Thames, from Creekmouth in the west to Shoeburyness on the coast. As Monty and Pom looked around they could see small boat-repair yards, net-makers, rope-walks and chandlery businesses crowded together and busy with labourers, traders and artisans.

They gave their horses to a small boy. Paying him sixpence, with the promise of another on return, but also dire warnings of painful retribution if he left his post, they entered *The Cog Inn* through a low wooden door. They were met by a frowst of stale air infused with the stink of bodies, ale and fish, and the hum of talking and laughter. Even though this September afternoon was sunny, the windows were too small to let in but a modicum of light. In the gloom, they could see men huddled round tables. As they made their way across the dirt floor to the bar, an uncomfortable silence fell. Conversation stopped as the customers looked suspiciously at these strangers. 'Who comes to Barking? They look like Londoners. No fish trader dresses so well!' The atmosphere was unfriendly.

Disconcerted, Pom put his hand on his sword, whilst trying to look unconcerned. Monty likewise clutched his weapon. From the back of the bar emerged a woman of middle-years, with the face the colour of a pickled onion, and a body of similar shape. She carried a large jug which she placed on the bar. 'What can I do for you gentlemen?' she asked sourly.

'Mistress Roberts—Plump Poll! Don't you recognise us. I know it's been some years, but surely we haven't aged that much!' She frowned and chewed her lip. Then as recognition dawned her green eyes opened wide and she broke into a beaming smile. 'Why—it's Mister Appleby and Mister Pickle!' Then with the relish of a fishwife she said, 'God's bollocks! Whatever are you doing in Barking? Fuck me! You're the last people I would've expected. Come to buy some fish? That's what most people do!'

Monty shook his head, 'No, Poll, our business isn't fish— we've come to seek you out for information.' There was no point in wasting time with pleasantries. Monty had been given three days by Master Caxton to fulfil his quest. 'Back by Thursday, Mister Pickle, we have much work on!'

Monty added hastily, 'Of course, it's good to see you after all this time, Mistress Roberts—and clearly doing well.' He remained, as always, a polite man.

'Yes, the place makes me a tidy penny.'

'Where is Master Roberts?' asked Pom, looking around for her spouse.

'He died two years ago. I'm on my own, but as I say, doing well.'

Monty dropped his voice, 'Are you still in the same trade?'

'What—running a bawdy house?' And to his embarrassment, Poll laughed and so did the customers, who by now were following the conversation closely. 'Occasionally I might provide certain services, but I can make more money selling drink than favours; and I own a fishing boat. Putting no finer point on it—managing barrels and fish is easier than managing whores! Is there anything I can do for either of you in that area though—I am still in touch with the trade?' Pom assured her hastily that they were on an entirely different quest. In fact, looking for a man.

'Crosby—Peter Crosby. You must remember him, Poll. He came to Sir Tom's Newgate cell looking for evidence of treason; you were there when he searched my basket for letters and found a leg of pork instead!'

'I've never forgotten any of those days, Mister Appleby. Great times we had with old Sir Thomas. I tell my customers some of the stories and they hardly believe it! Now, this Crosby. Of course, I remember him—he was the Lord Chancellor's secretary and I certainly remember that old goat Stillington! Is he still Lord Chancellor after all this time?'

'No, Poll, he went out of favour with the old king and is now just the Bishop of Bath and Wells.'

'Churchman or not, what a hypocrite he was—regular in the Stews! I couldn't stand the man, although I gave him services. He tried to recruit me to spy on Sir Tom and I pretended to go along with it, but never gave anything away.'

Mindful of the time and anxious not to take a long trip down memory lane, Monty returned to the question, 'Have you any idea where Peter Crosby lives? We've been told it's somewhere in Romford, which is a day's walk from here I believe.'

'Yes, that's right. Some of my customers live there,' and before he could reply, she turned to the room and shouted, 'anyone know of a Peter Crosby? Said to live in Romford?'

There was a silence, then a lanky and filthily dressed man of middle-years stood up and said, 'Might do! Is it worth a drink?'

Pom quickly intervened, knowing that his trusting friend would take the man at his word, get out his purse and buy him a tankard of ale before he had the information. 'It might be, stranger,' he said. 'Tell me what you know and there'll be something more than a pint for you.'

'There's a Debra Crosby who lives in Romford. She has a man living with her she says is her brother, but no one believes it.'

'Have you seen the man? What does he look like?' asked Monty eagerly.

'About forty—long dark hair, small—bit rat-like. They say he writes thing—po—po…'

'Poetry?'

'That's it—rhymes. Doesn't do a day's work. No one knows how he gets his money. Lives off the woman, I suppose.'

Pom muttered to Monty, 'That's him! We've got him!' He turned to the fisherman, 'Sounds like our man. Can you give me an address?'

'You mean—where does he live?'

'Yes, that's it; where does he live?'

'Let's see the money first!' And Pom took out a sixpence and laid it on the bar, whilst keeping his finger on the coin. 'Go to the end of the main street—three cottages. Mistress Crosby lives in the middle one. Tidy little place it is—good garden with plenty of—', but Pom cut him off before they were treated to a horticultural appraisal. He slid the coin towards the man and said, 'Thanks stranger. That's for your trouble!' There was a murmur among the audience and expectant looks as they gazed at their friend who was now "in funds". To their disappointment he placed the precious coin in his pocket and sat down again.

Turning to their hostess, Pom said, 'We'll be travelling straight to Romford from here, but can we get something to eat first, Poll? It'll give us a chance to catch up. We've much news—especially of Meg and Tony!'

'That I can't wait to hear! Certainly we can feed you—and on the house.'

'What's on offer, Poll?' asked Monty.

'What do you think? Fish—what else!'

\*\*\*\*\*\*

They left *The Cog Inn* in the late afternoon, having debated whether they should ask Mistress Roberts to put them up for the night, or head for Romford as planned and seek an inn there. The decision was made to follow the latter option for two reasons: Plump Poll's tavern was none too clean and both men knew the rooms were likely to be dire; secondly, they would spend less time on the quest if they were already in Romford by the next morning and could go directly to Crosby's house. While enjoying a surprisingly good fishy meal with the lady, they passed on as much of the news from the last twelve years as they had time for. At four o'clock, they bid Poll farewell and promised to return the next day with more tales of their wanderings in France and Burgundy. 'My, you gentlemen have travelled further than I could imagine and such lives you're leading!' She had been particularly impressed with Meg's rise in the world. 'So, Six-toed Tanner kept his oath and married her!'

'Why are you surprised, Poll? He's a man of honour.'

'A rogue who could tie women in knots around his little finger! I had a yen for his blue eyes myself, you know! He could do anything he liked with—'

'Indeed, Poll,' burst in Monty, not wishing to hear any more of Tony Tanner's prowess with women. 'But he's now respectably married and has two sturdy boys. Time's moved on for us all!' And he skilfully brought the conversation onto other matters, like how long it would take them to ride to Romford.

'She said under two hours and she was right!' Pom looked about him as they entered the main street of the village. He sniffed the air, 'If you could distinguish the trade in Barking as fish—then here it's leather! Jack Worms would like this.' And it was true. Romford was well known as a place dealing in the treatment of hides and the selling of leather-goods in its substantial market, which was not operating on that day. In fact, the town was quiet since it was past six and everyone was indoors or in one of the two taverns.

Poll's directions were helpful, 'If you'll take my advice— you'll head for the *Market Tavern* in the main street. Tell Master Gabbett you know Mistress Pauline at the *Cog*. He'll find you rooms, even though it'll be late when you arrive. They're as suspicious of strangers there as they are here.' Her advice was sound. Once they'd introduced themselves, the master of the house welcomed them warmly and showed them to a decent room at the back—one bed, but they had shared on many occasion and, as it was for one night only, they made no objection. They had another meal—a roast capon between them—and turned in early with the object of rising as soon as it was light and seeking out Mister Crosby. They had not confirmed with their host that Peter Crosby was a resident of Romford; gossip spreads rapidly in small country places and they had no wish to alert their quarry that there were strangers enquiring after him. They had already decided the element of surprise could only be favourable to their cause.

The next morning they retrieved their horses from the stables at the back of the tavern and, following the fisherman's directions, headed off eastward towards the far end of the street and the outskirts of the town. 'I hope the rogue hasn't cheated us and sent us on a wild goose chase!' growled Pom. 'I paid good money for that information; if he has, I'll seek him out on the way back—you can be sure of that.'

'Before you start grumbling, I think he was telling the truth. Look—there are the three cottages. The one in the middle has a decent garden, just as he said.'

'So, what do we do? The shutters are open; they must be up and doing! We'll knock and see what we will see! After all these years we may be getting close to the truth.'

'I sincerely hope so,' sighed Monty. Perhaps it would all have been in vain. Perhaps Crosby was never involved and had no idea where the manuscript was. Ten years was a long time. *A long time to keep a promise. But I made an oath and will fulfil it*, he muttered to himself.

'What's that?' asked Pom.

'Nothing—let's knock and see who answers!'

****** 

'Another day of boredom and no visitors I suppose!' Peter Crosby stretched and thought it was time he rose and faced the day. He could hear his sister crashing about downstairs with pots and pans, grumbling to herself as usual about how put-upon she was. Well, he needed his breakfast, so the sooner he got up, dressed himself and went downstairs, the sooner he could eat and withdraw to the pokey chamber she had grudgingly allocated for his use. His "book-room" as he liked to think of it, was meagerly furnished with a rickety table and chair, knocked up by a local carpenter who skills mainly lay in hammering together market stalls and sheds of rough wood. Using the same raw material the man had nailed up a few shelves on which there were fewer books. Crosby's recurring desire was expressed thus: *If I had the money, I could fill these spaces—preferably with my poetry, leather-bound, with my name on the spines in gold leaf.*

For the fisherman of Barking was correct; Peter Crosby did style himself "a poet", certainly nothing as unrefined as a balladeer. He had always had a yen for the art since university, where he discovered the works of the great Italian poets and acquired a special admiration for Petrarch. To his great dissatisfaction he was not born with the wherewithal to become a fully-fledged versemonger but, obtaining a law degree, had subsequently made his way in life as secretary to a variety of government officers, working his way from assistant to the Clerk of Works, to right-hand man and dogsbody for Robert Stillington, Lord Chancellor, who he continued to work for after that man's loss of office in '73 and until his serious fall from grace in '78.

*If that stupid bastard hadn't insisted in meddling in dangerous matters with the Duke of Clarence, he would still be in a proper job and so might I*! was the recurring sour theme in Mister Crosby's consciousness. It had been a time of great danger when the soldiers had gone to Chiswick, where Stillington was living, and arrested him "for high treason". What a shock it was when a servant had rushed to Peter's lodgings and told him their master was being rowed down the Thames to the Tower at that moment, and 'they'll surely have his head, Mister Crosby. You should look out for yours!' And he did, by making a run for it to Essex where he took sanctuary with his much older sister who had never liked him. For the last five years, they'd lived uneasily and disharmoniously; she resenting this intruder; he hating the place—it's flatness, stink of animals, and the dullness of its inhabitants. *There's no one here to have an erudite conversation with. For two pins, I'd move back to London*! But he knew this was a dream. He needed a roof over his head and a cheap housekeeper. Debra Crosby might grumble, but her brother paid his way. The Barking fisherman was wrong in one respect—Peter did not live off his sister. When he had turned up on her doorstep five years ago, he had assured her he could pay rent. And where did the money come from? Well, in his pocket was the grand sum of £20 which, if you have been paying attention dear reader, was the very amount Lord Rivers paid to one Doctor Makepeace for a manuscript entitled *The Tale of King Arthur* or, as we recognise it, *Le Morte D'Arthur*. This had been in the year '73, five years before Stillington's downfall. Being in gainful employment, Crosby, with remarkable self-discipline, had squirreled away the cash rather than indulging his bibliophile cravings; the reason had been practical and prescient: *I might need the money one day. While I'm in work on good pay, I don't have to use it, but times being as they are employment may not necessarily remain secure. When the time's right, I'll spend it on books*!

Stillington and he had hatched the original plan to get hold of the manuscript, which they both recognised as uniquely valuable. Indeed, Crosby had undertaken a perilous journey overseas, paid for by the state, in pursuit of this quest. When he returned and was quizzed by his master as to his success, he reported failure with a doleful, regretful face, while secretly congratulating himself on his cleverness. As we know, he sold the manuscript on, the proceeds going directly into his cash box and by-passing Stillington's, who accepted his secretary's word and considered the matter closed. In '78 their paths had diverted—Robert Stillington to the Tower for a few weeks, then the wilderness of disgrace until, after Edward IV's death, he had been invited to join the new young king's council; Crosby to the home of his cross patch sister and obscurity.

Romford was not a town where Euterpe, the muse of the lyrical poet, was wont to visit. In the five-years Crosby had lived there, she had steadfastly refused his invitations and gone on her capricious way to other places worthier of her time and effort—erotic Coventry for example.

*Fuck it*! muttered Peter, one winter's day in the year '79. *I'll never have any of my work recognised while I languish here. These hands were not made for chopping wood*! he cursed, as he hacked at a pile of old timber his sister had bought from a bankrupt chandler. But soon there was a glimmer of hope. Later in the spring of that year, word reached Romford of the printing of Master Chaucer's Canterbury Tales; a set of stories familiar to most sections of society, if only for their saucy bits. Most of that good market town's inhabitants knew nothing of presses, other than those which produced wine, and cared less. The momentous implications of "The greatest invention since the wheel", as it was relayed to them via London traders, had passed over their heads and, with studied and understandable indifference, they expressed more interest in the current market-price of doe-hide. But Crosby was not indifferent. In fact, he was positively aquiver with the news. He had been aware of the arrival of Caxton's enterprise in the year '76 while he was still resident in London, but it had not registered as relevant to him. In fact he had dismissed it as "a fancy" which would soon be surpassed by another "good idea". However, when news of Chaucer's work being committed to print was casually filtered through to him by his sister he had an epiphany. He told her, 'Debra, this is it! The opportunity for poets to disseminate their works. I must be part of it!' Visions of leather-bound volumes of well-thumbed poetry in the vernacular by Peter Crosby, Master of Letters (Oxon)—the new Geoffrey Chaucer—flashed through his mind and raised the hairs on the back of his neck. But Debra Crosby was as unmoved as her neighbours, 'I can't see why you're making such a fuss, brother. It's all going on in London; it'll never catch on in Romford.'

'That's why I intend to move immediately to London and set up as a writer.'

Now Miss Crosby was dismayed. Much as she resented her brother's lazy ways, which all stemmed from this poetry nonsense, she enjoyed the rent he paid which she was putting away for her old age. 'I wouldn't make too many hasty decisions, brother,' she advised soothingly. 'Why not wait and see how this new—new—er—press, printing press is accepted by the nobility.' Miss Crosby had great faith in the judgement of the nobility, who must know what's what. If they thought such an invention worth their interest, then the rest of society could safely embrace it. 'Would it not be a good idea to write some poetry first and send it off to this—who was it?'

'Caxton, William Caxton.'

'Yes, send off your work and see if he likes it!'

Much as Peter Crosby despised his sister for her lack of literary skills and complete uninterest in his own work, he had to admit she might be right. Printing was very new and might not be accepted in the highest places. She was also correct in reminding him he had little work to show anyone. He inwardly admitted he had been idle too long. *But this is the spur I needed to get me going again! I'll work on new stuff and send off a manuscript when I have enough to make it worthwhile.* The thought of "a manuscript" jerked his memory to *Le Morte D'Arthur. I must be sure of making copies of all my works before I send them anywhere. I won't be caught out like that caitiff Malory and his minions—a life's work unrecognised because the old fool wouldn't make copies "in case they got into the wrong hands". Well, it did, and thank the Lord for it! I'll also stay here—it's as good a place to work from, cheap and with a ready-made housekeeper. I can avoid some of the harder work by insisting my time is better spent with a pen than an axe and I'll promise the old cow some of the proceeds.*

Thus we find the charmless Mister Crosby, versemonger manqué, who once described himself to his former master, the one-time Lord Chancellor, as "a bit of a poet", but who had now elevated himself to the status of "serious writer".

\*\*\*\*\*\*

'You knock, I'll look out for him. The bastard might try and make a run for it!' Pom was looking stern, but Monty thought this approach unnecessary and said, 'Surely he won't recognise us after all this time?'

'He'll still have a guilty conscience.'

'We don't know he's guilty of anything!'

'Of course he is. As Sir Tom would say, 'As guilty as fucking Judas!' There's only one way to find out—knock on the door and see if he's in.'

Monty obliged, giving a couple of gentle raps on a studded oak door. It opened within seconds, and a small, grey-haired woman in her fifties opened it and looked out suspiciously. The Crosbys had few visitors. 'Yes?' was the unpromising response.

'Is—er—is Mister Crosby at home?' Monty asked, politely he hoped.

'What is it you want?'

'To speak to him, please.'

'Who is it who wants him and what is it about?'

They had still not agreed how they should identify themselves or their business. Pom was all for an open admission of who they were; Monty thought they should introduce themselves as old acquaintances from London. As the latter seemed to be in control of matters across the doorstep, he said, 'We knew Mister Crosby when he was in London and have come to see him on er—'

Pom stepped up, 'On matters of great importance—financial matters.'

Now, if anything can get a woman—or man's—attention at their front door, it's the term "financial matters", as expressed by a well-dressed, respectable gentleman. Miss Crosby was no exception, but her thoughts flew immediately to problem rather than profit.

'What do you mean, "financial matters"? We owe no one anything. I'm in charge of "financial matters" in this house, and we are free of debt.' Why is it the stranger on the doorstep who is there to discuss money issues, however well-dressed, must be a debt-collector? Debra Crosby had the acute fear of debt common to people of the middling sort. The word had connotations of all the expressions summed up in "dishonourable". It was not to be borne that either of them owed money to anyone, other than their landlord; but Debra had never been in arrears of rent.

'Are you saying my brother has run up debts?'

'Certainly not—well, not as far as we are concerned. No, it is about something else entirely. Now, is he in or not!' Pom became assertive.

With a sense of relief, Debra called to her brother who, cloistered in his study was trying to ignore the evident sounds of conversation floating upwards. Sighing at the interruption, he made his way downstairs to the front door, where he saw his sister and two men—men he vaguely recognised but was not sure.

'Brother, these men want to speak to you of "financial matters". Is there anything you haven't told me?' she asked accusingly.

'No sister! I have no idea what this about. Who are you?'

'May we come in? Our business may take some time,' said Pom. Now, an Englishman's home is his—in this case—tiny cottage—and Peter was not prepared to allow invaders across the threshold without good reason. 'Tell me what you want, and I'll consider it.'

Monty stepped forward. *Le Morte D'Arthur,* he said. 'We want to know where it is!'

There was a silence. Debra looked at her brother with a frown and blank expression; Peter looked at Monty with wide-eyes and a bewildered expression. Then recognition dawned, 'I know you—Malory's creatures! Don't tell me—I'll remember in a minute!'

'Mister John Appleby and Mister Montmorency Pickle! Let's not waste time, Mister Crosby. Are you going to let us in, or shall I tell your sister here the whole sordid story on the doorstep?' Pom had his toe against the door, and Debra had stepped back hastily into the hallway.

Within seconds, they were in Debra's good parlour sitting on uncomfortable wooden seats.

'Debra, there's no need for you to stay. I'm sure you have better things to do!'

But the words, "sordid story" had more than stirred her curiosity; it had rung a loud warning bell in her head. 'Certainly not brother. You may need my help. These men seem rather—er—rather—'

'—Angry, Mistress—er—' said Monty helpfully.

'—Miss—Miss Crosby.'

'Miss Crosby, I beg your pardon!' said Monty. 'Yes, we are angry and have travelled many miles to get answers to a long-standing matter which concerns your brother.'

'Well, would you like to explain then? What has he done—or is accused of—which is what you seem to be hinting.'

'He stole a unique and precious document and we are here to find out what he did with it and if it can be retrieved and returned to its rightful owners.'

'Brother, what are they talking about. What is this document?'

'Nothing that need concern you, sister. Do as I say, go into the kitchen or somewhere; leave me to sort this matter out.'

'They're accusing you of theft! I have a right to defend you brother!' She turned to Pom, 'Sir, my brother has been a respectable and respected officer of the crown. He was secretary to the Lord Chancell—'

'Yes, Miss Crosby, we are aware of your brother's previous position. All we want to do is question him about the theft of this valuable document in which we are certain he is implicated.'

'Do you have any evidence?'

'Circumstantial—but serious and credible enough for us to seek him out. If we could all calm down and then my friend Mister Pickle and I will put certain questions to him. That way he can prove his innocence, or we can prove his guilt!'

Debra looked hard at her brother and recognised a shifty look when she saw one. He had always been a little sneak—and a thief as a boy. Stealing her trinkets and selling them to the tinkers when they came. He told lies too, denying misdemeanours for which he knew he'd get a thrashing; even

117

blaming her so that she received the whipping. Despite her protestations on his behalf, she didn't like him at all, and only tolerated his presence because "Blood is thicker than water" although what that meant she had no idea. Now she said sharply, 'Brother, unless we are to play host to these men all day, I suggest you do as the man says, and answer his questions; that way you can prove your innocence—or not.'

Crosby looked defiant but, as his sister pursed her lips and frowned, he realised he was cornered. Better to try and weasel his way out of the situation and deny everything. They had no proof against him. In the end, if they did have any solid evidence, he could offer money in recompense on the understanding they went away for good, and never involved him in the business again.

It was so unfair! All he had ever wanted to do was write poetry.

\*\*\*\*\*\*

'The piece of cod!' And Pom chuckled as he turned his horse's head away from the stables at the *Market Tavern* and they headed back towards Barking.

'Which passeth all understanding!' said Monty. 'Why are you quoting Philippians at me?'

'Not "The peace of God", you fool! "The piece of cod"— the fish that made you ill in Bruges!'

'Ah, yes! that was a craven act, but clever how he got away with it; not so clever how easy it was to get him to admit he stole the manuscript.'

'Of course, it was his sister who really clinched it, Monty! She doesn't like him at all, does she?'

'I have some sympathy with him—my sisters had no time for me—being the youngest and smallest. But you're right, she was certainly hostile to him. God help him when we left. I wouldn't be surprised if she doesn't throw him out bag and baggage!'

'Well, if she hadn't been there I'd have beaten the truth out of him. Pity she was—I would've liked to have given him a good thumping!'

'I could hardly believe how devious he was—poisoning my food like that, and almost in front of me!'

'The truth will out, even though it's taken ten years!'

For, just as Tony Tanner had wished, Peter Crosby had been squeezed of the facts while cornered by three adversaries, although fortunately it had been unnecessary to handle his genitals. Once the story had been laid out by these two strangers, Debra Crosby, recognising her brother's facility for scheming, was as keen as they were to wring the truth out of him. In the end, it was as the Newgate Fellowship suspected; Crosby admitted he had gone to Monty's lodgings disguised as a doctor and gained exclusive access to the sick room for eight days.

As he explained, 'I searched for days for the key to the only locked cupboard; it wasn't easy to find hidden away in your secret pocket—and then, once I had the manuscript I substituted blank sheets for the real thing and took it out in my bag—right under the nose of your wife!' It was the only time Crosby looked pleased with himself, for Pom stepped forward menacingly, and Peter's sister tightened her lips and glared at him, until he lowered his eyes and looked sheepish.

'The question is, Crosby, what did you do with it then? Or have you still got it?' asked Monty.

119

'I brought it back to London and sold it.'

'To whom?'

'To Earl Rivers!'

'How much?'

'—Er—£10.'

'How much?' And Debra stepped forward with a glint in her eye; she knew when her brother was lying. 'When you came here, you said you'd saved £15 working for Lord Stillington, and you'd use it to pay your rent. I wouldn't have taken you in for that long otherwise, so I know it was more than £10, brother!'

'All right—£15.'

'Are you sure?' And she loomed over him.

'Yes!' He would hang on to the £5 if it killed him!

'Earl Rivers obviously knew the manuscript was valuable to pay that much for it,' Pom said thoughtfully.

'He was very excited when he saw it. Couldn't wait to get his hands on it.'

'Did he say what he was going to do with it?'

'No, but I suppose he would put it in his library.'

'Hmm,' mused Monty, 'when and where did this transaction take place?'

'April '73, in his lodgings in Westminster.'

'Was anyone else present?' asked Pom. Rivers was dead, and it was crucial they found someone who would know what happened to *Le Morte D'Arthur* afterwards, now the Woodville estate had been broken up.

'His lawyer Andrew Dymock knew about it. I had to go to him for the cash—oh, and there was a steward there as well.'

The conversation continued until Pom and Monty were sure they had levered every detail from the rascal. After an hour's questioning, they left him to the mercy of his sister. As for the money, he assured them the £15 had been spent long ago, so there was no possibility of redress there. When Pom enquired how Crosby made his living if the money was no more, Debra advised him that her brother acted as a scribe for some merchants in Romford. 'He makes a living, but only enough to pay his way,' she said with pursed lips, glaring at Pom and defying him to insist on reparation in instalments.

As they jogged along the track towards Barking, Monty said, 'It's the meddling with the fish that astonishes me. Crosby certainly has a devious mind and a deal of patience. To get to know the cook at our regular tavern and then spin him a story about how I'd taken his girl and he wanted revenge by making me "slightly ill".

'Then giving the cook a purgative to slip into the cod— any taste masked because Henri had already smothered the fish in his familiar onion and ale sauce. Crosby would assure him it was harmless, and the cook would think of it as a joke. Surprising Henri didn't mention it when he heard you were ill.'

'Probably scared stiff the stuff might kill you—and I'd wager Crosby paid him to keep his mouth shut,' said Monty.

'He certainly was desperate to get his hands on *Le Morte*!'

'Not as desperate as we are, Pom!'

'Well, let's return home and discuss all this with the Fellowship. See if our friends can come up with any ideas of how we progress.'

'I think we should speak to Master Caxton. He had a very good relationship with Earl Rivers—they were friends to the end. He might know what Anthony Woodville could have done with his library—who he bequeathed it to.'

'Let's hope it's not been broken up and scattered among friends and enemies, Monty! Knowing the facility of the nobility to take revenge on one another, as we suggested before, the earl's collection could've been burned out of spite!'

'Jesus Christ! I hope not,' and Monty turned pale and briefly fumbled with the reins. The horse stumbled and snorted disagreeably.

Pom frowned, 'No point in troubling trouble—'

'—Until trouble troubles you—yes, I know all the old wives' saying but it doesn't ease my mind. We may have solved several mysteries today—but I fear it is not the end of the quest!'

# Chapter 5

We return to London and follow the fortunes of Lady Tanner
and her sewing basket;
Members of the Fellowship hold earnest conversations
with significant men;
Tony and Meg find more than they expected;

The second week of August and Meg was making her way
into the Abbey on her customary route. The guards at the
postern gate were so used to her visits they let her through
unchallenged, other than a lewd comment or two which she
persistently ignored.

The routine inside was unchanging. The basket was taken
into the queen's private apartment, linen exchanged, and then
returned to the seamstress, who was then taken to a small
anteroom, ostensibly to be paid, but also to conceal letters and
small packages in the pockets of her chemise. If there was to
be any random checking of the basket, either in or out, all the
guards would find was pristine linen, beautifully
embroidered. In truth this was not Meg's work, for she was
unpractised with a needle and thread. The original work was
that of an expert; the garments, sheets and kerchiefs simply
rearranged for each visit. For it was confidently assumed that
simple-minded guards would have as much knowledge of

exquisite point-work as a seamstress would have of fletching an arrow.

This day was different. Meg arrived and, instead of waiting outside the queen's chamber, she was ushered in. Queen Elizabeth had evidently been crying, as had the three ladies with her. There was an air of deep misery in the room and Meg was uncertain of what she should say or do. She curtsied low and waited for the queen to speak.

'Mistress Limpett, we have had grave news and there will be no exchange of linen today. I—I—' and her voice faded. She put one of the beautifully embroidered kerchiefs to her face and turned away. One of the ladies-in-waiting stepped forward and said, 'The queen has another task for you,' and she turned to a chair across which lay a simple blue gown. 'She wishes you to change into this dress and wear it home. The hem and waistband must be altered to suit her majesty. It is considered you are almost the same height and therefore makes sense for you to try it for size.'

'I understand, my lady,' but Meg was confused. Why couldn't she try it on in front of the queen and then carry the dress home in the basket as usual? Why did she have to wear it herself? Seeing the confusion on Meg's face, the lady-in-waiting said, 'As you can see, her majesty is indisposed and cannot involve herself in these trifles; that is why we wish you to wear it home. Also, we do not wish the dress to be crushed in the basket; it belonged to the queen's mother and is very precious to her majesty. The hem is the important area for you to work on, but the waist needs alteration too. Now, go to the anteroom and change. There are also written instructions for you,' and she looked meaningfully at Meg, who nodded and bowed her way out.

Wearing the cast-off dress of a woman once deemed a witch, Meg walked back towards the postern gate. She thought to herself, *Jacquetta may have been a duchess, but she had a poor taste in dresses! The garment hangs badly and the waistband's too thick. It completely ruins the line of the gown. But who am I to grumble, I've never worn a garment graced by a duchess before!* She walked casually as usual past the guard at the gate, but immediately she was outside into Broad Sanctuary, a figure approached her from the shadow of a wall close by.

'Mistress Limpett! One moment if you please!' She turned in surprise to see who it was addressing her. To her complete astonishment, she recognised Robert Stillington, erstwhile Lord Chancellor, but, in Meg's memory, frequenter of the Stews and seeker of the services of its whores. 'I want a moment of your time, woman. Bring your basket and follow me!'

\*\*\*\*\*\*

While Meg in her ducal blue gown was, with trepidation, obediently following the plump priest out of the abbey and towards Westminster Palace, three of the Newgate Fellowship were reunited in the back of Jack's workshop. It was a convenient place to meet, for Monty and Pom, newly returned from Essex, wanted to make an appointment with William Caxton to discuss what to do about the manuscript. But first they recounted all the details of the visit to Jack Worms who was particularly incensed at the vile treatment of Monty in Bruges. "The fucking caitiff!" was his assessment of Mister Crosby, and, since Master Worms was not one to use expletives to any great extent, it was an explicit show of his disgust.

Monty brought them back to the most important matter, 'So, we can be certain *Le Morte D'Arthur* went into River's collection, and he paid fifteen pounds for it! My, I always thought it was worth money, but not that much! But we still don't know where it is. It seems to me that the only man who can help is Andrew Dymock, Rivers' lawyer. Is he still alive—or has he gone the way of his master?'

'Caxton may know, Monty,' Jack said. 'He had many personal dealings with Lord Rivers. I suggest we wait and see what he says about how to proceed.'

\*\*\*\*\*\*

'The question is, mistress, how do we proceed?'

'Proceed in what, sir?' Meg took a haughty stance. Apart from another layer of fat from good living, Stillington hadn't changed so much in twelve years and she wondered if she had. If not, there was a chance he might recognise her. He had never been one of her customers, for Meg had worked out of Gropecunt and Popkirtle Lanes—even a rampant old goat like him avoided those dangerous streets, where lecherous men could end up with a sore prick or a knife in their guts, probably the latter following the former. The Stews were marginally safer, and Master Robert's *The Unicorn* was safer than most. Meg had only worked for Plump Poll at the bawdy house as a barmaid—her beauty valued for the marriage market. Poll had never put her to work, despite Master Robert's protestations that 'she's more of an asset on her back than in the marriage bed, where we'll only get paid once for her!' But Stillington had been a customer when Meg was taken to *The Unicorn* and she had served him wine and sweet cakes on several occasions. Her young beauty was not to be forgotten, and he had cast many a-leering look her way. Although now approaching thirty and with two children, her face retained those intrinsic structures of enduring beauty which would remain with her into old age.

However, there was no recognition in those bird-like eyes as Stillington licked his dry old lips. 'Proceed to discover what secrets you conceal in this basket of yours.'

'Sir, I am a humble seamstress with orders to fulfil—the fact that I serve Queen—'

'That whore's no longer queen.'

Meg was shocked at the vitriol, but kept her composure, '—Serve she who was queen, is nothing secret. Search for whatever it is you are looking for, and then let me be on my way!' She held out the basket and he took it; thick, plump, ringed fingers pawed through the lacy garments. He held some up to the light, in the way Meg had seen some men hold up the intimate garments of the whores, but he resisted sniffing them, as those same men might do. Meg shuddered as she thought of Queen Elizabeth putting on the linen, unaware of whose podgy hands had fingered them. *'I'll wash then all when I return home,'* she vowed.

Sounding disappointed, Stillington looked up at Meg, 'Nothing here—but there is other linen to examine,' and he regarded her with raised eyebrows. 'Take off the dress!'

'Sir! I protest most vehemently! You have no right to insult me so!'

'There's some plotting here—my sources tell me—and I'm following up everyone who enters and leaves Elizabeth

127

Grey's apartments. I can assure you I have not singled you out for special treatment. Take off the dress!'

'My lord, if you are to continue with this gross discourtesy, then I would wish for a woman to act as chaperone! I refuse to undress in front of a man alone, other than my husband!'

'But, Mistress Limpett, I am the Bishop of Bath and Wells—a celibate man with no inclination or intention of ravishing you!'

*Liar*! she thought, but said robustly, 'I don't care if you're the Archbishop of Canterbury, my lord! I will not take off this dress unless I am behind a screen and in the presence of another woman.'

'I seems I shall have to call in the guard and order him to strip you!'

'If you attempt it, I will scream for help and then traduce your name all over the city. "The old goat Stillington at his old tricks!" As soon as she said it, she realised she had made a terrible blunder. How was she to know of Stillington's visits to the bawdy houses?

He stopped and eyed her suspiciously. 'What are you—'

She thought on her feet, *Seize the initiative Meg! Get in first*. She looked him in the eye and said, 'My lord, like many others, I've heard the things that are put about—palaces are breeding grounds for gossip. Your visits to the South Bank are well-known! I can say no more—but you have left yourself open to such accusations. I make no judgement as to whether it is true, but that is what is said—and by respectable servants here and elsewhere in London—and perhaps Bath and even Wells!'

Stillington frowned. She was right, and he was aware some of his colleagues guessed he frequented the Stews. He denied it, of course, and even though he was not believed, since others deemed as "gentlemen" and even "noblemen" pursued the same activities, the sexual proclivities of the bishop were generally ignored. But the idea of the facts being posted up in taverns and market-places—and the doors of St Paul's was a different matter. He looked back at Meg's steely face. 'Very well. Sergeant!' And he called in the guard. 'Find one of the female scullions and bring her here at once!'

They waited a few minutes during which time Meg and Lord Stillington stared defiantly at each other across the small chamber. When the guard returned with a scared and scruffy kitchen maid, Meg said, 'You won't forget the screen, sir?' And another few minutes passed while the sergeant searched the palace. 'It took some finding, sir!' he grunted as he pulled the folding partition into the room. 'I had to go all the way to—'

'Never mind that—just put it here! Now, Mistress Limpett, I've fulfilled all your conditions, perhaps you will fulfil mine and take off the dress.'

Meg stepped behind the screen and undid the buttons on the gown. Slipping it round her feet, she stood in her chemise and boots. 'I will throw it over and you may examine it. But I can tell you, there are no pockets in queens' dresses—they spoil the line!'

'Never mind. I want the undergarment too!'

'You go too far sir! The girl may come around and search the chemise for you; I refuse to stand naked in a chamber housing a bishop—screen or no screen!'

129

'Very well. Girl! Go behind and search through the woman's chemise. Look for hidden pockets!'

By this time, the girl, no more than eleven, was scared out of her wits and clueless as to what was occurring. She came behind the screen to find Meg standing in only a pretty linen shift.

'Come girl, don't be frightened, you're not in trouble. Here, I have one pocket in this chemise—search it and take whatever you find to the bishop.' The girl nodded and took out of the generous compartment a small slip of paper. She looked at Meg, who nodded encouragingly.

'Have you found anything girl?' Stillington was becoming impatient. He would have liked to search the woman personally, but this would have to do.

'Only this, sir!' And the kitchen maid handed him the paper. Triumphantly he grabbed it and said, 'I knew it!' Unfolding it he frowned as he read. 'Dress and show yourself to me, woman! We surely have evidence of Elizabeth Grey's treason here!'

Within minutes, Meg stood fully clothed and unsmiling before him. 'What is it you think you have, sir?'

'A secret code—figures!'

'Indeed, sir, and what do you think these figures mean?'

'I want you to tell me, woman.'

'Me sir? How would I know what any code means?'

'Who is it for? Who do you pass it to? By the Lord Jesus whom I serve, you'll end up in the Tower for this!'

'In the Tower—for jotting down measurements?'

'Measurements? What are you talking about?'

'The secret code you are excited about is concerned with measurements,' and she took the paper gently from his hand.

'Let me explain: 25inw-r is to be the finished size of the waistband of the dress you were so anxious to examine—Lady Grey's waist has thickened—all those babies I suppose. The next figure, 10inh-d, is what is required to be taken up at the hem. The number 32rn-p is a marker for a length of ribbon to be sewn on; the other letters indicate type of stitching—'

Stillington grabbed the paper back and looked suspiciously at it. Meg continued, 'We poor women cannot carry such figures in our heads, our brains being so much smaller than those of men. I have always taken the precaution of writing all measurements down as they are taken. That way I can never be accused of carelessness; call it a professional safeguard. I'm sure you take such precautions—especially with risky procedures where others are involved who may be less scrupulous than yourself—sir.'

The kitchen maid had been agog as this conversation flowed. *I'll never be able to remember it all to tell the others*! What came out was a muddled account to the "others" in the kitchen of how Bishop Stillington had stripped a lady of her gown, rummaged through her underwear, discovered some writing, copied it down, then, losing his temper had knocked over the screen and rushed out of the room cursing loudly. 'I didn't know a bishop could swear like a cook! The best part was that the lady told me I'd been a good girl and gave me sixpence for my trouble!'

\*\*\*\*\*\*

While Meg was rewarding the young scullion with kind words and ready money, Monty, Pom and Jack were sitting opposite Master Caxton in his study at the back of his Westminster press shop.

'An interesting tale, gentleman,' was his comment after Pom had related all that happened in Essex, and the true story of the loss of *Le Morte*. 'I take it you will be pursuing the matter with those administering Lord River's estates?'

'That sounds expensive, sir!' said Jack. 'We certainly can't afford lawyers and court action.'

'I take your point Master Worms and you are right. Litigation would be costly, and you might never make your money back, even if *Le Morte D'Arthur* was printed. You know well we are in the early stages of marketing our books and the outlet for them is limited to those who either appreciate them and can afford to buy our editions or pay us to publish their works. It is a somewhat awkward circle—we can publish many editions but sell only to those who can read. When literacy becomes commonplace, our books will be valued widely and prices must surely fall. But until that time, the circle is closed as we have only a limited market.'

Monty spoke up, 'Master Caxton, my only concern is to find Sir Tom's manuscript and take it to Winchester, as he requested and as I swore I would do. Now we are certain it lies somewhere in one of Lord River's properties, it is a matter of searching for it and making an offer to buy it back—'

'—Although why we should I can't think!' interrupted Jack, thumping Caxton's table. 'That caitiff Crosby stole it from us and profited by his larceny.'

'Calm yourself, Master Worms, please!' said Caxton, who did not like liberties taken with his furniture. 'You must remember, Earl Rivers purchased the manuscript in good faith—as far as his estate is concerned, it is his property. He would surely have taken the precaution of obtaining a bill of sale—even though Crosby would know it was worthless. That would be his argument in court; he trusted this spurious Doctor Makepeace—Crosby in disguise—as a man of Oxford and therefore of honour.'

'Claiming to be "a man from Oxford" and talking well can evidently take in a noble lord!' growled Pom sceptically.

'People generally believe what they want to believe, Mister Appleby!' said Caxton with a sigh. 'Lord Rivers wanted the manuscript badly enough to be taken in by a mountebank in an academic gown. But to get back to the problem of retrieval. Dymock's your man; he's in charge of administering Rivers' estates, although there aren't many of them. There's a property in Kent—The Mote—which his family own outright and cannot be taken by the crown. He was fond of the place and told me how he was spending large sums having the tower raised and some dais made bigger and grander, all by the king's mason no less.'

'You knew the earl well I understand, sir,' Monty looked hopefully at the printer's face; Caxton's curly and abundant beard held a fascination for all who viewed it and Monty always wondered how such a growth was managed, his own adult life having mostly been led clean-shaven. The pink lips above the beard formed themselves into a smile, 'Extremely well, Mister Pickle. You know yourself how much work he put our way. His vernacular translation of the sayings of the philosophers was the first book we printed in England in the year after we arrived—although, of course, our first *work* was the Abbot of Abingdon's Indulgence for—'

'Yes, sir!' Jack received a frown from Caxton for his interruption, but Master Worms was sure they didn't need a

133

catalogue of Westminster editions since their arrival in the country in '76 and he continued, 'Nonetheless, the question is who inherits his books?'

"Master Worms", and Caxton looked sternly at him with raised bushy eyebrows which were almost joined to the aforementioned beard, thus making a frame around his face, 'another problem to consider, is whether the Woodville library has been scattered since the earl's execution. My guess is that it won't have been. The new king is a northern man of war, not a sophisticated man of letters—although he's not completely illiterate, I understand. Some say Richard III, as we must call him, is a pious man. But my instincts tell me he is like all grasping noblemen, on his knees when it suits— likewise piously handing out cash for masses and charitable institutions. It's all politics! But I digress. I would say it's unlikely that King Richard will make it a priority to plunder the Woodville literary legacy, especially with this trouble in the southern counties. I would advise that your first call would be on Andrew Dymock, who is still here in Westminster; I saw him about the palace two days ago. He's an affable man, but busy as you can imagine. However, I'm sure if you put your request to see him in writing he would look favourably on it. You can but try! What you then ask him I leave to you, but you may have to prepare yourselves for a demand for the original sum to be paid back, and with interest—if Dymock is prepared to sell. Who knows? He may have looked over the manuscript and seen a profit to be made from it. As one of the estate's executors he is honour-bound to seek the maximum advantage for the legatees.'

The trio looked one to another. *This is practical advice*, was their concerted thought. When they were back in Jack's house sipping a well-earned Burgundy from Pom's warehouse, Monty said, 'We must draft the letter to Andrew Dymock now. Let's not waste any time on further discussion—let's get on with it!'

\*\*\*\*\*\*

'"Off with it!" that's what the knave said!'

'The devil he did! That bastard bishop—I'll seek him out and deal with him, slowly and painfully when I get the chance.'

'I was concerned he would recognise me from the old days, but he was more interested in having me stripped and searched. How he's found out about our device for passing messages I can't think. It was the first time in many visits I've been challenged.'

'Magpie, the authorities are on the alert to everything which might mean plotting; these recent uprisings against the king in the south and south-west have rattled him. I'm not surprised at Stillington's action; as he said, everyone going in and out of the abbey to visit the queen must be suspect. You weren't singled out and he obviously didn't recognise you, otherwise he would have told you and challenged you even more. But enough of that rascal, take off the gown and let's look at it.'

Meg had arrived home angry, but relieved. Tony was equally relieved to see her, having waited anxiously, for she was an hour late. After explaining all that took place in the palace, she passed him a sealed letter and the slip of paper. Upstairs she began to undress, taking off the blue gown carefully. 'Bring it down and we'll look at it together!' he shouted at her as she disappeared into their bed chamber. When she returned, he laid out the dress on the table and handed Meg the paper with the measurements on it.

'These numbers and letters—did the lady-in-waiting say what they meant?'

'Just that they were "measurements which I would understand". It was obvious from her manner that the dress is very important; the fact they insisted I wore it confirms it.'

'Well, can you see anything different about it—different from any of your gowns?'

'What do you mean "any"? I only have two, neither of them silk!'

'Look at this one. Try and remember what the queen's lady said Magpie.'

'Well, she wanted the hem and waistband adjusted and these were the measurements for the alterations.'

'Let's look at the hem, shall we?' And, before Meg could stop him, Tony had grasped the fine silk, made a hole with his canines, pushed his finger into it and tore at the bottom of the dress.

'Shame on you, Tony. How can you waste such a fine gown?'

'Pass me the scissors then,' and he began to cut at the tiny stitches of the hem. She watched him as he prised the material apart until, with a grin he looked up at her and said, 'Very fine—look here!' And between his fingers he held up what looked to Meg like a small stone, the size of her little fingernail. She peered at it.

'It's a diamond, Magpie. My guess is the "d" in 10inh-d means 'ten diamonds concealed in "h" for—'

'—Yes, I begin to see what it means. So, if there are ten diamonds in the hem, are we looking at twenty-five precious stones in the "w" or the waistband?'

'I believe so and my guess is it's "r" for rubies.'

'And thirty-two rnp—p? Yes! Pearls, and somewhere else, beginning with "n". This one is not so clear. Obviously, the alteration of the length and waist of a gown is not unusual. There's nowhere else which might be changed—necklines don't usually alter, but this one is decorated with ribbon!' cried Meg, triumphantly.

'That's it, Magpie! Ribbon round neckline—with thirty-two pearls.'

'How clever of the queen to think of this, Tony. You know, she had been crying and was obviously very upset about something.'

'You can be sure she was, Meg. There's no point in concealing it—she heard three days ago that her two sons are dead—murdered by some child-killer on instructions from our new king.'

Meg was stunned into silence for a few seconds. Then she said, 'The poor, poor woman! As a mother of two boys almost the same age, I can only imagine how she must feel. Who did it? How did it happen and when?'

'No one's sure—one of Richard's henchmen I suppose; certainly, someone who the king relies on to keep his mouth shut. But these things have a habit of seeping out—tower guards with loose tongues and short of cash; kitchen staff who are badly paid and will sell anything for a few groats. As yet it's not widely known, although, of course, the rumours have been circulating since they were incarcerated in that grim place. As for how it was done—it's presumed they were poisoned or smothered and buried somewhere in the grounds—or walled up.'

'Poisoned—smothered! Two young boys! How dreadful—and what thoughts must be going on in the queen's head! How long has it been known?'

'I had it confirmed five days ago from a contact I have in the tower itself. I'm convinced the source is sound and these are the facts. But I'd surmised from Stillington's shifty manner last time I saw him that this was the case. When the murder was carried out, I'm not sure. Possibly 30th or 31st July.'

'And you've kept this to yourself, Tony?'

'I didn't want there to be any risk you would mention it to the queen or anyone else in the abbey. How else would you have found out about it if it wasn't from an internal source? The whole business is shrouded in absolute secrecy and anyone in the know is forbidden to mention it. Richard is remaining tight-lipped and insisting the boys are "in good health and happy"! Could you believe the utter evilness of the man?'

'No wonder she was so upset this morning. I can only admire her for finding the strength to pursue this plan you talk of.'

'She's a desperate woman, Meg and will be driven purely by revenge—possibly the strongest motive for anyone, especially a grieving mother. But now we must consider this gown and what it conceals. We should take the whole garment to pieces and recover whatever she has hidden inside it!'

Within half-an-hour of careful snipping and cutting, they were rewarded by the sight of a small pile of precious gems and flawless pearls lying on a cloth on the table. They both stared at the size and magnificence of the jewels; Meg had never seen a diamond, let alone held one.

'What are they worth, Tony?'

'The proverbial king's ransom—but this isn't a ransom, rather a marriage portion I suspect, Meg.'

'Marriage portion? What do you mean?'

'Better you don't know—and I have one more task for you before I tell you everything—and I promise I will. I want you to return to the abbey and confirm verbally to the queen we have retrieved the jewels and know what we are to do with them. That will be the last time you visit the place, Meg. I feel sure you won't be accosted by Stillington or anyone else. There'll be no documents to exchange, so no risk. Just deliver the linen, and the message. The queen will be expecting it.'

'You haven't told me what was in the other letter, Tony. I risked a good deal to keep that clenched in my hands while the maid searched the pockets of my chemise!'

'My orders, Magpie! As I told you, your visit is the last you will make and will provide her majesty with reassurance that the plans now laid will be carried out. I'll tell you everything soon—just make this one last visit for me— please!'

\*\*\*\*\*\*

'We've been asked to visit him in his lodgings in Fetter Lane,' Monty was reading aloud a letter from Andrew Dymock, who had been courteous and replied very quickly. 'We can take a wherry from the Westminster quay to the Inner Temple and walk up Middle Temple to Fleet Street. Fetter

Lane joins it near Clifford's Inn; some of my best lawyer-clients came from Clifford's.'

'We better go armed then!' said Pom cheerfully. 'We all know what these young student lawyers are like! When does he say Monty?'

'Two days' time—Tuesday.'

'I suppose Master Caxton will give us time off?'

'We'll probably have to make up the hours! But, no matter. We have the interview; we've made a start!'

Now, on the day appointed, they stood rather nervously in a well-furnished chamber smelling of scented beeswax. A small fire was burning in the grate and the whole atmosphere was one of comfort and order. Mistress Dymock had been polite and offered them refreshment, which they declined. Her husband, she explained, was with another client but should not be long. They were rather early.

At the stroke of ten, Andrew Dymock appeared; a tall, slender man with thick greying hair and a long rather equine face; Monty estimated he was in his early forties.

'Good morning gentlemen! You have me at a disadvantage as I do not know your names. Which of you is, let me see,' and he consulted their letter, '—ah yes, Mister Montmorency Pickle?'

Monty stepped forward, bowed and then introduced his companions.

'Now we know each other, please take your ease and let me call for wine?' Pom was not going to refuse a second time, and Dymock rang a small bell. A servant appeared, took the order for "a decent wine" and their host settled back in his well-upholstered chair. 'You noticed I ordered a good Burgundy because I recognise your name, Mister Appleby. If

I'm not mistaken, you are the owner of a wine shop and a wholesaler of good repute. I've had some of your quality vintages and have not been disappointed. I would never serve inferior wine to an expert!'

'That is very courteous of you, sir!' said Pom with a smile. Monty and Jack exchanged uneasy glances; this was no time for deviation to matters of viticulture. They knew Pom would easily be distracted into a long discussion on the merits of different grapes and their sources.

Monty took the initiative as the servant returned with a tray, a jug and four glasses. 'You will remember from our letter, Mister Dymock, our business concerns the late Earl Rivers' library. It was Master William Caxton who advised us to contact you as the chief administrator of the earl's estates.'

'Ah yes, Caxton. I had dealings with the man when the earl was alive. Lord Rivers was a man of learning and letters and he wrote considerable amounts of philosophy and poetry. Caxton printed several of his works and I was sent to the print shop to negotiate terms and editorial matters. I believe I saw you there on occasion, Master Worms and Mister Pickle!'

'You would have had the advantage of us, Mister Dymock,' and Jack smiled. 'Master Caxton took exclusive control of Earl Rivers' manuscripts. I merely printed them off and bound them into volumes.'

'And very fine they were, Master Worms.'

'Were? Do they no longer exist?' And Monty leaned forward, anxiety clearly in his face.

'I speak in the past tense of their production, Mister Pickle. As far as I know, my master's library remains untouched at The Mote. We moved the last of his most precious manuscripts and books to Kent last year. He had a strict routine—once he had perused a work at his lodgings in Westminster and deemed it fit for his library, he would send myself or his servant Butside with it to be stored there. I believe his reasoning was that he spent much time away from London—on pilgrimages abroad and official business and that his collection would be safe from theft, fire or damage which might occur at any time in the city. He remembered when the old Duke of York's house was looted and burned to the ground; I told him that was thirty years ago, but he said, "You can never be too careful, Andrew!"'

Monty was anxious to get down to the point of their visit. 'We are most certainly interested in the late earl's collection, and one manuscript in particular.'

'I'm afraid I may not remember individual items; although the collection is not huge, there are possibly over one hundred works of varying sizes and subjects. One thing which may help, my master maintained—or at least his steward did—a catalogue of every work down at The Mote.'

'That is good news. But you may remember a certain very large manuscript called *Le Morte D'Arthur*. It was in vernacular English and ran to some eight hundred pages. We believe Earl Rivers acquired it ten years ago, from a Doctor Makepeace who claimed he was a Doctor of Letters or Theology from Oxford.'

Dymock sat up. 'Claimed? Do you mean he was an imposter?'

'Yes, I'm afraid he was, and he had no right to the manuscript—in fact he had stolen it.'

'That is a serious accusation, Mister Pickle. Yes, I do happen to remember the occasion, mostly because I was concerned that his lordship was spending money on luxuries which he could not afford. I even remember the sum involved which was twenty pounds—in my opinion, too much for a book—any book!'

'That caitiff said he got fifteen pounds for it!' Jack flushed with anger.

'Whoever the caitiff was, I can assure you it was twenty. Anyway, it will be entered in the catalogue and my accounts. It was a large sum at a time when his lordship was in debt for almost one thousand pounds.'

'May I ask where the manuscript is now?'

'I am certain it has not been moved from The Mote during the last ten years. Earl Rivers may have had some plans for it and discussed them with his steward. As I remember, it was in a rather dog-eared state—as though it had been carted around from one place to another! It is certain that he has never presented it to Master Caxton—otherwise you would have known of it. Once the earl was busy as the young Prince of Wales's governor, he rarely spent time in Kent. As well as his frequent pilgrimages, he was mostly in Ludlow and the midlands for those ten years, until his unfortunate end in June.'

The Newgate trio maintained a suitably respectful silence for a few seconds, then Jack asked, 'Who is heir to Lord Rivers' estates?'

'His brother Richard inherits the Woodville lands and title; other estates Lord Anthony held from his first wife's family, the Scales, goes to his brother Edward Woodville. But the property in Kent is still owned outright by Queen Elizabeth, the earl's sister and I presume the contents will pass to her, when the will is proved; unless the king interferes with natural law and seizes the properties to share them with his—

er—followers.' It was evident from his disapproving expression that Andrew Dymock had little time for the newly crowned Richard III.

'Mister Dymock, is there any chance we might be allowed to visit The Mote and Lord Rivers' library?' asked Monty.

'Are you thinking of trying to retrieve the document, Mister Pickle? I can tell you, as a lawyer, that his lordship had a bill of sale signed and witnessed by Butside and myself at the time of the transaction and the money changed hands. It will be very difficult for you to make a claim on the estate.'

'Might it be possible to purchase it?'

Jack looked mutinous—and was about to intervene, but Dymock said, 'There may be an opportunity to make an offer. As you can imagine, a man of such standing left a long and detailed will and, besides myself, he appointed ten other executors, including two bishops and two King's Bench judges! We are in the early stages of settlement of the earl's various bequests and debts. The landed estates are another matter, since it seems likely the king will confiscate many of them; as a Woodville, the heir Lord Richard will be disadvantaged by his name. But before we discuss any possibility of either Queen Elizabeth or the new Earl Rivers selling the manuscript, I would like to hear the whole story of *Le Morte D'Arthur*; not the tale itself you understand, but the manuscript's journey from the Newgate cell to The Mote in Kent. I have an hour to spare before my next appointment. Perhaps we could dine together. I will be able to place some of the missing pieces as far as you are concerned with the story of Doctor Makepeace and his appearance on the earl's doorstep! I'm sure you will find it all very diverting!'

\*\*\*\*\*\*

While Andrew Dymock was diverting members of the Newgate Fellowship with a certain tale of Mister Peter Crosby's doctoral subterfuge, and after Meg had returned from her last visit to the Abbey unmolested by a certain clerical caitiff, Sir Anthony Tanner was finalising certain plans which had been in train for some weeks. Meg had noticed how he was wont to disappear at uncivilised hours, although well within the curfew which had lately been imposed on the citizens, "in view of the unsettled times". For there was rebellion in the air in all counties south and west of a line from Bristol to east Kent and led by men who had been loyal household servants of the late king and were appalled by street-talk of the treatment of their master's legitimate heirs by the current occupier of the throne.

Lady Rumour, that ancient but persistently vigorous nourisher of discontent and revolt, was ably assisted by her libertine hand-maidens Dame Speculation and Goodwife Gossip, all busy about the streets, villages, towns, cities and counties feeding men's ignorance with dangerous part-truths. In the communal areas where men gathered in the warmth of balmy late-August days, such news as was circulating about the whereabouts of the two princes was picked over, re-cycled and passed on with embellishments.

'They've had their throats cut—then into the Thames with them!' said a master cutler with relish and authority, as one who claimed to fashion knives of fine quality and felt some ownership, if this had been the method of dispatch.

'No, you're wrong, master; their bodies would have been washed up with the tide!' said a woman who, anxious to be early to exchange any news, had come out onto the street as soon as one or more had gathered round the market cross. 'It's my guess they've been poisoned and buried in the Tower gardens.'

'That's poisonous talk put about by the king's enemies, woman! You should be careful what you repeat.' Undaunted the woman pursed her lips and said, 'If they're not dead, why can't we see them? It seems stupid to me that King Richard would not ease his subjects' minds as to where they are. All we ask is to see them alive and well—never mind claims to the throne. These are children after all! The idea of their uncle doing away with them, so he can place his arse on the throne is—is—'

'Not unusual, mistress! There have been many instances of homicide for gain.' Here was a black-gowned professional man—maybe an apothecary or a lawyer—who had seen the small crowd and with the inherent curiosity of his calling had joined it. 'I could name you several instances where—'

'That may well be, sir,' said another bystander sternly, 'but we talk of the present. Where are these boys? I agree with the cutler here—they are surely done away with and in ghastly fashion. The king is to blame!' A shudder circulated among them and then a murmur, half-fearful, half-assenting. But these words were dangerous in increasingly dangerous times and rapidly the crowd dispersed, its members anxious not to be party to such hostile expressions towards one anointed with the holy oil.

One who was not afraid to voice such concerns, admittedly in the safety of his own house, was Sir Anthony Tanner, who was certain he knew the truth: that Edward and Richard of York, boys of the tender ages of twelve and ten, had been done to death; smothered with a pillow and their bodies walled up inside the Tower of London.

'There is only one man responsible for this heinous action—Richard of Gloucester—our so-called king!' Anthony paced up and down his small living room, grinding his right fist into the palm of his left hand. 'That is why we must take action!'

'We?' queried Meg.

'The queen and—and,' he hesitated, '—others!'

'So, are you going to tell me what these plans are and who is involved—above all, what are the risks for you—and by implication—myself and our boys?'

'Sit down Meg. This is the time for me to call on your patience and support!'

'Any husband who starts a conversation in that mode is looking to convince his spouse he is going to do something she will violently disagree with!'

'I think, when you've heard me out, you'll be fully behind me.'

'I'll say nothing until you've finished—I promise no interruptions!'

'Good. The thing is, we must all return to France—you, me, Leo and Dickon—we must ride to Southampton and get a boat to Brittany within the next forty-eight hours.' True to her word, Meg said nothing, but her brain was working rapidly, as were her eyebrows, which shot up almost into her hairline. 'Our journey will be on Queen Elizabeth's business. We will be seeking out Henry Tudor Earl of Richmond at the court of Francis II of Brittany.' He paused, 'Aren't you going to ask me who he is?'

'I was waiting for you to tell me, husband!'

147

'Richmond is the son of Edmund Tudor and Margaret Beaufort and, through her line, has a lineage all the way back to Edward III's son, John of Gaunt. As the senior remaining male Lancastrian he has a slim claim to the throne; his mother is actively promoting him as our rightful king—a brave thing to do. He's in Brittany, which is where we are going with a proposal from the queen that Henry Richmond, as he styles himself, should invade England, seize the crown, marry her eldest daughter Elizabeth and unite the Houses of York and Lancaster.'

Meg was silent while she absorbed these unprecedented propositions; then she said, 'The jewels are part of this plot—am I right?'

'You are. We will carry them to Henry, so he can sell them and use the money to fit out a fleet and an army.'

'When is this invasion to take place?'

'As soon as matters can be arranged—clearly before the winter weather sets in.'

'This seems all very sudden, Anthony. Was it the murder of her sons which propelled her into action?'

'Very astute of you, Magpie! Once she knew her two legitimate heirs to the throne were dead she became determined her eldest daughter would become queen. There are others with a lesser claim to the throne—the Duke of Buckingham for one.'

'But he's a loyal supporter of Richard III, is he not?'

'He's wavering, Meg. The killing of the two boys has had serious ramifications for Richard. Men were sickened when they heard of it and Buckingham, despite all the honours and land Richard has heaped on him, is said to consider child-killing a step too far for ambition's sake. There are those working on the duke to bring him over at this moment. You have heard of the uprisings in the south and south-west? That is all part of the general hostility towards Richard and which the queen in banking on. If we can galvanise Henry Richmond with promises of marriage to Elizabeth of York and the greater prize of the crown of England, we have a chance to overturn this tyrant.'

'Strong words, Anthony! Are we sure Richard is responsible for the deaths of the two boys? No one has reported seeing their bodies.'

'And we wouldn't expect to! Richard would have them secretly disposed of; they haven't been seen alive and well since 9th July. They were a hindrance to his claim to the throne. No usurper wants to have the usurped king remain alive and able to muster opposition—think of Henry IV and how quickly he disposed of Richard II; likewise, Edward II was murdered on Queen Isabella's orders so that their son could become Henry III. Edward IV had Henry VI done to death to secure his throne—it's a common theme among murderous monarchs!'

'Yes, I understand, and it does look very bleak as far as young Edward V is concerned. But why must we go to Brittany? Why are you involved? And how long has it been so?'

'Briefly—I speak the language and I know my way around the court of the Duke of Brittany. Also I've met Henry Richmond. Don't forget, I'm trusted as a loyal follower of Edward IV for these past twelve years and I've been personally involved with the queen since she took sanctuary. I must tell you, she was extremely grateful for all you did, especially your clever resistance of Stillington's interference.

She told me that, if we are successful in our mission, then she will be pleased to give you an audience—and perhaps other rewards for your service.'

Meg was silent again, but her mind was racing around domestic matters and the potential dangers of the enterprise. *Our boys must be safe! That is the priority for us both*! she thought. Then she asked, 'Why must I go—and the boys? How long are we likely to be away?'

'That's impossible to say, but you will all be safely quartered in Francis's court while these matters are discussed. I want you all with me because I can't be sure what the king might do in revenge for any perceived disloyalty to him. He must surely find out what is in the wind very shortly and if I leave you in London there's a strong possibility you could be taken as hostages. You complain loudly enough when I go off without you so this time I want you by my side. I'll obviously come back with Henry Richmond when we invade—'

'—Part of the invasion?'

'Of course. I'm a soldier, Meg, first and foremost. I've pledged myself to the queen's service.'

'Why couldn't you share this with me sooner. Why spring it on me—forty-eight hours' notice to pack up and leave the country. What are we to tell Monty and Gisella, Pom and Jack?'

'The least they know the safer they'll be. That's the reason I haven't taken you into my confidence, Magpie. I didn't want you worried.'

'You were happy enough to involve me in passing secret messages to and from the queen. I take it these concerned the proposals you have described?'

'I will admit, I had some misgivings about using you—'

'—By the Blessed Virgin! I should hope you did!' Meg had passed through various emotions up to this point. She was now steeped in that of anger.

'Meg, Meg! Let's not quarrel. This is not the time for us to fall out. When we're in France, you can punish me all you like, but not now, please! Let's just concentrate on packing up and preparing for the journey. I'll talk to the boys and explain, so they understand but have no idea of what we are involved with. Small lads chatter and, as with our friends, the less they know the less they can let slip.'

'Very well.' Meg sighed, still aggrieved at the suddenness of it all. However, "for better or for worse!" had been a recurring theme in their marriage.

'Magpie?'

She knew a pleading voice when she heard it, 'Yes?'

'There is one thing I need you to do.'

'What is it?'

'We must conceal the jewels somewhere very safe and I know just the place.'

'Where's that?'

'I've just bought one of those new codpieces. It will be perfect as a hiding place; no man would lay hands on another's crotch without risking a severe buffeting, even if he was undertaking a search. If you could make a small pouch to be sewn inside so it fitted neatly round my—'

'Yes, I get the idea, husband!'

'You'll need measurements; using our code I've worked it out—it would be 9in-rdp!'

'Nine inches! As much as that! You sound very sure, husband! Are you confident that's accurate?'

'You should know, Magpie! You should know!'

# Chapter 6

*In which the quest for* Le Morte *is continued;*
*The Newgate Three venture into Kent;*
*Monty has a spine-tingling moment and Gisella has "a good idea".*

'Did Six-toed say when he was coming back?' Pom growled and looked unusually downcast; Monty had just brought him the news of the Tanner family's imminent departure.

'He was uncertain, Pom. He told me very little, other than "he was on an important venture and had to leave for the continent early tomorrow morning". He wouldn't even say exactly where they were going.'

'That's just it "they" are *all* going! He's taking Meg and the boys—which must mean he doesn't intend coming back.'

'We don't know that. You know what he's like, Pom. In his work, he has to keep things close to his chest.'

'That's all very well—but we are supposed to be his friends. Surely he can trust us!'

'You know what he always says—"the less you know the safer you are!"'

'That's fucking rubbish!' Monty winced. Since the demise of Sir Tom, whose liberal application of expletives was a vexation he'd had to put with, Monty noticed that Pom's usage of violent cussing had disappeared. It's re-appearance now indicated his friend was very upset.

Pom's distress was generated mainly by the thought of losing contact with Lionel and Richard of whom he was as fond as if they had been his own. As one of their newly-appointed godfathers, Jack Worms the other, he had taken his duties seriously. Perhaps less so as far as their spiritual welfare was concerned, but certainly he had stepped in as a father-figure on those many occasions when Anthony had been away from home for days or weeks. Meg would call their friend in to deputise, especially when there were brotherly disputes to be settled, or praise for exceptional effort required, besides the activities—swordplay, self-defence and horsemanship, which Pom demonstrated and participated in with a will and a certain amount of joint and muscular pain afterwards. He was on the dark side of sixty-five after all.

'Will we be able to see them off?'

'Tony said he wanted to "leave quietly and discreetly very early", just after the curfew is raised. He evidently doesn't want any attention drawn to them.'

'Do you know where they are sailing from?'

'No.'

'Can't I even say goodbye to the boys?'

'It seems not; it's too late for you to walk to Cornhill, because the curfew's on and it's too dark.' For Monty had only just had this news from Anthony, who had called in at his lodgings late in the evening of 21 August. He had avoided telling Pom directly for the very reason described above. 'Tell Pom the boys will write when we're settled. I'm sorry he won't be able to say goodbye properly, but we are in haste.'

153

Margaret Tanner had been as perturbed and distressed as Pom at the necessity for such a hurried departure. It had taken her a full day to arrange their affairs, including writing a list of instructions to their three friends as to what should happen to the house and its contents. Insofar as she had no idea when they would be returning, she told them to try to sub-let it, with all its contents, to tenants of whom they approved. That way at least they would have a home to return to—if they returned. She had spent much time selecting and packing small, precious items which she would never leave—a small creamer, the one item of value left her by her mother and which she had carried safely with her throughout all her travels. The jewels were now safely tucked away on her husband's person and he had made the inevitable and obvious quip as he settled the small pouch into the larger one: 'They add a certain improved dimension—the country's crown jewels hidden among my own, Magpie!'

And what was Lady Margaret Tanner's private view of all this commotion?

*This is what comes of marrying an inveterate conspirator, spy and all-round adventurer! Some may think it exciting, romantic, venturesome—like a story from Sir Tom's book. That's all well and good when one is young and free, but now we have a family I would trade it all in for some stability.* But she had sworn an oath of marital loyalty and she mentally shrugged off her dismay and continued the packing. That had been difficult since the boys could not understand why they shouldn't take all their belongings. There had been some argument, stamping of feet, mutinous looks; but Tony had finally intervened with a firm hand and reminded them, 'You must become young men from now on. This is a manly adventure and requires appropriate behaviour. Look and learn, boys!' In the end the promise of a two-day ride to Southampton and a sea voyage did much to ameliorate the distress of leaving behind a plaything or two.

Pom's distress was not ameliorated by any such prospect. For some days after the Tanners left, he was moody and, in his usual manner when discomforted, isolated himself in his work. A true professional, he never let his feelings show to his customers or employees—maintaining his customary affability which was the key asset of his business. 'See Mister Appleby, he'll do you a fair deal and pleasant with it!' was the general opinion of all who did business with him and one which had brought him success and long-term profits. He traded in a variety of goods—furs, wine, and lately the beautiful blue and white pottery from China—porcelain. *It does look like a cowrie shell*! he thought as he unpacked the lustrous chinaware so carefully wrapped in straw. *They are certainly a "good buy", although it takes years to get it here and breakages are a major problem. Still, a good mark-up on price covers that*! *People seem to want to pay abnormal sums for the stuff; it's a good job some of the nobility have more money than sense*! So now, in his shops at least, he shelved his sadness and concentrated on shifting new stocks of furs and anticipating the first fruits of the new wine season.

******

'That's it! Finished!' And Jack Worms sat back from his bench and looked at his work—a newly-bound volume, with the familiar and subtle smell of good soft leather, the cover and spine beautifully tooled with gold-leaf. 'John Gower would be delighted—if he was still here to see it! His *Confessio Amantis*, his first poem in English and now in print for the first time—with illustrations. You did a splendid job with the compositing, Monty.'

'It was a pleasure, but all the time I was conscious of the content—which contains many translations of Ovid and stories from the old days of Troy—rather like Master Caxton's own *History of Troy*. From that a chain of thought began which inevitably took me back to *Le Morte*, Jack. It's been almost three weeks since we visited Mister Dymock and we've done nothing about visiting The Mote.'

'Pom has been rather distracted by the sudden departure of Tony and family and it hasn't been the right time to ask Master Caxton for time off to pursue a private matter. But now the *Confessio* is finished, we could legitimately ask him for a couple of days rest! What are you working on now?'

'Varagine's *Golden Legend*; his lives of the saints.'

'Thrilling—although I personally can't stomach hagiographies! When does Caxton want it finished?'

'He says sometime in November.'

'Well, I think we've worked hard enough—and Inkin' Wynkyn looks worn out. We've put out about nine texts of vastly different sizes this year. It's time we all took a rest.'

'You're right. I'll speak to Master Caxton—and to Pom. I know this is a busy time for him with the new wine presses coming in—'

'Let's hope he's cheered up—it is his favourite time of year, all that sampling!'

'A visit to Kent will take his mind off missing Leo and Dickon. He's still a regular visitor to us—Thomas and the

156

girls love to see him, and he certainly loves them—spoils them too.'

'Pom should have married and had children of his own! Instead he was a sort of wife to Sir Tom! But I agree, Monty, we should make haste with our quest which has been going on for twelve years—thirteen next April; it's too long. I'd really like to see it in print and with binding designed and made by myself!'

'That is all any of the Newgate Fellowship want, Jack!'

\*\*\*\*\*\*

Permission granted from an unusually co-operative master, the Newgate Three found themselves riding towards Maidstone in Kent on the morning of Monday 8th September. A crisp day, warmth still in the air and the road south-east out of London providing a good dry track to ride on. It was a forty-five-mile journey, which they had no intention of trying to cover in one day; rather planning to stay at one of the many hostelries on the way.

'It's quite a coincidence that we should be travelling the route of Master Chaucer's pilgrims!' said Jack as they joined the Way at Otford, 'having just printed the second edition of his *Canterbury Tales*. Perhaps we should have brought some copies with us to sell. It would have pleased Master Caxton to have come back with some cash—or orders for his books!'

Any ideas of such sales' opportunities were dismissed by Pom and Monty as a distraction, much to Jack's disappointment. 'Sometimes your imagination outstrips your common-sense Jack!' Pom told him. 'I'm all for casting my bread upon the waters but selling books on the road will never take off!'

They spent an uncomfortable night in a cheap, flea-ridden inn where pilgrims were regularly fleeced by its owner. Leaving as early as possible, the three travellers arrived early in the afternoon on the outskirts of the fair town of Maidstone and asked directions to The Mote. They agreed it had been a pleasant surprise to be given succinct and reliable information by a local man with some intelligence. 'I usually pick someone who's either deliberately obstructive to strangers, or so garrulous I can't make sense of what they say!' laughed Jack. Within an hour, they were in sight of a castellated building surrounded by park land.

'It looks—er—er,'

'Like Camelot?' suggested Pom.

'Not quite, but I do feel I might come across a knight resting by a well and ready to have "a do" with us!' said Monty; but as they came nearer they saw a good deal of the building was covered with scaffolding. 'Sir Tom's stories never included a builder—or wheel-barrows—or hoists, pulleys and beams! But, as I remember, Andrew Dymock mentioned that Earl Rivers was having the tower extended upwards.'

'Let's go and ask one of the men which is the best way to get into the place,' and skirting their way through the debris of building materials scattered carelessly about, they approached a rough-looking labourer half-heartedly mixing some mortar. He viewed them with suspicion.

*They look like fucking lawyers*! he thought. *Let's hope they've brought some cash for us*! For Mister Dymock was correct. Lord Anthony Woodville had nothing with which to pay the builders and owed them substantial amounts. The builder here was in the not abnormal position of others working for customers with a lack of cash. Either they carried on in the hope of payment "one day" or sought work elsewhere, abandoning the project completely with no prospect of wages or payment for materials outstanding. This dilemma did not make them amenable to "gentlemen" of any standing, especially anyone who looked vaguely like perfidious lawyers; they generally arrived with bad news. Therefore, Monty's perfectly polite request for information was met with a surly grunt and a dismissive wave of the hand in a vaguely leftward direction.

After circling the building, they returned to a large door which appeared to be the main entrance. In the stone above the frame was the faint outline of a carving—but which was incomplete now the stonemason had left with his mallets and chisels and found secure work to chip away at elsewhere.

'What does it say?' asked Pom, looking up at the scratchings on the stone.

'It looks like the shape of a scutcheon, Pom', said Jack, whose eyesight was better than either of his friends'.

'Well, the owner has no use for such trappings now,' observed Monty. As they were staring up at the sad and abandoned signifier of noble ambition, the door opened a crack and a rubicund face appeared, followed by a squat body. 'Yes, what do you want?' was the unpromising response.

Monty dismounted and stepped forward, 'Good day, sir. We are visiting on the advice of Mister Andrew Dymock and wish to speak to Earl Rivers' steward.' He could already feel Jack and Pom's irritation at this obstructiveness by one who was evidently a menial.

'What about?'

'We will discuss that with the steward. Please take him this letter of introduction. May I ask whom I am addressing?' And Monty handed him the note in which Andrew Dymock had ordered the steward to "give them all assistance and hospitality".

'Lord Rivers' steward.'

'Really?' And Monty failed to keep the surprise out of his voice. The recipient of the letter glanced over it, nodded and, once he had opened the door fully, they stepped outside. In full daylight, they could see he was well-dressed and, despite his small, round physique, had a bearing of authority. 'Benjamin Trussell at your service,' and he gave a slight bow, and then signalled to one of the labourers, a small knot of whom had gathered a little way off, curious as to the business of these strangers, and ever-hopeful they would have brought with them a sack of cash. 'Arrange for these horses to be stabled!' ordered Master Trussell, and two apprentice masons took the reins and lead the mounts away, disappointment marked clearly on their faces.

'Now gentleman, please forgive the rough welcome, but we are suspicious of strangers for many reasons which I will explain over some refreshment.'

'This sounds better!' thought Pom, as he followed his friends into a great hall, but badly misnamed as there was nothing great about it—being filled with lumber and building materials.

'Please excuse the lack of comfort. As you can see, we have the builders in! How long they will stay is another matter, but we will take our ease in a chamber in the east side of the building which is undisturbed by the workmen.'

Within minutes, having introduced themselves, they were seated, glasses of wine in hand, in a pleasant room, admittedly dusty with persistent mortar, tiny motes of which floated in the air and settled at will on any flat bare surface. By this time, the Newgate Three were overcome with curiosity as to the state of the place, and the steward's evident suspicion of unexpected visitors. Pom, never one to skirt around a question—a trait he had imbibed from long exposure to Sir Thomas Malory's tactlessness—asked, 'Tell me, Master Trussell, what's amiss here? You seemed troubled when you first met us.'

'You must know that my master who was a tenant here, courtesy of his sister the queen—she who was queen—has recently been executed on the orders of the new king.'

'Indeed, it is common knowledge.'

'We live in fear of King Richard claiming the place for the crown—although he has no right—the property is owned entirely by the Woodville family. But in these uncertain times anything is possible. There is also the major problem of debt. Lord Anthony was up to his eyes in it—owing money here, there and everywhere. The masons and labourers haven't been paid for months. It's no secret; Lord Woodville died leaving debts of over two thousand pounds. I've been paying the kitchen staff from my own pocket—on the promise from the executors that I will be reimbursed when the will is proved. Queen Elizabeth hasn't been down to see the place, which is hardly surprising since she's wise to remain in sanctuary. Most of the Woodville lands have been confiscated by the crown, although, as I say, she owns The Mote outright and it shouldn't be touched. However, all the Woodvilles have gone to ground; again, hardly surprising under the circumstances of change of sovereign and one who is hostile to them; we have no idea whether we will see the new earl or his sister—or what is to happen to the building and the park. In its prime, the deer hunting was first class and Lord Anthony Rivers was very fond of the place.'

The steward was clearly grateful for an audience through which he could get his anxieties off his chest. But Monty, Jack and Pom were equally anxious to discover the facts about the late earl's library and Monty intervened gently when Trussell stopped for breath.

'As you have read in Mister Dymock's letter of introduction, we are particularly interested in the earl's collection of books and manuscripts. Is it still here and available for us to look at?' He held his breath, half expecting bad news—that the items had been destroyed somehow in all the upheavals of the past months; that the bailiffs had entered and exacted property to cover debts; that the material had been removed and stored elsewhere.

'I can assure you, the library is intact. I have made it my personal responsibility to keep it from harm and dust. I have been Earl Rivers' steward for many years and know how much his books meant to him. 'Trussell,' he would say, 'my manuscripts are my children. They would be the first things I would save in the event of a fire.'

'That is very good to hear, Master Trussell. Is it possible for us to see them?' asked Jack, who was becoming impatient.

'In what connection? I'm not sure of your status—are you professionally interested? Oxford or Cambridge men? Mister Dymock simply wrote that he gave permission for you to peruse the earl's collection.'

'Professionally interested yes—from the universities—no. It is rather a long and complicated matter. We are concerned with one manuscript only—*Le Morte D'Arthur* or *The Tales of King Arthur*, a substantial work of over eight hundred pages. You must surely remember it, a document of that size?'

'I can't possibly be expected to retain details of over a hundred works in my head. But I do have a catalogue of their titles, when they were purchased, from whom and for how much.'

'That is excellent, Master Trussell!' said Monty excitedly. 'Perhaps we may see the list?'

'Only if you tell me what your business is with this book—manuscript? Do you wish to purchase it? If so, you must go through the executors; I have no authority to sell any of Earl Rivers' property.'

Monty continued, 'It's a manuscript, and by rights does not belong to Earl Rivers's estate. It was stolen from me in January ten years ago and, for reasons which need not trouble you, my friends and I are anxious to regain possession.'

'Are you implying my master was party to a theft? That is a serious allegation, Mister Pickle and one I will refute vigorously. Everything listed is fully paid for, with receipts and details all very clearly documented. I shall go and find the catalogue so that you may see for yourselves,' and in an evident state of umbrage, he rose and left the room.

'Thank Christ he left the jug!' growled Pom, replenishing his glass. 'He seems rather wound up about this.'

Monty nodded, 'The man's obviously very loyal to his old master. The fact that he's keeping the place going from his own resources is laudable.'

Within minutes, the stalwart servant returned bearing a large roll of velum tied with a ribbon. He laid it on a small table and, holding the top end down with two great paperweights began unrolling it.

'Let me see—you say the document was stolen well over ten years ago? So, it could have come into my master's possession any time after January '73?'

'Likely to be a month or so afterwards, since it was stolen in Bruges and the thief needed time to return to England. If you check your dates from February onwards, you'll come across it I'm sure.'

Trussell continued to run his fingers down the velum until, with a cry of satisfaction he said, 'Here! Here it is:

*The Tales of King Arthur by Sir Thomas Malory 1471; 800+ pages, single-sided manuscript; purchased March 5th, 1473 from Doctor John Makepeace, (Oxon); price: £20. Somewhat dilapidated in appearance, although wrapped in oilskin; partly well-executed script by a practised hand, but with a few annotations and corrections of poorer quality by a second scribe.*

This must be the manuscript to which you refer.'

'It describes it precisely. I can tell you that the "practised hand" is my own and most of the annotations and corrections are those of the author, Sir Thomas Malory. We worked on this manuscript almost every day for two years. I know it intimately!'

Trussell said nothing for a few seconds, then, 'But that doesn't alter the fact that Earl Rivers paid twenty pounds in good faith to this Doctor Makepeace, from Oxford, who he evidently considered to be a man of letters and probity.'

'Doctor Makepeace was an imposter—a knave—a poisoner—' said Pom robustly, swallowing the remainder of the claret in his glass, then topping it up, uninvited.

'Indeed, Mister Appleby, if he was any one of these things he could be deemed a villain. Are you sure of this? Where is your evidence?'

'I'll tell you, Master Trussell! Under the guise of being a Doctor of Medicine he poisoned Mister Pickle here, stole the manuscript and then, under another doctoral disguise, duped your master into parting with twenty pounds for stolen goods! *Caveat emptor*! as my old master Sir Tom would have said. Earl Rivers should have heeded the maxim.'

'But Lord Rivers was not to know he was an imposter. He had his bona fides.'

'You mean he showed the earl his doctoral thesis and scroll from Oxford?'

'Of course not! But he said the man spoke well and dressed like an Oxford man! He was also knowledgeable about the manuscript.'

'Of course he was—he had a whole sea journey from Bruges to read it. Your master was duped; the manuscript rightly belongs to Mister Pickle here. He is one of Sir Thomas's executors; Master Worms and myself are the others, and we have sworn an oath to convey the manuscript to Winchester and into the care of the monks. It was one of Sir Thomas Malory's last spoken wishes to us.'

'I understand your concern,' said Benjamin Trussell soothingly, although he had become pinker in the face. 'But there is nothing I can do. You must take this matter up with the late earl's own executors. They will be in a position, perhaps, to sell you the manuscript.'

Jack, who had been unusually quiet, now spoke up most vehemently, 'We have no intention of paying a penny for property which is ours! We will go to court if necessary!'

Now both Monty and Pom—and Jack himself—knew this was a bluff. They had neither the time nor the cash to spend on a protracted lawsuit. It looked as though they had to choke on the realisation they would have to try to buy back *Le Morte*.

Monty brought matters back to the here and now. 'Whatever is decided, Master Trussell, we have come a considerable distance to find the manuscript and we would be obliged if we could at least see it.'

'I see no reason why not,' said the steward affably. Despite Jack's vigorous outburst, he felt no threat from the three gentlemen. In fact, he had some sympathy with their predicament. 'Come this way and I'll take you to the earl's book-room,' and he rose and led them through a maze of small corridors to the back of the building. Taking one of his many keys, he opened a low studded door and led them in. It was a small chamber but entirely lined with shelves on which were a notable number of bound books, manuscripts and piles of loose papers. Jack's eyes immediately lighted on a copy of *Sayings of the Philosophers*.

'Look, Monty—Pom, this is the first book Caxton printed in Westminster. Master Trussell, we didn't tell you, and perhaps we should have done, that both Mister Pickle and I work for Master William Caxton, the Westminster printer. Your master knew him well—in fact they were friends; we printed several of the earl's works for him.' He took down the leather-bound book most carefully, fingering the spine, 'I personally bound this for his lordship and he was very pleased with it!'

'Indeed, I remember well when he brought it here. I have never seen him so proud of anything, king's brother-in-law or not. "Trussell", he said, "this is the first book ever printed in England and it's all my work! Master Caxton is a wizard!" I remember the day very well, 19th November '77.'

'So you recognise how important these things are! This is a man's work—hours spent researching and writing. Think how his lordship would have felt if someone had stolen his manuscript and tried to sell it—or worse, pass it off as his own work!' said Pom darkly.

'Lord Rivers had no intention of passing anything off which wasn't his own,' and the steward went even redder in the face. Monty, seeing him bristle, said soothingly, 'Indeed he would not, being such a gentleman. The man who stole our manuscript was a caitiff of the first order and simply out to make money.'

But now he was anxious to locate *Le Morte* before the man became incensed and threw them out. Quietly he asked, 'Can we see the manuscript, please?' The steward, still smarting from this perceived insult to his late master's honour nodded curtly, 'Take a look for yourselves. You'll probably recognise it before I do!' he said shortly.

They cast their eyes around the shelves and there, to the left of the door on a middle shelf, still in an oilskin wrapper and tied with fresh string, was the bulky package which was *Le Morte D'Arthur*. Monty felt himself shivering from head to toe; his hair stood on end and the back of his neck tingled. It had been eleven years since he had touched it! He walked over and took it from the shelf, immediately reminded how heavy it was. 'To think I carried it first on horseback along the South Downs, then to Southampton, across the sea to Honfleur and then by horse across northern France to Bruges. No wonder the earl described it as dilapidated—twenty minutes crushed in a pork-barrel had done it no favours either!' He touched the oilskin and looked questioningly at the steward, who anticipated his meaning and said, mollified and his curiosity stirred, 'Certainly Mister Pickle; I'd be most interested to see it too. As you can see, on Lord Rivers's orders, I changed the old oilskin for a new one.'

Monty laid it out on a small table in the centre of the room and his fingers became all thumbs as, still trembling, he began to untie the string. Peeling back the oilskin he revealed the front page which, having been wrapped up all these years, had retained its original colour, the ink unfaded, although it was rather dog-eared. There was the familiar hand of Sir Tom— his writing spidery because of poor eyesight—but legible; the centre of the page bore the title of the first book: *The Tale of King Arthur and the Emperor Lucius*. Monty turned page after page, wondering at the detail within and remembering the hours of hard work, the arguments, the laughter and the satisfaction he had shared with the old man in that Newgate cell. Tears came to his eyes, and, for fear of them falling on the precious document, he turned away and wiped his face with his sleeve. There was an awkward silence, until Jack taking Monty's arm, squeezed it and said, 'We understand how you must feel, my friend. This is the moment we've all been waiting for since that terrible day in Bruges when you discovered it had gone. But now we know it's safe and still in one piece and for which we must give grateful thanks to the Almighty!'

'Amen to that!' Pom crossed himself.

Monty turned to Master Trussell, 'One thing which is perplexing; what did Earl Rivers intend to do with the manuscript? It seems to have been lying on this shelf untouched for ten years.'

'I think, once he had met Master Caxton and seen the Westminster presses—of which he was very much in favour—he would have offered it to be printed. But he became so entrenched in matters of state and, for those intervening years, was hardly ever at The Mote, that he forgot about it and the idea came to nothing. But one thing I am certain of, had it been printed, there would be no question but that he would have acknowledged Sir Thomas Malory as the author of *The Tales of King Arthur*. My master was an honourable man, I can assure you!'

Monty looked up from his examination of the manuscript, 'We realise that, of course. There was no intention to insult the integrity of Lord Rivers, I can assure you, Master Trussell. I want to thank you for taking care of the manuscript; it is now as it was on the day it was stolen, almost pristine. I mean, there's no damage other than what was already there, no alteration or additions by another's hand. My friends and I will obviously have to go away and discuss what we should do. In the meantime, I am confident *Le Morte D'Arthur* is safe!'

But Pom frowned, 'Monty, given the fact that this place is in the hands of executors—can we be sure they won't come here and sell everything that's not nailed down? These debts of the earl have to be paid.' He turned to the steward, 'Master Trussell, you've seen how much this document means to us, especially my excellent friend Monty Pickle here. He's already acknowledged your virtuous custodianship; would it be possible to persuade you to conceal—secrete—hide—whichever word you chose, *Le Morte D'Arthur* until we've arranged somehow to repossess it? Nothing dishonest—just move it out of sight of rascally bailiffs! They would never recognise its true worth—they might even sell it for burning if wood became short! They're not recognised as the most literate of men and will surely never appreciate such a work of genius.'

Monty and Jack looked surprised at this unexpected piece of initiative and the steward made no comment for a while. Then he nodded, 'As long as the estate eventually benefits I can't see it doing any harm, to "keep it by" for a future purchaser. I believe you are honourable men and accept your claim that the manuscript was stolen by a dishonourable caitiff, so long as you agree that my master purchased it in all good faith. Whatever is the outcome, I hope one day the work will pass through Master Caxton's presses and be launched into the world.'

'We would wish that too—and that the original manuscript reaches its true home—Sir Tom's Camelot in Winchester!' said Monty, grasping the man's hand and pumping it up and down. 'Thank you so much, Master Trussell!' he looked at Pom and Jack. 'I don't think we need impose on him any further.'

'But I would like to hear more of the story of the journey this manuscript has undergone. I must also offer you all some refreshment before you return from whence you came. We may be seriously in debt here, but we can still feed our guests!'

'I thought he'd never ask!' muttered Pom to Jack as they lingered behind their host.

******

'We must ask Andrew Dymock what we can do now,' Monty was sitting at his desk in Caxton's workshop and Jack had taken a break and was trying to persuade his friend to take one too.

'Why don't we walk around to Pom's and discuss it over one of his fine Burgundies?'

It was a week since they had returned from Kent, and Monty had been anxious to set in motion means to retrieve *Le Morte*. Gisella had listened intently as he shared the few options which were circling in his head. 'We could make an offer for the manuscript—say the price Lord Rivers paid for it—twenty pounds—or add a little more. Crosby was going to charge him twenty-two, but the earl beat him down.'

'But where would you get that kind of money, Monty?' his wife posed the obvious question. 'We've no savings to speak of, and only just manage to get by as it is. Are you thinking of borrowing it? If so, what security could you offer a lender? We've never asked for credit before. I'm not sure we have the wherewithal to pay back such a sum.'

'Of course, you're right, Gisella. It's a stupid idea!' but he looked so crestfallen, she put her hand on his knee and said, 'Here's an idea! Perhaps Master Caxton would be interested in purchasing the manuscript himself and printing *Le Morte*. As I remember, when we were in Bruges you suggested he should look over the manuscript with a view to printing it.'

'That's true, and it had crossed my mind also. But there are drawbacks. If he owns the manuscript, then he can do what he likes with it. What happens to the pledges we gave Sir Tom? Would Caxton be prepared to let me take the manuscript to Winchester, once he has done with it? What kind of alterations to the text and structure would he make? How would I be involved?'

'Well, as his best compositor, and part-author of *Le Morte* I would imagine you would be in prime position to set it up. That would mean a certain amount of control of its composing—wouldn't it?'

Monty thought for a moment. She was right; it was perhaps the only option, but he had to be certain that the book was for sale before he approached Caxton. He must also put the idea to his friends before he made any moves.

Sitting in Pom's small office, a place of seeming disorderliness but where the trader could lay hands immediately on the smallest invoice, order or despatch note, the three friends sipped on the latest pressings which had arrived from Germany. 'Try this new Riesling, Jack. Something different!' Pom would always ask his friends to taste any new vintages. He had become interested in a much wider variety of grape than many of his competitors; sometimes he was badly wrong and lost money; mostly he was on the right track. 'The business is full of risks, but that's what makes it interesting. Sir Tom would have relished being involved!' he would say with a grin.

Having agreed the German wine was "passable", the attention passed to the inevitable matter of the manuscript. Monty put Gisella's idea to them.

'I'm still not happy about paying for something which was ours in the first place!' scowled Jack, 'it's—it's—'

'—Unjust? Unnatural? But no one suggests life's fair; the law certainly isn't. "Finders are keepers", isn't that the common-law maxim?' was Pom's reaction to his friend's objection. 'If you're feeling that aggrieved, we could always steal it back again, now we know where it is! It wouldn't take much to break into the place—I noticed the doors were all open, labourers in and out. I don't suppose there's much of a guard at night either—perhaps a couple of dogs. Tony would do it, if he was here!'

'But he's not! And I'm not prepared to rob the steward—who I thought treated us well—'

'—His wine wasn't up to much!' Pom muttered.

'Never mind his wine—I felt he was on our side and would behave honourably—keeping *Le Morte* safe until we can decide what to do. So, what do you think of approaching Master Caxton?'

Jack shook his head, 'He's a businessman and not a sentimentalist, Monty. It's my guess he'd strike a hard bargain. Have you thought; the integrity of Sir Tom's original work might be compromised!'

'He's also a writer himself—and a good one. *The History of Troy* has been well-received—'

'For those who can get through seven hundred pages of classical mythology!'

'We could say the same thing about *Le Morte D'Arthur*, Pom. All these large works are aimed at special audiences.'

'Mostly people who sit around on their arses all day with nothing else to do, Monty!' laughed Jack. 'It's ironic that someone like me, who loves books and reading, has little time for it; those who have, simply want to show-off their shelves and never read a whole book in their lives! Sir Tom thought Lord Rivers was one such.'

'But Sir Tom was wrong—as he was about other things—but we won't go into that!' said Monty, thinking of the old knight's history of assault, robbery, adultery and general disregard for the Cardinal Sins. 'I suggest we write to Andrew Dymock and request another meeting. If he's prepared to arrange the sale of the manuscript, first having consulted with his fellow executors—'

'—That'll take some time,' growled Pom. 'Lawyers are not fast on their feet!'

'Regardless of that, we know the manuscript is safe—'

'—So long as Trussell avoids the piece of cod!' laughed Pom, and Jack joined in the laughter, having had the joke previously explained.

'Crosby is out of the affair, I'm convinced; there'll be no more disguises for him. When we left Romford, my feeling was that his sister had him under tight control and his days of scheming were over. No, I have no real concerns about the safety of the document, only how we try to raise the money to purchase it.'

'I still think it's iniquitous that we should be expected to pay for—'

'Yes, Jack, we know how you feel and we feel the same. But Trussell was right—the transaction was undertaken in good faith by the earl. Unless we're prepared to fight it out in court, I can't think what else we can do. I'm going to send a note to Dymock and ask him for an interview. Are we agreed?'

******

'*Festina lente*!' said Pom, as they left Andrew Dymock's chambers. 'I suppose we had no choice but to agree to be patient. I told you once the lawyers were involved we would "make haste slowly". It took us long enough to see him—how long ago was it we asked for an interview? At least three weeks!'

The long-awaited meeting with Earl Rivers' executor had been brief but positive. The attorney had promised to raise the matter of the sale of the manuscript at the next meeting of the eleven executors—sometime in December. 'I can't see there being any objection—but you never know with these learned gentlemen—they are not of the real world, bishops and judges. It maybe they think works of literature should not be bartered—as a string of sausages might be! But I'll do my best to persuade them. Of course, raising this will draw their attention to the rest of the late earl's book collection. I imagine they'll want to consult with the heir—Lord Richard Woodville as to what should happen to it. But my understanding of that gentleman is, firstly he does not have his brother's reputation as a bibliophile; secondly, we hear he's currently in the southern counties getting himself embroiled in the spasmodic uprisings against the new king. A dangerous strategy, especially for a Woodville. Undoubtedly, he will not be too concerned at present with the sale of a manuscript in his newly-acquired library, of which he probably knows little, having rarely visited The Mote. Let's hope he keeps his head, otherwise we'll be dealing with another will and a new chief legatee!'

As they left Dymock's chambers in Fetter Lane, Jack said to Pom, 'What's all this business about risings in the south of the country? Who's getting agitated—should I have known about this?'

'Well, if you'd keep your ears open, as I have to do in my business, you would know that various supporters of the late king are making trouble in most of the southern counties; in short they have no liking for Richard III. There's also a rumour that the Duke of Buckingham has fallen out with the king and may joined the rebels—as they are called in all the news-sheets posted up. I suppose you never read them, Jack?'

'I don't have time, Pom. But why is Buckingham revolting?'

'Sir Tom would have liked that, Jack! Revolting Buckingham—Fuckingham Buckingham! That's what he used to call the old duke, do you remember?' And he chuckled.

'Well, obviously this isn't the same one!' observed his friend.

'No, it's his grandson,' explained Monty. 'But I heard that this duke had taken against the king because of these rumours about the princes and how they have been locked away in the Tower and no one's seen them for weeks,' he looked about him furtively. 'Some say they are dead!'

'I've heard that too,' nodded Pom, 'and more—that the king had them murdered and bricked up in the walls. That's why Buckingham has fallen out with him. There's another rumour circulating too—'

'—What's that?' asked Jack, now all agog.

'That Buckingham's plotting with Queen Elizabeth to bring Henry Richmond back from Brittany and put him on the throne!'

'I'm glad this is a quiet street, Pom!' whispered Monty. 'This is not the right topic for open thoroughfares in broad daylight.'

Jack nodded, 'You're right. Perhaps we should wait until we are safely indoors!' And they drew their cloaks around them and put up their hoods, as though to keep their subversive thoughts contained, besides keeping out the chilling draught from an easterly wind.

# Chapter 7

We catch up with Tony, Meg and their boys on the high
seas;
The family make a home in Brittany; Tony's sons find
adventures are not always enjoyable.

Two character who so far have remained silently in the
background of our account are Lionel and Richard Tanner,
Meg and Tony's boys born in France in that period of the
Tanners' life-story which is yet to be told. In this year, 1483,
they were ten and a half and nine years respectively and fine
healthy specimens—Lionel, or Leo, with his father's dark
good looks and Richard, known as Dickon, favouring his
mother's beauty, with his brown curls and well-formed
features. Temperamentally they were similar—boisterous,
fearless and apparently unaware of the casual risks and
dangers life may throw up at any time; as the younger,
Richard was somewhat in awe of his older brother to whom
he deferred in times of crisis. In France, where they lived a
country life of freedom to roam, days of exploring forests and
fields and discovering the limits imposed on them by a loving
mother, a stricter father and older, graceless boys, they
advanced physically and in spirit. Sometimes they were the
despair of Meg who, since Tony was absent from home for

long periods, bore the brunt of their rearing. They adored her but knew just how to exploit her fair-mindedness and forgiving nature. If, for example, Leo had done something egregious, which was usually concerned with a breakage of some sort, or a forbidden activity which had been obstinately and covertly pursued and later discovered, Leo would hold up his hands and admit his fault, while Dickon would plead for his brother in the most winning way. This two-pronged strategy—remorse from the culprit, entreaty for rehabilitation by his defender—was always successful, unless their father happened to be home. Matters then became significantly more difficult for the pair.

Anthony rarely beat them, but since his appearances beside the family hearth were infrequent, the boys learned quickly to take time and effort to judge his moods and capabilities; such a useful social skill learned early will always serve well in later life. They were fully aware that he always kept to his word. There were no unfulfilled threats from their father; if he had warned of consequences for potential offences which were then committed, he would carry them out to the letter. Undoubtedly, Anthony loved his boys—almost as much as he loved Meg. He never considered his absences as in anyway detrimental to his sons' upbringing. Meg always knew he must lead an errant life—it was the trade by which he provided for them all. When he was at home, he made sure he spent time with the boys in manly pursuits, although he could often be heard grumbling to his wife after a day of frustration. 'They're a couple of harum-scarum little beasts! Dickon doesn't listen, and Leo thinks he knows everything. You spoil them, you know!'

179

Meg soothed her husband and, as any good parent would, made many excuses for her lads. There would follow the familiar plea from a defensive mother to an accusing father that, 'They're only young, Tony. It's God's blessing they have so much spirit!'

'Well, God should come down and try and teach them the intricacies of swordplay. As for their handling of horses— Dickon will end up with a broken neck unless he heeds me better!'

That spirit was somewhat curbed when the family moved from France to London. In the minds of both boys, the stinking streets of the city, and particularly its great sluggish river, had the potential as an invigorating and dangerous playground. But Meg, their hitherto kind, indulgent mother, suddenly became a tyrant, at first refusing to allow them out unless supervised by her. After a week of confinement, she agreed that young Thomas Pickle was "sensible enough" to guide them round streets very local to them, although she reinforced her original warnings every time they left the house: "This is not like the countryside; the streets are not safe, boys. Anything could happen. Caitiffs with knives, robbers and—and—" she nearly let slip, "pimps and whores", but fortunately stopped in mid-flow. She had no desire to allow the boys to pull on a thread of thought which would find its way to knotty questions. Any conversations on that subject could wait until later and be dealt with by their father.

Almost as bad as their early confinement within doors was the insistence by Meg that they should learn to read. When they argued vehemently against the idea she retorted, 'Do you want to be regarded as a pair of know-nothings? Laughed at by other boys!'

It mattered not a jot to either whether other boys might mock their ignorance—let them try! They would soon find themselves on the end of an angry fist or buffeted into the river. Meg struggled until rescue came from an unexpected source. Pom, their newly-acquired godfather, found he had a gift for mediation when it came to fractious lads and their frustrated teacher. By dint of quiet argument and a secret arrangement whereby there were certain "rewards" promised as lessons improved, Leo and Dickon settled to their hourly lessons without rancour, to their mother's great surprise and pride. Later in their lives they expressed their appreciation to their mother for her perseverance, admitting she had been right to insist; but never divulging the hand played in their success by Mister Appleby, now long dead.

The sudden uprooting from their comfortable lodgings in Cornhill had been taken in their stride. In France, they had been on the move regularly and were by now children well-adapted to change. However this time is different. They noted how their mother and father were closeted together speaking in the kind of low voices they themselves might use when planning some forbidden adventure. 'They're up to something, Leo!' said Dickon as they sat in their bedchamber, ears to the wall desperately trying to overhear what was being said.

'It's father's trade, Dickon. We both know he lives a life of secrets!'

The monumental events taking place around them had not gone unnoticed by either. Having partly conquered the written word, they were able to read the pithy comments and news posted up on tavern and church doors, although their understanding of the content was limited. But they did know that their father was somehow involved. Therefore, they were not surprised when he announced, 'We're leaving for France early tomorrow, boys. Pack up only those things which are necessary for your survival—no toys or keepsakes; just clothes and a knife each.'

There had been the inevitable argument about what constituted necessities for survival. 'I must take this model canon, father. Pom made it for me!'

'Leo, I've told you; we have no room for toys.'

'But it's not a toy, it's a skilfully crafted object of beauty!'

'A what?'

'That's what mother said, when Pom gave it to me.'

'I daresay it is, but skilfully crafted or not, it has no practical use. Now, I suggest we pack it away with the rest of our belongings, which are going into the care of your other godfathers Mister Pickle and Master Worms. It'll be quite safe with them.'

'Does that mean we're coming back, father?' asked Dickon, toying with a spinning-top and wondering if he could smuggle it into some clothing.

'Our venture is being undertaken with a view to our returning for good!' said Tony, equivocally. 'And don't even think about hiding that top in your clothes, Dickon.'

'Is that a "yes" then?' asked Leo.

'Yes—it's a "yes".'

'So, we will be coming back to Cornhill? When will that be?'

'I can't tell you when, or where we'll live, but we most certainly will be returning to England,' and they had to be satisfied with that. Dickon put the spinning-top back in the cupboard with a sigh and thought, *One day you won't be able to know what I'm thinking father. Then I'll consider myself a man*!

******

*When I'm a man I think I'll go to sea!* Leo looked about him at the raw grey waves on which their little ship was balancing; he found their constant movement fascinating. *Where do they go, these waves? Where do they start? Do they stay the same shape, or merge one into another? Why do they move so—what is their purpose*? he was a boy who always liked reasons for things. In his mind, nothing happened unless for a purpose.

They had come aboard yesterday at Southampton, riding fast from London. When they'd stopped last night in the great forest Meg had told them how she and their father had once made a similar journey to the port, with their three great friends, Monty, Pom and Jack long before he or Dickon were born. 'It was the first time I slept out under the trees.' Their mother was raised in their estimation by this revelation of outdoor adventuring.

'Why were you going to France, mother? You've never told us anything about your life in England before you left.'

Meg had no intention of launching into any family history. Her colourful past could wait until they were both old enough to listen and make their own decisions about her, although she was confident it would be a positive one. She made a soothing remark—something about it being "too long and complicated just now".

'That's what you always say!' protested Dickon but, noting the disapproval on his father's face, decided discretion was the better part of curiosity.

Two days later, as his brother was looking over the side of the ship and mentally catechising the properties of one of the unending ocean's natural features, that young man came up quietly behind him and gave him a hearty shove in the back. Unfortunately, Leo had been standing on a pile of ropes to gain a clearer view of his subject and was therefore only checked by the rail from the knees down. The momentum of the push had him tottering, arms flailing as his head went towards the water, followed by the rest of him. If it hadn't been for a passing sailor, who had seen what was occurring, and, with a quick head and quicker hands, grabbed for the boy and pulled him back on deck, Leo would have been bobbing about among the very waves he was considering.

'Steady, mister! We don't want anyone over-board; captain doesn't like it. It wastes time picking them up and we don't always bother,' he turned to Dickon, 'especially with brainless boys!'

On a small ship, nothing is hidden, and Anthony was soon present to investigate what his offspring had been up to now. The sailor shook his head, saying nothing, but raised his eyebrows quizzically as he handed the boys over to their father. Anthony recognised an unspoken criticism when he saw one. He bristled at the idea that a simple sailor should question his abilities as a father, and it made him even angrier with his sons. Taking them firmly by the arms he thrust them forward to the forecastle where the captain was standing four-square, viewing his immediate maritime kingdom and beyond. Tony asked for permission to visit the bilges, the brusque explanation being, "to teach these scape-graces a lesson!" Seeing this was an internal matter involving only passengers and having no bearing on any aspect of the running of his ship, the captain assented.

Tony took a lantern and, opening the hatches, led the boys down into the hold, and then further down via another ladder into the bilges. He had never ventured into these lower depths before on any sea-voyage. At the bottom of the ladder, they were immediately conscious of the slapping of water and then the inevitable wet feet. It was pitch-black and stank abominably, so they were soon covering their noses with their sleeves. Bent double in the confined space, Tony held the lantern as high as he could, and the boys could see more clearly their dismal surroundings. Standing hunched in three inches of water, they looked about and in the dim light became aware of the eerie grinding of the bare boards of the ship through which water was slowly oozing, despite the preventative calking which lined them. They realised they were below the water line; beyond these rotting boards was the Channel.

'Father, what's that noise?' a trembling Dickon clutched his father's sleeve.

'Don't worry, my boy, it's only the boards creaking as the ship rides the sea—and it'll be rats as well. They thrive down here and grow as big as terriers—because there are no terriers to catch them! You'll soon get use to them!'

There was a silence, 'Why will we get used them, father?' asked Dickon.

'Because you're going to stay down here for a time, in the dark and ponder on the stupidity of arsing around on a small ship in mid-ocean!' And turning abruptly and with no further comment, he walked to the ladder. When he reached the top, he extinguished the light and pulled across the small hatchway separating the bilges from the hold.

The darkness was so intense as to be palpable; the boys could determine neither shape nor surface once the lantern had gone. Instinctively they held out their hands in search of each other and once found, clung on tenaciously.

'The bastard!' said Leo.

'Mother wouldn't like you saying that—especially not about father!'

'Well she's not here to help us, is she? I bet she'll be furious with him when she hears what he's done!'

'Perhaps she'll agree—it was a stupid thing to do.'

'For you to do! That's what's so unfair. It's all your doing! I didn't throw myself overboard. You pushed me. Why should I be punished?'

In truth, Anthony knew this to be correct, but neither lad had acquitted himself well since they came aboard. The excitement of a new location led them into all kinds of mischief which had not endeared them to crew or captain.

'I don't understand it, Meg,' sighed Tony, when another complainant arrived to point out that it was unsafe for lads to try to compete as to who could be first to the masthead. 'It's not as if they haven't been on board a ship before. We had to sail to England, after all.'

'It's just high spirits, Tony!'

'Please don't say that again. They're a pair of ill-disciplined little brutes and if there are any more incidents I'll have to take drastic action.'

This was the drastic action. 'Let them rot in the bilges, until they're ready to acknowledge their faults. If time down there that doesn't dampen their spirits, I'll give permission to the captain for him to use his lash and in front of the crew!'

The rats were as curious as to the visitors, as the visitors were appalled at the thought of them. 'What's that round my feet, Leo? Something's moving, touching my leg!'

'We are standing in a deal of water, brother.'

'No, this is something soft and—my God! It's climbing up my leg!' And he disentangled himself from Leo's grasp and thrust his hand down towards his feet. There was a splashing and squealing as the soft-bodied creature was brushed off Dickon's hose and back into the stagnant water. 'Didn't father say they were as big as terriers?'

'Did it bite you?' asked Leo, secretly more curious than concerned.

'No, but I can hear others, can't you?'

'I'm trying not to think about it. How long will he leave us down here, do you think?'

'He was very angry. Do you think we've pushed him too far? I'd rather have had a beating than this.'

Leo had great resilience for a lad of almost eleven, 'Let's wait a little while and then bang on the hatch and say we're very, very sorry and beg his pardon—and the captain's and the sailors'—perhaps he'll let us out.'

Dickon saw the immediate snag in this proposal, 'How can we find the hatchway in the dark; how can we climb the ladder when we can't see it?'

'This is only a small place, if we feel around we'll surely get our bearings.'

'I don't want to feel around, Leo—not with large rats with large teeth.'

'Don't be such a baby!' scoffed his brother, warming to the task. 'Put out your hands and feel for the sides, then we'll work our way round until we come to the ladder at the entrance.'

For the next few minutes, they splashed through loose spars, old rope and other dangerous encumbrances until Dickon cried out with triumph, 'I think I've found the bottom of the ladder, Leo—I can feel the rungs!'

'I'm behind you. Climb up and see if you can open the hatch!'

It was only five rungs to the covering hatchway; Dickon put his small hands on the flat surface and began to heave, but he just wasn't strong enough to lift it. By a series of complicated moves which required some skilful manoeuvring on the ladder while they changed places, Leo pushed with all his might and to his relief, felt the hatchway move and through the crack saw a dim light from the hold. To his surprise the cover continued to move, seemingly unaided, until there was a gap wide enough for them both to clamber through. Standing looking down at them was their father. 'Had enough?'

Tony had no intention of leaving them down in that rat-hole for longer than half-an-hour and he hoped they would have learned their lesson before then. When they emerged, shamefaced and scared, he had felt somewhat guilty about his robust response to their escapades, but it soon passed. They were taken to the captain, to whom they gave abject and sincere apologies for causing him and his crew unnecessary work and worry; then they repeated the exercise to their parents.

As they lay in their tiny bunks—banished to their sleeping quarters early, before the sun went down, Dickon said, 'How long would father have left us there, Leo?'

'You never can tell with him, brother. But you noticed that he was standing by the hatchway waiting for us? I think he'd been there all the time and would have stayed there waiting for us to come up. Anyway, mother would have made him bring us up for supper at least! She always has the last word!'

'But, we'd better be careful from now on, wouldn't you say, Leo?'

'Until we're on dry land at least, Dickon. At all costs, I'm going to avoid contact with any dog-sized rats!'

\*\*\*\*\*\*

They reached the busy port of St-Malo on the west coast of Brittany in four days, delayed somewhat by adverse winds which blew persistently westward from the continent. The Tanner family were fortunate in that none of them suffered significantly with mal-de-mer, although to the boys' amusement, their father was often a little paler and groaned a good deal when the ship pitched and tossed excessively. Leo and Dickon's experience in the bilges had brought them to the realisation that "we'd better behave", and they were models of obedience for the remainder of the voyage. They struck up a friendship with a look-out boy, one of their own age, who was pleased to explain the intricacies of rigging and setting sails, using all the nautical terms at his command, to their intense admiration. It was agreed, "He knows everything!" They were particularly struck with his ability among the "yards" and "shrouds", as he termed the sails and ropes; this ten-year old boy could clamber up the rigging in seconds and, standing casually on the edge of the crow's nest, would wave nonchalantly at them, shouting words they couldn't possibly catch as they were borne away on the breeze. Strictly forbidden to follow him, Leo and Dickon could only crane their necks from the deck and wish they were there too.

It is the way of boys that one entertainment can rapidly supersede another, and the ship's boy and his maritime antics were soon forgotten when the Tanner lads set foot in St-Malo. This place of bustle, noise, smells and all-round diversions was a revelation. They itched to be set free to roam the busy streets and quays, but, just as they had experienced in Southampton, where the same temptations were on offer, they were hurried out of the port almost as soon as they landed. Horses had been hired and loaded; a hasty meal taken and within the hour they were on their way south towards Quiberon Bay on Brittany's Atlantic coast.

Again, the anticipation of the unexplored pleasures of St-Malo was soon exchanged for the exhilaration of riding free on good French tracks through deep forests. Riding skills had been inculcated from an early age on their father's insistence. Even when they were in London, their Uncle Pom had seen to it that horses were hired so that lessons could be taken twice weekly from an old friend of Mister Appleby who had been a groom at Greyfriars when it had been the Earl of Warwick's lodgings. All the skills they had acquired in France were still evident, and, although the horse-master was sometimes scathing about "the style of the French" he could not fault the youngsters' ability and enthusiasm. 'As fine a couple of horseman as I've not seen since Lord Warwick was a boy in Middleham. I came down to London with him, you know! He would have no other.' And off he would go in a reminiscence of "fifty years man and boy" as stable lad and then head horse-master to the noble earl.

Tony was proud of his lads' evident skills, although he knew any comparison with his late master was spurious—the man had been and remained, although dead, the best horseman of the century in England by a country mile. Now, as he watched them canter skilfully through trees and take the odd fallen trunk in their stride, he considered his work done. 'They'll never forget how to ride a horse, Magpie!' he grinned at his wife, 'however much you try to turn them into book-learning gentlemen!'

'I've long since realised that will never happen, husband. They're too spirited—like their father.'

'And like their mother, Meg! I never would have married you if you had been some weak-kneed woman.'

It was well over one hundred miles to their destination, the town of Sarzeau and the Château de Suscino, the home and headquarters of Francis II, Duke of Brittany and a place of refuge for young Henry Earl of Richmond since the year '71, when, as a Lancastrian, he'd been forced to flee when Edward IV returned to the throne.

'You see, he was a lad of fourteen when he came to France. Rather like you, he's spent much of his time here.' Leo and Dickon were intrigued to hear the story of young Henry and how he had become so important that their father was making this long journey to visit him. Tony made no attempt to describe the intricacies of Henry's family line, and how it had led him to be considered as a contended for the throne of England. It was sufficient to tell them that the current occupant was under suspicion of having done away with his nephews, and, 'There are many lords in England who are appalled by that idea and feel he should not enjoy the privileges of kingship.'

'Tell us about these boys in the Tower of London, father. How old were they and how were they killed? Was there much blood?' asked Leo, relishing the idea of a good killing in a dark dungeon.

'Edward, who should have been king, was nearly thirteen; his brother Richard would have had his tenth birthday in August this year. We don't know how they were killed, Leo. But it was a wicked, foul act and ordered by their uncle—'

'—I suppose so he could become king,' Dickon looked thoughtful. 'Is being a king so important that a man would kill another for it?'

'I'm afraid it is, Dickon, and our history is littered with examples!'

'But you said you'll support this Henry—er—'

'—Richmond,' prompted Leo, who had been paying close attention.

'—Yes, this Henry Richmond. You'll support him to get the throne away from this wicked Uncle Richard. So, will you have to kill the king that is now, to put the next one on the throne?'

'Yes.' Anthony could think of no other way to answer a straight question.

'What happens if Henry's no good as a king and people don't like him?' asked Dickon, with the unwitting perspicacity of youth.

'That is something we'll have to face if it happens.'

'You always say that when we ask a difficult question!' sighed Leo.

'My boy, there are some questions which can't be answered until the circumstances arise. That is one of them. Now, I suggest we catch up with your mother as she's well ahead. We've lingered on this conversation too long.'

'You always say that too—just when it's getting interesting!' protested Leo. But his father had spurred on his horse and cantered off up the track.

\*\*\*\*\*\*

Three days of hard riding found them close to Sarzeau, a small town on the Gulf of Morbihan, which they first saw from the outskirts of the larger town of Vannes on the north side of the bay.

'Look at all these small islands!' said Meg, peering out across a wide expanse of water, which was almost surrounded by land, making it a natural harbour with its entrance from the Bay of Quiberon. She was correct. Everywhere one looked there was a small island. 'Some say there are as many as there are days in the year!' laughed Tony. 'Some disappear when the tide comes in, but many are inhabited.'

'You seem to know a lot about it, Anthony?'

'You must remember? I came here a few times in my travels in France for Louis XI. He has a difficult relationship with Francis, and they've almost come to blows several times. I can't remember the exact years I visited; one time was just after Dickon was born—the year '74.'

'I remember those times well! You were barely home for more than a few days at a time before you were off again!'

'Well, this time perhaps we shall stay for a while and be together as a family. That was my intention. These are difficult times, Meg. I will admit, I'm taking a gamble here; I hope I'm backing the right man.'

'If what we have heard of King Richard is true, and it does seem likely from what you tell me, then you are most certainly right to support Queen Elizabeth, regardless of whether this Henry is an honourable man as you seem to believe he is.'

'Are any of them trustworthy? When it comes down to it, the only way you can tell a man's integrity is by looking them in the eye and trying to read their souls! But that's not fool-proof; I've had men swear on their mothers' lives that they are telling me the truth, and then I find they've lied and deceived. We'll see what we make of Henry, although I have committed myself to Elizabeth's cause. I carry her pledge between my legs, if you remember!'

'Only the jewels, husband! Only the jewels.'

'Well, let's sort our lodgings out and get settled. Tomorrow I shall ride to the chateau and introduce myself. I'm grateful the journey has been without incident. I have a feeling the coming months are not going to be so smooth.'

They found a small, clean tavern and settled into two rooms before going down for a welcome meal. Seafood seemed to dominate the menu, and soon they were enjoying a thick soup with all kinds of shellfish which Tony had great fun in describing to the boys. 'This one's a mussel—look they've left the shells on—so eat up!' Leo picked up the blue-black shell and looked at it dubiously. 'This as well?'

'Of course—the French are just the same as us—they don't waste a thing!'

All-trusting of his father's great wisdom in these affairs, Leo opened his mouth and prepared to take a bite. 'Stop!' said

Meg, 'your father's jesting. Of course you don't eat the shell, foolish boy!'

Leo scowled and threw the mussel back in the dish. Dickon sniggered until his brother glared at him with a look which said, 'Wait 'til we're alone.'

Attempting to rescue the evening from the atmosphere of sullen annoyance which had descended, Meg suggested they all went for a walk around the town after they had eaten.

'Let's explore its possibilities. After all, we are going to be staying here for some time.'

They walked out into the cool September evening and took a winding route across the flat land of scrub and shingle which led down to the seashore where they watched fishermen tending their nets. All the time they were within sight of the magnificent Castle of Suscinio with its series of rounded towers.

'It's been fortified and enlarged over nearly a century,' explained Tony. 'When I visited a few years ago Duke Francis invited me to hunt with him; for this place is a favourite of his—the woods are ideal for deer and boar.'

'So do you often hunt with dukes, father?' asked Leo, who had by now walked off his sulks over the mussel and was taking in the spectacular view of the château with great interest.

'Not as often as I would like, Leo, but I have known a few.'

'In which of those towers does Henry Richmond live?' asked Dickon, wondering what it would be like to live in an entirely circular chamber.

'I can't be sure, Dickon. Inside the castle isn't as large as it looks from the outside. I've been told that the young earl brought nearly five hundred servants with him, but the castle couldn't house that many, so most live in a village nearby called Kermoizin. I know this, because it's where we'll rent lodgings for the next two months.'

'Did you know all this, mother?' asked Leo, turning to Meg with a frown.

'Yes, indeed, your father told me he had seen to these arrangements before we left London, although I'm not sure exactly where we'll live, and what the lodgings will be like. But I'm sure we'll make the best of them, as we always do!'

And she looked meaningfully at Tony, as though to say, 'I hope you were thinking of us all when you prepared this, and that the boys and I are not to be housed in some out-of-the-way cottage in a dank marsh, while you leave us and enjoy the comforts of a duke's castle!'

Dusk was upon them and they walked back slowly towards the tavern. Later, in the bed-chamber when they were alone, the boys chewed over all they had heard—and embroidered on some things they had not. They agreed Sarzeau and its surroundings was not such a bad place to be.

Leo was most enthusiastic, 'We'll have the horses and can ride out each day to explore. Perhaps we'll be able to swim to an island—or find a boat—and set up a camp!'

'We may still have to do lessons. Mother has packed paper and ink you know,' said Dickon dolefully.

'We'll soon talk her out of that! She'll be too busy worrying about father,' said Leo confidently. 'I can wind her round all my fingers if necessary.'

'Do you think father is in any danger—is this Henry to be trusted? If he plans to kill another English king, perhaps it's not a good idea to make friends with him.'

'Dolt-head! It's not about being friends. Father's working for England and trying to save it from a—a—I can't remember the word, but I think it starts with a T—'

'—Tyrant is what you're looking for!' said a voice, and Tony peered around the corner of the door. 'As for twisting your mother round all your fingers, Leo—I don't think so! I shall be coming home regularly and inspecting your copybooks. So, if you think the next two months are going to be spent in idleness, think again! Now, no more noise. Good night!'

The door shut, and they heard his feet on the stairs. After a few seconds, Dickon broke the silence and whispered, 'Leo!'

'What?'

'Leo, how did he know—about the lessons and the camping?'

'Because he's a spy, that's how; he can hear through stone walls! We'll never get the better of him on that score. Still— we won't be doing lessons all day and he won't be here very much, despite what he says. Mother will have to let us out sometimes. Tomorrow we'll ride down to the bay, skirt round it and look out for some likely islands to conquer.'

'Leo!'

'Yes?'

'Do you think those two boys are still alive in the Tower? Perhaps their uncle didn't murder them after all.'

'Of course he did, stupid! How could he become king unless he got rid of the one that should have been? No question, it was the uncle who did for them!' And on that confident note of finality, Leo rolled over and went to sleep.

197

\*\*\*\*\*\*

There was no question of exploring the next day, or the day after. The family were involved in a move to the village of Kermoizin; a small place but it seemed overwhelmed with Englishmen and women—and soldiers. Tony had immediately sought out accommodation and been able to rent a small farmhouse on the edge of the village, two bedrooms and good-sized living quarters. 'There's poultry and a pig— milk from the people next door. Even a small garden, although it's the wrong time of year for planting.'

*Thank goodness*! thought Meg, who had acquired certain talents in that area.

'We have stabling for five horses, so we'll hang on to the four beasts we've hired. I took them for six months.'

'We seem to be spending rather freely, husband!'

'No need to worry on that score, Magpie. Before we left London, Queen Elizabeth furnished me with a generous sum, "To cover expenses you might incur while on our great mission", to quote her exact words. We're living well within our means! You might even get a new gown out of it!'

Overall Margaret was satisfied with the accommodation, although she felt the place should be thoroughly cleaned from top to bottom. Never one to shirk from getting her hands dirty she set to with a will, although Tony insisted they brought a young girl up from the village to help. Meg drafted the boys in to help carry water from the stream nearby and find a goodly supply of wood for fires. Once she was satisfied they had done their share she gave way to their pleas that they be allowed to explore. 'After all,' Leo argued, 'you don't really want us under your feet!'

With sighs of relief on both sides, the boys took their horses and rode off towards the Gulf of Morbihan. They had packed food and "essential supplies", being a knife each and a precious tinderbox which Leo secreted on his way out of the kitchen. 'We'll find a good place, set up a camp and light our fire.' When they lived deep in the countryside in France and were still small boys, Tony, at those times when he had been at home, had often taken them to spend a night or two under the stars. On those occasions, he had taught them how to make fire, always carrying the embers away with them for use at the next campsite. It was a skill they never forgot, and "sleeping out" was something they missed in London.

'This is the perfect place for it!' enthused Leo as they trotted towards the edge of the water and looked across at the myriads of islands in and around the bay. He reined in his horse as they approached a grove of trees stunted by the wind into weird ghostly shapes. It formed a half-circle, open where the waves lapped gently against a tiny sandy shore. Leo dismounted and tied his horse to a branch. 'This is a good spot—firm and dry with some shelter. Father would stop here I'm sure; there's wood for a fire too!'

Dickon, still mounted, was looking across at the water. He pointed and cried, 'Look, Leo—a tower coming out of the water!'

About two hundred yards from the shore rose a single tower of pinkish stone about thirty feet up from the water. As Dickon had noticed, it seemed to rise out of nowhere, but as they looked more carefully, they could see it was encircled by a few yards of green turf.

'It looks like an island prison, Dickon. Anyone trying to escape would have to swim for it.'

'Do you think there are any prisoners in there?'

'Well, they're not waving at us out of the windows! We'll make our camp here and keep watch.'

They settled down in front of a small fire which they lit because they could, and for no practical reason since they had brought cold food and water to sustain them. 'Tomorrow perhaps we'll ask mother if we can bring some soup to heat up!' Leo laid back, a thin stream of September sun falling on his face. 'This place is all right, but if we really want to keep an eye on the tower we should conceal ourselves better. I suggest we mount up in a minute and explore around the edges of the bay more thoroughly.'

'But we still want to keep watch on the tower, don't we?' asked Dickon, very intrigued as to who might be incarcerated there. Having absorbed the story of the princes shut away and murdered in the Tower of London, to come across such an isolated place, and so close, made him curious but fearful at the same time.

They placed some embers back in the firebox, remounted, and headed off on a natural track which skirted that section of the bay, all the time keeping the tower in view as it stood like a lonely sentinel. Within a few minutes, they came to a larger group of fir trees, almost a small wood which, like the grove they had just left, grew down to the waterline.

'There's plenty of shelter here and we can see the tower better!' said Leo triumphantly. This time they didn't bother to light a fire, the novelty having worn off. Instead they unsaddled the horses and, sitting with their backs against the trunk of a tree, began to ponder on the object of their curiosity. Why was it there? Who built it? Who used it? Unable to come up with any adequate explanations, they sat for a further twenty minutes, before growing bored with the lack of action. In fact, it was becoming decidedly chilly and, as nothing was happening, they decided to abandon their vigil for the day and return home.

Overall, disappointed to have found no villains, pirates or spies, besides any children who might have inhabited the tower and needed rescuing, they hoped for better luck on the morrow. But, as with all the best laid plans, the weather took a hand and it rained. They were confined to the house and lessons, but Meg did promise, 'Two hours hard work today and, if it's fine tomorrow, you can be excused and do as you please!'

'Mother, could we take some soup to heat up?'

'I don't see why not; but only if I know where you're going, and you return long before it begins to get dark.'

Feeling they had manipulated their mother to her full extent, they went to bed in anticipation that something exciting must happen tomorrow.

\*\*\*\*\*\*

'What is happening up at the chateau, Tony?' Her husband having arrived home late that same evening, evidently tired but exhilarated, she was determined there would be no shocks and surprises for her family arising from this venture. 'Did you manage to speak to Henry Richmond this time?'

'I did, and had a very warm reception, not least when I handed him the contents of my cod-piece.'

'I hope you only extricated the less-valuable contents, husband!'

'Those I left behind are for you to dally with. I presented him with the jewels in that small casket which we chose for the purpose before we left London.'

'Did he say what he would do with them?'

'Not exactly. After passing all the coded correspondence, I carried with me to his agents, he ordered I return tomorrow when he will hold a full meeting of his advisers. I'm expected to prepare a report of the situation with regards to rebellion in England by certain lords, the atmosphere at court and in the London streets, and the position of those noblemen at home who equivocate in their support for Richard III. In fact, a statement of how matters might stand should he mount an invasion. While I was with Richmond, I heard other important news; our old friend King Louis is dead!'

'Dead! What was it?'

'He's been unwell since his apoplexy two years ago and never really recovered. He had another severe seizure in the fortress at Plessy, where he died four days ago, on the last day of August. I'm sad for the old boy—a strange yet generous man. You remember how kind he was to us when we first arrived at his court, Meg?'

His wife was silent for a while. 'So, his son Charles is the new King of France now. He's still a boy though!'

'Yes, just thirteen. He's going to have a struggle—as all minority heirs to any throne do. His father wasn't popular in many quarters, and all kinds of factions will be waiting to grab whatever power they can. Not a happy situation for France, as we well know with our experience of that situation in England. But, that's a problem for the French and Charles VIII. We must concentrate on our great enterprise: the invasion of England.'

Meg was silent, then she asked, 'And will you still be part of this invasion?'

'Having gone this far in supporting Queen Elizabeth I can hardly back out now. The most important consideration, besides raising money for a fleet and an army, is the proposed marriage between Elizabeth of York and Henry. This effectively unites the Yorkists with the Lancastrians.'

'Which must be a good thing, Tony—surely, and bring an end to all these wars of greedy noblemen.'

'We may think that, others differ. Men always take sides in these matters, depending on how much they think they can get out of supporting one side or another. It's all about self-interest, as we know.'

'Has Henry any important noblemen willing to fight for him?'

'Some. Sir Edward Woodville for one, also Robert Willoughby, Charles Somerset and Giles Daubeney, plus several others. Those that are over here are quartered in the village. You'll see them about when they're not up at the chateau. Henry's agents in England have told him there are definitely those who would support him if he brought an army over to challenge Richard; the Earl of Oxford, for example, although he's locked up in Hammes Castle, Calais.'

'That is a risky strategy—to mount a challenge while not knowing for sure whether he will be supported back home. Men, especially noblemen, are fickle and could change sides on a whim. As you say, Tony, if they're promised enough they'll follow where the money or privileges are.' She sighed and shook her head. 'When is all this likely to happen, do you know?'

'Not for a month or so. It takes time to raise money; fleets are also difficult to organise, much less easy than men.'

'So, we will be staying for at least two months—as you said.'

'Most certainly. Henry Richmond has asked that I join his court immediately. It means I will be paid something—not much, as he's short of cash, relying on hand-outs from Francis.'

'Please don't tell me he wants you to move into the chateau!'

'Yes he does. Don't worry, Meg, it's only a few minutes away. I shall visit often—someone has to keep those boys sharp!'

'If anyone's going to be sharp it's me! I've done most of their upbringing since they were babes and it hasn't always been easy!'

'And no one appreciates it more than me, Magpie!' he said soothingly. 'You have done a wonderful job. But I have been thinking about their future and, when all these important matters of state are resolved, we'll discuss it and make decisions together—I promise!'

'Matters of state!' she scoffed. 'Matters of war you mean. More widows and orphans I suppose.'

'That's the way of the world, Magpie, and you know it has ever been thus!'

\*\*\*\*\*\*

'It's still the same, Leo!' Dickon was disappointed. During the two days which passed before they could ride out to the tower, he had built pictures in his mind of troops of soldiers guarding men bound in chains and a flotilla of small boats to ferry them across. The two boys stood at the edge of the great bay and looked out at the pile of rosy-coloured stone which projected eerily from smooth grey tidal water; there was hardly a breath of wind. They had set their camp within the small wood where they were sheltered from the weather, but most importantly, out of sight of any prying eyes. 'We'll take it in turns to keep watch,' ordered Leo—always taking command in these situations by right of age, although not necessarily natural talent. Dickon had a sharp eye and quick brain also, but as a rule he deferred to his older brother in decision-making; generally agreeing, although occasionally arguing against, just to make his mark.

On this occasion, lying flat on his stomach and keeping a close eye on the tower and water around it, Dickon, having been ordered as first watch, after half an hour spied visitors to the lake. Stiffening with excitement, he crawled round to his brother lazing on his saddle. 'Leo—Leo!' he whispered, although he was far away from any other ears, 'there's a boat—two men in a rowing boat and going towards the tower!'

Leo left off his daydreaming and crawled behind his brother to the waterside. He saw a small skiff heading from the water's edge to the small island. He could see the outline of the rower, a short, squat man pulling strongly on the oars. Sitting opposite was a man of great height who seemed to loom over the other. Thin and wiry, he was evidently giving instructions to the oarsman as to where they should land. Both men were dressed in light mail, but without head gear and even from their limited vantage point Leo and Dickon could see the shorter man was as bald as an egg; the tall one with a mop of flaming ginger hair which blazed in the sunlight. The boat came to rest on the small shore and the two men alighted and pulled the craft up beyond the waterline. It was high tide, the sea coming directly from the Bay of Biscay through the Quiberon Bay. The sward around the tower was at its least extension; for the moment a thin strip over which the men walked briskly until they disappeared around the far side of the building and out of sight.

'That must be where the door is!' said Dickon, squinting after them as though to force his eyes to see around corners.

'We'll wait until they come out!' said Leo.

'But they may be staying the night?'

'If we see any signs of a fire being lit, we can assume that's what they'll do. Otherwise they might be just visiting. It doesn't look like the sort of place one would want to spend the night.'

'Did you notice how they were dressed?' asked Dickon.

'They're obviously soldiers—but who do they fight for? I didn't see any badges. They must be mercenaries!' he said with authority because he knew Dickon probably didn't know what the word meant. He was right.

'What's that?'

'A man who fights for money, not a cause.' Leo quoted his father exactly, since he knew it would give a sense of adult endorsement to the explanation. He went on, 'Well, Dickon, it proves we were right. This tower is used for something by someone. What we must do now is find out what it is and who they are!'

'Why?'

'Because that's what spies do!'

'And are we spies now, Leo?'

206

'This is practice for the real thing. You do want to be like father and take up spying for your country?'

Dickon had never considered this as a possibility, uncertain how he viewed his life to come. But stirred by the discovery that two soldiers were furtively rowing across a mysterious lake to an even more mysterious keep, he felt the least he could do was go along with Leo's enthusiasm and see what came of it.

'Very well, but how will we find out?'

'Tomorrow we'll attempt to get across the lake and enter the tower!'

Dickon fell silent as he contemplated all the snags in this proposition, the most obvious being how they would engineer a crossing.

'You know I'm not as good a swimmer as you, Leo, and it seems quite a way and looks rather deep.'

'We'll wait until the tide is at its lowest, then wade and swim across.'

'What if the men come back while we're in the tower? What if—'

Leo frowned and said sternly, 'Dickon, if all commanders listened to their foot-soldiers asking, "What if, sir?" then there would be no battles at all.'

'Wouldn't that be a good thing, Leo?'

'Certainly not. It's how our father makes his living and puts food in our mouths. So be a man, Dickon and have faith!' Once again, a stern lecture from Tony had instilled itself in Leo's mind and was dredged up to stiffen the sinews of this doubting brother. Dickon looked chastened as he always did when chided. His brother clapped him on the back and said, 'Tomorrow we begin our campaign!'

******

'The campaign begins in earnest, Meg!' That night, Tony returned from the chateau at a late hour. Pulling off his boots, he looked up at her with a grin.

*He may be forty, but he's still a boy at heart*! was her verdict. True, lines were appearing at the corner of his eyes, and wasn't that a tinge of grey at the sides of his hair? But he still maintained a lithe body which could give her intense pleasure on those occasions when they had time to enjoy each other. The long absences were more than compensated for by the rapturous reception they exchanged when he returned.

'So, when is this invasion going to happen?'

'You know I can't tell you that, Magpie. In fact, I'm not sure myself. The unfortunate thing is—and you're not going to like it—in a week's time I have to be away for month.'

'A month? Surely you're not going back to England?'

'No, but there's no harm in you knowing that I'm being sent to Calais to canvas the Earl of Oxford's support for Henry Richmond.'

'I thought Oxford was in prison in Hammes Castle?'

'He is, but that needn't stop him planning an escape. I hope to help him with it! But that's all I can tell you. I'm sorry it will be so long, especially as we've just arrived and are still settling in. But I'm sure you'll make friends with neighbours—you have good French after all.'

'Tony, I've never grumbled about these adventures of yours—I've always known it's what you do. But a month is a long time and the boys will be disappointed. I think they were hoping you'd ride out with them and explore the place.

They've already come back excited by it all; you must have noticed!'

'I listened in on them talking about camps and fires. Perhaps I'll spend a day with them before I go.'

But this was not what our intrepid trainee-spies wanted at all! When their father suggested they make a day of it and ride out to the bay and to their camp, they were dismayed. This was their discovery and the last thing they wanted was a professional spy taking over. They were therefore very relieved when, on the day marked out for this proposed two-way filial and paternal bonding, the fog came down, followed by intense rain. There was no possibility of a ride that day and Tony was disappointed, since he had cleared his mind to leave himself available for a special day with his boys. He had planned trapping rabbits and game, showing them how to prepare them for cooking, making a fire and then, lazing on their saddles, eating and laughing together, while he told them of some of his exploits.

This paternal aspiration was wiped from his mind when he looked out of the window and saw the fog. 'That's that!' he told Meg. 'It's the only opportunity I have. There's so much to do before I leave. I won't be able to spare another day.'

Meg sighed, 'Well, I'm sure the boys will understand, although I know they were looking forward to it as much as you were.'

\*\*\*\*\*\*

'We had a lucky escape, Dickon!' Leo led his brother round to their vantage point on the edge of the lake. 'Father would have been very curious as to the tower and, if the men had appeared again, he would probably have wanted to investigate.'

The weather had cleared; Sir Anthony Tanner had returned to the chateau to receive further instructions; Lady Margaret Tanner was busy introducing herself to the neighbours, and the boys had decided to walk to their destination rather than ride. 'We'd have to leave the horses tied up for too long and there's always a chance they could get free and wander away!' said Leo. It was but a couple of miles walk and took them quarter of an hour at the fast pace, set by Leo with Dickon trotting manfully behind.

The question in the elder brother's mind was where the tide would be. He had, with considerable foresight for a near-eleven-year old, sought out the local fishermen and asked about tides. As he explained to Dickon, 'We can't get across to the tower until low tide. There's no point in hanging about waiting for it.' The first pêcheur had not been helpful, 'Les Anglais devraient regarder autour d'eux!' he advised as he spat expertly, hitting a hopeful herring-gull which shook its beautiful plumage and gave an ugly squawk of annoyance. By dint of persistence and a certain amount of charm, Leo discovered from a more helpful shrimper that the next low tide would occur at about two in the afternoon. On that understanding, the boys had set out after dinner at a brisk rate and soon came down to the edge of the bay. The tower loomed large and, in Dickon's mind, was even more threatening. For the first time, they had a full view of its base, for, as the obliging shrimper had advised them, the tide was now at its lowest ebb and therefore they could see the entirety of the island. The tower was built on a hump of ground with an

210

elevation of about twenty feet. The building, which on their first viewing seemed to rise completely from the water, was not as tall as they had observed, being about thirty feet; it's height distorted by the view at high tide when the base was unfathomable.

'Look!' pointed Leo. 'The tide's as low as it can be. There's only a few yards of water further off; the rest is muddy pools. We can easily walk across, although we may have to take our boots off.' He threw a large bag across his shoulder which contained a change of hose for them both, a water-flask, food packed by their mother and some small cakes he'd purloined from the pantry when her back was turned. His thinking was: *We don't know how long we'll be and we're bound to get hungry*! Then he selected a stout staff from a few branches lying under a tree. His facility for forward-planning really impressed his brother. Watched him stride off onto the muddy bed of the lake, he thought, *He looks like a sort of pilgrim—like mother has told us of.*

As they started off across their route, which at first was devoid of deep water, Leo said, 'Have you put your knife somewhere out of sight and safe?'

'Yes, but why?' Dickon, not sure of the necessity of such a precaution, and, rather disturbed by the underlying inference in the question, began to wonder if this adventure was as sensible as it had seemed. Planning a campaign in the comfort and safety of one's bedchamber was certainly not the same as the real thing.

'Spies always keep their weapons out of sight!'

After a few minutes, they came to a strip of water which they saw immediately might be deep and was certainly running fast. 'This is why I brought the stick. I'll use it to test

211

the depth,' and Leo walked forward, gingerly prodding the ground in front of him. He hadn't gone more than three yards when the stick disappeared several feet into the water. 'It's much deeper here—we'll have to go back and take our boots off.'

'Will we have to swim?'

'I don't think so; it shelves a bit as we get towards the island, but probably no more than up to our waists. We've brought a change of clothes, so it doesn't matter, but we can take off our hose and then put them on again when we're on the island. Once we're past the deepest part we start climbing up to it.'

It wasn't a warm day, and Dickon was none too keen to get his body wet without the provision of a fire to dry himself off. Leo, by now like a terrier on the scent of rats, was busy taking off his boots and hose and stuffing them in his bag. Dickon would never argue and handed over his own. Carefully they began to wade waist-deep and arms and bag aloft through the chilly grey water, stirring up soft sand which squelched between their toes; Dickon forbore to imagine what creatures might be lurking underneath the silt. Within a few minutes, they had come to the green sward which encircled the island, and for the first time they had a close view of the tower which loomed over them. They both gave an involuntary shiver. Far off and in the pale sunshine its pinkish hue might have seemed unthreatening, but to the two boys, now they were at close quarters with it, in their minds it exuded an atmosphere of dread.

'Leo!'

'What is it?'

'I don't like it here. I don't think we should go any further.'

'Well, having come this far, it would be foolish just to turn and go back again. We should at least walk about and have a look—even if we decide not to try and get in,' and he sat down and put his hose and boots back on. 'We'll just have a look and then go back!'

'Do you promise?'

'Of course!'

Fully dressed again, they climbed up the small hillock to the walls of the keep. They could see they were strong, smooth and had evidently once been carefully crafted by the stonemasons. Each side of the square tower was about twenty-five feet wide and, as they looked up, Leo estimated it possibly consisted of two storeys. 'Look, Dickon, you can see the windows are placed one above the other—four barred windows on this side. Let's go on and see what's around the corner.'

The east side of the wall was bare of door or window, so they proceeded to the north side which like the south, had four windows. 'There must be a door here somewhere—it should be around the corner.' Leo walked confidently on and cried out in excitement, 'Here it is, Dickon—a door at last!' Coming up behind him, Dickon peered at a low, stout, studied oak door which his brother was trying to rattle open, 'Damnation! It's locked!' cursed Leo.

'Which means someone doesn't want anyone to go in. Shall we go now?'

'I'm not so sure about that!' murmured Leo. 'This lock doesn't look very complicated; it's worth a try with the knife.'

'What if someone comes and finds us damaging it?'

'Dickon, just get your knife out and give it to me. It's got a thinner blade than mine.' His brother, now extremely uncertain as to the way the day was going, reluctantly fished for his blade and handed it over. Leo had a certain facility with locks. Uncle Pom had showed him how prisoners in Newgate had often been able to escape quite successfully by skilful working a blade on tumblers. The boy had twice practised on his father's front door, until he was caught, thrashed, and forced to work for a week chopping wood to pay for a locksmith's visit.

He got to work very carefully; as far as Dickon was concerned it seemed to take an age and much cursing. Then he heard a clicking and his brother's immediate yell of triumph, 'Got the bastard!' And the door swung open at Leo's push.

******

Meg immediately noticed the cakes were gone and sighed. *Leo only had to ask me! The boy is so wilful. I wish Tony wasn't going to be away for so long. They're both at the age of needing their father. When he's here, he's very good with them and they obviously adore him. But I do find them a handful on my own.*

They had been in Kermoizin a week and, at first, she had been too busy setting the house straight to investigate the village and its possibilities. The family next door, owners of a couple of cows, had visited and offered to supply fresh milk—at a price. They had been gratified that she spoke good French and, although they spoke with a strong Breton timbre, she knew that, as a stranger in this small village, the ability to

214

converse in French would be to the Tanner family's advantage; they were all fluent in the language and not shy of using it.

As far as going out to explore the countryside, there had been no time. The boys seemed to have plenty to occupy them, coming back from a day's excursion excited and dirty. They were sleeping and eating well and even settling to their obligatory lessons without too much complaining.

*Now we are settled in, I should offer to ride out with them and let them show me around. The countryside seems very pleasant.* But the two lads seemed set always to want to go off on their own and, with Tony constantly at the chateau, she found she had more time on her hands than she liked. It was at these times she missed her friends in London and wondered what Monty, Gisella, Pom and Jack were doing. *I wonder what's become of the Malory Quest?* she thought. *Will we ever be together to fulfil old Sir Tom's wishes, and ride to Winchester to deliver 'Le Morte'?*

******

On their own quest, the Tanner boys looked one to another. Then, pushing open the door, Leo walked into the ground floor of the tower, closely followed by a distinctly nervous younger brother. There was a dirt floor and at first viewing the place appeared empty in the gloomy light afforded by four smallish windows. Leo looked up and, pointing to the wooden ceiling said, 'I told you there were two levels.'

Dickon, somewhat bolder now he was sure there was nobody else about, had moved to the far end and whispered for safety's sake, 'Leo, look here—these covers. What do you think is underneath them?'

'Let's see!' And his brother pulled back some canvas sheets to reveal a half-dozen or more large chests and long wooden boxes. He pulled on the lid of one chest, 'It's not locked, help me heave it over!' And they pulled it up until it fell open under its own momentum.

'Look at this!' And Leo rummaged among the straw packing and pulled out a sword. He gave a whistle of approval, 'This is fine steel—and well-made. Don't you remember father telling us that not all swords are made the same. Some are much better than others. I can't remember how or why, but I do remember he told us the best ones come from Spain. Just looking at this you don't have to know about swords to see it's well-made.' He ran his finger along the flat of the blade and noted that, had he even gently pressed his finger on its edge, he would have easily drawn blood. 'Let's see what else is here; I'll open this one, you that small box there.' They began to investigate with a will.

'This one has arrows and bolts, Leo.'

'And here are the cross-bows to go with them!'

Within a few minutes, they had investigated the contents of every box and found they contained all the weapons of war any military captain would require. There was even a chest of hauberks and aventails carefully packed. 'There must be twenty or more here,' said Leo, taking out a hauberk and slipping it over his head.

'Do you think you should be doing that?' asked Dickon anxiously, as his brother wandered up and down, the too-long chainmail dragging behind him in the dust.

Leo took it off and placed it back with the others in the chest. 'You know what I think, Dickon?'

'What?'

'This is an arms store for someone. Those men we saw are keeping these things here for some reason.'

'It's probably the duke's up in the chateau.'

'Don't be stupid! He'll have his own armoury up there and it'll be well-guarded. No, I think this a private store and they've chosen this tower because it's a safe place.'

'We found it, Leo!'

'Yes, but we're spies and must investigate!' He looked up over their heads. 'See! A trapdoor leading to the next storey. There must be more arms up there and there's a ladder propped up against the wall—we'll go up.'

The trapdoor was designed so that anyone climbing had room to unbolt it, throw it back and climb through. Leo took the rungs eagerly, his brother more gingerly; Dickon was not fond of heights. Pulling his brother through, they both stood up and, to their disappointment found themselves in an empty chamber, apart from a rickety table, two small chairs and a fireplace whose chimney was built within the walls and up through to the roof. The ceiling was wooden, with another trap door leading to the top of the tower. The four windows, corresponding with those in the chamber below, let in some light.

'Someone's been here and lit a fire,' observed Dickon, looking down into the hearth.

'We could light one and warm ourselves while we eat. We could burn this old table! Let's see, we did bring the firebox with us, didn't we? I asked you to pack it.'

With a mixture of shame and relief, Dickon said, 'I'm sorry, Leo, I forgot! I went to the privy before we left and didn't think about it!'

'A fine spy you'll make! Stupid boy! What would happen if we were stuck out for the night and found we hadn't got any way of making fire. We'd probably die, and it would be your fault!' Dickon hung his head. Up on this first floor with just a ladder between them and escape, the younger Tanner was feeling distinctly exposed to every possible danger. Despite his brother's insouciance, ever since they'd entered the place he was conscious the men might return, or perhaps someone else might arrive. This was not the time for arsing about lighting fires.

Leo sighed, disappointed. A fire would have added a certain element of excitement, authenticity and even romance. It would be as though they had laid claim to the tower and its contents, made their mark on the place. He opened the bag and checked the food and water flask. 'We may as well eat here and then go back,' he said. 'But first, let's see what the view's like. We should be able to see the grove of trees where our camp is from here,' and he dragged the table underneath a window on the south side of the tower, climbed up and pulled Dickon up after him. They peered out through the four iron bars. They could see nothing but the skyline and surrounding water. However, this became an instant cause for concern.

'Jesus Christ!' Leo only cursed when Dickon was present and no other. His mother had strong feeling about boys taking the Lord's name in vain.

Dickon knew exactly what had prompted this violent expression of concern. 'Look, Leo, the tide's coming in—and really fast! The water will be all around us soon; it's already beginning to cover the bits we walked over. It'll soon reach our shore on the other side!'

'The bastard fisherman didn't tell us it would turn so quickly. We must have crossed at the time it started to come in. There's no way out of here until it ebbs again—which will be hours!'

'What will mother say when we don't come home? What will father do?'

'That's the least of our worries, brother. We're trapped. Let's hope the men don't decide to make a visit in the next few hours!'

\*\*\*\*\*\*

There was a tenuous link between King Herod and Sir Jasper Percy. As far as the Biblical Jewish monarch has any reputation, it is as a child-killer. Sir Jasper merely disliked anyone under the age of fifteen, as he intensely disliked animals, women and most men. In fact, he was an all-round misanthrope, where King Herod was possibly not. It was not entirely Jasper's fault; he had endured severe bullying as a boy, because of his pock-marked face and his unfortunate voice, which had never developed to its full manly potential; in fact he squeaked rather than spoke.

If the reader has been paying attention, they may remember we met him, and his companion in dishonour, the bull-headed Robert Costello, twelve years before in the forests between Honfleur and Bolbec in northern France, when the Newgate Fellowship was on the road to Bruges. The encounter had been short and violent; Percy bested by Sir

Anthony Tanner and left horseless, hoseless and hooked to a tree.[1] Immediately after this encounter, Percy had made haste to the French coast; sailed after Queen Margaret; caught up with her army and fought bravely at the Battle of Tewkesbury, where he witnessed his defeated mistress break down in great shoulder-heaving sobs when hearing the news that her son had had his throat cut by the Yorkists.

The intervening years had seen Percy and Costello constantly on the move as Queen Margaret, having failed in her attempt to regain the English throne for her husband, found grudging shelter from the King of France. Eventually the quietly disgruntled king paid Edward IV a ransom of fifty thousand crowns and took her into his court, with the status of "poor relation". Jasper Percy had always been one of her closest companions; she, unlike any other woman, appeared to like him, and he became slavishly devoted. There was nothing physical between them, just an unspoken loyal bond which remained until her death in August of the previous year. He was with her in the castle of Dampierre-sur-Loire, where he had seen her deteriorate, from a tough, strong-willed, argumentative woman to a dribbling, muttering wreck who constantly harked back to the past and seemed to have no structure to cling to in the present. When it was all over, and she had been buried alongside her parents in Angers Cathedral, as he walked away from the grave he said to Costello, as always right on his shoulder, 'Bob, we must shift for ourselves! We go to the highest bidder. The Lancastrian campaign is ended.' But, as he later discovered, he had been premature in his assessment. In November he heard, through

---

[1] See Malory's Quest

his many contacts scattered across France and in England, the rumour that young Henry Richmond, a Lancastrian living in Brittany, might—just might—make a bid for the English throne. 'At least, it's another Lancastrian waiting for a chance. Perhaps we should look in that direction,' he thought with relief.

But events were not kind to Percy. Richard of Gloucester got there first and had himself crowned. For some months in the first half of the year '83 Jasper and Costello wandered around unsuccessfully looking for enterprises by which they could put food in their mouths. Their luck changed when they met an errant Spanish sea-faring man, captain of a cargo vessel which plied its trade across the Bay of Biscay. He boasted he would 'carry anything which made money' and, to shorten the tale, Percy and Costello went into arms dealing.

'We'll make money in France—all these petty dukes vying against each other. We'll sell Toledo swords at a premium, as well as other arms and mail. We can't lose,' was Jasper's optimistic assessment of the possibilities.

They scraped the money together for one full shipload of war-gear and the arrangement with the captain was that he would stand off at the entrance to Quiberon Bay and Percy and Costello would arrange to have the cargo ferried into the Gulf of Morbihan. They scouted the area for a likely hiding place and came across the isolated tower whose access was subject to the tides. "Perfect!" had been the conclusion, as Costello exchanged the defunct old lock for a new one and screwed solid bolts on the trapdoor to the upper storey. When the tide was high, they spent days ferrying the arms, stacking the boxes and chests on the ground floor. 'No one's been here for years! It's obviously not used. This table and these chairs are wormy. Everything will be safe until we decide who to sell it to.'

On this day, Percy wanted to check his inventory. He had an idea that he might approach the Earl of Richmond and test his interest. The old rumours that Richmond might make a move and invade England had been revived and, if they were true, he would need arms. Getting an audience would be tricky, and even then, he would probably have to reveal his source which he was reluctant to do since there was the likelihood of further deals to be made with the Iberian trader. The business must be handled diplomatically and with all the cunning at his disposal.

Bob Costello had rowed them across from the small beach they used as a launch-way, pulling strongly, for the tide was almost completely up, although still running fast. Reaching the island, he leapt out, tied the boat to a post and they proceeded towards the door. Suddenly Costello put his hand on his master's arm, 'Look sir—it's open!'

'You must have left it unlocked!'

'You saw me lock it sir—I always check the lock works—it was a cheap one, remember? Someone's been here!' He pulled out his sword and Percy did the same. Stealthily they pushed the door wider and heard—nothing; then the faint murmur of high-pitched voices coming from above. They walked to the trapdoor and looked up at the ladder and the opening. Putting his fingers to his lips, as quietly as possible Percy mounted the ladder and made his way up. At the top, he poked his head through and saw what he never expected: two boys standing on the table and looking through the window. Softly and quietly as a cat he pulled himself out into the chamber, turned back and beckoned to Bob to follow.

The table had uneven legs and the boys were being extra-cautious in keeping themselves from falling off by clinging to the bars as they peered through. So hard were they concentrating that they failed to heed to the two men now standing in the room, until Percy stepped up behind Leo and squeaked quietly, 'Well! well! trespassers; this is a surprise!'

Bob Costello wasted no time and grabbed Dickon, who lost his balance and fell off into the man's arms. Leo was, for a few seconds, frozen with surprise and then fear. Percy pulled him down and held him firmly at arms' length while he scrutinised him. He wasted no time on pleasantries, 'Who the fuck are you? What do you think you're doing here?'

Leo gulped, 'We're just exploring, sir. We didn't mean any harm.'

'When people trespass, there's always harm. You know you are in deep trouble?'

Dickon was squirming in Costello's grip, 'I'm sure we wouldn't say anything about the weapons—.'

Leo groaned to himself, *Driveller!*

'—So you know about that? It seems you've been doing more than exploring the building—you've been poking your long noses into business which doesn't concern you. That's a pity!' Leo didn't like the threatening note in the man's voice at all. The man's voice—yes; even under these tense circumstances it occurred to him that it was very odd, *So squeaky—not like a man, but like boy*, he thought.

'Shall I slit their throats, sir?' Costello pulled out a long blade and pointed it towards Dickon's neck. Leo tensed as though he would spring to his brother's defence, but Percy laughed and said, 'Not yet, Bob. Let's find out a bit more about them first. Now, I'll ask you once again, who are you and where have you come from?'

'I'm Pierre and this is François. Our father is a fisherman.'

'I don't believe you; you speak English perfectly.'

'Our mother is English, but we can speak French too,' and, jabbering away to Dickon in French, he told his brother to say nothing at all. 'Laissez-moi parler.'

'I'm sure your brother can speak for himself. Now, you must be local to come to this place. Who else knows about it?' asked Percy, whose French was also good and could understand everything Leo had said.

Dickon, although stricken with fear, despite his brother's instructions, was minded he shouldn't duck out of his responsibilities and said, 'No one in the village comes here! Our friends think it's haunted—by ghosts.'

'That is usually the case, my boy. I see, so no one knows you're here?'

'No—'

Leo shook his head at Dickon with fury and said, 'Of course they do! My father will be expecting us soon. We were waiting for the tide to ebb and then go back to the village. If we're not back by dark, everyone will be out looking for us!'

Percy, who was very relaxed during this exchange, gave a small smile of thanks to Dickon; he was the weak link; the boy could easily be broken to tell them who they were and, more to the point, who might be looking for them if they didn't return home on time.

'François—that's right isn't it?' Dickon nodded. 'How long have you been here—have you had any food?'

Fooled into feeling there had been a change in approach, Dickon said, 'We have some in our bag, sir.'

'So, you were prepared to camp out here for the day, were you lad?'

'Yes, sir. It seemed to be an adventure!'

'I liked adventures when I was a boy.'

'Did you sir?' Dickon felt emboldened by this sharing of experiences but made a fatal error in mistaking the subtleness of Percy's conversation for friendliness. 'May I ask a question?'

'I might not answer it, but yes.'

'Can you tell me why you speak in such a strange way?'

The atmosphere, which was verging on the civilised, changed immediately. There was an icy silence and Percy's pitted pink face turned a deep shade of carmine. Bob Costello knew such an enquiry would incense his master, and immediately went across to Dickon and gave a back-handed swipe to the lad's face, so fierce it sent him spinning across the floor, his head narrowly missing the stone wall opposite. Leo lurched forward but was restrained in a vice-like grip by Percy. The boy beat back tears of frustration and anger; any attack on Dickon was an attack on himself.

'Your brother should learn better manners, the little bastard! Shall I cut their throats now sir? We can dispose of them easily enough out here. No one will ever find them.' It was no threat but seriously suggested; Percy considered it for a moment. Then he said, 'No, I think they might be useful to us in another way. Let's see what's in this bag first,' and he took out the spare hose, the food and the water-flask. 'You've come ill-prepared for a real adventure, boys, which was stupid of you—no firebox. But I see you have some food. Well, we'll leave you here while we consider what to do with you. Come Bob, we'll go downstairs out of earshot of our two ill-mannered spies!' Picking up the bag, he turned on his heels and disappeared down the ladder. Costello walked across to Dickon who was still lying in a heap shaking; he had unfortunately wet himself in fear. Leaning over the boy, the man took out his knife and pressed it at his neck, whispering, 'If I'd had my way you'd be out of the window and buried in the mud by now.'

Downstairs standing underneath the trapdoor, Jasper Percy, still inwardly smarting from a question which many would have liked to have asked, but few dared, said, 'Ransom, Bob. We can make some money from them. They're lying—fisherman's sons my arse! They're well-dressed, well-fed and well-spoken. I'll wager their father has money and will pay up to get them back. But of course, he won't get them back. We'll dispose of them as you suggested once we have the cash'

'But we don't know who their father is?'

'Not necessary. When these boys don't return home tonight, there'll be a hue and cry—the whole village will come out searching for them. We'll soon find out whose boys they are; we'll also lay a false trail well away from here—send the search party out in an opposite direction. I hazard we could make fifty crowns from this. We'll leave them up there, lock the place up and get off. There's no escape; the tide won't be turning for hours.'

They checked the contents of the boxes to see there had been no interference with the stock; Costello bolted the trapdoor but found the lock of the outer door was so badly damaged by Leo's inexpert picking at it, they had to leave it unlocked. Confident the place was too isolated for casual visitors to investigate, the two men walked out into the cool

September evening, retrieved their boat and headed back to the shore.

'Dickon, did you hear that?' asked Leo, who had his ear to a gap in the trapdoor. 'They intend to hold us for ransom, although not give us back even if father pays it.'

Dickon, who had by now somewhat recovered, apart from a cut on his face from an ostentatious ring on Costello's index finger, an eye which was blackening nicely, and hose which was uncomfortably wet, said, with quivering lips, 'What will father do when he gets the ransom note?'

'Go mad and come and rescue us of course!'

'But no one knows we're here, Leo. We never told mother exactly where we were going.'

'Well then, if we don't want to have our throats cut, we have to get out of here at once. Any ideas, little brother?' And he looked quizzically at Dickon, but with little expectation of a useful answer.

# Chapter 8

October '83, London: Caxton expresses an interest in *Le Morte*;
The Quest goes back to a rebellious Kent;
The manuscript is finally returned to its anxious custodian;
Caxton commits himself.

All unaware that his godsons were involving themselves in high-risk activities, their Uncle Pom was considering his own business risks and trying to decide how much the instability in the south of England would affect his wine trade. He was sharing his concerns with his great friend Monty Pickle.

'Anyway you look at it, Monty, supplies coming into Kent and Hampshire must be disrupted,' he said gloomily. 'The new pressings from France are ready and I like to be first to offer it, especially to my best customers. Sir Robert Billesdon has already put in a large order for claret; I just hope I can fulfil it—he is our mayor after all!'

'I don't think you should worry too much, Pom. These rebellions are localised—I don't think they'll come to anything.'

'The king doesn't agree with you. You know he's sent out commissions to hang any rebels.'

'Buckingham's still in Brecon I believe with Welsh troops. There have been no rumours that he'll desert the king—at least I haven't heard any.'

'He's not likely to pin up a notice, Monty! This is where Tony would come in useful. He'd be able to tell us what's going on.'

'Judging from their letter, the family arrived safely in Brittany. Meg writes that the boys have plenty of open spaces to explore. Tony's found himself a place with Henry Tudor who he says is a fair-minded young man—as far as he can tell. I did burn the letter, on Meg's instructions.'

'I miss them all, Monty!' sighed Pom sadly. 'Thank goodness I have your three to give me solace. The girls are charming and young Thomas is growing into a very sensible young man—just like his father!'

'He has his moments, Pom. They're on their best behaviour when their godfathers come to visit. Jack spoils them so, with his gifts. Gisella has to be very firm with him.'

'He can afford it. Caxton gives him plenty of work—"too much sometimes"—as he complains to me. Inkin' Wynkyn and he are really expert on the presses and have nearly finished at least ten large projects this year.'

'We still haven't decided what to do about *Le Morte*. I think it'll be worth approaching Master Caxton to see if he'd be interested in buying the manuscript with a view to printing it.'

'Well, he wouldn't want it for any other purpose. He'd have to be sure he could make money from it.'

'Let's ask Jack whether he thinks now would be a good time to approach Caxton. After all, the work on *The Golden Legend* is completed; Jack only has to bind the copies.'

'Very well, although you know Master Worms' opinion on buying back property which is ours in the first place!'

'Let's try and keep him off that subject. The most important thing is getting the manuscript back by whatever means,' and Monty sat back in his chair with the determined look on his face which his friend knew so well.

******

Two weeks later, on a Monday in mid-October, the three friends were sitting in Caxton's small chamber where he conducted most of his business. The Westminster Press was now a very successful enterprise; hardly surprising since it was the only press-shop in London and Master Caxton was anxious to keep it that way. However, the death of Edward IV and the subsequent loss of one of Caxton's chief patrons, Earl Rivers, was worrisome and the printer knew he would have to cast around for new royal and noble patrons. Queen Elizabeth would have been an obvious contender, but she had shut herself up in sanctuary and was not to be disturbed by approaches to endorse works of literature. She obviously had more pressing matters on her mind than the pressing out of books.

What Master Caxton had not told his compositor or his binder at the time, was that some weeks before he was executed and still a free man Earl Rivers had made a lightening visit to London from the midlands in order to attend to matters of personal business. While in the city, he had taken the opportunity to visit the Westminster print-shop. From the outset, he had been fascinated by the whole process which Caxton had brought to London and proud of the fact that he had been one of the first in line to benefit from this "wondrous invention", as its owner proudly described it. Whilst discussing literary matters with Caxton he mentioned, very casually, that he had in his possession "a mighty manuscript of many pages". Short of time, he never revealed the title or the author and Caxton, being busy on other projects, had not delved too deeply into this throw-away comment. However many months later, having followed the Newgate Three's tale of the tracking of the work and their confirmation that *Le Morte D'Arthur* was lying on the shelves of Earl Rivers' library in Kent, he realised this must be the same manuscript.

He listened carefully to Jack Worms as he put forward the proposition that his employer might like to purchase the manuscript from the Woodville estate and then, with Monty's total involvement, bring it to a point where it could be printed. Caxton sat back in his chair, stroking the ringlets in his substantial beard, 'Gentlemen I will confess an interest here. I believe Lord Rivers mentioned *Le Morte* to me some weeks before his death—and before you began your investigation into its whereabouts in Essex. I'm afraid I wasn't paying the attention I should have done to the vague words of a great lord; we'd been discussing other projects he had in mind. I do think, had he lived, he would have eventually brought the manuscript to me. If Earl Rivers was prepared to pay a large sum of money for it, then it obviously has a value—and not just a sentimental one, Mister Pickle,' and he looked sternly at his compositor and transcriber.

'Knowing everything you do of *Le Morte* would you be prepared to buy it—if the estate was prepared to sell it?' asked Pom, who always like to get to the point of a business deal.

'I would have to insist I was fully involved in the editing and production of the finished work,' and Monty leaned forward, blushing pink as he always did when excited or exercised over a serious matter.

'If, and only if, I decide to purchase it, of course, as my senior transcriber, and as someone who was directly involved in the production of the original, it would be stupid of me not to seek your expert eye. But, may I remind you gentlemen, twenty pounds is a great deal of money, and times are not favourable for printing. We appear to be almost in a state of civil war again—uprisings, plots, conspiracies, rebellion. Our lords and masters—those who have the fat purses—are thinking of matters other than the publication of new works. I have had a couple of enquiries from noble lords, Lord Daubeney—and the Earl of Arundel who, as we know, has generously supported the publication of *The Golden Legend*. But these men are rarities and now power has changed hands, Daubeney's out of favour having led rebellion in the south. Oh yes, gentlemen, I too have heard the rumours that the Duke of Buckingham, Queen Elizabeth, Lady Margaret Beaufort and her son Henry Richmond are plotting together to tip Richard III from his regal seat. Who can be sure of anything in these turbulent times—a rhetorical question because I'm sure none of us in this room can know the answer. On the other hand a non-rhetorical question is, "Can I risk that amount of money at this moment, even if Andrew Dymock and the other executors agree to sell?" I think you will have to leave it with me for a few days to come to a decision. If I agree to purchase, then I'll visit Mister Dymock and ask him to arrange for the manuscript to be brought to London where I can view it.'

'If that is the case, sir, could I ask if I might go down to Maidstone and collect it myself?' Monty's pink face flushed deeper and he looked appealingly into Caxton's face.

'This evidently means a great deal to you, Mister Pickle. That will most certainly be a possibility—if I should so decide.'

And the Newgate Three had to be satisfied to wait for the decision. 'This is such a long-drawn-out process,' sighed Jack.

'You do realise that if Caxton had told us about Lord Rivers mentioning "a large manuscript", we might have surmised that it was *Le Morte*,' said Pom. 'We could have saved ourselves a journey into the flat lands of Essex and all the expense we incurred!'

'But we wouldn't have had the fun of catching Crosby out and seeing how he would be punished by his shrewish sister!' laughed Monty, who was generally not a vindictive man but, in this instance, had enjoyed every minute of the thief's discomfort.

'Caxton said "a few days". By that time all these reported uprisings in the southern counties will probably be over and Buckingham will either be sitting on the throne or lying with his head over a block.'

'We live in exciting times, Pom!' And Jack with a grin.

'To be frank—I could do without it. It does trade no favours—ask any man of business. I wish they would sort themselves out and decide on a long period of peace and stability.'

'I'll say "Amen" to that!' agreed Monty, as they came to his front door. 'Will you come in to supper? Gisella will be delighted to see you.'

Never forsaking an opportunity for a free meal, the two bachelors nodded their thanks and prepared to enjoy one of "Gisella's finest".

******

'How do you like your first full ride out in the countryside?' Riding alongside his godson Thomas Pickle, Jack Worms was trying not to show his anxiety as he watched the young man guiding his pony through the Kent forest. Tom's prowess on horseback was "adequate" according to Pom Appleby, who had taken pains to teach the boy. 'He's not afraid, but sometimes rather hesitant, which gives his mount the wrong signals. Horses can immediately tell if a rider is confident. I think what the boy needs is a good long ride somewhere—not just a trot around the city. Do you remember how you were on a horse all those years ago, Monty, when we set out from Greyfriars' to Winchester?'

'I do, Pom. It took me many days before I felt I'd mastered the art!'

On this Monday morning, 3rd November, Jack, Monty and his son Tom were heading out of London towards the North Downs of Kent. Once they had crossed London Bridge and negotiated the busy streets of Southwark, they began to enjoy the fresher air of the county. The purpose of their journey was to collect Malory's manuscript from its custodian, Benjamin Trussell, the late Earl Rivers' steward of The Mote near Maidstone. Master Caxton had been true to his word, considered their request; decided it was viable; visited Andrew Dimmock and negotiated terms. He had not divulged to the Newgate Three how much he had offered for *Le Morte* but was quietly satisfied he had not taken too much of a risk. His experience with the printing of large works was such that he could envisage a market for these tales, but they were very expensive to produce. His seven hundred pages of the *History of Troy* had been quite well received, having the seal of approval from the Duchess of Burgundy and there was no reason to think these equally mythical stories would not be accepted by discerning readers. He had at least broken even as far as his investment in *Troy* was concerned; sales had been adequate to cover those high expenses. Hence, he had given Monty the promised task of retrieving the precious pages from The Mote and bringing them back to London, where Caxton would cast his eye over them. There was no question he would not publish it, having committed the sum of sixteen pounds which was paid in cash to Mister Dymock. Monty had the sealed receipt and a letter from the executor in his pocket.

It had occurred to Mister Pickle that this journey would be an ideal opportunity for his son to experience his first long journey on horseback and an overnight stay at an inn. Thomas had been three when they left Bruges for London and had little memory of the journey. Now very close to his eleventh birthday his father thought this was the ideal time for an outing which would entail a stay away from home. Jack had offered to accompany them, with Master Caxton's permission for absence, and the three had set off on a fine Tuesday with stores provided by an anxious Gisella, who kept her features firmly cheerful as she waved off her eldest on his first full ride.

There had been some doubt that this was an appropriate time to be travelling in one of the southern counties most active in the rebellion against King Richard. Earlier in the month it had been reported that the men of the Weald were "in arms" and threatening to march on London. No further such worrying news had been forthcoming, and on hearing the king had raised an army and successfully suppressed uprisings across the south, even the cautious Monty felt there would be no undue risks for plain travellers. Besides, the leader of the rebels, the Duke of Buckingham, had been unable to rally his supporters in the southern counties because of the severe October floods which prevented him crossing the River Severn. "Buckingham's water" as it was known to future generations, saw him forced to ride northwards to seek shelter with friends in Shropshire, where he was promptly captured and later taken south to Salisbury Castle.

'Travelling is always a risk—never mind rebels, we could be attacked by robbers or cutthroats of any variety! Remember, last time we went we were fearful that the new king's men would have ransacked The Mote before we got there; nothing of the sort happened. The most danger we faced was tripping over a wheelbarrow!' said Jack Worms cheerfully to Gisella, when she had nervously enquired about the likelihood of her son meeting up with a few hundred armed rebellious Kentish men. 'Buckingham's no longer a threat, so we have no need to worry, Gisella!' That lady was not so sure. Although she had been born in Bruges, her father was English and had taken a keen interest in the affairs of his countrymen. She had heard his tales of Jack Cade's invasion of London and how the county of Kent had a reputation for rebellion. 'Even though Buckingham's been captured, it doesn't mean the men of Kent aren't still angry and believe the rumours about the king killing his nephews.'

'We will be gone only a short while, Gisella,' said Monty soothingly, although he also had his doubts. But the desire to get his hands on the manuscript and show it to Caxton overrode his natural caution. As for taking Thomas, once he had casually mentioned the possibility there was no denying the lad; this journey to new places was not to be missed.

They took the same route as previously and stayed in the same cheap lodgings on the Pilgrims' Way. Anxious not to draw undue attention to themselves, subtly they enquired of a local man what the state of the county was in terms of "troubles". In return for several pots of sour ale, he was most forthcoming.

'We've seen many troubles, mister. About two weeks ago a whole party of our Maidstone men under two of our county's gentlemen, Dick Haute and Richard Gildford gathered on Penenden Heath outside the town; then they marched to Rochester to join with the men there—then all to Gravesend to join in a mighty affray. It was the day of the fair and some say there were as many as five thousand armed men crammed into the town.'

Monty looked at Jack and raised his eyebrows. Penenden Heath was close to The Mote.

'Why are they so angry?' asked Monty.

'Many reasons. This king killed his two young nephews and had our noble lords Anthony Woodville and his half-brother executed. Whatever anyone says about them, the Woodville family are thought well of around here. There's no liking for Richard of York,' and he spat a gobbet of beer stained spittle onto the floor. 'Anyway, there was much blood shed in the market square; a yeoman—Bonting was his name—cut the throat of a labourer called Mowbray after an argument. Then everyone waded in—many more were killed or injured; the place was in uproar and much drink was taken. There was no militia—they were all involved in the fight. The trouble lasted for a couple of days.'

'So, has it calmed down now? Is it safe for travellers to pass through the town?'

'Keep your wits about you. There are plenty of ner'-do-wells and men who have just come down here from London mostly to see what they can get. They have nothing to do with our cause.'

'What's happened to the five thousand men in Gravesend?' asked Jack.

'They've dispersed for now but are waiting for the next chance. We heard today that Buckingham's dead.'

'Dead?'

'Executed at Salisbury yesterday. A rider came through with the news this afternoon. That bastard James Tyrell oversaw it—he who probably killed the two princes.'

'So the Kentish men—and those in the rest of the south—have no leader now?'

'There's rumours that young Henry Richmond is coming over with a fleet and an army to take the throne back from that caitiff Richard. But no one's sure if it's true. It's all as my father and grandfather remember it in the year '50 when we rose against the milk-sop Henry VI. They tell me some tales about that!'

Anxious not to spend the evening listening to tall tales of murder and mayhem in the streets of London thirty years before, especially with young Tom present, Monty put the money down for a couple more pots of ale for their informant and made the usual excuses that they were "tired and had an early start". When they were up in their room, Jack said, 'Well, we seemed to have come down here precisely at the right moment! If we'd have come a fortnight ago we would have been in the thick of it. Hundreds of men gathered on Penenden Heath would have been a sight—all waving weapons and kitchen utensils! I don't suppose it was a well-organised army.'

'More like a rabble, but it sounded nasty in Gravesend.'

'What are these men fighting about?' asked young Tom, who had followed the conversation as best he could, but had still not got to the bottom of the "quarrel". All fights started with "a quarrel" of some kind—he knew that from his own experience. He'd had one or two skirmishes with Leo, and his young sisters when they'd particularly annoyed him. The man had said there were five thousand men fighting in a market place; that sounded like a battle out of one of Uncle Pom's stories.

'It's very confusing for us, Tom,' laughed his Uncle Jack. 'I couldn't begin to explain it all as we'd be up all night. Now we should get some sleep and make an early start. The sooner we collect this manuscript and get out of Kent the better!'

Tom finally went to sleep with a picture in his mind of his father standing alone and wielding a saucepan in a market place where thousands of men were advancing on him with swords and pikes. He woke with a great feeling of relief.

\*\*\*\*\*\*

The following morning they breakfasted before most of the other guests were abroad, paid the bill and sought out the horses from the ostler. 'You gentlemen going to Maidstone?' he asked.

'Indeed we are,' replied Monty.

'There's been reports of some bands of men, probably let loose from the Penenden Heath army, roaming about looking for trouble. Two pilgrims reported being attacked and robbed on the Way last night. Foolish them being out after dark.'

Now Monty was worried. Neither he nor Jack considered themselves "fighting men". They had never had battle training and were self-confessed novices with a sword. They each carried such a weapon but had never been put to the test. Neither lacked courage and when pushed to the extreme would probably take the normal route to self-preservation, using their fists. But, nonetheless, they set out nervously looking around for suspicious-looking characters. They jogged on for a few miles until, just as they were examining a way-marker, they heard voices and, looking up, they saw four men coming towards them on foot. Within minutes, the two groups were viewing each other—the newcomers from the ground; the riders looking down on them. Monty could see immediately they were shabbily dressed, thin faced with eyes which spoke of hunger and desperation. They all carried weapons of some kind—stout staffs, an old pike and cheap swords.

Thinking it would be best to take the initiative, Jack said as cheerfully as he could, but with his knees trembling, 'Good day, masters! A fine day for travelling.'

A small man with a face twitching like a terrier which had just scented a rat, stepped forward. 'You're strangers here; where are you going?'

'Surely you're used to strangers on the Downs—the most-used track-way in England!' replied Jack with a nervous smile.

'Surely you've heard the men of Kent are up in arms, mister. Not a good place for travellers.' His companions nodded and muttered agreement. Monty could see two of them had wandered round the back of the horses eyeing their packs and saddles. 'Got any food in those saddle-bags?' asked one particularly lean and hungry-looking individual.

'We've just come from the inn—no, we don't carry any food—we haven't far to go before we stop with friends for dinner.'

'Ah! Dinner is it? You're lucky then. Get down! Let's see what you have in those packs.' He went towards Thomas as though to pull him off his mount.

Monty's hand went to his sword, 'Don't touch that boy!' Tom had gone stiff with fear, and the man put his hand on his leg as though to manhandle him and said roughly, 'Get off!'

'The boy can't hear you—he's deaf and dumb,' and Monty looked desperately at Thomas to see if he understood what he must do. Fortunately, being in the frozen state he was, the boy was incapable of speech anyway, and just sat staring in front of him.

'Deaf and dumb? Can't hear or speak. That's an advantage for you—can't have any backchat! Must be difficult giving him orders though. 'Here, you!' and he shouted at Thomas, as though by raising his voice he could overcome the lad's disability. Tom continued to look straight ahead as though he had heard nothing. 'Well, you can get off that pony—we'll take it. It should fetch something.'

241

The terrier said, 'Same goes for you two; we'll take everything you have.'

Jack and Monty exchanged glances, both thinking the same, *Two against four and we have the boy to protect. Is it worth the fight? These men are desperate, and it wouldn't take much opposition from us for them to cut our throats. Horses and gear can be replaced.*

Monty however, wasn't going to give up so easily. While the men had been circling and eyeing up their goods, he remembered the man's words from the inn, "The Woodvilles are respected round here". He looked the leader in the eye and said, 'We are on a mission to The Mote and the House of Lord Woodville. A secret mission to revenge Queen Elizabeth's brother.'

'With a boy in tow? You think we're stupid?'

'How better to disguise a mission by appearing as a family. Who would think we were spies? I know that everyone in Kent opposes the tyrant Richard. We have come from London to help your cause. I can see you've been working hard—I suppose you've returned from Gravesend and the great fight in that town? We hear it was a marvellous victory for the men of Kent!'

There was silence as the men absorbed this information.

'Something else, not connected with "the cause" but you may find some sympathy in your hearts. After we have settled our business with Master Trussell—the steward—'

'—We know who he is.'

'When we leave The Mote—do you know where we're going?' The men shook their heads, interested now. 'We're going on a pilgrimage to Becket's shrine to pray for a miracle cure for my son here. The holy saint will look kindly on the

242

boy, I know it!' And Monty tried to look pathetic, hopeful, and stern all at the same time, but simply appeared as somewhat ingenuous to his audience.

'You mention Steward Trussell. What do you know of him?'

'We've visited him before,' said Jack truthfully, now fully in tune with Monty's artful approach. 'Last month—he had the builders in!' as though to provide evidence the statement was true. The men looked one to another, 'We are those builders!' said one with a laugh now.

The tension broke, and Monty and Jack sighed inwardly with relief. 'Tell you what! We'll escort you to The Mote. You can't be too careful—plenty of caitiffs on the road waiting to rob travellers,' and the leader roared with laughter, holding his sides.

Monty smiled weakly and nodded, 'That will be a comfort to us. Here's money for your trouble,' and he fished in his jerkin pocket and brought out a few coins. To his great surprise, the leader shook his head, 'No need for that—we don't ask for favours from those working against the tyrant.'

'I insist,' and Monty pressed the money into the man's hand. With a shrug, he held on to it and nodded thanks.

Within a few minutes, the strange party of two mounted gentleman, a boy bereft of speech and hearing staring straight between the ears of his pony, and four dishevelled unemployed ex-soldiers set off down the Pilgrim's Way towards the fair town of Maidstone.

******

Travelling the pace of the slowest, it took an hour to reach The Mote. As they approached the wide expanse of ground before the front entrance they saw the familiar sight of building work in abeyance. Tools, mortar, ladders, buckets all abandoned as though those using them had suddenly decided to down-tools and take off—which is exactly what had happened.

'The call came from our village to muster on Penenden Heath and we obeyed it!' explained the chief individual of the group—who, after his assumption as escort had introduced himself as Tom Parkes, labourer. 'This here is Francis, Peter and John, John's a master stone-mason,' he said, evidently proud to be associated with a craftsman. Within minutes, they were all on first name terms.

'It's just as we left it, Tom!' observed Francis, a man with a hair-lip and doleful demeanour.

'Well, no other bastards are going to take over Frank! At least we have work to come back to. Now, we'll knock up Master Trussell and see what he says about you two.' It was evident to Monty that the man had only half accepted his story and was waiting for verification. *This'll take some quick thinking*, he decided, as he pulled the bell rope by the door. A few seconds later the door opened to reveal a servant who Monty did not recognise, and who was evidently surprised to see strangers. He looked at them suspiciously, until John stepped forward and identified himself as the stonemason, 'Hired by Steward Trussell.'

Ignoring him, the servant looked at Monty and asked superciliously, 'And you gentlemen, what is your business here?'

'We are here to see Master Trussell on a matter of great urgency and importance,' and Monty looking urgent and trying to look important.

'In what connection?'

Jack stepped forward, 'That, my man, is no business of yours. Fetch your master immediately, or it will be the worse for you.'

The stonemason came to Jack's aid now and said, 'Walter, don't be a prick! These gentlemen are on a special mission concerned with the queen. Just go and find the steward.'

Even though reluctant to take orders from artisans, the servant said, 'If you give me your names I will enquire if the steward will see you.' He disappeared for a while and then returned, 'Master Trussell will see you two gentlemen—'

'—The boy comes too,' said Monty firmly.

'Very well!' He turned to the labourers, 'You men! The steward will see you later. He's none too pleased that you left without a word. There'll be no pay for the two weeks you've been away. This job was supposed to be finished last week.'

'It'll be finished when we get paid what we're owed, Thomson—'

'That's for Master Trussell to say, Parkes. Don't compound his anger by demanding favours.'

'It's not a favour—it's what we're owed—'

Monty did not want his business held up by a workers' dispute over pay and said emolliently, 'I'm sure Master Trussell will understand the situation when I explain how helpful you've been guiding us here. Now, we'll go in and carry out our business, Tom,' and he looked at the labourer meaningfully, who himself winked back conspiratorially, thinking he was now part of a grand plot to save the nation.

To the intense disappointment of the labourers, the servant Thomson slammed the door in their faces and then led Monty, Jack and young Tom into the great hall and then into Master Trussell's chamber. The steward was evidently pleased to see them, 'Such times we've had here, Mister Pickle, such times! Kent has been in an uproar.'

'We have heard all about it on our journey, Master Trussell,' said Jack rather brusquely, not wishing to hear it all again; rather wanting to conclude their business and get out of the county as soon as possible.

'We are delighted to be back again,' smiled Monty, always ready to smooth Jack's rough edges when it came to social niceties. 'We come from Mister Andrew Dymock, and our own master, William Caxton, the printer.'

'Ah! Caxton. My master Anthony Woodville considered him a "good acquaintance". Master Caxton has prepared and printed many of my late master's works, as you well know. Let me see—there was—' and he held up his fingers as an aid to enumeration.

With no intention of listening to a catalogue of works, with which he was fully familiar having bound them all, Jack once again interrupted their host rather ungraciously, 'He certainly was a bibliophile—your master I mean. We come with letters from the earl's executors, confirming that Master Caxton has purchased Le Morte D'Arthur and giving us leave to take the manuscript back to its new owner.' He felt he had been succinct enough for there to be no necessity for further elaboration.

'I see, well perhaps you should sit down, and I'll call for some refreshment. Your boy will have something? Some wine and cakes?'

'Indeed he will—Thomas say good morning to Master Trussell.' At the word "cakes", Thomas brightened up considerably and maintaining his persona, nodded. The day had passed in a blur and he was not paying much attention to the exchanges in this small room. His thoughts mostly centred on how it would really be to be deaf and dumb.

'You have obviously been travelling along the dangerous track of the Way and I hear, in company with some of my builders. You know, they just left one morning—not a word—mixed mortar left to waste!'

'If I may say, Master Trussell—'

'—Benjamin, please.'

'—Benjamin, they were most obliging and provided us with protection on the road.' Monty said nothing about the men's original intention to rob them but felt obliged to put in a word on their behalf. They had turned out to be amiable—not villains, simply hungry.

The steward sighed, 'They can't be blamed for following their fellows. Their lives are dull enough—any possibility of adventure must be tempting.'

'I don't think the thought of having their throats cut was too tempting, Benjamin!' laughed Monty. Jack began to fidget in his chair, 'Monty, show Benjamin the bill of sale and the letter from the earl's executors.'

'Certainly,' and he pulled out a sheaf of papers from inside his jerkin. 'It's all there, the signed bill of purchase,' and he pushed the papers towards Benjamin.

Breaking the seal of the receipt he said, 'Well, this is an interesting amount! Sixteen pounds—four pounds less than—'

Jack looked at Monty and raised his eyebrows. They knew that Lord Rivers had paid Crosby twenty, and Dymock knew that also. Caxton had evidently beaten him down on price; perhaps the executors were thinking "a bird in the hand"; who else would be prepared to pay even fifteen for it? In these dangerous times, when the fruits of the estate were ripe for picking by Richard's government, a quick sale would ensure the cash went into the safety of a locked and well-hidden treasure-chest.

'I'm sure the manuscript is in the same condition it was when we were last here, Benjamin,' said Monty with a smile.

'I've kept my word, Mr Pickle. It remains locked here in my chamber,' and he fished for a key, stood up and walked towards a large chest. Unlocking it and throwing back the lid, he lifted out the oil-skin wrapped parcel of papers and laid it on his desk. 'Here it is, exactly as we left it!'

Monty untied the string and uncovered *Le Morte D'Arthur*. Whenever he looked at it, so many memories of Sir Thomas Malory and Newgate came flooding back his head buzzed with them. Just the feel of the paper and the smell of the ink was enough to send him dizzy.

*Two years of my life spent on this work—the fun, the laughter, the outrage and the pain! Perhaps now, twelve years later, it can be put to the world as a masterpiece, and I can lay this precious manuscript to rest in Winchester, according to Sir Tom's wishes.*

Now, breaking the silence which had descended, Benjamin said, 'I insist you stay and dine with us. You will surely not want to return immediately to London?'

'We would gratefully accept your invitation Benjamin,' said Jack quickly, 'and then we must be on our way before darkness. You were right when you described the Way as dangerous. And we have the boy to consider,' and he looked meaningfully at Monty to back him up.

A pleasant dinner was served, and the supercilious servant was suitably servile. Benjamin Trussell had the manuscript repackaged and Monty placed it reverently in his saddlebag. 'I've never forgotten how heavy it is!' he laughed as they walked to their horses being held by the grooms. As they mounted up, Tom Parkes sauntered across and said, 'I hope your prayers to St Thomas are answered! How do I say, "Good luck" to the boy?'

For a moment, Monty had forgotten his son's presumed disability. 'Just mouth it—he can read your lips!' And to Jack's amusement, the labourer went across to young Tom, pulled on his sleeve and with exaggeration, formed the silent words 'Good luck lad!' slowly and deliberately. Young Tom played his part well and nodded and stuck up his thumb in acknowledgement and made a couple of grunts. Tom Parkes was immensely tickled by this, 'He understands! Good lad!' And he leaned forward, and slapped Tom on the shoulder, nearly knocking the boy over.

Mounted up they waved goodbye to the now friendly labourers who were standing among the wreckage of their tools and materials. 'No much work going to be done today, I'll wager,' said Jack. 'Remember, Tom, not a word until we're on the road!'

The boy stared through him as though he had heard not a word and continued to ignore him and his father for some miles down the track towards Otford.

'There's no need to carry it on, lad!' grumbled Jack after he had received no response to several questions; Thomas Pickle was still experimenting with the notion of how one copes without speech. But within three miles of their destination, he became bored. He didn't stop chattering for the rest of the journey.

'I preferred him when he was dumb!' growled Jack.

\*\*\*\*\*\*

'A significant size, but obviously it has been on its travels, Mister Pickle!' And William Caxton peered with critical eyes at the pile of papers released from their packaging. 'You say this is Sir Thomas's hand here—' and he pointed at a section, 'and this other is yours?'

'Indeed sir. Sir Tom had completed the work and I was hired to help him edit and transcribe it where necessary.'

'And it took you two years, you say?'

'Sir Tom was anxious that the work would be complete and perfect—according to his ideas anyway. He spent almost fifteen years researching from the original sources. It was a labour of love!'

'I know all about that! I felt the same with my *History of Troy*.'

'That is why we know you will appreciate how special *Le Morte D'Arthur* is—as a work of vernacular English. It incorporates many aspects of our island hist—'

'Yes, Master Worms, I'm fully aware of the content. That's why I laid out money for its purchase.'

Monty, Jack and Caxton were in the master printer's study perusing the manuscript which had now found its way back to

London. It was the second week of November and at last Monty had been able to corner William Caxton to discuss the printing of the work. It wasn't that Caxton had been deliberately awkward, just very absorbed with the last production of the year—*The Golden Legend*, the largest folio he had printed so far and running to just under nine hundred pages. The Earl of Arundel had been its patron and was anxiously waiting for the first copy. Jack Worms had promised a "work of art" and had not disappointed.

'Now the good earl is satisfied and has his personal copy on his shelves, I feel I have time to consider how we should proceed with Sir Thomas' great work. My experience with *Troy* was that it took at least two years to prepare, but that was in our early days when we were inexperienced. Time has smoothed the process. I estimate it will take a year for you to set it for pressing, Mister Pickle, bearing in mind you will have other projects on hand. I cannot give you time to devote exclusively to the printing and, we must consider that it will have to be amended somewhat to suit the printing process.' Seeing alarm on Monty's face, he said, 'But, as I promised, you will have control over the process, with my supervision,' he added. 'I'm sure we won't quarrel over it! The manuscript will remain untouched and will be the base for the stories. We will keep it safely locked in my chamber—only two of us will have a key, Mister Pickle, and I trust neither of us will be visited by strange doctors offering spurious cures for non-existent illnesses!' And a rare jest from Caxton raised a smile from his two employees.

'When shall we be starting?'

'Easter next year. My thinking is we look for completion by mid-'85. Does that chime well with you?'

'Yes, sir. May I say how relieved I am that the process will soon be underway. I am looking forward to it immensely.'

'I'm sure we all are. I commend you on your fortitude and constancy. I have rarely met anyone so set on anything—especially a work of literature! The story of the manuscript is worthy of a book in its own right. Perhaps you should consider writing it up, Mister Pickle?'

'Something similar was in my mind many years ago, Master Caxton, but time and events overtook the idea and I shelved it. Perhaps, when the book is published, and the manuscript safely stored, I will find time to revisit the notion. But I wonder if the world is ready for the tale of Sir Thomas Malory and his *Magnum Opus*?'

'From what you've hinted at—possibly not, Mister Pickle, possibly not!'

# Chapter 9

In which we return to our two young spies who make a leap of faith,

earning the admiration of a very important person.

'The moat, Leo; what about the moat?'

'Moat? What moat?'

'The moat at the manor house Uncle Pom told us about—you remember; the story of wicked old Sir Tom and how he swam across the moat to escape the duke.'

Having discovered they were locked in the upper storey of a tower surrounded by rising seawater, in desperation Leo had challenged his younger brother to come up with a solution for their escape. His question, "Any ideas" was a forlorn one as far as he was concerned. Of course Dickon would have no notion of how to get out, having a younger, smaller brain. It would be down to Leo to conjure up an answer to their predicament. In truth, he didn't have one and this bald reply took him completely by surprise.

Not waiting to be scoffed at, Dickon continued, 'Sir Tom and Uncle Pom took the window-frame out of the chamber where they were prisoners and jumped into the moat. Then they swam across to the other side where their friends were waiting and they all rode away. Why couldn't we jump out of this window and do the same?'

'For several reasons, dolt-head. These windows are barred, we're twenty feet up and you can't swim as well as I. Besides, we don't know what we'd be jumping into.'

Now Dickon was equally surprised at his brother's reaction. Normally it was Leo who took the lead, formulated the plans and urged his brother on. Warming to his idea he said, 'Leo, the bars on this side are shaky—when we were holding on to look through the window, I definitely felt them move. They look old and rusty. The water around us must be deep because, when it's high tide, the island the tower stands on almost disappears. If we swim together we can help each other!' And he looked expectantly at Leo, who stared back at him, with a look half of disbelief, half of admiration. *There might be something in this he thought; at least we could try and move the bars and then decide about jumping when we can stick our heads out and see what was below.*

'I don't often credit you with brains, little brother, but you may have come up with a good idea! Thinking about it, the only window we can try is the one we were looking out of before those bastards caught us, the one which faces our target—our grove of trees; we don't want to land on the wrong side of the tower and be swimming in the wrong direction!' He paused and then seemed to make up his mind. 'We'll get back on the table and look to see what state these bars are in.'

The table in place, they stood side by side pulling at each of the four bars to see whether they moved. The first was rigid and well-mortared into the wall. 'This one looks better!' said Leo as he tugged hard at the third in the row. 'If we can chip this one out, we may be able to squeeze through the gap, but it would be better if we could take two out and then there would be space for us to sit and push ourselves off. Let's see what this one will do,' and he put both hands on the second of the middle bars and pulled hard. To their great delight they heard a grinding noise as it shifted in its base. 'Look, Dickon! The stuff it's set in is crumbling! If we work at these two with our knives I'm sure we can loosen them enough to push them apart. But the thing is we don't have that much time; I don't know when the tide will turn. We can't jump unless there's enough water, otherwise we'll probably break our necks.'

'If we can't jump now, that means we'll have to stay all night and we have no food or water. Even if father pays the ransom I think the men will still come back and slit our throats!'

'Well, we'd better get on with it then!' And Leo fished deep inside his jerkin and brought out his knife. 'Find your knife and let's get to work brother!'

For quarter of an hour, they chipped, bored, scraped and tugged at the bars. At first, it seemed hopeless as the metal was more solidly secured than they had first thought. But suddenly there was a breakthrough as Leo gave his bar a severe tug and it cracked at the base where he had been attacking it. 'Got the bastard!' As he pushed it with a great heave outwards, the top became loose and began to shed its mortar. After some hard shoving, he was able to pull the bar out completely; he gave a grunt of satisfaction when he saw the gap. 'Dickon, let's see if we can do the same with yours,' and as his brother scraped away, Leo rattled, pushed and pulled until there was an equally satisfying sound of mortar crumbling and giving way. This bar was less rusty and weaker than the other and it took some effort before Leo was able to pull it out. Now they had achieved a gap large enough to take a small man and Leo was able to lay across the wide sill, with Dickon holding on to his legs, and peer over the side of the tower. The September sun was still up, and he had good vision of what was below.

'The water's still high—no sign of it turning yet. I think we can do this, Dickon.'

Now they had come to the point of carrying out his proposition to jump, Dickon was having second thoughts. Would he be able to launch himself into the unknown and cover a distance he had never swum before? Feeling his brother's concern, Leo said, 'Dickon, we'll go together and when we hit the water I'll watch out for you when you come up and we'll swim side by side. As I remember, when we walked over there were lots of shallows. I think the deepest part stretches about the first hundred yards and then we might be able to start putting our feet down. Can you manage that—with my help?'

Dickon was torn between bursting into tears and stiffening himself with fright. But with quivering lips he nodded. Leo pulled himself back in from the sill and stood on the table.

'First we must take off our boots. They'll only drag us down and make it difficult to swim.'

'Will we leave them here then? What will mother say when we go home with no boots?'

'Better we go home with no boots than not go home at all! Take them off!'

Dickon, more certain than ever that this enterprise was not a good idea, nonetheless pulled off his footwear and looked expectantly at Leo, who, fearing his brother's resolve was melting, wasted no time and pulled the boy towards him, holding him round his waist and helping him onto the sill. There the lad sat, body trembling, teeth chattering, legs dangling and hands clinging for dear life onto a remaining bar. With great care, Leo pulled himself up behind his brother, placing his legs either side of his arse. Gently he unclenched his brother's hands from the bar. 'Put your hands across your chest, Dickon.' With his own hands joined around his brother's waist, they were now poised and prepared for the launch through the gap. 'Ready?'

******

*The sun's already beginning to go down. The boys should be home by now.* Meg had been busy all afternoon and was now resting in a chair outside her front door, thinking about supper and what she could give them to eat. *They'll be ravenous as usual.*

She was glad the boys seemed to have found their feet and were obviously engrossed in exploring the locality. When she asked them where they would be, they were somewhat vague, but promised never to go out of sight of the village and to make sure there were always people around, "in case you were ever in any trouble".

'What sort of trouble, mother?' was Leo's innocent reply, although he knew exactly what she meant.

'There are lots of strangers here—English soldiers, mercenaries—men who are not always gentlemen like your father.'

'We'll run away if we see anyone who's not a gentleman!' said Dickon, taking her meaning literally, as always.

That morning they had seemed in a greater state of excitement than normal as they set off on foot with the food she had prepared. They waved as she stood at the door to see them off.

*I wonder where they do go exactly. It can't always be to the beach as they say. I'll ask them to show me where they do their exploring—we could all go together tomorrow!*

She was expecting them at any moment. They had only been out on their own for three days and had been very obedient and always returned home on time. Now she stood at the door shading her eyes against the setting sun ready to welcome them and ready to hear their adventures.

******

'Ready? Shut your eyes!' shouted Leo, and before Dickon could answer he pushed them both off the sill and into mid-air. A few seconds and they were plunging down into the water. To Leo's relief it was only moments before he hit the bottom and, kicking with his legs, was able to push himself up to the surface, where he shook his head, cleared his mouth, nose and eyes, took a deep breath and looked round for his brother. At first, he had no sighting because Dickon was behind him, but then he heard spluttering close by, and turning, immediately swam towards a pair of flailing arms.

'Calm down, Dickon, don't fight! I'm here,' and he took hold of his brother's jerkin and pulled him upright, clasping his chin in his hands until Dickon was in a state to propel himself forwards. With a flash of anxiety, Leo realised the pull of the tide was much stronger than he had anticipated. From their vantage point at the tower window, the waves seemed gentle, lapping on the shore of the far side; but once in the water he was aware of the strong undertow. Would his brother have the strength to keep going in a straight line and not drift with the waves?

'All right?' Leo shouted, and seeing a nod, trod water by his brother's side. 'Just keep going; we must paddle hard, but it's not far.' These simple words of encouragement were enough to keep Dickon afloat. Indeed, once he had been at it for a little while, he found his rhythm and so long as he could see Leo from the corner of his good eye, he felt he could keep going. He floundered once or twice and had to be supported by his brother. Worried that Dickon might not be able to manage much longer, and having swum about a hundred yards, Leo shouted, 'I'm going to try and put my feet down!' But to Dickon's horror he saw his brother sink like a stone. When he reappeared, he spluttered, 'Not yet, I'll try a few yards ahead.' Eventually, after two unsuccessful attempts, to his relief he could feel the muddy bottom, although the water still came up to his neck.

He called to Dickon, 'It's too deep for you to try. We'll go on a bit longer, but we're definitely out of the deep part and coming to the shallows.' For another couple of minutes, they paddled and gasped their way towards the grove of trees which was coming encouragingly closer with each stroke. Leo tried his feet again and found he was now up to his waist. 'Dickon, you can try and stand up now—have a rest!' Within a few more minutes they were upright and able to wade through ever-shallower water, until, up to their knees they were within ten yards of the edge and could see the individual trees which made up their campsite.

Leo turned to his brother and clapped him on the shoulder, 'You did well, Dickon! Very well!'

This rare burst of praise overcame Richard Tanner and to his disgust ever after, he burst into tears—briefly. On this occasion, instead of the merciless teasing he might had received from his older sibling, Leo continued to pat him on the back, nodding with approval. They walked onto the small shelving beach and lay down, soaking wet and shivering.

'We should get home quickly, Leo. Mother will be worrying!'

'Think about it, Dickon. We can't go home!'

'Why?'

'Those men will be around the village because they said they would find out who father was and ask for ransom. If we walk back home, we might bump into them.'

Dickon was very dismayed and very cold. Having made their spectacular escape, all he wanted to do was be safely ministered to by his mother with warm clothes, warm food and her warm embraces.

'But where will we go?'

'It's obvious! We must go to the chateau and find father. We'll tell him about the bastards who captured us and their store of weapon. It's not far—only a few miles.'

'Do you know the way?'

'Don't be stupid—everyone can see the castle from any point round this side of the Gulf. We'll just walk straight towards it. Father will know what to do!'

\*\*\*\*\*\*

Picket duty was not to be relished, especially round the side entrance to the Chateau de Suscinio where no one of any importance arrived to be challenged. Much better to be on guard at the main gate by the bridge across the moat; this was where the interesting people made their entrance. The Breton soldier ordered to the post was idling out of sight of his captain, who had just done his rounds and would not reappear for two hours. The trouble with picket duty was that he couldn't sit down in the tiny wooden shelter provided against the weather, unlike the guard room in the tower by the main gate where benches and a fire were on offer. The soldier was therefore not in the best of moods and when he saw two figures approaching he sighed and picked up his halberd, ready to repel the infernal beggars who frequented the gate looking for alms. *Je vais leur donner l'aummes*! he muttered to himself.

To his surprise, as they drew nearer, he saw they were not men, but boys, scruffy and bootless. *Alors*, he thought, *les mendicants envoient leurs bâtards maintenant*! He called out, 'Fuck off salaud ursins!' Tired, cold and hungry, Leo and Dickon had been relieved to arrive at the chateau, but after walking bare foot for more than an hour, they were dismayed at this hostile reception. Ignoring the Anglo-Saxon order, Leo came close to the sentry box and stood resolutely in front of the guard. In French, he began to explain who they were and their intention to see their father.

'Nous sommes les fils de Chev—'

In translation, the unhelpful guard said something to the effect of, 'I don't care if you're the bastard sons of the pope! You can't come in—so, fuck off back to where you came from!'

This was not a promising start, and Leo was just considering whether they should try the front entrance, when a second soldier appeared, and the lad could see he wore a different badge which his observant eye recognised as displaying the lions of England.

'Sir, are you an English soldier?'

'Indeed I am. And who are you?'

'Lionel Tanner, sir and this is my brother, Richard.'

'And what are you doing here Lionel Tanner—soaking wet and without your boots—and you,' he stared at Dickon, 'sporting a black eye. Are you begging? If so, do as my Breton friend here says and fuck off!'

His companion nodded and muttered, 'Salaud ursins!'

'We are no bastard urchins, sir! Our father is Sir Anthony Tanner and we have come to find him on—on—' Leo tailed off as he didn't want to go into a full explanation of all that had occurred.

'Yes? On what?'

'Family business, sir; can you please take us to our father?' The guard looked them up and down with a frown. On closer viewing, these boys were not "salaud ursins". They may have been muddy and bereft of shoes, but there was something in Leo's open-faced look and speech which told him they were the sons of a gentleman and not misbegotten sons of a local rascal. Besides, he recognised the name "Tanner". He regarded them both; the younger one looked almost dead on his feet—blue lips, chattering teeth and a swollen left eye.

'Laissez-mois cela,' he said to the Breton, who shrugged with relief that he wouldn't have to stir himself in any way. 'Follow me,' and the English soldier took them beyond the picket gate and through to the interior. He ushered them to a small chamber where there was a fire and benches. 'Wait here and I'll see what I can do. Don't either of you move! If you are spies we'll cut out your tongues and then you'll never speak of any "family business" again!' But, as though to ameliorate his roughness, he left them for a minute and returned with two coarse woollen blankets. 'I suggest you take off those wet clothes and wrap yourselves in these; you look frozen. I'll be interested to hear what you've been up to. I don't know what your father will say; he's with the Earl of Richmond on important business. Neither of them will be pleased to be disturbed. You'll probably get a whipping,' he said cheerfully, as he left them.

'Leo, do you think we will?'

'What?'

'Get a whipping from father?'

'Not when he's heard what we have to tell him. I expect we'll be knighted for services to the earl!'

Despite teeth which chattered and a body which shivered as much from nervousness as cold, Dickon contemplated the possibility of such a title. "Sir Richard Tanner" was something to look forward to. 'Mother will be pleased! Perhaps it'll make up for the boots.'

He was less sure of paternal approval when his father entered the room. Tony had, as the soldier mentioned, been closeted with other captains in the earl's chamber, where they were making essential plans. To have been pulled out by an anxious guard telling him that two lads were in the chateau claiming to be his sons was badly timed. 'They seem to be in a bit of a state, sir,' the man had told him. 'I'm not sure whether they are genuine, but they were soaking wet and had clearly walked some miles without their boots.'

Making embarrassed excuses to the earl, Tony had followed the man to the extremities of the building, fuming all the way. *If this is some jest on their part, they'll suffer for it! Meg should keep a tighter rein on them.* Then he checked himself, *I should keep a tighter rein on them*!

But his anger disappeared when he was confronted with his two wayward sons, who made a pathetic sight wrapped in blankets, Dickon still blue around the lips, his eye black and closed, and both boys' bare feet and legs scratched and bleeding.

'So, Leo, Dickon, what's to do?' he asked.

While they were making their way across rough scrub and shingle, Leo had vigorously instructed his brother that 'on no account are you to burst into tears when you see father. He won't thank you for acting like a girl. You must be a man and unflinching!' Now, faced with the man who had entered the room in high dudgeon, Dickon felt the state of "unflinching" might be difficult to achieve, but he bit hard on his lip and blinked his good eye. *I will not cry*! he vowed. Before his father waded in with the tongue-lashing and worse that was sure to come, mindful that the best form of defence would be attack, Leo said, 'Father, we have important news for you, which you will want to hear and take to the earl.'

Immediately taken aback, and outraged at this impertinence, Tony frowned and looked even more severe, but there was something in Leo's face which made him stop before remonstrating. Turning to the soldier he said, 'I'll deal with this—return to your duties.'

Disappointed that he might never know what adventures had befallen these two boys, the soldier returned to the picket gate and his surly brother-in-arms whose duties he shared. For the Earl of Richmond, supplicant at Francis II's court as he was, felt honour-bound to offer his men to take on general duties around the chateau with their Breton companions.

Particularly studying Dickon's face, Tony became aware of the boys' need for material comfort before they plunged into any explanations. He went to the door and called a servant, 'Hé! Apportez du vin, du pain et de la viande—et vite!' Within minutes Leo and Dickon were gulping down some wine and water and gobbling unceremoniously at the food; while they ate Tony questioned them closely until their adventure was fully revealed.

Their father experienced a mixture of responses while the tale was told: firstly acute outrage at the way his boys had been treated by these two caitiffs; secondly, pride at his sons' initiative and fortitude; thirdly, anger that they had put themselves in harm's way. He was also very intrigued by Leo's description of the men and, of course, struck by the boys' report of the store of arms.

'Tell me again, what these men looked like.' Leo gave a full description and Dickon was anxious to mention the lanky man's strange mode of speech. *There's no disputing it*! Tony thought. *It's that bastard Percy and his minion, Costello. They're still here in France and up to no good.* He asked Dickon to tell him what he remembered of the store of arms and, at their description, nodded with satisfaction. *We must lay hands on these and at once*! he determined to himself.

He turned again to Leo, 'Now, we must consider this ransom threat. You say they were riding back to the village to watch and see who would set up a hue and cry for you both?'

'Yes, father; the thin red-headed man said they might get fifty crowns for us!'

'That much!' laughed Tony. 'I wouldn't give five for either of you!' Dickon looked alarmed. 'Father's only jesting, Dickon!' Leo said. He hoped it was true, but sometimes they couldn't tell when he was teasing. But Tony was, in a clumsy way, trying to calm the boys and make light of what must have been a frightening ordeal.

'The first thing we do is find you some clothes,' and he called again to the servant to seek out garments which would fit the boys adequately enough for them possibly to appear before Earl Richmond. 'When I have told him of these events, I'm sure he'll want to question you himself. But first I must speak to him about dealing with these rogues, Percy and Costello.'

'You speak as though you know them, father,' observed Leo.

'Oh yes! I know them all right, but from years ago before you were born. I can tell you this, my son, they'll both suffer severely for what they've put you through. It'll be up to me to catch them and then they'll regret laying hands on my brave boys!'

\*\*\*\*\*\*

'I can see some movement, sir!' Bob Costello shifted his body on the shingle where he lay concealed looking out towards the thin lights coming from hamlets around the Gulf of Morbihan and turned his face to his master. 'Lights and bodies. It looks as though you were right—they've sent out a hue and cry looking for the boys.'

'We need to show ourselves and locate the parents. Let's move out of here and ride to the village. Be casual, Bob, no unnecessary rough stuff!' Percy knew his companion well. *He may be loyal, but he can be too heavy-handed at times. Subtlety is not one of his talents.*

It was six o'clock and the sun was still above the horizon, but the light was fading. The two men trotted towards what they soon identified as a small group of men and women carrying torches. 'Ho there!' Jasper called to the nearest. 'What's to do?'

'Two boys are missing—not home when they should be. Have you seen any signs—one's eleven, dark haired, the other nine—both tall for their age.'

Sir Percy looked at Bob, 'Well, we did see two boys earlier, larking about on the beach.'

'How long ago?'

'About half an hour. We asked them what they were doing, and they said they were going home.'

'Which direction were they going?' asked a man who had evidently taken the role of organiser.

'East, towards Sarzeau. We didn't think anything of it— surely the parents know where they are?'

The searchers looked one to another, 'East's not the way home—what were they doing going east?'

'Sorry we can't be of more help. Perhaps we should speak to the father, just to make sure we have the right boys. It might be a comfort for him to know we've seen them recently.'

'Their mother's at home waiting in case they turn up. By all means—you'll find her at the farmhouse at the end of the village. The family is part of the English contingent quartered here.'

\*\*\*\*\*\*

'*Where are they? They must have come to some harm*!' Meg, with the anxiety of a frantic mother could only think the worst. 'They have been so obedient, coming home on time every day. Something has happened to them; I can feel it.' She paced the kitchen, looking at the meal she had prepared for them congealing on the plates. The villagers, especially the English had been very obliging, but soothing when she had first expressed concerns about her sons' whereabouts.

'Don't, worry, mistress, they'll come back when they're hungry—boys don't always appreciate the time.' But, as the light dimmed, she began to really worry, and soon her neighbours set aside their insouciance and it was agreed it was time to send out a search party. 'Perhaps you should send to the chateau and ask their father to return,' was the general opinion when the boys were overdue by two hours. This was precisely at the time Leo and Dickon were relating their adventures to Tony.

Meg was just pondering whether she should ride to the chateau herself when there was a knock on the door. 'Mary Mother of God! They've found them!' And she rushed to answer. To her acute disappointment two strangers were standing outside in the gloom.

'You must be from the village. Have you any news?'

'Indeed we are, and we do, mistress. May we come in?'

For a few seconds, Meg was confused, but then something in her brain leaped to the fore.

*That voice, I know it*! It was unmistakeable, but it couldn't be—not at this time. She peered at the pair and saw a short, squat, bald fellow standing with an exceptionally tall and thin man who took the initiative, noting immediately her confusion.

'I think you'll be interested in what we have to tell you. Perhaps it would be best if we speak inside. We have news of your two sons. We'll come in, shall we?'

\*\*\*\*\*\*

'These are your sons, Sir Anthony—Lionel and Richard?'

'Yes my lord. I apologise for their attire, but they are in borrowed garments for the reasons I have told you.'

'No, matter, Sir Anthony. But I suggest you ride back to the village to catch these scoundrels who are seeking your boys' ransom. It'll be dark in an hour and the hue and cry will be up. Take a posse of men and bring the two caitiffs back. They obviously have information that will be very useful to us. Leave your lads with me, for I would dearly like to hear the details of their adventure!'

For the next half-hour, he plied his questions. Leo and Dickon, who, gazing up into the face of this earl—a new experience—were disappointed to find he was a man like any other; not as tall as their father, with a nose quite long and straight, eyes deep brown, hair mousy-brown and chin pointed. Overall, they found him neither threatening nor proud, as they might have expected a senior nobleman to be and, should you ask them how old he was, they would have replied "old", in the manner of the very young for whom anyone approaching twenty is ancient. In fact, Henry of Richmond was young and agile at twenty-six, a well-trained soldier; son and grandson of sturdy Welshmen and, although an exile in a foreign land, well-liked by his generous host, even though he seemed to have taken over Francis's chateau and turned it into a fortress. But eleven years of being a guest in someone else's castle had taught him consideration and subtlety. He took pains to learn the language and, as we have seen, insisted his soldiers took their share of duties about the place. The locals, who had to make way for "les inconnus Anglais", gradually became accustomed to their ways and it took only a few years for them to be accepted.

Having examined closely the two ruined knives which they had used to hack at the bars, the Earl of Richmond looked quizzically at the boys. 'Tell me once again the story which inspired you to jump out of the tower window.' Dickon, not aware of what "inspired" meant, but making a guess, said, 'Uncle Pom told us how his friend Sir Tom and he jumped into a moat and escaped some soldiers. I thought that was a good way of getting out.'

'It most certainly was—and did your uncle and his friend escape in the end?'

'They did for a time but were caught later.'

'You know that is exactly what happened to a great friend of mine a few years ago.' The boys leaned forward in their chairs; they loved a story.

'My friend—an earl like me—was imprisoned in Hammes Castle, which is in Calais—you've heard of Calais?' They nodded. 'Unlike your story, when your uncle and his companion escaped the same night, my friend was imprisoned for three years and no hope of escape. Then, one day, he saw a chance. I don't know the exact details; perhaps the guards weren't paying proper attention; but he was able to get out of a window—just like you did—and climb down a little way before jumping into the moat and swimming for the other side. It seems this is a popular way of escaping from towers!'

Leo frowned. 'I wonder how far he had to jump, sir?'

'How far did you jump?'

'I'm not good at telling heights, sir—I thought it might be twenty feet.'

'Well, I'll wager you jumped further than my friend John de Vere, and, unlike you, he was captured again pretty quickly.'

'Where is he now, sir?' asked Dickon.

'Back in Hammes Castle. Now, I'll let you into a secret and it must never be divulged to anyone—on pain of being locked up in a castle without windows with rotten bars!'

The boys drew even nearer, wide-eyed, mouths agape. 'Your father's next mission is to try and rescue Lord John and bring him here to me. What do you think of that?' And Henry Richmond smiled as he looked at the intent expressions on the boys' faces. There was no harm in them knowing something which everyone in Chateau de Suscinio was already aware of, but he noted how seriously they seem to take his word about secrecy.

'We will never tell, sir, we swear it!'

'I believe you and you know, you're a credit to your father—'

'—And our mother!' Dickon burst in, ignoring Leo's frown of disapproval.

'And your mother, who I hope to meet very soon. In the meantime, I have things to do—prisoners to rescue, countries to save and many other noble deeds. You are to remain here until your father comes to collect you. I will ensure you have plenty to eat and drink while you enjoy this fire. Oh, and I've been told one of the castle bitches had a litter of pups last week—I'm sure we could arrange for you to see them. Would you like that?'

'Yes, sir. Thank you, sir!' And Leo stood up and gave an awkward bow—Dickon followed, so far forward his nose was only inches from the ground.

When Henry Richmond left the room, Dickon said, 'Leo, what do you think he meant about "saving countries"?'

'I don't know; but why did you have to bring mother into it? We might have heard more about what father's doing here if you hadn't interrupted.'

'Mother is as important as father, Leo. She just stays at home and doesn't have any excitement. I wanted the Lord Earl to know about her.'

Leo felt it would be disrespectful to argue the point, but sometimes he wished Dickon would keep his mouth shut and let him do the important talking.

\*\*\*\*\*\*

There was much important talking going on in the farmhouse in Kermoizin and, to Meg's ears, it was very unpleasant talk indeed and from two very unpleasant men.

'Are you telling me you've captured my boys and are holding them somewhere?'

'That is the truth of the matter, madam. Don't worry, they're in safe hands. Once you've paid us for them they'll be released unharmed.'

'Pay you! You are so low you will ransom two small boys!'

'Not so small—both fine sturdy specimens. I'm sure you want them back—or do they eat you out of house and home?'

Meg fell silent; how should she respond? 'Why should I believe you. You could have seen the hue and cry and come in here with such a story just to get money.'

'You're right, we could. But perhaps this will persuade you,' and he nodded to Costello who brought out the boys' bag from behind his back and threw it on the table. 'I think you'll find there's a quantity of food—and cakes—good cakes for we sampled some—as well as changes of clothes.'

Meg could see immediately it was the bag she had help Leo pack that morning; she also recognised the two pairs of hose.

'Now, it is evident from your face you recognise the bag and must believe what we say. We want fifty gold crowns by tomorrow mid-day. You'll meet Mister Costello here in the village church where you will give him the money. You will come alone—just you, not your husband—where is he, by the way? Out searching I suppose. When we have the money, my friend here will bring you to the boys and all will be well, you have my word; but only if you come alone. We have several men surrounding the village on look-out. Any sign of interference by any others and the boys will have their throats cut.'

'Your word!' scoffed Meg, trying to hide her fright and anguish. In her mind she fumed. *Where is Anthony! Has he heard? This squeaking caitiff!* She considered Percy's pock-marked face. *Older and uglier than ever! I hadn't reckoned on seeing you again*, she thought. But she gave no hint that she recognised him and evidently he had no remembrance of their encounter twelve years before in the forest of northern France.

'This is a business deal, madam. I'm sorry—I have no idea of your name. Your boys simply introduced themselves as Pierre and François—aliases I'm sure, but they did have remarkably good French—for English boys. Just for the record as I can't go on calling you "madam"; who are you?'

'Mistress Limpett. That's all you need to know. If any harm has come to my children, I will search for you and kill you—I do not speak idly sir!'

'I'd expect nothing else from a frantic mother, Mistress Limpett. I admire your spirit and I'm sure you have the resourcefulness to acquire the necessary cash. We will see you—'

At that moment, there was a sharp knock on the door and a voice called out, 'Madame, j'ai des nouvelles de vos garçons. Puis-je entrer?'

Percy and Costello exchanged looks. This was a trick. The villagers could have no news of where the boys were. 'Go to the door and tell them you'll come out to speak to them. If you want to stay safe, don't let them in. Bob, we'll leave by the back entrance and then merge in with the crowd before slipping away.'

'What about the horses?'

'We'll come back when things have died down. In all the disturbance, no one will notice two stray mounts. Now mistress, give us a minute to make our departure then open the door. Until tomorrow then. Now not a word; remember you're being watched!'

\*\*\*\*\*\*

Accompanied by four fully armed soldiers, Anthony rode at full gallop back to the village where he could already see lights and hear anxious voices calling. Among this crowd could be Jasper Percy and his henchman Costello.

As they arrived outside Kermoizin Tony shouted, 'I must speak to my wife and reassure her the boys are safe! We'll go to my house first and then set about seeking out these bastards. They won't be hard to find—a lanky pock-marked villain and a short ugly varlet. They go by the name of Jasper Percy and Robert Costello. We'll comb the village for them!'

Arriving at the farm house they immediately noticed the two horses tied up outside. 'Who's are these? Anyone recognise them?' for in this peninsula most horses were known, being valuable commodities. The soldiers shook their heads and Tony's suspicions were immediately aroused. 'I don't like the look of this, John,' and he nodded to the captain. 'Knock on the door and tell my wife you have news of the boys. Two of you cover the back. We'll stand waiting to see who's inside once my wife opens the door.'

The captain dismounted, tied up his horse to the fencepost alongside the two others and rapped on the door, giving the message in a loud clear voice. Tony heard no response from Meg, until the door opened slowly, and she stood looking out with the most abject expression of misery. Tony, by now dismounted, rushed through the door, followed by two soldiers, and immediately looked round the room to find there was no one. At the same time, there was the sound of fighting from the back yard, and Tony said, 'Follow me! I think we've caught the bastards!' And he plunged through the house to the back kitchen and out into a small yard where Meg kept her fowls, and the single pig, comfortably housed while waiting for its throat to be cut some time soon.

They almost tripped over four men brawling in the dust. Jasper Percy, with the advantage of his great height and gangling limbs, was using his long sword to fend off a soldier with short arms who was lunging ineffectively at him when not pinned up against the hedge. The second man-at-arms was having more success with Costello, who had always preferred skill with a knife in the guts to elegant swordplay. Sword drawn, Tony went straight for Percy and whistled—'Hey, ginger! Try me, you fucking poxy bastard!' And went for him with raised blade which he brought down flat on Jasper's wrist. Caught unawares, Percy flailed for a few seconds, but gathered his wits and prepared to parry Tony's strikes. They fought and for a while it was evenly balanced. But Tony was more concerned with capturing the man than besting him in swordplay and called for assistance to bring Percy down. Soon he was lying full length on the ground with a soldier's knee in his back. Tony looked down at him, 'They'll be plenty of time for me to take my revenge and at my leisure,' he growled.

Percy looked up and since it was now dark, with only the illumination from a few torches, he couldn't recognise Tony—but it had been twelve years. Tony continued, 'I have several scores to settle with you, but you have no idea what I have planned for someone who would dare lay hands on my sons.' He turned to Bob Costello, who was standing between two soldiers, arms pinioned. 'As for you, I understand you hit my boy—gave him a black eye and probably a scar for life. Here's a scar for you,' and he took his knife and ran it slowly and deeply down Costello's cheek. There was a screech and the blood poured down the side of the man's neck and his jerkin was soon darkly stained and soaking wet. 'Put a pad on it—we don't want him to bleed to death before we hang him!' said Tony cheerfully. 'Take them back to Earl Richmond and tell him I'll be returning to the chateau behind them—and bringing my wife with me!'

******

'You know your boys were in more danger than they realised?' The Earl of Richmond looked thoughtfully at Tony Tanner. 'They jumped into a tidal bay where the currents are exceptionally strong and were lucky not to have been drawn into Quiberon—or drowned beforehand. Had it been rough weather and a faster tide, I don't think they would have stood a chance!'

'Please, my lord, don't let my wife hear you say it! It was difficult enough for her to get over the ransom business. For her to know our boys might have been swept into the Atlantic would be too much to bear.'

'Well, what's certain is that young Leo probably saved his brother's life while they were swimming across. I doubt Dickon could have achieved it alone. Your eldest son has much fortitude and courage. You should be very proud—of them both, for the younger one has spirit and loyalty—speaking up for his mother in that way.'

The two men were walking the walls of Chateau de Suscinio; it was the best place for private conversations and laying plots and stratagems. They had discussed the impeding journey to Calais before the earl turned the conversation to Tony's two boys. 'I'm full of admiration for them. If I have lads, I would like them to be the same.'

'Your marriage to the Lady Elizabeth will surely be fruitful, my lord!'

'If it happens. I haven't heard anything recently about matters in England. Tell me, your wife has seen the Lady Elizabeth, and has the advantage of me, for I haven't ever met her—not even a portrait.'

'Lady Tanner only saw her in the chamber with her mother; she didn't speak to her, my lord.'

'But still, she could give me an idea of her looks—her presence?'

'I'm sure she would be delighted to try.'

'Then I'll invite her to dine with us tomorrow. Turning to other matters—what progress have we made with Percy and Costello?'

'Nothing to speak of, my lord, but a turn of the screw may produce something—the name of a contact for the arms perhaps.'

'I'll speak to the officer of the watch and tell him to get to work on them. In the meantime, we should set about retrieving the arms from the tower. According to the boys, there will be no difficulty breaking in—the varlets used cheap locks. I must say, your sons have been a mine of information; if it hadn't been for them we would never have learned of this store of arms and armour. It must be worth a few hundred crowns and if we can discover the source, we may solve some of our supply problems.'

'Let's hope so, my lord. We also need men for the invasion—they'll need paying.'

'It always comes back to money, Sir Anthony. Duke Francis has been very generous allowing us to stay here all these years, but there are those in his court who are hostile to us and politics will change now that Louis XI is dead. Who knows how his son Charles VIII will view us. Will he support Richard, get behind my claim, or stay neutral? It's all unknown. The sooner we get on with the invasion, the happier I'll be. Let's hope word comes from England soon. In the meantime, see if you can use your skills to extricate John de Vere from Hammes Castle—but tell him on no account is he to jump into the moat again!'

\*\*\*\*\*\*

Of course, there had been rapturous scenes of joy when Meg Tanner was reunited with her sons. No remonstrations about "putting themselves in harm's way"—that could wait until later. She was just relieved they were unscathed, apart from Dickon's black eye and scratched cheek.

'Mother, we are all right!' insisted Richard, as she stroked his arm and scrutinised his face again. 'We have been congratulated by Earl Richmond for our forti—forti—'

'—Fortitude is the word you're seeking Dickon,' laughed Tony, 'and he's quite right. You have both done well, although you shouldn't have left home without telling your mother exactly where you were going. But I think we can forgive you for that—as long as it doesn't happen again.'

'We promise always to tell you both where we are going, don't we Leo?'

There was a marginal hesitation from his brother, but graciously he nodded and said, 'Indeed we will, father.'

'Good! Now you are to change your clothes and smarten yourselves up. We dine with the earl at mid-day.'

The food was good and plentiful, and the boys were very gratified to be the centre of attention once again. There was no doubting Tony's pride in them, although he reminded himself that the sin of pride always came before a fall. 'I'll prick their bubble slightly at the right time. Can't have them getting above themselves!' he told his wife later.

After dinner, they were led into a small anteroom where wine and small beer was served. The earl rang a little brass bell; a servant appeared, and he whispered in the man's ear. A minute later he reappeared with a tray on which was a cloth-covered bundle.

'Lionel and Richard Tanner, in recognition of the service you have performed for my cause, the danger you placed yourselves in and the fortitude and quick-thinking with which you acted, I present you with these,' and he unwrapped the cloth and brought out two fine daggers, with gold leaf at the metal hilts and beautifully tempered blades which glinted in the firelight. 'These are not for hacking at iron bars, but to be looked after and kept sharp. I think you have shown you are now men enough to use them properly.'

The boys were overcome, and even Leo blushed and appeared awkward, desperately looking at his father as though asking how he should respond. Tony stepped in, 'Thank you, my lord.'

'Yes, thank you my lord,' said Leo, handling his knife with the utmost care.

Dickon was more forthcoming, 'Thank you very much, sir. Our knives are useless; we will certainly take care of these. May we keep them father, or will you look after them?'

The earl smiled, 'A knife is to be carried, young man. You must learn to take care of it yourself. One day it may save your life, just as these did,' and he took up one of the two battered daggers which the servant had also brought in. 'But that is not all I have for you,' and he rang his bell again. The servant reappeared, this time carrying very familiar objects. 'Here are your boots which my men found where you left them! I'm sure your mother will be relieved to have them back,' and he smiled at Meg. 'Footwear is as important as knives; a man cannot get far without them; that's why I make sure my soldiers have stout boots. Although of course, under the circumstances, your boys were right to discard them.'

'Sir, we walked five miles without them,' said Dickon.

'Indeed you did and look at the state your feet were in when you arrived here!'

Tony began to fidget, thinking Dickon had just about pushed his luck with his observations. 'My lord, I think it's time the lads went about their lessons.'

'Ah, yes, lessons. I understand you are teaching the boys yourself, Lady Tanner.'

She nodded, 'I am, my lord.'

'And do they make progress?'

'When I can get them to concentrate—although the pull of the outdoors is stronger than the enticement of the written word.'

'It was ever thus with energetic lads. I was none too keen on being tutored, although I have realised its great value since. But, with that in mind, I have had thoughts about your accommodation while Sir Anthony is away in Calais. I would like you and the boys to move into the chateau. I have already spoken to the duke,' and he turned to Leo and Dickon, 'and have told him about your adventures. He is not so well presently and says it would be entertaining for him to hear them from you personally. He is delighted to be able to offer accommodation here. While you are away, Sir Anthony, we can keep these boys out of mischief. Time with one of my captains in the tilting yard and the pell—as well as some lessons with one of the clerics here. You will at least know where the lads are, Lady Tanner!' And, if this was a subtle criticism of her supervision, she did not take it as that intent.

'My lord, I thank you with all my heart. This will be a haven for us while Sir Anthony is absent. I couldn't be more pleased.'

'We will talk also of your visits to Westminster Abbey and your contact with the queen and her daughter. As for this being a "haven", let's hope so, Lady Tanner, let's hope so!'

# Chapter 10

London 1484 and Monty prepares the manuscript;
Gisella has an idea; Jack expands on it;
Caxton organises it.

There was a dismal atmosphere about the capital city in the first weeks of the year '84 and it was not connected to the persistent foul miasma which arose from its myriad middens and the rank River Thames. These were constants in the lives of the citizens to which they were inured over generations. There was also the permanent pall of smoke from thousands of winter fires, fuelled by anything combustible and which lingered over roofs and then infiltrated the lower reaches of the streets, alleyways and courts; finally permeating nostrils, clothing and skin.

No, the intangible ambience came directly from the appalling events of the previous year, and the citizens' belief that two young boys, princes of the royal blood, had been incarcerated in the Tower of London and subsequently murdered. There was no doubt in most minds who the culprit was.

'Have you seen this latest rhyme? It was first on the doors of St Paul's—now it's stuck up everywhere?' Jack Worms came into the print shop where Monty was sitting at his table, composing-stick in hand and storage bins full of newly-cast letters from which he was making his selection.

'No, but I suppose you're going to tell me,' Monty frowned at the interruption. He was finding preparation of Caxton's translation of Geoffrey de la Tour Landry's *Knight in the Tower* particularly vexing and time-consuming, having lost his normal rhythm of working. *It's all very well insisting I have it ready by May; unless he improves his handwriting, it'll be next Christmas before it appears. It gets more spider-like by the day*, he thought as he painstakingly searched for the character he required.

'Listen: "The Cat, the Rat, and Lovell our Dog, Rule all England under the Hog." What do you think of that?'

'I don't think anything of it, Jack. We all know Catesby, Ratcliff and Lovell are universally hated, but, as they are such favourites of the king, no one dares touch them. As usual, their enemies take to pinning up doggerel to make the point.' He sighed, 'It's about all that can be done these days—recourse to terrible poetry! They tried rebellion and look what happened—bodies swinging from gibbets.'

'Things are not getting any better on the streets. There was that business of the Earl of Richmond and his failed attempt at an invasion last November. Some people were disappointed that it came to nothing. There's also unrest because it's said Buckingham's head is still on a pike on Salisbury's walls after two months and the king won't allow it to be joined with the rest of the body for burial. That's an act of real spite!'

'I'm sure you're right, but there's nothing I can do about it. Worry about those things you have control over—the rest is irrelevant, Jack.'

'You do sound sour this morning, my friend.'

'I've been having a succession of difficult interviews with our mutual employer, Master Caxton.'

'Don't tell me—it's about *Le Morte* I'll wager.'

'He's finally read it cover to cover, says he wants to print it, but that it needs "great emendation".'

'Oh dear! We always knew there would be risk he would meddle—he does own it after all and is entitled to do what he wants with it.'

'But I always thought he would be true to the original; he promised I would be the chief amender. All right, if he wants to change the odd word here and there, I'd have no objection; I don't even mind that he wants to write a preface of some kind, as he suggests. But he's working on cutting by half the section on Arthur versus Emperor Lucius, which I know Sir Tom was very proud of and enjoyed writing; also he's shortened the story of Sir Tristram—he suggests it can be reduced to a quarter of the length.'

'Well, Monty, as I remember you did complain that the section was "somewhat tedious in parts!"—I think that's what you said. It was certainly long—well over two hundred pages.'

'I'm surprised you can remember that, Jack!'

'Well, as a bookbinder, I take an especial interest in the size of a book—I leave clever men like you to sort out the quality! But I take it that most of the rest of Malory's work is included—that it won't be a completely new book?'

'By the time I left him, I wasn't sure. I agreed with him that the form the final book takes could be tidied up. But he wants to set it up in books and chapters and make a single work out of it, which counteracts Sir Tom's attempt to produce a series of self-contained stories. I'll give you an example—Sir Tom's tale of Sir Lancelot is a much better read than the French version because he makes it a complete single story instead of breaking it up as the French author had it. I can tell you, it must have been a very difficult job for Sir Tom to translate from the French sources, which were very elaborate. It was no fun editing it in English either; we—'

But before Monty embarked on a full explanation of the difficulties he had experienced while closeted for two years in a Newgate cell with his sometime-ungracious employer— which Jack was fully aware of, having shared many of those experiences—the bookbinder intervened and said, 'Well, I appreciate it's going to be difficult, but I do have some news that will cheer you up. I received a letter—addressed to us all—from Meg, who I believe is still in France somewhere.'

'Believe she's there? Was there no address?'

'No, and she was very vague about what Six-toed Tony is doing.'

'That'll be because he's spying somewhere for someone. Do you think it's the new king of France?'

'Who knows? Tony could be back in England working for King Richard!'

'He certainly won't be doing that! I take it Meg and the boys are well?'

'She says they are growing by the minute and have "frightened her witless with their escapades", and I quote. Whatever they've been up to, they still sound the spirited pair we know and love.'

'My Tom misses them, I know that!'

'I'll leave the letter with you and you can pass it on to Pom when you've read it. It doesn't sound as though they'll be returning to London any time soon. I can't say I blame them. If I had the choice, I'd leave the city for a while. It's a dangerous place—people muttering together; northern soldiers swaggering on the streets. This scrap of verse tells us all we need to know about how people feel about King Richard and his—'

'—Henchmen?'

'You can say that—I think I'll resist it, Monty. You never know who's listening!'

\*\*\*\*\*\*

'Meister De Worde, sit down!' William Caxton waved vaguely towards a seat on the other side of his desk. His one-time apprentice, now master printer, had retained his youthful look on an unremarkable face: pug-nosed and with a determined chin. The two men's relationship had remained business-like; they worked together but did not play together, hence the formal greeting. Caxton had strict views about keeping a distance between himself and his employees. Annually, immediately after Epiphany, he would take each of his senior men to one side and appraise their work and discuss future projects. Wynkyn de Worde, or "Inkin' Wynkyn" as he was more familiarly known on the shopfloor, had been longest in Caxton's employment—he was about to start his twelfth year with the master printer. Originally recruited in Cologne, he left the Rhineland, accompanying Caxton to Bruges and then across to Westminster in the year '76. Although young when Caxton recruited him, Wynkyn had good previous experience in the home of printing, where Meister Guttenberg had originated his new techniques.

Caxton was lucky to find the young man and he had not disappointed.

'Ten works last year—many of them major, like the second, corrected edition of *The Canterbury Tales* and my own repeated *Game of Chess*—'

'Both with woodcuts, sir.'

'Yes, and they much enhance them I think. Looking ahead, we have several editions almost ready and patronised by some of our noblemen—thank God for them!' And Caxton crossed himself.

'On that point, sir, this change of kingship in your country—will it affect us? As explained you have to me on many occasions, we can produce the books only if supported we are by the men with money and influence. Men like Lord Rivers and Lord Daub—Dab—'

'Daubeney. Quite right! Lord Rivers is especially a great loss to us. I try to avoid any talk or involvement with politics, especially now when there is much unrest among the populace. You must have noticed, Meister Worde, Englishmen can be easily roused when they scent any kind of injustice. It's safer to concentrate on our own affairs. We have been fortunate that the art of printing has been slow to catch-on here among English stationers and booksellers. When we arrived seven years ago, I imagined many in Paternoster Row would have rushed to set up on their own account. But no, the field has been left to us.'

'Apart from Masters Lettou and Machlinia—the only other printers in London I think.'

'But they have been but a short time in the field and, as you know, they only work with religious and scholastic manuscripts; they're no competition to us. The same can be said for the two new printing houses in Oxford which rely on the masters and clerics for work. Besides, we had a head start; patronage from her grace the Duchess of Burgundy was crucial and so was her letter of introduction to Lord Rivers.'

'A cruel blow for the head of the man to be lost it is, Master Caxton!'

'However you choose to phrase it, I take it you're being ironic, Meister Worde!' It was a source of irritation to Master Caxton that his master printer occasionally lapsed into inappropriate Germanic syntax even after nearly twelve years in his service.

'Ironic, sir?'

'Never mind—if you haven't yet learned the subtlety of our spoken language, you probably never will. But I can't fault your vernacular productions; I am most pleased with the quality of the printing which you and Master Worms have achieved. And talking of Lord Rivers, this coming year I will be translating Alayn Charetier's *Curial*—a French book of manners written for the author's brother's first appearance at the French court. It's of no great length and will be a pleasure to work on. Sadly it was one of his lordship's last requests to me—for which he paid me in advance I might add. Then there's *Aesop*—'

'Your translation and, again, with woodcut illustrations, sir?'

'Indeed, I've also enjoyed preparing that for your presses, Meister Worde; those old moral tales still ring true with me. In addition we have another important work to bring out which I've almost finished translating from the French: Geoffrey de Charny's *Order of Chivalry*, a large and complex work which is taking much of my time.'

'Is it as large as *Le Morte D'Arthur*, sir?'

'Ah, *Le Morte D'Arthur*! I wondered when that would be mentioned. Have Mister Pickle or Master Worms been bending your ear about it?'

'Bending my ear?'

'Forever talking about it, Meister De Worde; bringing it up in conversation.'

'Quite often mentioning they do.'

'Obsessed! The pair of them are continually harping on it. "When are we to start work on it? Who is to supervise the amendments?" It's all very well, but we must find a patron for it first. They know I can't embark on such a large work without cash for materials and labour. I agree with them—it's a fine piece of work, but it needs considerable reduction; there is much repetition in it.'

'Mister Pickle once told me he thought Sir Thomas sometimes for no good literary reason embellished.'

'From what I've heard of the man, he was a demon to work for and would never take criticism. But I'll say this for Mister Pickle, he has been stalwart in his loyalty to his old master. Twelve years of involvement with the manuscript is remarkable, although not unknown; look at my *Troy*, which I worked on for years. But, as far as Malory's work is concerned, I will admit to almost shedding a tear when Mister Pickle finally retrieved it from Kent and brought it to me. However, it took me some months to read it cover to cover and I could see immediately where the emendations should be made. Convincing Mister Pickle of them has been very difficult.'

'Does he agree now, sir?'

'I think so. Never let it be said I cannot compromise—'

*An English word neither of them with familiarity is*! thought Inkin' Wynkyn, but of course did not say so, however awkwardly he might have done it. Instead he smiled and looked back expectantly at Caxton. 'Compromise, sir?'

'I've told him we will keep the majority of Sir Thomas Malory's original text, just sharpen it up when it appears too overblown. I have insisted though that I write a preface, but that can wait until the presses have done their work.'

'How many pages will there be?'

'Seven to eight hundred.'

'Costly in paper that will be, sir. Why are there no paper-makers in England?'

'A good question, but I have no idea what the answer is Meister De Worde. I'm sure one day someone will be enterprising enough to journey to the Low Countries to see how it's done, just as I did to discover printing. Until that happens we must continue to import the stuff at great expense. That is why I must be sure of a patron or patrons for *Le Morte*. I can't guarantee printing without one.'

'Disappointed Mister Pickle will be, sir!'

'Disappointed he will be, I'm afraid Meister Worde. But we run a business and must make money, otherwise there is no bread for our children. Talking of children, how are yours?' And the conversation dwindled briefly to domestic matters, before Caxton cut it short and sent his master printer back to his presses.

******

'He'll print this year or next—if we can find the money; but it's impossible!' Monty shook his head and Gisella

291

stroked his hand. 'Have you any idea how much is needed, Monty?'

'There's no precise way of costing it. Eight hundred sheets of good quality paper, plus ink, binding, just for one copy—and then there's the labour costs.'

'But you could take less in wages—and perhaps Jack would also?'

'I still have to put food on the table, Gisella. I suppose if I agreed to work in my own time, Caxton wouldn't mind.'

'Since it's his property, he'll be the one to take any profits. I understand how desperate you are for *Le Morte* to be printed, but before you start thinking of working for nothing, discuss with him the possibility of a share. He could look on your contribution of labour as a kind of patronage—not hard cash, but expertise and time.'

'You're right, Gisella. Noble patrons don't always pay us cash. The Earl of Arundel promised Caxton an annual fee of a buck in summer and a doe in winter, and that he would take "a reasonable quantity" of the books if Caxton persevered with *The Golden Legend*. You remember me telling you how the task of translating such a huge work made Master Caxton half-desperate to finish it. He was certainly difficult to work with at the time!'

'Thinking about it, I have another suggestion.'

'Yes?'

'Pom.'

'What about him?'

'You know he's now one of the richest merchants in the city. Last year his income was in the region of twenty pounds'

'Yes, he told us; it was one of the best year's trading he's had, despite the troubled times.'

'People still need wine—and furs, Monty. Lands and estates may pass from one nobleman to another, but their value in terms of rents remains the same. He says there's been an especial interest in the new pottery—porc—porcelain he calls it. "I'm making a killing with it, Gisella!" he told me last time I was in one of his shops.'

'I'm beginning to see where you're going with this. You're suggesting he'd patronise *Le Morte*?'

'Think about it. He's a bachelor, no family heirs to leave it all to. He already has an historical stake in *Le Morte*; it's been a part of his life longer than your connection with it— nearly thirty years according to him. He and Jack have supported you in retrieving the manuscript so that it can be published, and I'm sure he'll be with you when you fulfil Sir Tom's wish and take it to the monks in Winchester.'

'He's certainly seen the project through some difficult times. Think of all those years he was locked up with Sir Tom in various London jails! You're right! I think it might be an idea to at least talk to him.'

'There's another thing which occurred to me. As a well-respected and nobly-patronised merchant, he has numerous contacts with important people—people in and around the court and people with money.'

'Not all of them want to spend it on books, Gisella. Most would rather purchase a new horse, hawk or hound! The nobility is not generally known for its literary tastes!'

'I'm not so sure, Monty. The number of editions Caxton's Westminster Press produces increases by the year. What was it last year, ten or more? Most of them were projects brought to him by the great and the wealthy—ordinary people just can't afford it. Books are becoming a symbol of—er—'

'—Power?—Intelligence? No, I don't necessarily agree with you. It's more likely a fashion which is followed because it's agreeable to have it known one owns a library. Admittedly, it's led by people who do have a love of literature—Rivers and Arundel, and even the old king, Edward IV.'

'But he didn't have a reputation as a bibliophile; he was more a hunter than a reader!'

'That is true, but simply including his name in the front of a book as an acknowledgement of his support makes it a desirable object. But that's my objection—that these are kings and noblemen, not merchants. They may have the money, but it's the regal or noble name that counts, surely?'

'I'm not so sure Master Caxton will see it that way. I remember you telling me how surprised you were when a mercer brought him Chaucer's *Boethius* to be printed.'

'Master William Pratt—I remember him, although it was five years ago. I thought at the time, it just shows one shouldn't judge one's fellow man by his occupation! Two others have brought in works to be printed—both merchants. Hugh Bryce is one, although he is an alderman.'

'So, it's not beyond the realms of possibility that Master Caxton would welcome patronage from a lesser mortal—one who earns his money rather than inherits or grabs it!'

'Not when you put it liked that!' laughed Monty. 'Perhaps we should invite Pom and Jack for supper sometime soon and get some plan together.'

'Perhaps we should, husband!' And Gisella smiled at him, relieved she had moderated his concerns, and given him new avenues to follow. *Le Morte* was a weight on them both, and not one she wanted to bear forever.

******

Gisella was correct. Mister John Appleby was now a man of substance; a well-respected merchant with several shops, significant numbers of employees to run them, and many satisfied customers, among whom were a sprinkling of nobility and plenty of those from the class of "gentlemen" or "the middling sort" with money in cashboxes under their beds. He prided himself on the quality of his wines; his organised "tastings" had become a feature of the London trade, when he encouraged the fraternity of wine merchants to mix with their customers, trying the products of fresh vines and new vintages. His affability was such that these occasions became as much social gatherings as business opportunities and were anticipated eagerly by everyone who appreciated "a good wine". Of course, there was much nonsense talked about "scent", "ambience" and "bouquet", but most of the merchants were experts in their trade and were trusted in their judgements by their customers. However, Pom was probably the best of them all, having regularly imbibed great quantities of Burgundy since a boy. Unfortunately his face and body were beginning to show the effects of this long-term indulgence and whereas he would once delight in training Monty and Anthony's boys in swordplay and other manly skills, those days were diminishing as his hips, knees and elbows creaked in protest after every bout.

'I think I must hand you over to another captain, Tom,' he panted, after a session of defence training with young Thomas Pickle. 'I'm too old!'

'He's getting too good for me, as one approaching his seventieth year!' reported Pom as he sat at Gisella and

Monty's table, anticipating the usual good supper, for she was an excellent cook. 'I'll seek out someone who will take him on; he has all the makings of a fine soldier.'

Monty looked dismayed, as did his wife. A military career was not what they had in mind for their son, now in his twelfth year, although the lad seemed to relish the idea. "Something in the book world, after a university education", was the joint opinion of his parents. It was, after all, the coming thing— printing and book production. There was surely secure employment in it. But that was for another day, tonight they were to discuss the proposal that Mister Appleby become patron, or one of them, of *Le Morte D'Arthur*.

Knowing Pom's heathy appetite for food as well as wine, Gisella had done her best to ease the evening by producing some of his favourite dishes: they started with mushroom pasties, followed by poached fowl and bacon served with her speciality: a pudding of herb mixture, finely chopped neck, liver and heart from the bird, mixed with breadcrumbs and stuffed into the skin of the neck, and then boiled with the fowl and bacon in cider.

'What will you be giving them for a dessert, Gisella?' asked Monty, hopeful it would be one of his own favourites.

'Cream custard tart, although I'll have to seek out some saffron—just a few small strands, nothing too expensive,' she said reassuringly, for this was one of the costliest of ingredients and she rarely indulged in its use.

'This is all delicious, Gisella!' said Pom approvingly.

'Good wine too—as usual!' laughed Jack, who as a bachelor always enjoyed the prospect of "home cooking". His housekeeper was adequate in the kitchen, but hardly inventive. Shrewd as ever, he knew when Monty was on edge and wanted to get something off his chest. He finished his last mouthful of cream custard, laid down his spoon and sat back in his chair. 'Now Monty, what's on your mind? I can tell you've been boiling up to something all day, and it wasn't the thought of our estimable company round your table—which we do more times than we should; all down to your great hospitality, Gisella,' and he lifted his glass to their hostess.

'You know me too well, Jack,' laughed Monty.

'I don't even have to guess what this is about—it's *Le Morte*, isn't it?' growled Pom, reaching forward and re-filling his glass.

'Isn't it always?' agreed Monty and then proceeded to lay out what was in his mind. When he finished, he looked hopefully at his two greatest friends. 'I—we—Gisella and I—see this as the only way by which Sir Tom's work will get out into the world. This whole printing business coming alive at this time seems like fate's wheel has turned in our favour; or perhaps it's providence. Whatever it is, the time is right to settle the business. Once the manuscript has been composed to print, we can fulfil our pledges, take the original to Winchester and lay it all to rest.'

'Then get on with our lives,' said Gisella with more meaning in her heart than she expressed in her words.

'You're suggesting Pom dips into his vast wealth and supports the publication of *Le Morte*?'

'Well, yes, Jack. But as I said, he may know of others who would be prepared to do the same.' He turned to Pom, 'You have contacts with some of the nobility, and numerous wealthy gentlemen customers. As we know, Caxton's taken work, and money, from merchants in the city and been happy to do so. There doesn't always have to be a great name in the front of a book. If the work is worthy of his time and effort, and he thinks it will sell, he's not too fussy about its patrons.'

Pom was silent for a few moments and stared into his glass as though seeking inspiration. He looked up, 'Everything you say rings true. Over and above the practical matter of finance, I still feel very responsible for the safe deliverance of Sir Tom's work. Thirty years was a long time for me to be involved with his obsession. Now I have it within my means to promote it, I can do nothing else. Of course I'll help! I'm only surprised you hadn't asked me before, Monty.'

'Once we'd retrieved the manuscript, Caxton had to read it and consider whether he would publish it anyway. This is really good news, Pom!' And he stood up, went around the table and grasped his friend's hand.

'This notion of others being involved—I believe it's a good one!' said Jack. 'It will do the book no harm to have many subscribers. As Monty said, you have many contacts in the city and Westminster. Despite the upheavals in the country, as I understand it many of King Edward's ministers and officials have been retained by his brother in their court roles.'

'That's right,' said Pom. 'King Richard seems to prefer experience rather than abject loyalty. I think almost half the officials who served under Edward are still in place and I know many of them.'

Monty nodded, 'Could you make a list of those likely to be interested? Then we can take it to Caxton and see what he thinks.'

'It seems to me that if it means him making money, and promoting the Westminster Press, then he'll be delighted,' said Jack. 'Now, having settled matters, is there any chance of more of that custard tart, Gisella?'

\*\*\*\*\*\*

'So, this list—' and Caxton pulled it towards him. The Newgate Three sat opposite, looking expectantly at the master printer. Also with them was Meister Wynkyn de Worde, who Caxton had insisted was present as an "objective voice". 'He's not so bound up in the work as yourself, Mister Pickle, and will give us a fair idea of the cost and effort it will take to bring the manuscript to print.'

Privately, Monty and Jack knew this to be spurious, since Caxton had himself brought to print several weighty tomes and knew precisely the cost of their production. *Inkin's here to make objection to any fanciful ideas we have of having the book illustrated, or produced in too luxurious a form, which we have never contemplated*, thought Jack shrewdly.

'These gentlemen-customers of yours, Mister Appleby, have you approached them regarding their support?'

'I felt you should look over their suitability first, sir. Some of them are well-respected aldermen, but not entirely in the class of gentlemen, although they are wealthy merchants like myself.'

'Where is the nobility in the list? I don't see a single duke or earl?'

'Whilst I supply several of the most noble in London, my contacts are with their stewards and treasurers, sir. But don't forget, *Le Morte* was recommended by one of the greatest ladies—her grace the Duchess of Burgundy, and then his lordship Earl Rivers.'

'Hmm, may I remind you that her grace is domiciled in the Duchy and Lord Rivers is buried somewhere in the north!'

'There's nothing to stop his name being used posthumously, sir.'

'The Woodville name may be a bar to others becoming involved, given current events. Let's see, who else is on the list, apart from the ironmonger, draper and mercer—?'

'—As I said, all well-respected city officers,' replied Pom, beginning to sense disapprobation of the list which had taken him some time to compile. It was true, he didn't have direct access to the great magnate names in London and was certainly not on intimate terms with many of the senior officials. But he ran his finger down the list and with a slight note of triumph said, 'Here are two officials who are very close to the king: Sir John Kendall and Sir John Wood.'

'Those names are known to me. One is treasurer to the exchequer and the other is the king's secretary. How do you come to know them?'

'They have been kind enough to patronise my businesses with orders for wine and, on occasion, have been present at my wine tastings; I found them affable and approachable.'

'But are they interested in books and printing, Mister Appleby? They may enjoy your wine, but will they patronise our printing press? I think we need more great names and some assurances that they are prepared to support our enterprise financially.'

Monty intervened here, as he could see the situation slipping away. 'Master Caxton, it's a well-known fact that noblemen may have great names, lineages and historical provenances, but they are generally short of cash. Merchants, like Mister Appleby here, may not have the background, but they do possess the money. It's been the way of the world for centuries. The mayor and aldermen of the city of London are essential to the running of the place. If you cast your mind back to last year, before Richard of Gloucester became king, he found it necessary to consult with and gain the approval of the city officials before he could claim the crown. He may have asked the peers first, but he could not proceed without the support of these humble merchants, who, as is well known, have always provided money which keeps the monarch in funds—besides our taxes of course,' he added hastily before one of the others reminded him.

Caxton was silent for a while; looked the list up and down again, and then pushed it back to Pom. 'Given that, according to your judgement, these are fit and proper men to back our project, how did you wish to engage with them?'

Jack said, 'We've thought of that, sir and would propose inviting them to one of our demonstrations of the presses—run off a few pages of *Le Morte* for them to peruse at their leisure. We can explain the process, how intricate the composing work is, and then show them some of the finished works in our collection. As we know from experience, many of them won't have seen a printed book before.'

Caxton was silent again, then, looking across at Inkin' asked, 'What do you think, Meister de Worde?'

'Any opportunity to promote the Westminster Press must a good proposition be, sir. I should also say very successful with our other large folio works we have been. There have been customers for them and money not lost. I have read *Le Morte D'Arthur* and its potential I can see. It's an exciting book, fast-paced and highly descriptive and I think to ladies as well and gentlemen it will appeal.'

Monty was pleased at that comment, even if it was in mangled English, for he had done his best to encourage Sir Tom to imagine there was an audience among females for his work. 'Perhaps we should ask some ladies to come along,' he suggested. But the silence which followed indicated the idea of the ironmonger's wife rubbing shoulders with a very senior court official was perhaps not advisable.

Pom intervened swiftly, 'We could promote it as a gathering of like-minded men who are anxious to promote the advance of learning and literature in this new format. There are people now who like to consider themselves as free-thinking pathfinders. We could make it as much of a social gathering as a business one. I will be willing to supply some wine.'

'I'm not sure I would want people supping liquor in my printing shop, Mister Appleby. I foresee all kinds of disasters arising. But that aside, I'm minded to agree; we could promote ourselves in this way. Having paid a goodly sum for the work, there's no doubt we can't leave it mouldering on the shelf any longer. Discuss with Meister de Worde when will be a convenient date for this gathering to take place. But no Burgundy, however fine, Mister Appleby!'

\*\*\*\*\*\*

'That was highly successful! I take full credit for the idea,' and Pom looked round triumphantly at his two great friends, and their companion Inkin' Wynkyn. They were sitting in a Westminster tavern to which they had strolled immediately after the demonstration. 'I still say Master Caxton made a mistake not agreeing to serve wine. I'm sure it would have loosened the pockets of some of the new patrons!'

'Never mind whose idea it was, it would seem *Le Morte* has attracted a good number of gentlemen to support it. A very good job with the pages you did, Monty, and Jack—the looks of amazement on their faces when the page peeled from the press they saw and hung up to dry,' and Wynkyn de Worde looked approvingly at his workmates and friends.

This was by no means the first demonstration in Master Caxton's printing shop. As soon as he had established himself in Westminster he recognised that, for the business to progress, those uninitiated into the mysteries of the workings of this innovative system for the expansion of literature would have to have them explained, even though it would mean exposing the knowledge to possible competitors. The risks of the latter were reduced because setting up such a business from nothing required a substantial investment, as well as men of skill, and, until it could be shown that it was a viable and profitable business, the stationers and bookbinders of Paternoster Row, being a cautious breed, sat back and waited to see how long it would be before Master Caxton failed.

Since his arrival in the year '76 he had become a competitor in the London book trade, selling his own books, as well as the manuscript works of other writers. His customers, as Jack knew, having most to do with them, ranged in social class from merchant to marquis, although the latter were rare. Despite the doubt of the fraternity of booksellers, his business was thriving and interest certainly growing in the new process. One of Caxton's earliest visitors had been the late King Edward, who had been pressed by his wife to make the short step from Westminster Palace to the Westminster

Almonry where the printer had set up his works. Not only did the king and queen visit, but they took their numerous royal children, who initially ran rather wild about the shop, but then, frowned on and growled at by their father, became suitably awed by the smells and clatter from the strange devices and sat on the floor as quiet and still as dead mice while the demonstration was in progress.

This early attempt at the engagement of the public alerted Caxton to the need for some formality in the process. It would not do for the visiting crowd to act like a mob and cluster round the presses at random, risking their structure; it would be bad for business, as well as a calamity if one fell on top of them; just the kind of negative incident which would be remembered and do nothing to enhance sales. Therefore he insisted everyone was positioned in rows, as at a lecture, and watched much of the demonstration while seated; he borrowed chairs from all and sundry for the purpose. There was a strict procedure for the demonstration. After a short introductory speech by the Master Printer, Monty would pass round a small quantity of the metal letters and characters, then he would move on to explain the composing process. Wynkyn and Jack would operate the press while giving commentaries of its workings. There was always a gratifying sound of wonder when at last the finished page was peeled away and held up to view. Examples of these pages were only presented to those who had commissioned pieces of work or were willing to patronise Caxton's own projects; these sheets were considered very valuable by their owners and brought out at their own social gatherings to be admired and discussed; some changed hands for agreeable sums. Although this unofficial trading was, to Caxton's mind, a disagreeable consequence, he had to admit in the end that it was all grist to his mill, and the approbation necessary, for there were still many nay-sayers in the book-trade who wished the whole business would be damned and disappear and tried to undermine it.

'It's too expensive to set up,' they would tell their own customers when they enquired. 'It'll never catch on. Everyone wants quality handwritten, well-illustrated manuscripts on vellum. There's no market for these thin paper copies in black and white and clumsy wood-cut drawings.' For most of the citizens who had never read, owned or desired either manuscript or book, the whole business passed them by, and those who did hear of "the Westminster machines" thought they must be another of the Devil's works, akin to the dubious alchemical experiments practised in dark cellars in the back alleys of London by equally diabolical men.

On this day, at least twenty worthy citizens arrived at the sign of *The Red Pale*, with Caxton's monogrammed plaque proudly displayed above the door. They were ushered in by Pom and two of Jack's apprentices, dressed smartly for the occasion. Caxton was at the back of the workshop, ready to make an entrance, for on any occasion of business he was something of a showman. Jack and Inkin' Wynkyn had set up the press with the first page of *Le Morte D'Arthur*, newly composed by Monty to Caxton's instructions. Within minutes the doors were closed, the audience seated. Among them were a couple of bishops who, having business with Caxton's landlord, the dean of the abbey, had invited themselves, hearing of the enterprise occupying abbey premises. 'We'd better make sure the business is appropriate to a religious house' was their excuse for attending; although the real reason for the visit was curiosity as to what all the fuss was about.

Caxton made his entrance and welcomed one and all to the Westminster Press. After a few emollient social niceties, he reminded them they were here to make a little history and to be some of the first to own or share in these remarkable works. A little shiver of pride and self-satisfaction circulated the room and members of the audience looked one to another with a certain smugness. Exactly the response Caxton was looking for.

'I've played them like fish, Mister Pickle, now it's up to you to engage their attention for twenty minutes before slipping them into the net. Don't let it go on for too long. These people will soon become bored with too much information. Make sure they handle the typeface and you must stress the intricacies required to produce them. Awe and wonder is what we are looking for!' All this said in a whisper as Monty took his place by his composing table which had been carried onto the platform.

Montmorency Pickle drew breath and began, 'Good morning, my lords, ladies, gentlemen and gentlewomen,' for the objection to the presence of such as the ironmonger's wife had been overruled because, as Monty pointed out, Sir Thomas Malory himself had beseeched: '...*all gentlemen and gentlewomen that read this book of Arthur and his knights from the beginning to the ending pray for me...*'

Passing a few around, Monty began to explain how the tiny type-pieces, the actual individual letters, were carved out by a very skilful hand from hard metal using a drawing of the letter as a guide. The letter was then punched into soft metal to leave a reversed impression.

'This we call the matrix and the process "type-casting". The matrix is then placed in a mould and hot metal poured over it.'

A fashionably dressed man put his hand up and asked, 'How many letters can be made in a day?'

'A good question, sir. The individual letters may take half a day to prepare.' There was an appreciative gasp of surprise. *That long*? was the collective thought. Monty continued, 'From the matrix, in a day a skilful type-caster can produce upwards of four thousand, but not all of them are useable; some have flaws and must be melted down again for reuse, for we waste little here. The essential point is that the matrices produce letters crisp and sharp enough for use. You will see at the end of the printing process why Master Caxton's print is lauded for its clarity. But let's not get ahead of ourselves! The next stage is the composition of the page ready for printing, which is one of my tasks. After the manuscript has been laid out to fit the page-size required, with the help of others, for it is a long process, I will assemble the letters first into this composing stick,' and Monty took up a small piece of wood about nine inches long, the middle hollowed and smoothed out to take the letters which were formed, in this instance, into four rows of sentences of a width to fit the page. 'I will pass this among you and you will see how the letters are placed from left to right, upside down and backwards. This is not a stick from *Le Morte D'Arthur*, which will be a book in the folio size. This stick is part of a single indulgence manuscript commissioned last week—something their lordships the bishops will appreciate I'm sure!' And he smiled as he walked to the front of the audience and handed the stick to a sober-looking gentleman. The man took it gingerly at first, as though Monty had handed him an explosive weapon; then he peered with interest and tried to decipher the upside-down, back-to-front words. Finally he shook his head and passed it to his neighbour. 'I can't make head nor tail of it, friend!'

The composing stick well on its way round the audience, one of ladies put up her hand and asked, 'How do you manage to remember to set these letters so? I'm sure if I tried, I'd simply fall into the way of putting them in so that I can read them. This must be an almost impossible task!'

'Another interesting question, mistress' said Monty diplomatically. He had been asked the same thing innumerable times. 'All I can say is, one gets used to it and soon it becomes second nature.'

'Do you make many errors, sir?' asked one of the aldermen, a jolly-looking mercer who had brought his wife. She was peering closely at the words, and, tugging at his sleeve said triumphantly, 'Look, John—I can read it. There's the word "spiritual"!'

'Very clever, wife; but we might have expected to see that in an indulgence.' Crushed, she passed the stick on with a sniff. After a few minutes, everyone who was interested had examined this composing stick and Monty turned to show them how others were then placed in large trays called galleys. 'We assemble all the sticks in the trays, in the right order, and then they are ready for the printing process.'

The mercer persisted, 'What happens if you make a mistake; put the wrong letter or sentence in the wrong place?'

'Obviously it would be very expensive to make an error and then print it innumerable times; such a waste of paper and ink. So it is at this stage that the final detailed checking against the original manuscript is done. Master Caxton insists many pairs of eyes peruse the galley before the type is moved to a special iron frame called "the chase".'

'Why "the chase"?' asked a lady.

'I'm afraid I can't answer that because I don't know,' admitted Monty. He could feel Caxton's eyes on him. He had overrun his twenty minutes and Jack and Inkin' were waiting patiently by the side of the press ready to take over. 'This is a young business, but, as you can see, we are already building up a new vocabulary to explain it; a fitting situation in this magic world of metal letters. Now I'll pass you over to my colleagues, Master Printers Wynkyn de Worde and Jack Worms,' and all eyes turned to the printing press which stood close by.

Caxton stepped forward, 'Now my colleague Mister Pickle has explained how the type-setting process is accomplished, we move on to the production of the printed page. Meister Wynkyn de Worde, a very experienced master printer who came to England with me from the cradle of printing—the Rhineland—and my senior printer and bookbinder Master Jack Worms, will demonstrate by producing a page from the proposed edition of *Le Morte D'Arthur*.' And he gave a nod to Jack who stepped forward.

'Good day to you all. Now, the text having been thoroughly checked, we transfer the type from the galley to the iron frame—the chase—where wedges and filler pieces are used to tighten it all up so there is no slippage. This is called "the form"—another word for you to ponder on! Perhaps at this stage it might be easier for you to gather round to view the process. Please! there's no need to rush, there's room for all to see!' There was a rapid move to get to the front for the best vantage point, and when everyone was settled, the two printers laid the frame with the type on a large press stone and Inkin', appropriately, took up two large, padded balls on the end of sturdy handles, rolled them in a puddle of black and sticky ink and proceeded to apply them evenly to the surface of the type.

'An interesting fact is that these ink balls are covered with the skin of dogs. Has anyone any idea why we do that?' asked Jack. A silence and people looked one to another, shrugged and shook their heads. 'I'll tell you. It's because dogs don't sweat through their skin, so the ink is not absorbed into the sheep's wool with which the balls are stuffed.' There was a nod of understanding by the crowd.

'It looks very thick—the ink?' observed one of the bishops, who was finding the whole demonstration fascinating.

'That's because it contains oil rather than water—for obvious reasons. If the ink was made with water, all the type would smudge and become illegible as soon as it was exposed to rain or any kind of dampness. The oil-based ink dries solid and water-resistant, which means these documents will last until—forever! The only risk to them is fire, but that is a hazard for everything in our lives, is it not?' And there was a general murmur of agreement.

'Now, we come to the final process, the actual pressing of the page. Would anyone like to volunteer?'

The interested bishop stepped forward, rustling his silk gown importantly. 'I should very much like to try, Master Worms.'

'Excellent, there's nothing like the seal of approval from a bishop!' said Jack with a laugh. Fortunately the cleric had a sense of humour and smiled as he stepped forward to the press.

'Before we wind down the screw, we attach a damp sheet of paper with pins to a tympan. For those of you struggling with the vocabulary, you may associate that word with the skin of a drum—and this tough piece of cloth is held in place by a frame called the frisket, so the whole thing is entirely stable under the weight of the press; essential as we don't want any smudging, rather the sharpest and cleanest imprint we can produce. Now we come to it. My lord, if you would step forward and take the handle, you may turn it to make the stone and wooden platen slide under the screw.' The bishop obliged. 'Good, nicely done! For those who are interested in such things, it works by means of a windlass mechanism. Now perhaps someone else would like to operate the pressing screw?' Not to be outdone by a bishop, the Treasurer of England himself, Sir John Wood stepped forward. 'I see nothing amiss in an official of the exchequer applying pressure!' he jested. There was a ripple of laughter and everyone waited expectantly.

'Perhaps it will be more appropriate for a layman to wield the screw, for the handle which attaches to it is called "the Devil's Tail" and possibly not suitable for a bishop to push or pull,' and Jack added to the mood, which was now companionable. Sir John grasped the Devil's Tail without any perceived apprehension of hellfire and pushed it forward. People watched carefully as the pressure was applied for a few seconds, then, when Jack nodded, the system reversed, the pressure released with the screw pulled back; the bed with the tympan and frame slid back to its original position.

'Now we have the moment of truth; let's see what's been produced,' and Jack, raised the tympan and frisket, unpinned and peeled back the sheet of damp paper. The atmosphere produced by concentrated minds was palpable. Jack gently held up the sheet with both first fingers and thumbs. 'As you can see, it's wet, so will be pegged out to dry. But I have here one we made earlier for you to look at.' He took a sheet on which were printed four pages, 'This is our folio size and one you may possibly have seen elsewhere. I will lay it out on the table presently and before you leave you can take a closer look. Now, if you would return to your seats Master Caxton will have a final word. Thank you for your attention.' There was a ripple of applause and everyone moved back to their chairs.

Caxton took centre stage and explained the process of patronising such works, emphasising the great opportunities for them to participate in these historic events which, as he said, must be marked out in the future as a turning point in literary progress. He gave them a flavour of the content of *Le Morte D'Arthur* and a little of its history. 'Sir Thomas Malory devoted much of his life to compiling these ancient stories from the French and early English sources. It is a work of great imagination and will appeal to many of you I'm sure. Those who decide they would like to be part of this venture will be presented with a page of the work for them to keep as a memento of their day at the Westminster Press. I will leave you with my employees to discuss how you wish to proceed. Thank you for your attendance today. The Westminster Press is always open to those whose minds are also open to propelling this important work forward.'

The audience sat for a few minutes, and then to Monty's relief, he saw the Lord Mayor, Sir Robert Billesden, haberdasher, and Sir John Wood approaching him. 'How do I become involved and lay my hands on a copy of this new work?' asked the mayor. As sheep follow the bellwether, the members of the audience began to form an orderly queue.

'It was music to my ears, Gisella,' Monty said when he arrived home. 'We've signed enough patrons to ensure the book can be brought out; sixteen of them! You have no idea how relieved I am!'

'Oh yes I do, husband, oh yes I do!'

# Chapter 11

We return to Brittany and catch up with important events,
such as a new addition to the Tanner family and a failed
invasion attempt.
In England Richard III is vexed and in Brittany
the English exiles are threatened and forced to make a
swift exit.

And what of our friends in Brittany? We move backwards to
late September '83. The Tanners were fully accommodated in
the Chateau de Suscinio and Sir Anthony was waiting for
orders to advance to Calais in the rescue attempt of the Earl
of Oxford, John de Vere. He had made his preparations and
wondered why he had not had the order to move out.

'Something's up, Magpie,' he commented. 'Henry and his
uncle Jasper Tudor seem worried and I can't get an audience
with either. There have been some visitors from England who
have been closeted for days with Duke Francis.'

'I'm sure you'll be told in due course, Tony.' His wife was
soothing as ever when she perceived her husband to be "in a
state". He hated inaction and waiting about for days did little
to enhance his usual good temper. However, Meg persuaded
him that the time could be well spent with his boys, instead of
pacing their chamber anxious for news. Leo and Dickon were

delighted to have their father's attention, although they were perceptive enough to understand his mind was not always on their training.

'Father let me take him to a fall when we were wrestling this morning, Dickon. There's something on his mind. He would never do that!'

All was revealed a few days later when Henry and Jasper Tudor sent for Anthony.

'Sir Anthony, there's been a change of plan—you will no longer be going to Calais. We have had intelligence that Richard has tightened up the fortress's defences considerably and the Calais Captain, Lord John Dinham has been given express orders that Oxford should be kept under strict supervision. Also, there's no indication that the garrison there will rise and support us. We think an attempt at rescue would be a waste of time.'

Jasper Tudor, fifty-two, fit, stocky, a determined Welshman and still with a complete head of deep auburn hair nodded and said, 'Even so, Richard is evidently worried about the growing support for my nephew. Duke Francis had a visit earlier this month from a confidential agent of King Richard—one of your counterparts, Sir Anthony—one Doctor Thomas Sutton, although I don't know what he's a doctor of—anyway he came to sound out the duke's attitude to our band of exiles here—especially Lord Edward Woodville and his "pirates", as Sutton apparently called them.'

'I've heard something of the man. What did the duke tell him, my lord,' asked Anthony, disappointed at the loss of the commission and wondering where it left him.

'The duke, as you know, is not a well man and has lapses of memory. But it was reported to us that he was "noncommittal" about supporting Richard of Gloucester, as I will always think of him. Francis did ask Richard for four thousand archers from England for his defence from the threat of a French invasion—which never goes away, although has not happened for some years.'

'Are you saying we can assume the duke is still supporting us, my lord?'

'There's no chance Francis will have us bound and sent back to England, if that's what you mean!' laughed Henry. 'As far as he's concerned, I am a valuable pawn in his game with France as well as England. It's all high politics.'

Jasper Tudor said, 'Let's move on to the real practical business, Sir Anthony. We have enough supportive Englishmen of military experience here to mount the invasion sometime soon.'

'The invasion imminent, my lord? I take it you've intelligence from England that you will be well supported when you arrive?'

'Not universally, but certainly in the west and south-west.'

'Where will the ships, men and arms come from?'

'Some of it will be money from the jewels you smuggled in. We also have the small hoard your two excellent boys discovered, and, thanks to the judicious use of Duke Francis' "persuader", we've managed to get out of Jasper Percy and his henchman Costello the name of their supplier. Our men have already contacted him and arranged for more deliveries.'

This didn't sound very promising—a small store of arms and promise of more from a dubious source. Jasper Tudor read the thought on Anthony's face and said, 'Of course, that's not enough, but we are ready to go to Duke Francis and ask him for money, men and ships. If we catch him on a good day,' and he looked meaningfully at his nephew, 'we're confident he will give us the necessary funds and equipment.'

Anthony returned to Meg with the good news that he would not be away in Calais for possibly months on end, but the bad news that he would inevitably be included in the invasion fleet which was to sail, "as soon as the ships and money are organised", according to Jasper Tudor.

That time did not arrive until the second week of October, when Henry Richmond and his band of exiles sailed from Brittany in a tiny fleet of five ships donated by Duke Francis, along with three thousand pounds and three hundred and twenty-five fighting men. They travelled perhaps more in hope than expectation, although the intelligence was that full support for Henry would come from the Duke of Buckingham in Wales and other disaffected noblemen in the south and western counties. The intention was to land at Exeter and gather men and arms on their way into the west to meet Buckingham and his army.

'But it was a total failure, Meg,' and Sir Anthony Tanner shook his head in sorrow and frustration when he returned to tell his wife the dismal facts. 'Everything was against us, including the weather. Buckingham didn't show, and we learned later he had been caught and executed in front of Richard at Salisbury. We were held up because of a violent storm in the Channel and all those waiting for us in Exeter gave up and ran. Richard caught Sir Thomas de Leger, our man leading the army on the English side, and had him executed on the spot. I believe many of the rest of our supporters are making their way to Brittany to join us. I'll be glad when they all arrive. Not everyone in the duchy wants

Henry here. If you look at Breton politics closely, it's a mess of intrigue and petty jealousies—the usual nonsense!'

'But the duke seems so supportive of Henry, and us all. Look how kind he's been to the boys.'

'He may be kind, but the duke's an ill man and not always right in the head. He's easily manipulated, especially by his chief minister, Pierre Landois, who's very tough and a nasty bastard.'

'Oh yes, I've heard of him and seen him too. He seems to strut about the château as if it belongs to him.'

'To all intents and purposes it does, Magpie! Francis has given over the running of things to Landois and he takes every advantage. He's as slippery a customer as I've come across in all my dealings with such men. He sways with the wind— whichever way it blows so long as it's in his favour. I knew from brother agents in England that he had many secret dealings with King Edward, trying to keep Brittany independent from Louis XI who was anxious to bring the duchy under his control. If Brittany was going to be under anyone's control, Landois wanted it to be his. Nothing will have changed on that score even though Louis is dead.'

'So what will happen now? Will Henry try again— another invasion?'

'Of course! And, as I said, we have more supporters here than ever. They say nearly a hundred gentry have sailed from the south coast and are on their way to join us.'

'Is there a danger that Richard could attack Brittany?'

'Not a chance! It would start a continental war; Charles VIII—or his advisers, since he's a minor—would wade in to protect French soil. Besides, Richard has no money for foreign wars. What he will do is step up action in the Channel against the Breton pirates, who are making themselves very unpopular with merchants in England—I would in his position.'

'But that doesn't answer my question, Tony. What will happen *now*—to us I mean?'

'I must stay here and wait for orders. You're happy, aren't you? The boys seem well!'

'Anthony, there's a matter I need to talk about with you.'

'When you say that, and with a solemn face, it means the boys have been up to something and you want to protect them from a beating.'

'It's nothing the boys have done, but you mentioned how the duke is kind to them.'

'Mmm,' murmured Tony with a frown.

'Well, he wants to give them a dog.'

'A dog!'

'When they first came here, one of the castle bitches had pupped. They became besotted with them and begged me to ask the hunt-master if they could have one.'

'What breed? Not a fighting dog I hope?'

'No, the master of the hounds says they're a special French cross called an "Alaunt Gentil"; it's got greyhound in it and used for hunting. They're very pretty and sweet, Tony,' she said lamely.

'I'm sure they are; all puppies are pretty and sweet, but like people, some grow to very ugly and bad-tempered and large. How big do these dogs get?'

'Well, I suppose large greyhound-size.'

'And you say the duke has offered them one?'

'Yes. You know he's very taken with the boys and was captivated by the story of their escape from the tower. He also wants to reward them for discovering the arms and armour.'

'I can hardly say no to the duke, I suppose. All right, tell them they can have one—a dog not a bitch. But there are three conditions.'

'Oh?'

'Yes, there's to be no fighting over it and they're to make sure it gets proper exercise.'

'I'm sure they will. And the third?'

'They must clear up any shit it leaves around the place. The first time I tread in one of its turds, back to the kennels it goes!'

\*\*\*\*\*\*

Mid-December and there was an uneasy atmosphere around the Château de Suscino, and it didn't just revolve around the shitting arrangements for the new addition to the Tanner family, the grey puppy with "the adorable eyes", as Meg described him.

'What will you call him?' asked their father.

'We thought of Neville, father,' said Dickon.

'Neville? Why Neville?'

'Well, you've told us so many stories about the Earl of Warwick, how brave and strong he was. Also that he was the best horseman in the kingdom and was never in one place for very long. We thought, Neville was right for him—he is already very fast, father.'

'I approve; good choice, boys! Now, take him out and give him a run. Wear him out! I don't want him padding round the corridors all night, whining.'

The two boys and the wilful puppy, for he was wilful, headed out towards the beach; the boys whooping and the dog barking—all wildly. With a sigh of relief, Tony and Meg sat together in front of the fire. 'There's something you should know, Meg. Henry's planning to attend a mass at Rennes Cathedral on Christmas Day.'

'A long way to go for a mass, Tony.'

'A three-day ride this time of year. Anyway, it's not just a mass; he intends to gather all his supporters together and ask them to be witnesses.'

'To what?'

'To his solemn pledge to marry Elizabeth of York once he's acknowledged King of England. They'll be expected to make an equally solemn pledge to support his efforts to gain the crown. It'll be a public show on Henry's part that his intentions are serious and that he's confident he can achieve it; that confidence will go a long way in persuading Duke Francis to continue his support, despite the failure in October.'

'Will you be going with him?'

'Certainly. I must.'

'So you won't be here for Christmas?'

'I'm afraid not, but we'll have our celebration when I return.'

Meg sighed, but she was used to such disappointments. They had been a feature of her married life and the price she paid for being married to a "confidential agent" as Sir Anthony now styled himself.

'Very well, Tony. Leo, Dickon, Neville and I will have to make the best of it!'

\*\*\*\*\*\*

Someone who was finding it difficult to make "the best of it" was Richard III who viewed the activities in Brittany with increased alarm. Despite his success in halting the rebellions in southern England, catching the arch-traitor Buckingham and despatching him publicly, as well as driving out the invading Tudors, admittedly with the assistance of the weather, according to some observers he was "vexed and tormented in his mind with perpetual fear". This vexation and torment did not lead to paralysis of action; rather he plunged into a series of measures designed to curb the activities of the Bretons as far as their piratical exploits were concerned. Throughout the summer of '84 squadrons of his ships were sent into the Channel to resist the depredations of the Bretons, and Richard made it known that their hostile attitude to England and English ships was a dangerous one and would be paid back measure for measure. The vigour with which the English flotillas dealt with the Breton pirates was successful and prizes poured into southern ports, the Breton ships suffering much damage. The response was so overwhelming, the inhabitants of Brittany living on the coast were warned to maintain a persistent watch for a possible invasion.

The kindly Duke Francis was a man ailing in body and mind, and when bouts of disorientation came upon him, Pierre Landois put himself firmly in control of the duchy. Confronted with the dangers in the Channel, the chief minister favoured an alliance with Richard and sent an agent to sound him out. After much deliberation, Richard agreed to send Francis a thousand archers on the condition that Henry Tudor was captured, with his uncle and other Lancastrians and all returned to England, preferably in chains.

On the evening of 3$^{rd}$ October '84, Tony returned to their chamber in a state of great agitation.

'Meg, I must leave immediately. The game's up I'm afraid. Pierre Landois has ratted on us and will be sending soldiers to arrest all the English.'

'Where will you go? What about us?'

'Well, there's only place I can go and that's across the border to France. Henry and Jasper are close by in Vannes and will leave for the border from there, once they've thrown themselves on the mercy of Charles VIII. Let's hope the French don't play fast and loose with us. I'm going to join them with a few of our men. Now, I want you to go back to the village and our good neighbours, who I'm sure will give you lodgings as long as necessary.'

'As long as necessary? How long is that?'

'I can't be sure, but I've been assured you'll be protected by the duke, despite Landois and his grudges against the English. No harm will come to you. Now, get the boys here and I'll explain. It's likely you'll follow after us very soon.'

'What about Neville, if we have to go to France? They won't leave him behind.'

'We can't spend time arguing about it. If it's necessary, they must leave him behind. Who knows, we might all be back and soon.'

'They're going to be very upset—'

'Look, Meg, unless you want to be a widow and our boys orphans, I suggest you stop fretting about the damned dog and help me get ready. This is no jest. I leave in a half-hour.'

There had been a short row, but Tony played a heavy hand and threatened them with a beating if they didn't promise to take Neville to the kennels, if it came to it. However, when he saw them looking chastened and unhappy, he told them there was a great chance they would follow their father into France. 'Perhaps we can get you another dog.'

Leo and Dickon exchanged glances, knowing exactly what the other was thinking. *Why doesn't he understand—we want this dog!*'

As soon as the sun disappeared, Henry, with Anthony and a small crew, left the chateau quietly and discretely and headed the sixteen miles to Vannes where he found Jasper Tudor had already left for the frontier, as ordered, with all the English nobility in train, ostensibly to visit Duke Francis who was residing near the borders of Anjou. 'Don't hesitate Uncle Jasper,' Henry told him. 'When you arrive, just take the whole party across the border into France. The rest of us will follow in a day or two.'

Two days later, accompanied by five "servants", including Anthony, Henry rode out "to visit a friend in a nearby manor". After a five-mile ride, they withdrew into a wood and Henry changed into a serving man's clothes. The party then took the road to Anjou. Pierre Landois, who had planned orderly dawn raids the next morning imagining it would be totally unexpected, was somewhat lax in his deployment of guards and his quarry slipped across the border unseen.

\*\*\*\*\*\*

'Thank God for John Morton, Sir Anthony! He may be a bishop, but he's not afraid to get his hands dirty spying!'

'This is the bishop who is great friends with Queen Elizabeth, my lord?'

'Yes, indeed, and passed her letters to us when the idea that I should marry her daughter was first proposed. He's been a stalwart in all the business and has sharp eyes and ears. If he hadn't found out about Richard and Landois' plot to capture us, we would have all been arrested and certainly sent home and executed. Of course it was my mother, Lady Beaufort who alerted him to the danger, God bless her!'

Tony was sitting close to a good fire in a chateau just across the border. After a fast ride through the night, the next day they crossed into France without hindrance and gained a muted welcome from a local milord who became more enthusiastic when money changed hands.

To Henry's regret, at least three hundred English men were left in Vannes at the mercy of Landois. But within a week or so Duke Francis had temporarily recovered his wits and provided the wherewithal for the English party to join Henry in France. Among them was Edward Woodville. One evening in Angers, prior to an important interview with the young king of France as to how matters should proceed, Henry's inner circle sat contemplating the future.

'Doesn't it all depend on King Charles now; which way he'll jump, my lord?' Anthony mused.

'Rather it's his sister we must deal with, Sir Anthony. She rules as regent,' said Henry Tudor. 'I've been told she's a tough intelligent woman.'

'Is she the daughter Louis described as "the least foolish woman in France"?' asked Edward Woodville, stretching out his long legs and staring into the flames. Unlike his sanctimonious brother, our late friend Anthony Lord Rivers, Edward exuded an aura of dash and devilment and at the age of thirty-three had a reputation as "the last knight errant". If his brother Anthony had tried to uphold the values of piety, Edward took the same approach to piracy, not to mention chivalry. His sea-going exploits were legendary, especially among the exiles in Brittany where he had arrived in May '83 from England with a chest full of purloined gold, two ships captured from King Richard's fleet and a fund of stories which kept everyone entertained for many an evening. Duke Francis, always captivated by tales of heroic deeds, gave him a monthly pension.

As far as Tony was concerned, continental politics was so abstruse that he wondered if anyone had a clear idea how the situation between the powers of England, France, Brittany and Burgundy really stood. As a man for whom "deeds not words" was the preferred motto, Tony had no wish to listen to convoluted discussions about old treaties, new promises, and broken oaths. Instead he tried to bring matters back to the present and how they were to proceed in the enterprise to gain the crown for Henry Richmond.

'How do things stand in England with your supporters, sir. What about Queen Elizabeth?'

'Now she's out of sanctuary my mother says the queen has had discussion with Richard, but although there was a worrying suggestion she might abandon us, we heard she's still with us, as is her son the Marquis of Dorset who's here in France.' He smiled at Tony. 'My spies are everywhere, Sir

Anthony and this is where you'll be useful, with your knowledge of France and its kings—and you speak the language well. Tomorrow we'll arrive in Montargis in the train of the French court; like his father, Charles's court seems to be permanently on the move; necessary in a country of this size I hazard. I want you to ride ahead of us, taking letters explaining our intent, which is friendly to France. Remind Charles, or his sister, how Richard has supported Duke Francis with archers and could possibly be intending an invasion of France with his new friend.'

'But the Duke of Brittany has been so good to you; to have him painted as an enemy is—'

'—Is politics, Sir Anthony. You see I'm learning fast. The real power in Brittany is Landois, not the poor old duke who's losing his mind, and like the bastard Landois we must sway with the wind. French support for our cause is the key to our success. Tomorrow you will ride ahead of us and pave the way for the next episode of this great adventure. Here's to success!' And he raised his glass, the mouth in his young face set in a determined line, his pointed chin almost quivering with anticipation.

# Chapter 12

In which many matters are concluded.
In London the Pickles have a surprise visitor and plots are plotted.
In Paris the exiles experience the resentment of the natives.
*Le Morte* takes shape.

A new year and expectations were that '85 would see the culmination of many hopes and desires. London was, as usual in this cold season, frozen, inhospitable and grim. Foul smoke, thin air, damp fog left the act of breathing difficult for the very young, very old and quite a few in the middle. Occasionally in the mornings, bodies were found and left unclaimed, as early workers tentatively made their way to their places of occupation along frozen uneven paths. "Another one gone!" was the common observation at the sight of a body stiffly curled up in a doorway or laid out on the river solid with ice. Death was a constant visitor—not haunting tentatively or sneaking about, but open and defiant, ready to embrace the weak, reckless, drunk, plain stupid or penniless who had not the strength, wits or wherewithal to find their way home to a fire and a hot meal.

On such a night, Monty and his family were enjoying their own warm fire and hot meal, and he sat back with a sigh of contentment.

'An excellent supper, Gisella. Just what was needed. I really appreciate how well you manage! This weather is unremitting and makes life hard, not least the water supply being frozen solid.'

The remedy was rationing and to keep many buckets and containers full within the warmth of the house, and to replenish the supply at the slightest hint of a thaw. There was always a queue of hopeful collectors standing at the aquifers and conduits; usually a crowd of young boys eager to earn a penny or two as icebreakers and watercarriers.

Gisella stood up ready to go to the kitchen and bring in a bread pudding, when there was a quiet knock on the door. 'Visitors—at this hour after the curfew?' she said.

'I'll go,' and Monty walked through to the front door. Caution was the watchword after dark. Respectable friends and neighbours rarely walked the streets, and even less frequently made social calls at this time without pre-arrangement. The streets of any large town or city at night were highly dangerous.

He opened the door a crack and said, 'Who's here so late? What is it you want?'

'For fuck sake, Monty, let me in! I'm frozen!'

At first, the voice was not recognised, and Monty hesitated, so that the man pushed the door wider and said, 'Jesus! It's me—it's Tony! Tony Tanner!'

'Tony!' He held open the door and a cloaked figure with a wide-brimmed hat pushed his way through and stood in the hallway.

'Tony—I can't believe it. How long has it been?'

'Too long, old friend. Is there any chance of a drink and a warm fire? I've been hiding outside waiting to make sure you were still here.'

'You're lucky—we're at supper. Let me take your cloak. Now come in and meet the family again!'

It had been almost eighteen months since Tony and Meg departed for Brittany. There had been very few words from them to their friends in England, and it was a nagging worry which never left the Newgate Three as to where their friends were and what they were doing. The feeling was increasing that Tony might well be dead. 'Considering his work, it seems likely he has fallen foul of someone,' growled Pom.

Monty shook his head, 'Surely Meg would have written and told us?'

'Perhaps she's not able to. Perhaps she's been captured or something. They both seem to attract danger.'

'No, Pom, I don't believe that. She has the two boys to consider. She wouldn't put them at risk. I think they're both alive and Tony's probably up to his neck in plotting with Henry Richmond.'

'Well, Monty, I can confirm you are right!' laughed Tony, when Monty reported the concerns of his friends. The children: Thomas, Gisella and Isolde, had been ushered off to bed, much to their disgust. The appearance of this lithe stranger with a bright pink nose but dangerous blue eyes had stirred their young imaginations, particularly since he had come out of the darkness, like some fey spirit from one of their mother's stories. 'I've spent the last eighteen months in the service of Henry Tudor. I'm one of his confidential agents.'

'Confidential agent! Hmm, is that what they're calling spies these days?' Monty raised his eyebrows. 'Are you here to spy, or is this a social visit?'

'Henry's sent me to England for the usual reasons, to find out the likelihood he would be supported.'

'Supported in what?'

'An invasion.'

'Again, but he failed last time.'

'That was the weather and—'

'—And King Richard was waiting for him.'

'You're not saying you support Richard? Surely not, not after what he did—to the princes I mean?'

'No, of course not. But these constant battles over the crown of England. Will we never be at peace?'

'Henry's a good man and he's no child-murderer. I think he'll be a breath of fresh air and, if he marries Elizabeth of York as he intends, then the two Houses of York and Lancaster will be united. Only then can peace break out, you must see that?'

Gisella, who had been sitting quietly and observing her husband and this man, who was not too well-known to her, but of whom she had heard many good things, said, 'Monty, he has a point. Anyone who can unite this fractured country must be supported.'

Monty was silent for a few seconds, then he said, 'I'm sorry, this isn't much of a welcome for a man whose friendship I've always valued.' He took up the claret jug and refilled Tony's glass. 'Before you begin to tell us all that you have been doing, let's drink to that friendship and pledge that it will never be broken.'

'Amen to that!' said Tony and raised his glass. 'Any chance of some food?'

\*\*\*\*\*\*

'Secrecy is all, my friends. I can't be recognised. Even though it has been some time since I was in London, there will still be many who know me.'

Tony had stayed the night and the following morning Monty hurried out, firstly to Pom's lodgings and then with him, onto the Westminster Press where he took Jack to one side and told him of Tony's return. Having made their excuses to Inkin' Wynkyn that they were called away on "an urgent matter", the three men returned to Monty's house and were reunited with their errant friend. To save time, and his voice, Tony had postponed a résumé of his activities in France until the friends were all together.

'The best news we've had, apart from Charles—or should I say his sister's—support, especially with money, is John de Vere's escape from Hammes Castle. He joined us in November. My two boys were very disappointed that there was no jumping into the moat this time—he simply walked out with the captain of the castle, James Blount and a porter. They collected disaffected men from the garrison and hot-footed it to meet us in Paris.'

'How are your boys—and Meg? How is she? As stalwart as ever I suppose. She will always be a remarkable woman to me,' said Pom.

'As I said, I had to leave her in the château in Suscino with the two boys—and the dog—don't ask—but the duke gathered up his wits again and overruled Landois' orders that

332

all English exiles were to be detained. Meg rode out with all the remaining English and joined us at Charles' court at Montargis just before Christmas. You've no idea how relieved I was to see them! That's where they are now.'

'So, what are your plans—or should I say your orders?'

'Somehow, I must see Lady Margaret Beaufort, Henry's mother. She's been the prime mover of the whole enterprise to place her son on the throne and has been a constant source of information from the English court.'

'You may find that difficult, Tony,' said Pom. 'Her husband Lord Stanley, Richmond's stepfather, was interrogated as to his wife's activities and ordered to keep her close. You know Richard stripped her of all her titles and estates—although he passed them to her husband. You may find it difficult to gain an audience.'

There was a long silence, then Monty stroked his chin and said, 'There is a possibility Caxton could help—not in person, but through the Westminster Press.'

'How can that be?'

'In '83, before you left for Brittany, Lady Margaret came to the press shop to see a demonstration.'

'I remember it, Monty!' burst in Jack. 'She admitted that she was no scholar in Latin and regretted it. She was very interested in Caxton's collection of French and English manuscripts and hinted she might possibly purchase one or two to be printed. One of them was *Blanchardin and Eglantine*, yet another French poetic romance. But it didn't come to anything. Caxton shelved the possibility of her patronage; I think this business of Lady Margaret losing her estates and income has rather put him off; he is a businessman first and fore-most!'

'That's as maybe, but there's nothing to say the work can't be resurrected; we can nudge Caxton's memory, remind him he needs noble patrons more than ever. Lady Beaufort is just across the way in the palace, lady-in-waiting to Queen Anne. She may be under scrutiny, but her husband is well-thought of by the king; he's now Lord High Constable of England and a Knight of the Garter. If Caxton agrees to revive the business, we can arrange for correspondence about it to be sent to her ladyship and use it as a cover for contact. What do you think, Tony?'

'I'm surprised it's you who suggest such a thing, Monty.'

'You always thought I was a dullard!'

'Certainly not, only an upright, respectable citizen.'

'Having heard everything you've told me about current affairs in France, the machinations of kings, princes and so call nobility everywhere, I've come around to Gisella's view that this country needs a future of stability. Until these two great warring houses are united that will never happen. There'll always be some petty claimant plotting to overthrow the last one. I hate war, but if it takes just one battle to bring peace, then God protect the right!'

There was a silence; Tony, Jack and Pom exchanged glances and eyebrows were raised at this unexpected opinion. Then Jack clapped his friend on the back, 'Well said, Monty! I'm with you all the way. But what Master Caxton would think about his precious Westminster Press becoming a centre for spies and confidential agents, I don't like to think!'

\*\*\*\*\*\*

334

It was a matter for serious consideration. Jack's observation that Caxton could be unwittingly drawn into treasonable plots would be a situation the printer would rightly deplore. Before any move was made to put a plan into operation, Master Worms went away and thought carefully how that might be avoided. Within a day, he had come up with a solution.

'The answer is, as I said originally, nudge Caxton into reviving the work and let him contact Lady Beaufort. She's still in the palace and her post as lady-in-waiting to Queen Anne. I've heard, and it may just be a rumour, that the queen is unwell—very unwell with the scrofula. Few people survive that. But even if Anne dies, Lady Beaufort will probably remain in London with Lord Stanley.'

'So, how should we proceed?' asked Monty.

'I'll suggest to Caxton that the manuscript she was interested in is worthy of printing and that it's been some time since he looked at it and would it be worth contacting her ladyship about it. Looking at our work in hand, there are just two manuscripts in preparation—'

'—And *Le Morte*,' Monty reminded him.

'A large work, I know, but when you consider how much we put out last year, three is hardly going to stretch us. No, I'll suggest we could look at *Blanchardin and Eglantine* again.'

'According to Tony, Lady Margaret Beaufort is a key figure in the move to establish her son on the throne. King Richard is hardly likely to let her roam about without significant surveillance.'

'What could be more innocent than a letter of invitation from Master Caxton for her ladyship to visit his printing works to discuss matters of literature? There again, she need never come here; instead we pass her extracts of the manuscript in which we hide correspondence. We send in regularly some bona fide pieces for any of Richard's spies to look at and then, when they've been satisfied nothing untoward is happening, we can smuggle in the letters. We'll overwhelm them with pages of French poetry which will discourage them from investigating too closely; unless they happen to be keen on verse, which I doubt!'

'It sounds very risky to me, Jack,' Monty said with a frown.

'I thought you were in favour.'

'I was—I am—but these are difficult times. The king has his spies everywhere; you've heard the rumours of how he's tormented with fear. That's all because of Henry Tudor.'

'Look, we don't know what's in these letters. They may just be a son's loving sentiments to his mother.'

'You don't believe that, Jack! Tony wouldn't come over here at great risk if he wasn't carrying something vital. But I have agreed to go along with this and I won't break my word. I'll speak to Master Caxton—for all we know he still may not be interested in Lady Margaret Beaufort as a patron. After all, she comes with some taint of treason, besides having lost her estates.'

'But for all Caxton knows, she may be the next king's mother. Like us all, he has to take a gamble.'

\*\*\*\*\*\*

Astute businessman as he was, Caxton took his time to decide whether to write to Lady Beaufort, for the very reasons

Monty had laid out. 'She's branded almost as a traitress, Mister Pickle. I do take an interest in who is riding high at court and who is viewed as suspect. We rely on these people to patronise us, and it's as well to know these things. Lady Margaret—admittedly a charming, pious and intelligent woman—is regarded as somewhat of a threat to his majesty. I have heard there are still plots to replace King Richard with her son, Henry of Richmond, despite his failed invasion. I don't know how serious they are, but can I afford to do business with his mother?'

'But sir, that's what this is—purely a business matter. Nothing to do with politics,' said Jack, who had come along with Monty for two reasons, one: moral support, and two: to stiffen his friend's sinews if necessary. Jack felt they had given their word to Sir Anthony who was a founder member of the original Newgate Fellowship.

'Since you feel there is an opportunity for us here, and, as you point out, we aren't exactly rushed off our feet with work, I agree to think about writing to her on the matter. That is all I can promise. I'll let you know my decision in a couple of days.'

****** 

'Jesus Christ! At last! How long does it take him to make a decision? I've been here almost four days without any progress.' Tony was fuming; he had been staying with Monty in the guise of a "country cousin", keeping his head very low and hardly stirring out of doors. Monty's children had been entranced by their "Uncle Tony", although told not to discuss him with their friends, just to say he was a kindly relation who they liked very much and was staying for a few days. Tony told them some of Leo and Dickon's exploits, omitting names of places, just vague waves of the hand and "somewhere over the sea" descriptions. There was no mention of the Château du Suscino.

Monty returned from Westminster with the news that Caxton had written to Lady Beaufort, inviting her to the press shop to discuss her original interest in the French romance. 'There's no guaranteeing she'll come, Mister Pickle,' he said as he sealed the letter and handed it to Monty. 'If she does, and she's interested, I'll do all the preliminary work and then I'd like you to take on the business of keeping her informed of our progress. The usual facilities offered to a patron— extracts and generally keeping them up to date with the process.'

'Indeed, sir. It will be an honour,' and Monty sighed with relief. 'This is exactly what we wanted, Jack!' he told his friend afterwards.

'Let's hope she comes. If she does, how will you let her know about Tony?'

'I've been thinking about that. After Caxton has done all the politesse and smooth talking which he's so good at, I'll invite her into my chamber to set up arrangements for sending documents. I'll tell her outright about Tony, how he is our long-standing friend and his position as one of her son's confidential agents. I'll tell her he has documents from Richmond and is ready to carry letters of information back to Paris.'

'So no holding back then? Do you want me to be there?'

'Perhaps it would be advisable, then you can back up my story. She may think it's a subterfuge by King Richard, to compromise her. There must be something Tony can tell us about Henry which will show her he's come straight from her son.'

'That's a good thought, Monty. Let's hope he has something solid to convince her.'

\*\*\*\*\*\*

Lest our reader thinks we are ignoring them, the remaining Tanner family are at this time safely ensconced in lodgings in Paris. Reasonable lodging, not luxurious, but in a quiet and safe quarter of the city. But there had been adventures beforehand.

When Tony left them in such a hurry on that night in early October, the next morning Meg packed up such belongings as they had and went to the stables to find their horses. Pierre Landois' guards were ahead of her, mounting up and ready to ride in pursuit of the errant Englishmen.

'There are no horses to spare, madam. I suggest you return to your quarters. Chevalier Landois has ordered all English men—and their women and brats to be kept in close captivity. You husband should know of this—unless he's one of the renegade bastards who have cleared out with the traitor Henry Tudor and his uncle.'

Meg made no reply but turned on her heels and walked back to their chambers very worried indeed. This Pierre Landois was reputed to be a cruel, selfish man who had manipulated the good duke while he was in intermittent states of physical illness and madness. For the family to be in his hands and alone was not to be relished and she feared for her boys and herself; Landois was aware she was the wife of one of Henry's close companions.

'Lionel, Richard,' the boys looked one to another. Their mother only called them by their full names in times of trouble—trouble by them or trouble for them.

'What is it, mother?' asked Dickon with a worried look.

'We'll be confined to our rooms for a while. I'm not sure what's going to happen. I had hoped we might go to the village while father is away, but it seems the duke's chief minister has other ideas; he's a powerful man and doesn't like Lord Richmond's friends. You must stay inside and—'

'—But how can we exercise Neville? He must go out!' protested Leo.'

'I think we must get permission to take him back to the kennels—just until matters are sorted out.'

'No, mother! We'll never get him back. This man, this powerful man you talk about who's in charge will keep him, out of spite if he doesn't like us.'

'But Leo, it will be cruel to keep such a large dog penned up in a small room. I'm sure the master of hounds will look after him—he was very friendly when he gave Neville to you. He'll see you get him back when the time comes. It will be for the best.'

'You always say that when it's not, mother!' said Leo accusingly. 'Why did father have to go away *again*? If he was here he'd tell this minister or whatever he is to fuck off!'

There was a silence. Dickon's mouth dropped open and Meg's eyes widened with shock and horror. Cussing was a normal part of military life, and there was no doubt living in a fortress the boys were regularly exposed to soldiers' profanities. But neither of them had dared to use such expressions in front of her. *It just shows how Tony's frequent absences have affected these boys. They would never swear in front of me if he was here—or available to punish them.*

At that moment, she was angrier about this lack of respect than she was frightened of their position as prisoners. She stepped forward, raised her hand and slapped Leo hard on the cheek, leaving livid images of her palm and fingers. Her son gasped, and immediately tears sprang from his eyes.

'Never ever use language like that to me again, Lionel! God knows I've let you have enough freedom, and only once taken the whip to you, but you take advantage of it. Now apologise.' And she also started with tears, which fell slowly down her cheeks.

Shocked into silence, Leo felt the stinging on his face, but the stinging rebuke and then tears from his mother was far worse. The fact was he had not sworn at her but used a common expression to describe exactly what his father would say to any villain. However it seemed this fine distinction was ignored by his mother. 'I'm sorry mother, I didn't mean to upset you. I apologise for not—not—'

'—Being respectful to mother,' and Dickon stepped in, thoroughly upset by the scene, and in tears himself. He always shed them when he saw his mother crying—a rare event and this time more shocking for the tender-hearted lad.

'For not being respectful, mother. I'm sorry!'

Meg was as shocked at her response as her boys. She had never slapped either of them in fury. Yes, once, when Anthony had been long-absent, she had taken the whip to Leo when he had seriously bullied his brother, but nothing for some years, as she accepted they were growing boys and needed a degree of licence. She preferred to use other methods of correction than chastisement. The question was, should she pursue this and ostracise Leo for some time—to get the message through? Or should she take him in her arms and apologise? She decided she had no reason to take the latter course, which would surely dilute the effect; but equally there was no point in pursuing the punishment. 'Leo, I'm sure you understand why I was—am—so angry. You should never use such words in front of a lady—any lady—queen or servant. When you are a man and work and live among other men, you may adapt your language to suit the occasion. But remember, not every man cusses either. Some men don't like it, so it's up to you to judge when it's appropriate.'

'What does appropriate mean, mother?' asked Dickon, now recovering in concert with Meg, although his face was tear streaked.

'It means suitable for the time. If you were in a guard-room full of soldiers, it would be acceptable to swear. If you were in the cottage of a laundress, or the parlour of a merchant's wife, or the chamber of a countess it would be inappropriate. Do you understand?'

'Yes, mother,' said Leo, chastened and regretful.

'So, never forget it! Now I suggest we go to the kennels together and ask the hounds' man to look after Neville until we know when we can leave.'

They left ten days later after Duke Francis had again recovered his wits and realised how badly his remaining English guests had been treated. He ordered them to be allowed to follow the exiles across the border without further hindrance. Meg, her sons, and the dog which ran most of the way, although sometimes snoozing in the carts, in company with the other exiles caught up with Tony at Charles's court in Montargis from where, some months later, they all arrived in Paris.

Meg never revealed to her husband either the incident or her response. *It's over; I dealt with it and I'm convinced it'll never happen again*, she reasoned when she deliberated whether to tell him. *They were both so shocked when I slapped Leo, I can't think either will ever show disrespect to me in that way again.* And Leo, for a while anticipating a beating from his father, until he realised with relief that his mother had said nothing, never used such language in front of her or any woman again.

\*\*\*\*\*\*

'There is a problem, Monty,' Jack advised his friend a week after the letter had been sent from Caxton to the palace. 'Lady Beaufort is here, but she's brought someone with her—as well as a palace guard.'

'Perhaps it is just a companion. Great ladies don't usually go about unaccompanied.'

'I don't think this one could be considered companionable. They don't act together as friends, in fact Lady Beaufort hardly bothered to introduce her civilly. It's my guess she's been sent to spy on her ladyship.'

'Are you sure? I can understand the guard being present, but why would they send a female to supervise a countess?'

'Because they don't trust her. So what can we do? You obviously won't have chance to speak to her ladyship alone.'

Monty thought for a while. 'Find out if this woman speaks French. We know that Lady Beaufort can. If the woman

343

doesn't have the language, then I can speak to her ladyship freely.'

Jack disappeared and within minutes returned with a look of relief on his face. 'I spoke to the countess in fast French and the woman clearly couldn't understand what I was talking about, and asked me to translate, which I did.'

'Right, give me a minute. I'm going to unseal these letters from Richmond and read them to her ladyship in French; also explain Tony's involvement. I'll need time to present them as though they are documents from the manuscript.'

'Should you be doing that? They're confidential letters after all.'

'How else are we going to let her know we have them? It's obvious we can't pass them to her, sealed as they are.'

'You're right. Very well, I'll give you twenty minutes and then I'll bring them in. I'll entertain them with some extracts from *Le Morte*.'

'Always the salesman, Jack!' said Monty with a smile, but not feeling entirely happy. He was thinking, *Is my French up to this? It's been some time since I spoke it in the vernacular. Reading and translating it is one thing, vocal fluency another.*

Jack returned to Lady Beaufort and primed her, in immaculate French by pretending to read from a sheet of *Le Morte*, that there was information to be passed which was strictly for her ears only. The possibility that she would be mistrustful, and on her guard, had already been discussed. Tony came up with the name Christopher Urswick. 'He's Margaret's confidential agent. I've met him and know about his involvement with Bishop Morton. He was instrumental in getting word to Henry Richmond of Landois' proposal to have the English exiles arrested and detained. Tell her we've

344

worked together in the past and she can use my name next time she is in touch.'

Fortunately Jack was dealing with one of the most intelligent and quick-thinking of women. He inserted Sir Christopher Urswick into one of Malory's list of Arthur's knights, as 'un fedèle serviteur avec chevalier Antoine Tanner qui est aussi à votre service,' and she responded in equally good French, 'Je crois comprendre la situation.'

The accompanying woman was quiet and unobtrusive, pale faced with a receding chin, who hardly spoke and sat quietly in the room as Monty took up the documents and cleared his throat.

'My lady, I have the French version of *Blanchardin and Eglantine.* I thought it would be useful to read a page or two in the French and then translate for you into the English. You may have comments to make on the flow and structure. Would that be acceptable?'

'Certainly, Mister Pickle, that seems a sensible way to proceed,' and Monty cleared his throat again and began to read the first paragraph of the work in perfect French. Then he seemed to take a natural pause and began again, but this time reading out the letter from her son which contained details of proposals for a second invasion; the arrival in Paris of the Earl of Oxford with men from the Calais garrison; news of French support with money and men; and a brief resume of the convoluted politics of France, Brittany and Burgundy which could impact on his actions. He commended Sir Anthony Tanner as one of his confidential agents and implored her to respond as quickly as possible with news of her own health and well-being, the position of her husband Lord Stanley, and any other news she might have of prospective support for their "great enterprise". All this cleverly achieved by using the rhythm and cadence of the poetry, which made the countess smile with pleasure.

'C'est trés bon, Mister Pickle!' And she clapped her hands. 'Your French is perfect.' She turned to the lady-in-waiting, 'It's a pity, Joan, that you do not understand the language. It is so beautiful in this form of poetry. The words flow so elegantly.'

The woman sniffed and shook her head. 'I have never been able to pick it up, my lady. But I will be interested to hear it in our native tongue, if Mister Pickle will be so kind.'

'Certainly, madam, I'll offer the translation which Master Caxton has already worked on. See what you think.' And the session went on for a further half-hour while Monty read in English the fine thirteenth-century French verse. By the time they were ready to leave, Lady Margaret Beaufort had a full and detailed account of how her son was faring in France; instructions to gather further intelligence, and how it could be communicated. 'We will return in a few days to hear more, Mister Pickle. Perhaps we can take some of the sheets to look at in our leisure time? Je vais reviendrais des nouvelles.' She laughed and looked over at her companion and said, 'I just told Mister Pickle we'll return with news of any changes I think are necessary.' The woman nodded, and, looking very bored said, 'Indeed my lady, I'm sure it will be delightful to visit again.' Her face showed her words did not accord with her thoughts.

\*\*\*\*\*\*

'That went well, Monty!' Jack sat back with a look of satisfaction.

'So long as we're sure the spy-woman really couldn't speak French,' Monty replied.

'I tested her thoroughly and she was clearly confused. I don't think we should worry.'

'Now all that remains is to see if Lady Beaufort can find some privacy to write back. We have no idea how overlooked she is in the palace. Her letters will surely be read.'

'Pages of poetry in French will put off any prying censor, I'm sure. She strikes me as an unusually intelligent woman. She is very used to subterfuge and I have no doubt she'll find a way to fabricate a response for Tony to take back. Do we know how long he intends to be here?'

'As short a time as possible, for he has no wish for anyone to become curious about him and start asking questions.'

'I suppose he's comfortable in your lodgings. The children must find it strange to have him as a lodger—one who they know has a house of his own in Cornhill. They visited often enough when the family were here. They must have asked questions.'

'I just tell them he's visiting on business and because the house has been let to another family, Gisella and I invited him to stay. They're more than satisfied, especially when he has been entertaining them with stories of Leo and Dickon, who seem to have been having a very adventurous time.'

'Life around their father can't be anything less than adventurous, Monty!' said Jack with a rueful grin. 'I don't mind him involving us in his conspiracies, but it's the way he suddenly appears after months or even years of absence. We don't hear a thing from him, or Meg, and then he's on the doorstep in the dead of night looking like a conspirator!'

'It's the way of his work, I suppose. According to what he's told me there's a succession of spies, agents or whatever you want to call them passing backwards and forwards over the Channel. The king has men on the watch, but these agents are clever and know exactly how to merge into a crowd.'

'Dangerous work Monty!'

'And we are involved at some risk to ourselves.'

'You must have considered that when you agreed to help Tony—the effect on your family if it all came out.'

Monty nodded, 'My mind always goes back to the Cornelius Plot—you remember, back in '68—the reason why Sir Tom was in Newgate. King Edward decided to swoop on some possible Lancastrian spies and had them all arrested. Some were hanged. My only worry is King Richard will take it into his head to do something similar and round up anyone connected to Lady Beaufort. She must be of great concern to him.'

'That's why he sent the woman with her. What do we know of Lady Beaufort's husband? Where does Lord Stanley stand in all this?'

'Since we don't move in the exalted circles of the court, I have no more idea than you. He must be treading a very dangerous line, Jack—loyalty to his wife while keeping himself in favour with the king. He has a son George who's in his early twenties. Tony knows him. He's a nephew of the late Earl of Warwick. The Stanley family are all quartered in the palace under Richard's eye—when he's here that is. Our king spends much time up and down the country—seeking out traitors I suppose.'

'Well, the sooner Tony returns to France with the information the happier I'll be. I feel anxious for the Countess of Richmond. She seems a very noble lady,' Jack observed.

'At forty-one she doesn't look her age, I think. Not a beautiful woman, but a face that gives off warmth and humour.'

'She certainly appreciated our subterfuge. When do you think she'll return?'

'She hinted at a week: "Quand elle reviendra avec des nouvelles". It seems Tony will have to entertain my children for at least that long!'

\*\*\*\*\*\*

'I'll keep these letters in the French, as the countess presented them. Tomorrow I'll ride to Southampton and take ship to Honfleur, then onto Paris. I hope Charles hasn't decided to move his court again.' Tony bundled the letters together and wrapped them in oilskin, before storing them away inside his doublet.

Jack frowned, 'I presume you don't carry them so obviously on your person when you're on the road?'

'No, I have a special place designed for them in my saddle—don't worry, Jack, I've been doing this so long it's second nature!'

'We should have a grand supper together this evening, to send you on your way. The Newgate Fellowship reunited briefly!' suggested Monty.

'I've been remiss and not thoroughly enquired about your progress with *Le Morte*. Now you have it in your possession and persuaded Caxton to print it, you'll be thinking of making the journey to Winchester to fulfil Sir Tom's request?'

'We have a long way to go yet. I'm busy preparing it for printing but it's such a large work it takes a good deal of time. Although Master Caxton said it would be mostly in my hands, he is inclined to give his opinions rather forcefully at times. But he owns it after all, so it's difficult for me to object. As we speak, he's busy writing a preface. I've no idea what he's going to put in it. I just hope he remembers where the work came from originally!'

'Does he want many changes? I mean, do they alter the book substantially?'

'Not really, just stripping out some of the longer passages and putting it into books and chapters.'

'The question is, what would Sir Tom think?'

Jack laughed, 'Something like "Let's get the fucking thing printed and see what the world thinks!" All he wanted was for it to be acknowledged as a great set of stories and to become more famous than Chaucer's *Canterbury Tales.*'

'Will it?' asked Tony.

'I don't know. Chaucer has a head start—plenty of people know his work, especially since we've printed it; it's in its second edition, and he's written other things too which are now published. Those acquainted with the name of Sir Thomas Malory probably only remember him for his outlandish escapades and crimes.'

Tony frowned, 'Perhaps Caxton will eliminate his name from the finished book.'

'Caxton's a fair man and would never steal someone else's work. In any case, I intend to ensure Sir Tom's given full credit—even if I insert something in Caxton's preface myself!'

'Well said, Monty. How many years have you been involved with this work?'

'I joined Malory in his tower in Newgate in April '69, so that's over fifteen years.'

'That shows a great degree of loyalty.'

'Well. It's not just me. Pom was with him from the age of fourteen until Sir Tom died at fifty-seven—forty-three years is a long stretch of service—'

'—And he wasn't an easy man!'

'He certainly wasn't, Tony!' said Monty with a smile. 'But there was something about Rogue Malory which I couldn't help liking. He was a force of nature all right! I'll send the kitchen girl round to Pom and invite him tonight and we'll have a long talk about the old days.'

'That could go on for hours, Monty!' laughed Tony. 'As long as you remember I have an early start!'

\*\*\*\*\*\*

'You're earlier than I thought, Tony. Not that I'm sorry to see you, but you said it might be a month or so.'

'Business in London went very well, Meg, and I was able to conclude it early. Anyway, you sound as though you're not pleased to see me.'

She put her arms around him and pulled his face down for a kiss. 'Does that convince you?'

'It begins to, but something else would confirm it!' And he pulled her to him and began to fondle her breast. To his disappointment she pushed him away. 'Later, Tony! First, I want to hear all the news from our friends in London. Did you visit the house? Is it still with the same lodgers? Is it still standing!'

'What do you expect, Meg? That it's been burnt to a cinder? It's still there and looks well-tended, although I obviously didn't make a social call. I spent two weeks living with Monty and his family in rather cramped conditions. But I'll say one thing, he and Jack came up trumps and made my job so much easier.'

'That was brave of them—getting mixed up in your dangerous business.'

'Yes, I was surprised—it was Monty who suggested a very cunning plan and he and Jack carried it through like professionals!'

'Well, I'm grateful to them for allowing you to come home early.'

'So, wife, where are my boys? Why aren't they here to welcome their father?'

'Because they didn't know you were coming. They've gone off riding with some of the other English boys.'

'Not on their own, I hope?'

'Certainly not. While you've been away, they've been taken under the wing of James Blount—now the Earl of Oxford's great friend since he helped his lordship escape from Calais.'

'What do you mean, "taken under his wing"?' asked Tony with a stab of jealousy.

'He's just keeping a friendly eye. You know it's a close community here in Paris—we English exiles are inclined to keep together and not mix too freely with our French hosts.'

'What's his age—about fifty-five?' he asked, knowing very well it wasn't.

'About your age—and a very dashing gentleman he is too!' she said mischievously.

'I see, and you say he's taken an interest in our boys? I hope that's all he's taking an interest in, wife!' Tony was always acutely aware that, even now, just in her thirties, Meg was an exceptionally beautiful woman. In the early days of their marriage, whenever he went away, he was always mindful of her colourful past, and at the back of his mind was the anxiety she would be tempted to stray. Those feelings diminished with time, since there had never been a hint of unfaithfulness, and it was rare that he felt any jealousy. But for James Blount to take an interest in Leo and Dickon might just be a ploy for him to get closer to their mother. He looked carefully into her face, but could see no guile, no guilt.

Instead, knowing exactly what he was thinking, she laughed, 'Tony, he's a gentleman and offered to keep the boys amused for me while you were away. Other English lads go too—they hunt in the woods—obviously with the king's permission. It's all perfectly innocent—if you're worried he might have designs on me!'

'Of course I'm not, Magpie!' he said more brusquely than he meant to. Then, brushing such thoughts aside, he asked, 'How's that damned dog?'

'Neville? Eating us out of house and home. That's why I'm glad they go off hunting—at least we can feed him from the kills. He's too big to have in the house now. We had a kennel built and he sleeps outside. Sometimes he howls— there have been complaints, but mostly he's such a character people make allowances.'

'I hope he's not shitting all over the place,' Tony growled. That was the problem of being away for weeks on end; when he came back his family's life had moved on and he felt left behind. He was always torn between a feeling of admiration for Meg and how she had coped all these years when she was on her own, and regret that it wasn't he who always made the decisions for their domestic comfort. Who had made the kennel for her? Who did she ask? How much had she paid? The fact that she was a master of organisation should have been a matter a pride, but sometimes it grated.

In truth, she had done well as part of "les inconnus Anglais" in Paris. Like all exiles beholden to their hosts, they had to tread the difficult line between deference and subjugation. There were about four hundred living on the left bank of the River Seine which divided the city, and they clustered in small dwellings as close to each other as possible. The indigenous inhabitants were mostly hostile, with their inbred suspicion of the English. After all, it had been less than thirty years since their armies had been driven off French soil—Calais excepted—and memories were still fresh. Joan of Arc was regarded as the heroine and saviour of France and there were still men alive who had fought in campaigns to wrest their country back from the hated invader. But there was the persistent threat they would return. Their recently deceased monarch Edward IV had several times threatened an invasion and had the temerity to give himself the title of King of England, Ireland, Wales—and France.

Now there was another invasion, admittedly low in number, but nonetheless taking up housing and resources in an already overcrowded city and seeking money and arms from their king for some rash adventure by a presumptuous

English earl seeking to unseat an oil-anointed king. Their taxes and tithes were being used to pay for it.

'Here's a question for you, neighbour,' said a man of his friend in a tavern. 'Why have the English had three kings in twenty years—one of them twice on the throne but only for a few months? Now this upstart earl comes along asking for help to tip out the current king onto his arse!'

'And he's brought a crowd of the bastards with him!' nodded the neighbour, draining his pot and wondering whose round it was.

'Why can't they just accept who's next for the throne—civilised like us; when our kings die we have a new one ready. None of this fighting over it. Good old Charles VII had it for forty years—if you don't count the fact at the time the English said their fool of a king Henry VI was king of France too. Charles's son, old Louis XI hangs onto his crown for twenty-two years, dies decently and his son takes over; there's nothing difficult about it. Why do the English make such a meal of it?'

'Are we going to have another?' asked his friend hopefully. The man rose and felt in his pocket, 'Lend me a couple of sous and I'll get them in. I'm running short; there's no money about and little work. I blame these English exiles.'

'They've stirred up the English students at the university; there are plenty of them there.'

'That's another thing—they come over and take places which should go to good French students. Why do we have to have them here—that's what I want to know. We must keep an eye on our women, you know. Englishmen are born ravishers.'

'How do you know?'

'My grandfather was at Orléans in the war—he had many a tale about what they did to French women—especially nuns,' and he crossed himself and spat squarely on an unfortunate cockroach who was padding by, minding its own business looking for something nourishing to nibble among the detritus on the dirt-floor.

'I haven't seen any Englishmen lurking round our abbeys, friend!' laughed his companion. 'Mostly they seem to stay indoors—or go out in groups hunting.'

'That's another thing—the king gives them permission to hunt in the royal chases, but if we so much as snare a rabbit we're dead men.'

'Well, there's nothing we can do about it. We have to hope the king knows what he's doing—or his sister, who seems to be in charge.'

'One night I shall go out and slit a few throats—just to show who's really in charge round here. The next Englishman to come swaggering down the street and not move out of my way will—'

His friend intervened soothingly, '—Let's hope they'll all be gone by summer. If it gets hot and the plague comes back, I think they'll move out soon enough.'

Their grumbles had a certain amount of substance. The largest European city, Paris was, like any other great centre of population, an overcrowded filthy place; its exceptionally narrow streets and alleys dangerous at any time. Unemployment was high and, as in London, Parisians would wake up each morning to find bodies in doorways or floating in the Seine. Stark starvation as well as sickness and disease which haunted the streets, had seen most of them off, although some were victims of robbery and murder. The exiles, any

356

exiles or influx of strangers, were prime targets for resentment and occasional "retribution" simply for not being French.

Self-preservation meant those supporters of Henry Richmond who had followed him to Paris soon learned the places to avoid and that it was much safer to band together. But the very action of banding together caused resentment, especially in matters of accommodation. There was also a language problem; although some of the English nobility spoke decent French, many others did not. It was bad enough the university being "overrun" with English students who, as young men of any nationality on the loose from home and control, were "une doleur dans le cui", with their roistering behaviour, arrogant voices and permanent drunken states during holy days. The Parisians were not happy and there was tension in the atmosphere whenever an Englishman appeared.

Henry Richmond, anxious to carry out his objective, was mindful that he could not outstay his own welcome. Since the death of Louis XI the politics of France regarding her neighbours were as difficult and convoluted as ever, and the young earl found himself mixed up in factions and internal struggles of which he knew little and secretly cared less.

'It is always the problem with minority rule, as we know well enough from our own experience back home, Dorset' he sighed as he sat with the marquis of that county in the apartments Charles had found for them in one of the French palaces. 'But we were lucky to be given the chance to appeal to the French parliament for support in January, and even more fortunate that they finally agreed. We must be very careful though not to be seen to take sides in any of these domestic disputes but concentrate on raising forces and gathering a fleet together. We must be ready by the summer.'

'The arrangement for your marriage to my half-sister Elizabeth, still holds I suppose, sir?'

'So long as your mother keeps her promise—you haven't heard anything different from Queen Elizabeth, have you?'

'Oh, no sir!' said the marquis, but Richmond thought for a fleeting moment his friend looked shifty.

'I've recently had word from my own mother that matters are still progressing on that front. Support is growing in the southern counties, and Wales is certain; William Herbert and Rhys ap Thomas are definitely with us.'

'What of your stepfather Lord Stanley, sir. We heard he has been given honours and titles by Richard of Gloucester. He holds large sway in his lands in Cheshire and Lancashire—plenty of men. Is he still with us?'

'One of my confidential agents newly returned from England tells me Richard of Gloucester sent out a warrant in January ordering all knights, esquires and gentlemen of Chester, Lancashire and Glamorgan—in fact, wherever Lord Stanley's writ runs—to follow him in the event of an invasion "of rebels" as the usurper calls us! His lordship has a ready-made army for us.'

'Will he turn sir? I mean, will he swing to us when we invade?'

'I think we can rely on my step-father's promises, Dorset,' said Henry sternly. 'I just hope we can rely on those who say they are our friends!' And he frowned as he looked across at his noble companion. 'We all need to rely on our friends at this time, Dorset, don't we!'

'Indeed we do my lord!' And Thomas Grey smiled back blandly.

****** 

'Listen to this, Monty!' As ever Jack was first with the news, rumour or gossip. 'It's said that King Richard is planning to marry his niece, Elizabeth of York!'

Monty looked up from his composing table, 'Good morning Jack! Two things come to mind—firstly Queen Anne only died a week ago, and secondly how can an uncle marry his niece—the Church will never stand for it. It's pure gossip put around by his enemies, Jack!'

'I know that—you know that—but the man in the street will believe anything posted on a door. I saw it for myself—on the local tavern wall. Someone put it up.'

'Just to make mischief. I'm sure the king has no intention of even suggesting it. The pope would be incensed at the very idea! It's all part of this move to brand the king a devil. But it's his own fault; if he'd been open about where the young princes are, or were, people might not have taken against him.'

'You're right, Monty. This is pure mischief and we should pay no heed to what is written up on doors and walls—but as there are no other sources of information, people will continue to read such things and believe them!'

'Talking of reading things, Master Caxton has given me a draft of his preface for *Le Morte*.'

'And—is it good? Appropriate?'

'It's better than I expected, although there is one serious omission. But read it for yourself if you have time,' and Monty handed him a few sheets of manuscript.

'I have an hour to spare. I'm waiting for some spines to dry. You know, Monty, we're not as busy this year as we have been. You don't think the printing business has peaked? That people have lost interest because the books are quite expensive?'

'Not at all, Jack. I'm fully confident we're in the right business at exactly the right time! It's fortunate that we aren't so busy—gives us more time to finish *Le Morte D'Arthur*.'

'How many copies is Caxton prepared to produce? Have we had any advanced orders?'

'We can be sure of the Duchess of Burgundy, and the Countess of Richmond among the gentry. Her ladyship has told me she is putting the word about "concerning this important piece of literature which anyone of genteel mind should purchase". I know she was grateful for our involvement in her son's business in January.'

'It's all gone very quiet—this possible invasion by Henry Richmond. As usual, not a word from Tony!'

'I'm not sorry, Jack. Conspiracy and spying are not really for me!'

'I enjoyed it, Monty. Broke up an otherwise dull week!'

'You wouldn't have enjoyed it if we'd been caught! A stretch on Exeter's daughter in the Tower would have been anything but dull! I've been in a cell in that place, and although it only entailed the loss of a finger, the thought still haunts my dreams sometimes.'

'I suppose you're right. I'll take this preface and read it through. You say it's a draft? Is he willing to change anything do you think?'

'I'm not sure anything really needs to be changed. He's given Sir Tom part of his due, possibly rather buried it in the text. The old man is at least acknowledged but I am going to challenge his one omission in the text itself. However, I think you'll be amused by Caxton's opening paragraph. But I'll leave it with you!'

\*\*\*\*\*\*

'Magpie! We're on the move again!' Sir Anthony Tanner returned from an audience with his master, Henry Richmond to find his wife standing over their two sons while they painstakingly copied from a Latin grammar. 'Just try not to get ink everywhere, Dickon. You load your quill with too much of it. Wipe the surplus off on the cloth before you start writing.'

'Sorry, mother,' and Dickon sighed. Leo smirked, but kept his head down at his labours; it didn't do to irritate his mother now father was back. The boys wondered at these exercises, complaining to each other that they were, 'A complete waste of time. We should be out exercising Neville or down by the river with the other boys!' Their friends had set up a fishing group and were even now after a salmon of great size said to have been seen under the Bridge of Notre Dame. Meg was reluctant to let them join in. There were many groups of French boys who were as hostile as their parents to the English visitors and fights had broken out—some youngsters had been seriously hurt.

'There's no point in looking for trouble, Leo!' his father had said, when the boy begged to be allowed out.

'But we don't look for trouble, father,' he protested. 'It's the French boys.'

'It's always somebody else who starts these things, Leo! You must remember we are visitors here.'

'It's not a gentlemanly way to treat visitors—trying to ambush them and beat them with sticks or throw stones at them. We wouldn't do it if they were in London.'

'I'm not so sure. You wouldn't, I know—your mother has brought you up as real gentlemen! But others wouldn't be so scrupulous.'

'What does scrupulous mean, father,' asked Dickon, who always liked to roll these strange words round his tongue later.

'It means "fair and careful" and that's what you should be. So, stay in the house and, if you are good, I'll take you riding tomorrow.'

But it was as usual. Tony's promises were hardly ever kept because some event or problem would intervene. In this case, it was orders for the English exiles to follow King Charles to Evreux.

'Where are we going, Tony?' asked his wife with a sigh. She had only just finished settling the family in their lodgings. Everything had been put away and domestic routines established.

'About one hundred miles west of here—a place called Evreux. Henry says important events will take place there which will affect his plans. It's thought there's to be a reconciliation between two of the factions in this permanent fractious business which is French politics. I considered our civil war was complicated—but the French make it look like an orderly change of government. I don't know the details, and I don't want to, but it's divide and rule I think. If these two groups of so-called noblemen, who are thorns in Charles VIII's side, lay down their arms, he'll be less distracted and more likely to help our cause. He has a permanent fear of invasion from England and it make sense for him to back

Henry with troops and money and have a grateful French-friendly king on the throne, do you see?'

Meg nodded, 'I suppose it makes sense,' she sighed.

'So, we must pack up and be prepared to leave in the morning. Make sure the boys feed and water the dog before we go—and get them to clear up the yard. We don't want the next French occupants to think we leave our dogshit around. They think badly of us as it is!'

Early the next morning the contingent of four hundred or so English exiles joined Charles VIII's procession which made its way out of the city and onto poor tracks west towards Evreux. The day was wet, and the English company were not in the best of spirits. Some of them had spent years in exile and were beginning to wonder if they would ever see home again. Neville lolloped beside Leo and Dickon, who rode behind their mother. She was after all these years of travelling an accomplished horsewoman and needed no chaperone, although Tony hired a groom who would see to all their horses when they stopped and camped for the night. The journey was uneventful, and they arrived in the cathedral town in the afternoon of the third day.

Tony was immediately involved with his master, closeted together with the Earl of Oxford, James Blount and the Marquis of Dorset, as well as other senior gentlemen who were riding in Henry's cause.

'It's good news, Meg!' Tony told her later. 'The reconciliation has taken place and the warring parties laid down their arms. We move to Rouen where there will be celebrations. Henry hopes there'll be talks as to how Charles and his government can help us. We'll be asking for further help, especially with money.'

'I'm glad to hear it, Anthony!' As usual in times of crisis she called him by his full name. 'I hope this means you'll receive payment at last?' For Tony had not been remunerated for some weeks and, although she was doing her best, debts were beginning to mount up.

'Don't worry, Magpie,' he would laugh when she brought her concerns to him. 'Everyone knows I work for the future King of England—we've never defaulted with any tradesmen. We paid our dues before we left Paris, didn't we?'

'Yes, but we have horses to feed and stable, as well as two servants who need their wages. They'll leave us if we can't pay them.'

'Of course they won't. They know they'll be all right in the end—it would be too big a gamble for them to walk away and lose everything.'

But Meg was worried that Tony was gambling their own future on a success which was by no means guaranteed. It was not like him to put all his eggs in one basket, and she wondered what it was that made him do so this time. If there was an invasion and if Henry Richmond came off worst in any battle, all those who supported him would lose their heads, unless they could get out and go back where they came from. She had no wish to become a permanent exile in France. She wanted her boys' future to be in England; for them to become English gentlemen. Besides, however long she'd been away, she missed London and her friends. It would be two years in August since she left. Monty's boy would be thirteen in November and their daughters eleven. She had received a brief report of their friends from Tony following his last visit, but she longed to sit with Gisella, Monty, Jack and Pom and hear all their news. She was very fond of Monty's wife and their children. She knew that Thomas Pickle was held as a friend by Leo and Dickon. All that would be put at risk if this venture failed.

*I knew what it would be like marrying a rascal like Tony*! she sighed. *It was exciting to begin with, but his many absences and the perils of his work have caused me more anxiety than I should have to bear. Things must change when—if—we get home. We must have a settled life. But that's only possible if Tony has backed the right side*!

\*\*\*\*\*\*

'This preface, Monty. I think you're right; there's nothing to take issue with here. Caxton's been fair, although he does go on a bit about the Nine Worthies and whether Arthur really existed.'

'Did you note his reference to "Many noble and divers gentlemen came often and demanded why I have not made an imprint of the noble history of the Grail"?'

'Yes, I did, and I wonder who these "divers gentlemen" were! Perhaps he was thinking of our demonstration to the treasurer and the mayor.'

'No doubt. But you noticed how he has given credit to Sir Tom?'

'Yes—this phrase here—' and Jack took up the manuscript. 'It says: *Under the favour and correction of noble lords and gentlemen.* You know, Monty, he seems very fond of these oblique references to great men while naming no names! I wonder why that is? Anyway, he goes on: *…enprised to imprint a book of the noble histories of King*

*Arthur, and of certain knights*, and then we come to it, *after a copy unto me delivered, which copy Sir Thomas Malory did take out of certain books of French and reduced it to English.* I take it "reduced" is not in the pejorative sense of "lessen the quality"?'

'No, he simply means "translated".'

'There's no further mention of Sir Tom.'

'Unfortunately not until the very end. We originally had Malory's two references to himself as author, and I say had, because Caxton's taken one of them out.'

'Which one was it?'

'At the end of Book 4, Malory put in a sentence which seemed to suggest it was the end of the entire book, but, as he explained to me, it was simply the end of the story of how Sir Lancelot and Sir Tristram came to Arthur's court. There was a direct reference to Sir Tom being a prisoner. Listen:

*Who that will make anymore, let him seek other books of King Arthur or of Sir Lancelot or Sir Tristram; for this was drawn by a knight prisoner, Sir Thomas Malory, that God send him good recovery.*

'It seems rather strange for Sir Tom to have put it there, Monty?'

'He said he wanted to whet the readers' appetites and ensure they continued to "enjoy the book". I think he also wanted people to know the conditions he was writing the work under.'

'So do you think Caxton's taken it out because of this reference to Sir Tom being in jail?'

'Perhaps; I don't know. But I'm going to ask him.'

'But he left the second reference in?'

'Yes, at the very end where Sir Tom rounded the whole work off and asks the reader to pray for his soul etcetera. He also gave the date the book was completed. Caxton's left all that in, so perhaps the first omission's not so serious.'

'Do you agree with the rest of it—the preface I mean?'

'I have no argument with it. Although I thought I'd make things easier for the reader by inserting a table of contents, and Caxton has agreed. There were two additions to the book I would have had included—I suggested them to Sir Tom many times, but he always turned them down. I thought we should have a glossary of some of the more arcane words. There are many terms connected with chivalry, for example, which may be unknown, especially to female readers—and remember, Sir Tom always meant the book to be read by both sexes.'

'That sounds reasonable to me, Monty. What was the second?'

'That we had a list of characters at the back—who they were and who they were related to. There must be well over two hundred different names in the story—there are upwards of one hundred and twenty knights of the Round Table for a start—not to mention the multiple dwarves, giants, and the many ladies which appear. I find it confusing and I helped prepare it!'

'Why did Sir Tom turn down the idea?'

'He said it would be patronising for his audience, but I think he was just too lazy—or exhausted with it to bother, although I offered to do it myself. Caxton was equally dismissive, but that was because of time and cost.'

'Well, perhaps Sir Tom was right. The readers will be so enamoured of the stories they'll keep up.'

'The irony is he always reckoned that modern audiences have very short attention spans. "Mister Pickle", he told me, "there are too many fucking distractions these days. People can't concentrate!" He put it down to dicing, dancing and dogfighting!'

'It sounds as though, overall, Caxton will do our friend justice. I thought the preface read well, and, if you can iron out this problem with Sir Tom's comments at the end of Book 4, in your position I would be happy with it. How long do you think it will take you to compose it and get the pages set up?'

'I'm a third of the way through. Inkin' is helping me and I'm working on having it ready for you by the beginning of July.'

'So, it's mid-May now—that gives you six or seven weeks.'

'We're hoping you'll do a presentation copy—perhaps for the king?'

'Which one—King Richard or King Henry?'

Monty put his fingers to his lips, 'Dangerous words, Jack! But who knows?'

# Chapter 13

The month of August brings fulfilment for all; Jack plays an
ace;
Henry Richmond gambles everyone's future.

Nobody did know. By mid-June in the year '85, uncertainty
was in the air—but as usual with matters of great "weight and
importance", only those who had anything to lose were
agitated over them. The citizens of London went about their
daily business, grumbling as usual about prices, taxes, wages,
street crime, idle youth, foreigners and, of course the weather.
The fact that there may or may not have been a vast army
collecting on the other side of the Channel ready to invade
was neither here nor there to them; life with all its irritations
would roll along as usual. This side of the water some men
saw it as an opportunity—money to be made selling their
skills or hiring themselves out to the highest bidder; others
were anticipating being mustered to fight whether they liked
it or not. The king issued an order for everyone to "be
prepared", although exactly what the preparation would be for
was not explained, apart from dire warnings concerning "the
king's rebels"—the language not exactly clear here either:
were they rebels *of* the king, or rebels *against* the king?
Richard had also issued stern predictions of what would

happen should Henry Richmond, of non-regal stock on both sides of his family, be successful in helping himself to the crown. Not only was this mongrel prepared to sully the royal line, but information hastily posted up told the citizens that, to win French assistance, the beggarly earl had surrendered all rights of England to the throne of France and had even offered to hand back Calais—an unthinkable and perfidious action.

As those libertine companions Lady Rumour, Dame Speculation and Goodwife Gossip made play in the streets, avoiding the stern disapproval of the austere Duchess Fact, inside the hum and clatter of the Westminster Press Monty was busy composing the last pages of *Le Morte D'Arthur* or *The Most Ancient and Famous History of the Most Renowned Prince Arthur King of Britain* as it was ostentatiously displayed on the first page. But as he sat at his table he wasn't contemplating how he would feel when the last letter was placed in the last line of the last page, although that thought had occupied his mind of late. He was more concerned that there was something up with Jack Worms.

'Gisella, he's not himself. He seems distracted, which isn't like him at all. Especially now we are nearing the end of our great enterprise. He's always so sharp and to the point. For the last three weeks, he's been very vague and disappears for hours on end. We invited him for supper last week and he made an excuse. Have we ever known him to turn down an offer of one of your meals?'

'No, Monty, I was surprised. You don't think he's ill and doesn't want to tell us?'

'No, he's not worried in that way—just not very communicative. But it's these disappearances which are intriguing. I've no idea where he goes.'

'It's a woman, Monty! Or else he's got religion!'

'Religion? Jack's just about as religious as the rest of us—attends mass, confession and the rest, but I'd hardly say he was pious. Are you suggesting he's become devout? I see no signs of it! But a woman—well, that's just as unlikely. Jack's a perennial bachelor and, although I know he likes women, I've never heard him say he wished to change his status.'

'These things can happen late in life. Look at us. You always said that marriage had never been something you thought about.'

'Until I met you, and that completely changed my mind, Gisella! If it is a woman, I hope he finds as much happiness with her as I have with you. But I don't think you're right. He would have told me—after all I see him every day and consider myself to be his greatest friend—with Pom of course.'

'What does Pom think?'

'I haven't mentioned it to him—I didn't want to worry him. He has enough on his mind with this threatened invasion, and all the activity in the Channel. He was grumbling that it has disrupted trade badly.'

'Well, if you're so concerned, there's only one thing we can do—ask Jack what's wrong straight out. Why don't we invite him for supper—with Pom—and get him to talk to us.'

'I'll talk to Pom first, but Jack's gone very secretive; I'm not sure he'll come.'

'You won't know until you ask him.'

'I'll try, but don't be disappointed if he refuses.'

******

There was a certain measure of disappointment in Rouen among the followers of Henry Richmond. Tony pulled off his boots and unlaced his doublet with a sigh. He'd just returned home from a meeting of the regional court. 'This is all taking so long; I don't think Henry will get as much money as he needs.' It was the end of June and there had been intense negotiations between Charles VIII's ministers and Richmond and his friends. 'There's to be a final meeting tomorrow and then we'll see what the French are prepared to give us.'

'Will it be men and money, or just money?'

'Richmond's trying for both—and ships.'

'If he gets what he needs, when is the invasion likely to take place?'

'These things take time to organise, but I would say sometime in August.'

'And you will be among the earl's party?'

'Of course, Meg. He's offered me a captaincy and two hundred men if we get them. I'm to serve under the Earl of Oxford with James Blount.'

Meg was silent. She was expecting it; Sir Anthony Tanner would not be denied a part in any action. It would be pointless to object, so, as a good soldier's wife, she made no comment, just nodded and said, 'Make sure you speak to Leo and Dickon before you go. Answer their questions honestly, because I don't want to dissemble when they ask me what you're doing and why.'

'The politics of this adventure are too complicated for young boys, Meg!' protested Tony.

'They're old enough to understand that a soldier must do his duty. It's up to you to explain where that duty lies.'

'Are you questioning whether Henry Richmond has the right to claim the throne of England?'

'I don't know enough about it. All I can say is, should you not return, I wouldn't like Leo or Dickon to think you died for a treasonable cause.'

'I'm convinced Richmond's right to oppose a child-killer—you must agree with that?'

'It's all a matter of evidence, Tony. We've been too far away from it all and have heard only one side.'

'But we've been through it many times—we can be sure he didn't do the deed himself, but surely he must have given the order, whether directly or obliquely like Henry II did to the knights who murdered Thomas Becket. Either way he was responsible.'

'Well, whatever happened, the truth will come out one day, I'm sure. For now, I just ask you to talk to your boys.' She didn't add, *In case you never see them again.* There was always that possibility.

\*\*\*\*\*\*

'That was excellent, as usual, Gisella, thank you!' And Jack Worms sat back in his chair and beamed at her. 'Thanks to you too, my friend,' he said, turning to John Appleby. 'As usual, you have provided the best wine a man could enjoy!'

'My pleasure, Jack!' And Pom raised his glass. 'I endorse Master Worms comments, Gisella, another tasty supper! How we two bachelors would manage without you, I don't like to think.' He looked meaningfully at Monty as though he felt he had paved the way for his friend to introduce the topic on both their minds. Monty drew a deep breath and simply said, 'Is everything all right with you, Jack?'

'Yes, why shouldn't it be?'

'I was saying to Pom the other day, I thought you seemed to have something on your mind—apart from work, which you always take in your stride. I sensed you might be worried about something.'

'Ah—I see. I wondered why this invitation came unexpectedly.' He turned to Gisella, 'I know I take supper here at least once every two weeks, but this was a surprise— and to have Pom here as well, when we know he's very involved with his businesses. Well, they say you can't keep anything from good friends—or curious wives! And, speaking of wives, you might as well know—I'm getting married!'

There was a predictable audible intake of breath from his friends, then a silence borne of total shock and which lasted for a full ten seconds. When Gisella had mentioned "a woman", Monty had quietly dismissed the idea. Jack had made no mention or shown any recent sign of an interest in women generally and certainly no one in particular.

Pom broke the silence, 'So, are you going to tell us about her—her name, how you met—when you met—for you have been very silent on this, my friend?' It sounded almost like an admonition and Jack nodded, rather shamefaced.

'I apologise for springing this on you. I was going to announce it at the same time as I introduced by betrothed.'

Monty stood up immediately and grasped his friend's hand. Pumping it up and down he said, 'I'm delighted, Jack. This couldn't be better news!'

'You mean I shall avoid a bachelor's lonely old-age—no disrespect, Pom. You're such a confirmed singleton and have all of us as a family; life with a wife at this stage would probably kill you!'

Monty thought this was typical of Jack's capacity for tactlessness, as though Pom had never had it in him to sustain a marriage. But the old man took it as a great jest, laughed and slapped Jack on the back. 'Congratulations you old dog! I only wish Sir Tom was here—he would know exactly what to say—probably something like *Fu...*' But Monty gave him a warning look, and Pom, remembering he was in company, thought again. 'Something like "Good for you"!' he said lamely. 'Now, tell us all about her.'

'She's a widow, thirty-six and her name is Maria Tewkesbury.'

'Tewkesbury—that's somewhere in Gloucestershire, isn't it?' observed Monty.

Pom nodded, 'Yes, there was a battle there—Edward IV defeated Queen Margaret back in '71, less than two months after Sir Tom died.'

'Yes, but my Maria,' and Gisella marked the "my", 'has nothing to do with that town, although the family might have hailed from there in the past. No, she runs her own business. She's a milliner.'

Pom sat up very interested, 'Ah! I thought I recognised the name. Is she the proprietress of a shop on Lombard Street?'

'Yes, she's been there some years. Do you know her?'

'I've heard nothing but good things, Jack,' Pom said reassuringly. 'I don't deal in millinery myself, but as traders we meet sometimes at the guildhall and other places. I don't know anything about her husband—when he died or whether she has children.'

'She's been a widow for five years and has no children.'

'I'm interested in how you met, Jack,' said Gisella with a smile. 'I can't imagine you frequenting a milliner's!'

'Would you believe she came to see Mistress Maud Caxton—about trimmings for hats. She came into my section of the works to ask how to find Caxton's wife and I escorted her to their living quarters.'

'The elusive Mistress Caxton!' Pom frowned. 'I wonder why we hardly ever see her—or their daughter?'

'Never mind that, Pom, what happened after that? When was this anyway?'

'About six weeks ago, Monty. We seemed to like each other instantly, although we have nothing in common—'

'—Except you both have businesses,' Pom reminded him.

'But I know nothing of hats and Maria knows even less about the book trade!' And Jack looked round at his friends, wondering what they all really thought. *It's probably: Silly old fool—looking for someone to take care of him in his old age!* This was categorically untrue; for the first time in his life he felt a strong passion for another person. He woke in the morning with a sense of joy that he would see her later and went to sleep at night with her name on his mind and an image of her face in his head. *Is this romantic love?* he asked himself. It was certainly different from the lascivious emotion which he had seen active in the Newgate Tower when Sir Tom entertained his whorelets. Which reminded him there was the physical side to consider, and he was not a little daunted at the prospect of lying with a woman for the first time. *I'll have to ask Monty; he'll know because it happened to him later in his life*. He didn't relish the interview, but neither did he want to make a ham-fisted attempt at marital congress on their first night. But for now, he was pleased that his friends seemed to be delighted for him. He promised to bring Maria to meet them all as soon as it could be arranged.

After their guests had left, Monty turned to Gisella and said, 'I didn't see that coming! But you were as astute as ever, wife; well done!'

******

'This is not well done, Master Urswick! Not the news I was either expecting or hoping for. Is this rumour, speculation—or does it come from a reliable source?'

'I heard it discussed in the corridors of Westminster as I left, my lord. Your mother the countess fears that Queen Elizabeth may have been persuaded by Richard of Gloucester to support him.'

'Why on earth would she do that? The man who killed her children?'

'This is what is said, my lord. I cannot explain it.'

Henry Richmond punched his right fist into the palm of his left hand in a fury; then he rang a small bell; within seconds a servant appeared. 'Bring the Marquis of Dorset here!' As the man departed in a hurry, Richmond turned to his mother's confidential agent. 'He'll answer for his mother if this is true.'

Minutes passed and there was no sign of the servant. In a temper, Richmond rang his bell again. Another servant appeared. 'Where is the bastard Lord Grey—I sent someone for him long ago.'

'My lord, we are searching the palace for him, but he's nowhere to be found.'

'Fuck it! Check the stables—see if his horse is gone. If it has, ask the guards at the gates whether he's passed through—and if he has, how long ago.'

The servant, thoroughly scared and fearing a whipping, nodded, hesitated and then said, 'My lord, I saw him but a quarter of an hour ago. He was leaving his chamber with his servant.'

'Was the servant carrying anything?'

'Yes sir—a pack, and the marquis was in his outdoor clothes.'

'He'll be heading for Le Havre; but have all the roads checked around Rouen. I want the man found and brought to me! But make it seem like I've sent him on a mission, changed my mind and want him back. There must be no gossip put about that the marquis has defected. Urswick—how long has this been going on—this treachery?'

'My most recent intelligence is that six weeks ago Richard of Gloucester issued a list of your supporters and denounced them as traitors. The marquis was not on that list. This was what alerted your mother to the possibility he had changed sides.'

'Clever woman, my mother. I only wish I'd known earlier. But we'll catch the caitiff and squeeze the truth out of him. However, even when we do catch him, we have a problem in England if Elizabeth has changed her mind about the marriage between myself and her daughter.'

'There was this story put about the city that Richard planned to marry the Lady Elizabeth of York himself.'

'Even I don't believe that! An uncle marrying his niece—unheard of except among the ancient Egyptians! No, Richard's offered her something worth her forgetting he murdered her two boys. But I can't imagine what it is!'

'Does this change your plans in any way, sir? If so, perhaps I should return immediately to England and tell your mother, Lady Beaufort.'

'It hastens them, Urswick. I must go to Charles and settle the money question immediately; impress on him the need for a decision. If he agrees the sum he's prepared to lend us, I intend to bring the invasion forward by at least two weeks. You can tell my mother, all things going well—at least better than they are at present—I intend to cross the Channel at the end of July.'

******

'End of July you said, Mister Pickle!' And Master Caxton sat back in his chair looking expectantly at his translator and compositor.

'Indeed, and the first copy will on your desk on 31$^{st}$. Master Worms has it in his vice as we speak and is already cutting some beautiful leather—deepest brown. It will be a—a—'

'—Long time coming, Mister Pickle! Tell me again, when did Sir Thomas Malory finish it?'

'The actual composition was completed at the end of the year '70, but we finished checking it in March the following year. Just before he died, sir.'

'It sounds like it finished *him* off!' laughed the printer, who rarely made a jest.

Monty smiled wanly. He remembered well the days after Sir Tom had laid down his pen—how bereft he was. 'You may well be right, sir. Fifteen years of one's life devoted to one work must certainly leave a void.'

'Well, I look forward to seeing the book on my desk as soon as Master Worms has worked his magic. By the by, I hear we must congratulate our friend—on his forthcoming marriage to Mistress Tewksbury; I understand she's my wife's milliner. Have you met her?'

'Yes sir. My wife and I entertained Master Worms and Mistress Tewksbury to supper a few days ago. We were very taken with the lady.'

It was true. Monty and Gisella had found her charming. A quiet well-spoken woman, small and plump, with impeccable manners. She exuded an air of capability which obviously came from her status as a business woman who managed her affairs with competence. Pom had discreetly asked about her among his trading friends and the report was that she was solvent, honest and well-respected as a woman in business. The respect came from the fact that she paid her bills fully and on time—an asset highly-valued among the merchant community in any commodity, be it wool and wood or hats and haberdashery.

At first a little shy, understandably so when she was being discreetly scrutinised by Jack's "greatest and long-standing friends", as he introduced them, she soon warmed to their welcome. She knew something of Pom and his reputation as a well-respected city merchant.

'I hear there is a rumour you may soon be elected an alderman, Mister Appleby—'

'—Pom, please! Yes, I have been approached.'

'You said nothing to us, Pom,' Jack sounded reproachful.

'It's only just been put to me.'

'Next step it'll be Mayor Appleby,' laughed Monty, 'and well deserved too!'

'Let's not get ahead of ourselves! Rather we should concentrate on Jack and Maria's wedding. I presume we're all invited! You're not planning to elope, Jack?'

'That would be romantic—but entirely unnecessary! No, we plan to marry in Maria's parish church of All Hallows on Lombard Street.'

'Have we a date?'

'The 7th August. I will have long finished binding *Le Morte* and have already arranged with Master Caxton to take a break for three weeks.'

'I take it he's invited?'

'Certainly, and his wife and daughter.'

'I wonder if they'll come?' Gisella frowned, and then said to Maria. 'Master Caxton's wife is rarely seen. We have invited them both to supper several times; he has come, but she always has some excuse—illness mostly. But of course, you'll know more about her than us,' and Gisella looked hopefully at Maria.

'I've only just started attending on her. As you say, she is a very retiring woman—polite and well-bred—but seems reluctant to go abroad. She has never visited my shop; I always visit her.'

Monty nodded, 'She never comes to the print-shop. I wonder what she does all day. Her daughter is a pale skinny thing, about fourteen I would say. She's painfully shy and never goes abroad without her mother.'

Jack said, 'Caxton has already accepted an invitation for all three, so we'll see if they turn up.'

'Have you any relatives in London, Maria?' asked Gisella, anxious to know as much about their new friend as possible.

'Not in the city, but I have a sister in Highgate and she has several children. She's married to a master carpenter. She'll be coming, but apart from them and yourselves, it'll be a small gathering.'

'There's no chance of Tony and Meg being there I suppose?' asked Pom.

'We haven't heard a word since he went back to France,' said Monty. He wondered how much they should discuss these things in front of a stranger. Had Jack divulged to Maria all he knew of their friend and his employment in the service of Henry Richmond? Monty considered that he probably had. *Jack's an open type of fellow. He wouldn't want to have secrets from his future wife.* All the same, Monty decided to err on the side of caution and be circumspect in what he said. He therefore steered the conversation away from the current tense situation in the city to more pleasurable domestic matters, like the latest achievements of his two daughters.

By the end of the evening, they were all assured of each other's good intentions and gratified at the chance of new friendships. Pom, Monty and Gisella were particularly happy for Jack, who throughout the evening sat beaming, and when he wasn't helping himself to the excellent food on top of Gisella's table, sat holding his future bride's hand beneath it.

\*\*\*\*\*\*

'They caught him in Compiegne, Magpie, riding away from the coast. It seems he was heading for Flanders. Anyway, the French have taken Dorset and are using him as surety for the money Charles has now agreed to lend Henry— forty thousand francs.'

'So you'll be off then?'

'Well, not immediately. It'll take time to muster the men and get them to Harfleur. I would say we'll be leaving here in a week.'

'How many men?'

'About three thousand French and a thousand of us.'

'That's hardly enough for an invasion, Tony!'

'The good news is that Lord Stanley has twenty thousand men waiting for us in Wales, where we'll be landing. One of Lady Beaufort's agents arrived this morning with the news. Richmond's face was a picture—beaming from ear to ear! He can't wait, and neither can I, Meg. This is what we've been planning for months.'

As always, Meg smiled and nodded and kept her anxiety to herself. At this time, her thoughts were with her boys and Tony's promise to "talk to them" before he left. 'You'll find time to do it, won't you?' she reminded him later.

'I'll do it tomorrow evening—take them fishing. Will that make you happy?'

'It's not a matter of making me happy; it's you doing the right thing by them, Anthony.'

'When you call me Anthony, I know I must pay attention, Magpie. Don't worry, I'll keep my word.'

\*\*\*\*\*\*

'Well, Master Worms, you kept your word and here is the complete *Morte D'Arthur* finished on time.' Caxton fingered the smooth polished chestnut-brown leather of the cover of the folio lying on his desk and sniffed its aroma. He opened it up and grunted with satisfaction at the sight of the first page; he then turned to the Preface.

'I think the first sentence is important, Mister Pickle. You see the purpose in it?'

'I do, sir. It does the Westminster Press no harm for its patrons to know you have: *Accomplished and finished divers histories*—'

'—*As well as contemplation of other historical and worldly acts of great conqu*erors and I mark the next words as also important: *And also certain books of example and doctrine.* I want our patrons to know we are not only concerned with histories but can compete in some areas with our friends in Oxford. You note I have confirmed my part in all this. The final words are vital too,' and he turned to the last page of the heavy volume. 'I think you will agree with me, *Caxton me fieri fecit* leaves no doubt that the work comes from my presses. You are pleased with the work, Mister Pickle?'

In truth, Monty didn't know what to say. He should have felt overwhelmed with the occasion but was concerned that it all seemed somewhat of an anti-climax. He had waited and longed for this day; Sir Thomas' work was safe—it could be disseminated without risk of plagiarism—he had faithfully transposed the work to type-face which made it almost indestructible. The original manuscript was safe in his hands and he could fulfil the promise of the Newgate Fellowship and deliver it to the monks in Winchester—Malory's Camelot. He looked at the pristine pages, the crisp black print, every word legible. And Jack had done his best work with the binding. But he had the same feeling he remembered when he and Sir Tom had looked around the small Newgate cell where small piles of the completed manuscript occupied every available surface. *Where do I go from here*? he thought.

However, he had no intention of diminishing the occasion and said, 'I am very satisfied, Master Caxton. When Sir Tom put the last word down—with a flourish as we might have expected!—I had no thought in my head that it would be one of the first books to be produced using the new method. You know, when Sir Tom first told me about printing I was horrified. I thought it meant I would be obsolete as a manuscript writer; lose my livelihood. He was more confident and, had he lived, would have embraced printing with total enthusiasm.'

'I think he would have been pleased with what we have accomplished, Mister Pickle.'

'This presentation copy, sir. To whom will you dedicate it?'

'I had thought of a posthumous dedication to Earl Rivers, but after careful consideration that might not be wise. I propose to present it to the king.'

'King Richard will be pleased, sir, although he has much to concern himself.'

'I've heard the rumours. The Earl of Richmond is in the southern Channel heading towards Wales. So, when I say "king" I think we should wait and see!'

\*\*\*\*\*\*

'Who will it be, father? Who will win?' asked Dickon, getting straight to the point.

'Father and Lord Henry, dolthead!' scoffed Leo. 'The earl will have—er—', and he began to tot up with his fingers.

'Twenty-nine thousand men!' said Dickon triumphantly. He was much quicker at addition than his brother. 'Three thousand Fr—'

'—Yes, yes—we know the numbers. How many men will you have in your charge, father?'

'Two hundred men-at-arms, Leo.'

'Can we come?'

His father looked sternly at his boy who was standing knee-deep in the shallows of the River Seine, supposedly on the look-out for the monster pike which had been eluding hopeful spearfishermen for weeks. 'Certainly not.'

'But Lord Richmond himself called us "resourceful"; we could be of great help.'

'I think escaping from a tower, however courageous, no way compares with what is needed on a battlefield. Besides, whatever would your mother say if I agreed? And that was what I wanted to talk to you about. While I'm away, you must heed what she says—no wandering off without letting her know exactly where you're going. Take complete responsibility for Neville and clear up after him—it's not for your mother to organise it. You will have to be the men of the house—'

'—I'm the man of the house because I'm the eldest.'

'There's truth in that, Leo, but Dickon is sometimes more sensible than you and worth listening to, especially when you're seized with mischief! Even though I'm not at home so much, I know how your mind works, lad. When I return, if I have bad reports, you can expect the worst!'

'You will be coming back then?' And Dickon looked up at Tony with a slight frown.

'Why shouldn't I—I've always come back!'

'Mother says this time it's very serious and if Lord Richmond loses then you'll all be executed on the battlefield—heads chopped off!'

'Dickon, I'm sure your mother said nothing of the sort! Anyway, I intend to keep my head on my shoulders and Lord Richmond intends to win.'

'Will he be king then?'

'Yes, King Henry VII.'

'How long for? The others haven't lasted too long, according to what mother told us.'

'Edward IV did well—twelve years with a short break,' said Tony.

Leo frowned, 'Richard has only been king for a little while, and now he might lose his throne. Why does it keep happening? Is it because he killed his nephews? That's what the French boys say.'

'If I was to try to explain we'd be here long after this old pike was dead and rotting in the mud. All you need to know is, when we win it will be the start of a new life for us all.'

'A new life?' echoed Dickon. 'What do you mean?'

'We'll be able to return to England and I expect Lord Richmond, or King Henry as he will be, will show his gratitude and—'

'—What's "gratitude"?' asked Dickon.

'Show how pleased he is with me—us.'

Leo grinned, 'Give you money you mean?' There was a streak of mercenary shrewdness in Tony's older son.

'Yes, and perhaps land.'

'Will he make you an earl? After all, if he's king, who'll be Earl of Richmond?'

'No, I'm sure he won't make me an earl. A baron perhaps.'

'Is that better than a knight?'

'It can be.'

'What will mother be?'

'A baroness. But boys, we run before our cart to market. I return to my order to you which is to take care of your mother and cause her no distress. She is going to be worried during the next weeks, and you must be a comfort to her. I need your word and your hand,' and he held out his own and Leo, with some ceremony, took it firmly and shook it. His brother did likewise.

'Right, we all know where we stand. Let's see if we can sort out this fish!'

But the pike had plans of his own and was far away pursuing them in a different stretch of the river entirely.

\*\*\*\*\*\*

The 7$^{th}$ August. A date of great importance to all members of the Newgate Fellowship. It was the day of Jack and Maria's wedding. Also on that day Sir Anthony Tanner, in the service of Henry Tudor, Earl of Richmond, landed with his master on the coast of Wales at Milford Haven.

It was a dull day in London, but Mistress Tewkesbury, with all the trimmings to hand, had decked herself out with a bright array of colours and a hat which she had fashioned with her own fingers. Apart from the bride, and her brother-in-law who was to give her away, the rest walked together as a merry party to All Hallows where the two were waiting with the priest outside the doors. Mistress Caxton and her daughter had regretfully declined the invitation, but Master Caxton was present, smiling through his beard. The usual customs were observed, rings exchanged, pledges made before they entered, and a mass said for the couple.

Gisella, with Maria's help had offered to prepare the wedding feast and two other unexpected offers followed; one from Mistress Tewkesbury's sister who brought a purse of silver as contribution to the expense and the other from Master Caxton who offered one of his workshops as a venue, having it cleared out, cleaned and decorated at his own cost. 'I can do nothing less for a loyal and valued employee,' he explained when Jack sought him out to thank him. The bride and groom were, as they announced when the toasts were made, "overwhelmed by the kindness of their friends". Gisella was also happy, since Maria made her a new hat and gloves, and expertly trimmed one of her few gowns, making it "very special" according to the recipient of the milliner's kind thought.

It had been decided that Maria would move into Jack's house, which, although a bachelor residence, was spacious and well fitted out.

'Will you be keeping the shop now you are married, Maria?' asked Pom.

'I see no reason not to, Pom. It will provide us with another income.'

Gisella wanted to ask if Maria had considered children, but felt it was not the time or the place. She knew Jack and Monty had talked about these matters, for her husband had confided in her when they lay in the darkness of their bedchamber. 'It was all very difficult, Gisella. He came to me for advice on very intimate things which I found hard to discuss.'

'But, pardon me for reminding you, you were in the same situation when we were first married—inexperienced.'

'Well, I had a patient teacher!'

'I was as new to it as you were, husband, and unlike me, Maria's been married before and knows what to expect. I'm sure she'll be gentle with him! But, I'm curious; what did you say to him?'

'Just that as he has expressed how much he loves the woman, once he lies with her, nature will take its course!'

'That was it—that's all you said?'

'Well, it wasn't for me to tell him what goes where, Gisella! Surely he can work that out for himself!'

'But there are certain actions to go through beforehand; ways to induce a woman to pleasure.'

'Really, Gisella! I couldn't start going into that kind of detail.'

'You old hypocrite! You've had enough practice.'

'It's not the kind of thing one man tells another—unless it's father to son, and my father never even mentioned it. I had no idea women were any different to men until I was fourteen and I caught sight of one of my sisters swimming naked in the local lake. It was a shock I can tell you!'

'That was daring of her!'

'It wasn't so much a voluntary swim, rather one of my other sisters had pushed her in and her shift fell off when she struggled to get out. They were a bad-tempered set of girls! Is it any wonder I wasn't keen on women—until I met you of course!'

'Talking of fathers and sons, this is a conversation you should be having with Thomas. I noticed him taking more than a passing interest in one of Maria's nieces when they came to visit. He'll be thirteen in November.'

'Yes, I realise. Not to be put off then?'

'No, it must be tackled, Monty, and soon. Seize the day!'

\*\*\*\*\*\*

'*Carpe Diem*! Wasn't that one of Sir Thomas Malory's favourite sayings?' The Earl of Oxford had come up behind the leading troop to find Captain Tanner. 'I've heard many of the stories about the old caitiff. I never met him, but Lord Warwick knew him and held him in some esteem I believe.'

'Indeed, my lord. Sir Thomas was a loyal supporter of the earl, even from his prison cell in Newgate.'

'Well, we have certainly "seized the day". Tomorrow we should reach Shrewsbury before pushing on to meet Lord Stanley and his troops.'

It was 14th August and they had been on the march for a week, through Wales and across the border into Shropshire. If Henry had hoped for recruits to join him on the way, he was disappointed. Few men came out for him, in fact there was uncertainty about the right of his cause; his claim to the throne was very indirect. Besides, men had had enough of this perpetual scrapping for the crown. Harvest was coming; this was not the time to down-scythes and take up arms. There was equal reluctance to respond to Richard's call for "all sound men to muster to their lords".

'Let them get on with it and cause us as least disturbance as possible. We're paying in taxes for this war; I for one won't pay with my blood. I lost two uncles at Towton—and for what—it all happening again?' This was the general tenor of comment around the parish pump and inside the parish tavern.

'Have we heard anything about the size of Richard's army?' Tony asked Oxford.

'The rumour is it's anything between four and seven thousand. He's been in Nottingham recruiting—mostly his northerners.'

'We have Lord Stanley waiting, my lord.'

'We can no longer be sure of him, Sir Anthony. We heard this morning that he can't join us.'

'Can't or won't—why not?'

'Richard's holding Stanley's son George as hostage for his father's loyalty, although, of course, Stanley's brother William is possibly with us; we know he has three thousand men.'

'But we're without the twenty thousand Lord Stanley promised?'

'You know as well as I that an army's number doubles every time it's spoken of. I never believed that figure. As things stand, if William is loyal to us, both sides could be evenly matched. The only difference is that, besides probably having more artillery than us, Richard has ordered a large supply of handguns, which we don't have, at least not many and certainly not men trained to used them.'

'My experience of such ordnance is that it's "miss and hit"—miss with the thing and then hit the enemy over the head with it!'

Oxford chuckled, 'I agree. The other advantage for Richard is that he has loyal English soldiers and we're relying on French mercenaries. Let's hope they can fight as bravely for money as they can for a cause.'

'Where do we march to after Shrewsbury, my lord?' Tony asked.

'There will be a meeting this afternoon to plan our tactics. It's my guess we'll move east towards Richard's army as he's moving towards us from Nottingham. It will come to a fight soon, no doubt of that. We know from our scouts that the Duke of Norfolk is on his way up from Framlingham to join Gloucester; we have no news of the whereabouts of the Earl of Northumberland, but he must be riding down from the north as we speak. Both will bring Richard substantial numbers.

'Will you answer a straight question with a straight answer, my lord?'

'I'll try, Sir Anthony.'

'What are our chances of winning?'

'Slender, captain. Is that straight enough for you?'

\*\*\*\*\*\*

'Have you thought of going straightway to Winchester with the manuscript, Monty?' Jack Worms in the first flush of married life, sat with his friend in a tavern in Westminster after their day's work.

'It has been on my mind, Jack. There seems no reason why we shouldn't fulfil our oaths and see it safely stored at Sir Tom's "Camelot".

'Is Master Caxton happy for it to be stored there? It is his property after all.'

'Yes, he has been very generous about it. 'Mister Pickle,' he said, 'the manuscript must go where its originator intended. It will be safe with the monks of Winchester.' As far as us getting it to them, the more I consider how and when that is to be done, the more inclined I am to make it a substantial journey.'

'Substantial? How do you mean?'

'This was always about the Newgate Fellowship—you, me, Pom and Tony. We now have additions to that fellowship—wives and children. I would like to make it a real occasion—celebrating everything we've been through in the last sixteen years. I'd like us all to go.'

Jack thought for a moment, then said, 'I can have no argument about that, Monty, except Tony's not here. I presume he's somewhere marching towards a battlefield. And then there's Meg. She must still be in France otherwise she would surely have come here.'

'Hmm, that is so. What I propose is we wait and see the outcome of the invasion by Henry Richmond—'

'—Will he win or not? The odds are not in his favour, according to tittle-tattle.'

Monty frowned, 'Yes, but that's precisely what it is—gossip. There's been little reliable news coming through. The last I heard, Richmond was in Shrewsbury to meet Lord Stanley, and that was from a doubtful source—a chapman who heard it from a tinker who heard it from someone else, who heard it from—you know how it works!'

'I'm wondering what will happen to Meg if Tony is killed—or executed. It will be impossible for her to return here. She has no family and we are her only friends.'

'One of us will have to go to France to tell her, Jack, and help her make arrangements. Of course we'll all band together to help her and the boys, but I don't think Tony has any spare monies. He never was one to save!'

'Perhaps we're being too doleful. We know Tony has survived many battles and tight corners! Let's presume he comes out of this well, goes back to France and collects his family and then returns to us.'

'That would fit in perfectly with my "great idea"! We could all travel to Winchester together—like a band of pilgrims.'

'On the Pilgrims' Way. I like it, Monty!'

'Obviously we can't set aside a date until we know the outcome of the business between Richmond and the king, and that Tony's safe.'

'Let's hope we hear something soon, Monty!' And Jack drained his pot and stood up. 'Another?' And the two men sat for a further half-hour making plans.

\*\*\*\*\*\*

'The plan was to continue down Watling Street towards London, but our espials told us last night that Richard is marching to intercept us.' Henry Richmond had called his captains and sergeants to him. It was 19th August. 'Gloucester's turned off the Fosse Way and is heading towards Leicester. We march on to Merevale where we'll stop and spend the night in the abbey there. The Stanleys will join us and I hope to persuade them to stand with us—or at least not stand against us.'

'How far is Merevale from Leicester, my lord?'

'About a day's march, Captain Tanner.'

'So we're likely to engage with Richard the day after tomorrow?'

'It looks like it—or the day after that. We'll use the abbey as a base and send foragers out into the surrounding farms. I want you captains to ensure there's no pillaging. Make an account of what's taken and tell the farmers compensation will be paid. It's essential the locals don't see us as a ravening army.'

That evening Lord Stanley and his brother entered the abbey looking stern and left a half-hour later looker sterner.

\*\*\*\*\*\*

Early morning of 22$^{nd}$ August '85. Flat, open, wet fields somewhere in Leicestershire; the weather clear and bright. Richard's army, drawn up on the north-west side of a small river had been in position since the previous evening; his archers under the Duke of Norfolk already having prepared trenches and stakes against Henry's cavalry.

'Surprise—we'll take him with surprise tactics!' Henry looked out across the meadows. 'There seems to be little movement round Richard's quarters—hardly anyone stirring. Oxford, this marshy ground is very soft, so advance your men north at a medium pace. We'll have the advantage of the sun on our backs!' The captains dispersed back to their crews. De Vere walked across to Tony.

'Captain Tanner, you heard the earl's order. We advance round the marsh and confront Norfolk's archers, having deployed our own and artillery to cover our advance. While the enemy's archers and ordnance are thus engaged, bring your men up and be prepared for the duke's advance with his heavy cavalry. It's obvious even from here that Richard's deployed his army in wedge-shape—Norfolk in the van, Richard in the main and Northumberland rereward. The wedge means there'll inevitably be a mêlée, so, at all costs keep your men close-up to their standards; no man less than ten feet away from one, that way we'll all know where we are. Take your men to the right, I'll to the left. The object is to overwhelm Norfolk's archers and get them to run away. By the way, when were you last on a battlefield, Captain Tanner?'

'Apart from skirmishes in France, it was at Barnet in '71, sir.'

Oxford was silent for a moment, then he said, 'Well, it's not something one forgets—fighting in array! But, in the end it generally comes down to hand-to-hand, however organised we try to be. As Lord Richmond said, the best tactics are surprise and attacking the enemy's weak points, which is usually the flanks.'

Tony was not sure whether Oxford was giving him a short lecture on military tactics, or just testing his competence as a commander. What he did know was that it was Oxford's men who were partly instrumental in Lord Warwick's defeat at Barnet, when men in the earl's army mistook de Vere's star for King Edward IV's sun in the fog and began firing on their own side—at which Oxford's men ran off shouting "treason".

397

Perhaps he had been tactless to mention Barnet; but Oxford seemed unperturbed.

'Well, Tanner, you have your orders. Go to it!' And John de Vere cantered off to position himself for the first phase of the action. As Henry had observed, the sun was behind them and they could see it glinting on the armour of Norfolk's heavy cavalry. Tony peered into the distance, 'I estimate he has twelve hundred bowmen ready to engage us, sergeant.'

'Are those spearmen round the archers, and is that artillery, sir?'

'Certainly—and I think the artillery's chained—evidently to stop us penetrating beyond them. But we must overcome the Norfolk lines by going around them and get to the main army under Richard of Gloucester.' Tony held up his arm ready to give the signal for his men-at-arms to move out. The horses began to snort and pace the ground in anticipation. Tony had experience of war-horses' temperaments and knew they had a sixth sense when a battle was about to begin. He steadied his mount, a sixteen-hands gelding, part-armoured for action, as he was himself. The horse and all the gear were borrowed; he had no money to lay out on expensive trappings for war.

Tony heard Oxford's bugle and the order to fire. He was aware of the whine of arrows and the bangs of artillery from his own side, but the unreliable cannon balls widely missed their marks. Immediately there was a response from Norfolk's men. A stream of arrows came through the air with the familiar sound, and then silence as they glanced harmlessly off the armour of his men, before another stream came across. Having raised his arm to steady his men he dropped it and shouted, 'Let's to it!' kicking his horse into a canter and then a gallop towards Norfolk's flank and out of range of arrows and cannon. He saw immediately that the duke was at the back of his cavalry, sword drawn ready to fight, his horsemen now dispersing to seek individual quarries. He was aware of men on his right and left beginning to engage, some already on the ground battling hand-to-hand. Without a second thought Tony drew his sword and, singling out the senior nobleman, made a direct charge towards him. *Kill or be killed, Tony*! was the last thought in his mind as he yelled at his quarry, who turned in his saddle and saw a visored horseman bearing down on him.

John Howard was sixty-years of age and an experienced soldier. Anthony Tanner was almost forty, less competent as a strategist but fitter and quicker as a fighter. The younger man lunged forward, striking Norfolk across the back and almost dislodging him from his horse. The duke held up his sword to parry the next blow, but Tony was too quick and lunged again, this time using not only his weapon but his arm and fist to push the man out of his saddle. Norfolk landed on his arse and, heavily armoured, found it almost impossible to rise quickly. A young standard bearer also on his feet tried to assist his commander up, but Tony had now dismounted and, thrust his sword at the man's neck, who dodged and fell over backwards. 'Fuck off soldier—save yourself!' Scared and uncertain, the young man hesitated for a few seconds before turning his back and joining the rest of his brothers-in arms, who, seeing their commander was down had not stayed to assist him, but galloped off to another section of the field of battle. Tony turned to the duke who was still feebly attempting to rise, and he held out his hand, 'Will you fight?' Norfolk, wheezing heavily, nodded pulling on the proffered hand and getting to his feet. He recovered his sword and stood at guard. 'Come on, whoever you are—you fucking treacherous son of a whore!'

'Not so much of the traitor, your grace! Let's to it!'

They fought for a few minutes only. The duke was heavily built and slow and Tony parried his strokes with ease, nimbly enticing his opponent into mistakes and wasting energy. In the end, Tony pounded Howard's sword arm so that it hung uselessly, until the weapon was grounded. The tired old man began to buckle at the knees and, seeing his advantage, with little effort the younger man was able to pin the older to the ground, his knee on his stomach. John Howard looked up into the face of his assailant and shook his head. 'If you're going to do it, make it quick! Who are you by the way? It's good to know one's executioner.'

'Sir Anthony Tanner, your grace.'

'Never heard of you. A nobody—fucked over by a nobody!' He closed his eyes, took off his helmet and nodded his head, as though giving consent. Tony despatched the duke as he had often done before when putting wounded men out of their misery after a battle. A swift strike of a dagger to the neck and it was all over. The duke's eyes remained open staring back at him, until Tony gently closed them and then made the sign of the cross over the body. 'God send you to a peace, old man.' He stood up and took his horse from one of his men who, having ridden up to assist their captain, stood looking on with others of his crew. At the same time, the Earl of Oxford appeared.

'Fuck me! Is that the Duke of Norfolk you've just killed, captain?'

'It is, my lord.'

400

'We must ride to Lord Richmond and tell him. By Christ! This won't do you any harm, Tanner.'

'Have you any idea what the state of the battle is now, sir?'

'There was a bit of a lull. Both main armies withdrew for a while, apart from some small skirmishers.'

'Have we sustained many losses, sir?'

'Very few—no more than forty or so on our side,' said de Vere. He looked round, 'Good—now men, their commander despatched by your captain, I can see no signs of Norfolk's standard. I imagine the men left standing will have retreated to join Richard of Gloucester. We'll mop up the rest of the vanguard as we find them, then go and find out what's happening.'

******

What was happening was that Sir William Stanley had opted to join Richmond after all, although his brother remained uncommitted on the side lines. 'It's good to have you with us, William,' and Richmond grabbed Stanley's hand and pumped it up and down. 'How many men with you?'

'Two thousand horse, my lord, well-trained and keen. I've deployed them to the south-west of both armies, ready to cut in between Gloucester's main body of men and the Earl of Northumberland's army in the rereward. My brother still stands aloof—he'll not risk the life of his son, although he assures me he'll not lift a sword-hand against you.'

'That is—.' Richmond's opinion was left hanging in the air as a rider came up, horse and man breathing heavily. 'My lord, the king—I mean Richard of Gloucester—is leading a small band of cavalry and charging directly towards us.'

'How far away is Northumberland, Stanley?'

'Not near enough to intervene, sir.'

At that moment, the Earl of Oxford and Sir Anthony Tanner arrived with the news of Norfolk's death and the capture or flight of most of his men.

The king gripped de Vere's hand, 'Best news so far, Oxford—that means their van's obsolete. With Northumberland seemingly undecided, it's just Gloucester's cavalry and ourselves. You say it's a small group of horsemen with Richard, soldier?'

'Yes my lord. I would say he's outnumbered three-to-one!'

'It sounds a strange thing to do—perhaps he's run mad!'

De Vere frowned, 'He's after you, sir; we all know once a leader is bested the battle's over. We'll all be watching your back.'

'Let's to it then! With odds-of-three to one we can't fail,' and Richmond spurred his mount and, with increasing speed rode off towards his enemy who was charging towards them. The two groups soon engaged and to Tony's horror he saw Henry's standard bearer, Sir William Brandon cut down. The man was only a few feet from Henry himself, but who was immediately surrounded by supporters. Then ensued fierce hand-to-hand fighting, with Richard of Gloucester in the centre of the mêlée. What happened next, as Tony told his friends afterwards, 'Will be talked about by generations to come! Henry's man, Sir John Cheyne—a fighter renowned for his strength and stamina, was overcome by Richard himself, but as he was about to apply the coup-de-grace, one of Richmond's men close by turned and killed Gloucester's horse, which dropped and threw off its rider. A man-at-arms dismounted and quickly offered his own horse to Richard, shouting, "Escape your majesty—the day is lost! Go while you can!"'

'Richard seemed dazed and shook his head, turning to take on the next opponent, his sword raised. What was most surprising that in all this confusion, he still had his battle coronet on his head! Although overwhelmed by numbers, Richard continued to fight on foot, hacking his way through the mêlée and doing some damage. Finally a Welsh soldier floored him from behind with a single blow from his halberd and Richard of Gloucester lay dying. There were no final words, for the mouth was filled with blood, just the rattle of death. The fighting stopped almost immediately, and we were all aware how a strange silence descended.'

There is no dignity in death in battle. It is the fate of the vanquished commander to be especially humiliated; stripped of every article of clothing; the body exhibited to both sides present as proof of death. In this case, there were those ready with a blow or a stab to the lifeless body—marks of hatred so violent that they deeply penetrated the flesh and hit bone. Standing over the mud-covered corpse, Tony saw how small the victim was and how the slight curvature of his spine gave him his lack of symmetry when upright.

*All men look diminished when naked. Kings particularly, when their trappings are removed*! was Tony thought, as he looked down. Suddenly there was a shout and de Vere came across, blowing and red in the face. 'My lord, the coronet! It was found on a bush—just hanging there!' He went down on one knee and handed the small gold circlet to Henry Richmond.

As Tony told his friends later, 'To tell you the truth, it was a bit of an anti-climax. We were all exhausted and looking at this small piece of metal I wondered briefly what we'd been fighting for! It didn't last, of course; Henry took the thing and placed it on his head; it barely covered it, Richard being a much smaller man. But ownership is all! It was there and that's where it'll stay!'

The list of the three hundred dead showed that Richard sustained the most losses—especially among the circle of his immediate supporters. As the Earl of Oxford reported afterwards, 'As well as the Duke of Norfolk there was Brackenbury, Ratcliffe and Sir Robert Percy. Catesby was captured and executed in Leicester two days later. Four of Richard's senior men escaped, including Thomas Stafford and have not been apprehended. The Earl of Northumberland is under house arrest—Henry was lenient since the earl took no part. As for Richard—his naked body was slung across a horse and slowly processed to the House of the Franciscans in Leicester for a quiet inglorious burial. Richard III's reputation has been destroyed, a blot on the escutcheon of the country. Later generations will probably view him harshly: a child-murderer and usurper.'

Almost immediately after the battle, while still in Leicester, King Henry VII composed a letter which he ordered to be circulated throughout the kingdom and posted up, giving details of his victory and a list of those killed. Within the letter, he specifically ordered that: *No manner of man rob or spoil no manner of commons coming from the field; but suffer them to pass to their countries and dwelling places with their horses and harness. And moreover that no manner of man take upon him to go to no gentleman's place...nor pick no quarrels for old or new matters.* The most important sentence concerned the demise of Richard of Gloucester: *And moreover, the king ascertaineth to you, that Richard Duke of Gloucester, lately called King Richard, was lately slain at a place called Sandeford, within the shire of Leicester and there was laid openly that every man might see and look upon him.* There would be no possibility of misunderstanding in the market place.

Later the venue for this historic event was re-identified as the Field of Bosworth.

# Chapter 14

The manuscript comes to Camelot.

'You're sure you have that manuscript safe, Monty?'

'Do you know, Pom, you asked me almost the same question the last time we set out on this mission—fourteen years ago!'

The two men fell silent as they considered those years and all the events since the day the Newgate Three—Pom, Monty and Jack—set out from Greyfriars' stables in London and made their way towards the Downs Way on their journey to Winchester. Malory's death, the oaths sworn to protect his work and see it safely delivered; the flight to Burgundy and the subsequent theft of the manuscript; its loss for many years and its final recovery. Now *Le Morte D'Arthur* was in print and ready to be launched into the world.

As soon as Jack Worms had bound the first printing, Monty had begun thinking how they could fulfil Sir Tom's wish and deliver the manuscripts to the monks in Winchester and was still wedded to his idea that the Newgate Fellowship should travel together to fulfil the quest.

'We'll make a pilgrimage of it—we'll become Chaucer's characters!'

'I suppose I would be the merchant?'

'Except he had recently married and wished he hadn't since his wife gave him much grief. You're a bachelor who greatly admires women, most of them anyway!'

'As long as I'm not the merchant in Chaucer's Shipman's Tale—cuckolded by a monk!'

'I don't think we should mention the "C" word while we have custody of Sir Tom's work,' said Monty. 'You know how he felt about Master Chaucer.'

'Yes—"Just a fucking civil servant, Pom!" he would say,' laughed Pom.

'We all know Sir Tom was wrong about that—as he was a lot of things. Chaucer was a brave soldier and even ransomed and saved by whoever was king at the time. He may have been a civil servant, but he was a highly thought of and successful one. Since Caxton printed *The Canterbury Tales* and *Troilus and Cressida* his stock's risen even higher.'

'Sir Tom must be grinding his teeth—wherever he is!' laughed Pom. 'All the more reason to make this new adventure a success.'

They were sitting in Pom's small parlour in his house of modest size for a successful merchant, who was rumoured to be worth "a deal of money" according to those who speculated about such things. Years of fair-dealing, probity and co-operation with his fellow traders had left him regarded as a man of great esteem in his merchant-world and among his wider circle. Now almost seventy-one he had put on a considerable amount of weight and exhibited a rubicund face which clearly indicated his liking for good wines. He had maintained a decent head of hair which was silver-grey, as was his small, neat beard. When Monty first met him in '69, Pom had sported a massive black beard which gave him the look of a stubby corsair. During their later travels maintaining it became inconvenient and finally, with the regret one feels at losing an old friend, he was forced to shave it off, painfully without soap and in cold water. He never attempted to grow another hirsute appendage of that copious size, rather settling for a small growth easily managed.

His reputation as "a plain-dealer" was such that he anticipated being elected as an alderman by his peers. His friends felt this was only the first step on the way to the mayoralty, although he modestly dismissed this with a laugh. 'I'll be below ground before that happens, Jack!' he told his friend, who shook his head in vigorous disagreement.

'You were born to it, old friend. There would be no one better.'

Monty and Pom were busy making plans for themselves and their friends, who were at that time uninformed of the details, although all the Fellowship had agreed the journey should be made. As soon as a date was decided Pom suggested that Monty should write to the Prior of St Swithun, the Benedictine priory in Winchester where Malory wished the manuscript to be housed. "They have a fine cloister library there, Mister Pickle. Those monks appreciate good books," Sir Tom explained to his scribe when he was laying out his last wishes for *Le Morte D'Arthur's* final resting place.

Monty said, 'We'll give the prior good warning of our arrival, Pom. Tell me, Tony and Meg are due back from France next week—is that right?'

'Yes, he sailed a week ago for Le Havre and then rode to Paris to collect them and bring them home. After the excitement of events in Leicestershire, he asked for permission of the new king that he be given leave of absence to sail to France for that purpose. I had a letter saying he hoped to take a ship immediately and be back with us for Winchester.'

'Today is 14th September. We could plan to leave London on or around 1st October. I don't think we can leave it much longer; the hours of daylight will be diminishing, but Tony should have returned by then.'

'He'll want to be back by 30th October because King Henry plans to hold his coronation then. As one of the heroes of the defeat of Richard III, Sir Anthony will be expected to attend.'

'He'll want to, in any case—now he's been made a baron.'

'So Meg will be a baroness! Who would have thought it!' And Monty's mind went back to a scene in Newgate where a certain very young woman with a mass of dark curls had flashed her bare thighs and arse at him as she tumbled out of Sir Tom's bed before 10 o'clock in the morning. *I must try harder to erase that image from my mind! It was many years ago and no one would now suspect the dubious nature of Lady Tanner's past—thank God!*

Pom was doing some additions. 'By my reckoning, there'll be thirteen of us, including Wynkyn de Worde.'

'Yes, I'm glad Jack thought to include him. He's been instrumental in getting *Le Morte* printed and has been a very good friend; but thirteen's an unlucky number, Pom.'

'Fourteen if we include the dog!'

'Ah—I'd forgotten Neville! Jack almost asked Caxton if he would like to come, but he's an old man—'

'—I'm older than he is!' protested Pom.

'Yes, but you've been a soldier, as well as still travelling widely as a merchant. I doubt Caxton's horsemanship is that good, although I know he was once a diplomat and, in his younger days, often backwards and forwards to the continent. But I think it was wise of Jack not to ask him.'

'So, there will be the four Tanners, plus the dog, your family of five Monty, Jack and Maria, Inkin' and myself, plus three servants and two grooms. That's eighteen in all. I'll arrange the horses—the ladies will ride hackneys and we men will use coursers.'

'It's not going to be cheap,' Monty frowned and looked a little worried.

'Look, Monty, you'll have to swallow your pride and let me pay for most of it. I have no dependents, plenty of money laid by and made a promise to Sir Tom. I can't think of a better way of spending a small amount to keep that promise while having a very jolly time with all my friends—can you?' And Monty was forced to agree.

\*\*\*\*\*\*

It was a jolly party which set out from Westminster; such was its size it drew a crowd of onlookers outside Master Caxton's shop, the members of whom were not slow in their speculations as to what was occurring.

'I hear they're on their way to Canterbury. This is a clever way to encourage the sales of *The Canterbury Tales*; Master Caxton's a wily business man,' one man commented to his friend who, nodding and pursing his lips said, 'Mercer Appleby seems to be in charge—he's an old man to be taking on such a journey! The Pilgrims' Way's a dangerous road, I've heard.'

'I've never wanted to do a pilgrimage myself—can't see the point!'

'Well, neighbour, whatever reason they're doing it, they make a fine sight on a dull day!'

Which was true because the ladies wore brightly coloured cloaks and new hats, courtesy of Maria Worms, who was never one to miss a business opportunity. 'If we are to be on show, then all the better, husband,' she told Jack when he enquired as to what all the material was for and why she and her seamstresses were working through the night. The recipients of her labours were delighted with the results. 'It will be worth the discomfort of a long ride just to be seen in such apparel, Meg!' laughed Gisella.

Monty had been concerned that Gisella had only minimum skill on horseback. Like many inhabitants of cities it was an unnecessary expense for the Pickle family to keep a horse. Monty lived close enough to walk to Caxton's workshops, and Gisella had a servant who went on foot to the shops and markets. It was only when they travelled out of town to visit friends that they would hire a couple of hackneys. She considered she was competent up to a point. 'Don't ask me to gallop, Monty! I'll be fine trotting along at a respectable pace.' Their children were more skilled horse riders than their parents because Pom had taken it upon himself to give Tom, young Gisella and Isolde regular lessons. 'A vital skill, Monty! Remember how nervous you were when we made our first journey to Winchester. "I've not been on a horse for twelve years" is what you said, if my memory serves.'

'I can't argue with you there, Pom. I'm glad the children can ride well; it's something they'll never forget and always be grateful for.'

The Tanner boys were by now expert young horsemen, having spent a great deal of time travelling in France. Tony selected mounts which were spirited but would respond to firm handling, which he knew the boys were capable of. 'There's no point in hiring a couple of plodders, Pom!' he explained, when the good old man queried his choice as "too lively". 'My boys have come on so much since you used to trot them round the stable-yard at Greyfriars. Wait and see what they can do when we're out on the Downs.'

Jack and Monty had also improved and mounted up with no fear or nervousness. Pom selected two well-schooled coursers who responded to a light touch. Both men knew how horses can judge the competency of a rider. 'Just show him who's boss!' Pom gave the same advice as always as he handed Monty the reins. To Jack's surprise his wife was no mean rider.

'Master Tewkesbury insisted I learned when we were first married. "Maria", he said, "who knows when you'll need to mount up and go somewhere? We will keep two mounts stabled—hang the expense. Merchants must have transport available!"'

There was no intention of making a race of this journey. It would be an amble and without too much urgency. 'I estimate it'll take us four days or so, depending on the weather. For the sake of the ladies, we won't ride in the rain,' Pom told them when they were mounting up ready to set off.

'I must be back in London a few days before the coronation, Pom. It's important I'm there beforehand.'

'We understand that, Tony. Congratulations on your elevation! You must have done something spectacular in Leicestershire. The new king is evidently very impressed! I look forward to hearing all about it while we make the journey to Winchester. In fact that has given me an idea—something which will help to pass the time as we travel.'

Now they were leaving the city and heading on the old route, first to Kingston-upon-Thames where they would spend the night, then on to Leatherhead where they would join the South Downs Way leading directly to Winchester. The weather was dry but there was a keen easterly breeze; fortunately there had been little recent rain and the tracks were dry and hard.

'If the weather continues like this, the going will be easy, Monty!' shouted Jack as they picked their way carefully between potholes and stones. Inkin' Wynkyn was no mean horseman and had chosen and paid for his own mount, a substantial and lively grey rouncie, which to Monty's mind took up too much room on the track for riding companionably side by side.

'Can't you keep that beast from bumping into me, Inkin'?' he grumbled, as the horse brushed past eager to try his paces.

'He's like the good German horses I rode back in Cologne as a boy. Chances to ride I have not had since I have been in England and good it is to get out into your countryside!' And he cantered off to catch up with Leo and Dickon, to whom he had taken a liking. 'Such lively boys!' he told their father, who just grunted, 'Hmm!' Leo and Dickon had been too lively since they returned from France. They were extremely happy to be back with their friends—especially Thomas Pickle and their "uncles" Pom, Jack and Monty, who, although not blood

413

relations, were as close as they could be. Neither Tony nor Meg had any living relatives and their wandering life style had not lent itself to making lasting friendships.

'We have so much to tell you, Tom. You won't believe what happened to us in Brittany.'

Pom was riding behind them and called out, 'Save it for this evening, boys. We're going to do as the Canterbury Pilgrims did in the old days.'

'Who were they, Uncle Pom?' asked Dickon.

'Christians who rode along another part of this track to worship at the shrine of St Thomas Becket, a Christian martyr if you didn't know—'

'—I know who he was—he was killed by some soldiers in the cathedral,' said Tom.

'He was and it's an interesting story. But the pilgrims in Master Chaucer's book told other stories as they journeyed from London to Canterbury. I thought we could do the same when we reach the inn tonight where we're going to stay. All of us have interesting stories to tell.'

'Especially you, Uncle Pom. My father has told me some of Sir Thomas Malory's tales, but he says you know lots more.'

'Yes, and I thought your father was going to write them up into a full story, but I haven't heard him mention anything about it for many years. I wonder what happened to all his notes?'

In truth, Monty had always intended to collect together everything Pom had related to him about Sir Tom's colourful past, but events had intruded and as time passed the urge to complete it died away. He still had some notes, and bits and pieces he had added as they came into his mind; but nothing in a coherent form. *One day—when I'm not so busy!*' he told himself. *It's a story well worth telling.*

They arrived at the first tavern in Kingston at about six o'clock and the hostess was grateful to receive such a large party. 'You're fortunate; we have plenty of rooms available, if you're prepared to share. We can accommodate three of you gentlemen with the three boys together—two beds, three apiece. The ladies and girls can share one room. The rest of the gentlemen can share a couple of closet rooms—small but clean I can vouchsafe that. Usual arrangements out at the back for your servants and grooms.'

'Plenty of stabling I hope, mistress?' asked Jack.

'And plenty of hay and straw this time of year, sir.'

They met for supper in the tavern parlour which was small and only just accommodated them around tables pushed together. The food was passable and the wine "drinkable" according to Pom's critical taste.

Not only did Pom supervise the wine, he organised the story telling and insisted everyone drew straws to determine the order of telling. Leo and Dickon who drew the shortest straw, felt obliged to present their major adventure together, although secretly Leo would have liked to tell it alone without his brother's inevitable unhelpful interruptions. The Pickle ladies were next; Isolde, Gisella and their mother also wanted to present their story in concert, partly because Gisella knew her girls were shy in company and partly because it was a shared experience. Then came Tony, followed by Jack and Maria who had a joint tale to tell about how they had met; then young Tom, Pom, Meg, Inkin' and finally Monty.

'This is going to take some time!' observed Jack.

'I suggest we keep the stories short and to the point,' said Pom.

'Will there be time for questions?' asked Monty. 'There may be facts we're not clear about?'

'Monty, this is a story-telling, not an inquest!' replied Pom severely. 'We'll be here a twelve-month if everyone's to be interrogated.'

'All right, but I wonder if it would be an idea for us all to find a moral in our tale—like Chaucer's pilgrims?' suggested Monty.

There was a silence, as everyone considered whether their tale was weighty enough for such an outcome. Pom nodded, 'Yes, Monty, a good idea—not obligatory, but interesting none the less.'

'What's a moral?' asked Dickon.

'Did something good come out of it, blockhead!' said Leo.

'That's no way to speak to your brother, Leo,' frowned his father. 'But he's right, did you learn something from your adventure?'

'Jumping from—' began Dickon, but he was roundly interrupted by his brother.

'We haven't started yet! Don't give everything away!' Dickon looked chastened, but only for a few seconds. Leo's attempt at dominance never lasted long with him and he was determined to have his full share of the occasion.

'We may as well start with these two scamps!' suggested Pom, seeing that they were both itching to take the floor. 'Off you go, tell us a story Leo and Dickon.' There was an attentive silence and for a rare moment the two boys were the centre of the adult attention. Eleven expectant faces were turned towards them.

'It all started when we down by the bay—'—The Gulf of Morbihan,' said Dickon, who had a better memory for facts than his brother.'—Look! Am I telling this or are you?' grumbled Leo.

'I thought we both were!' protested Dickon. Pom intervened and tactfully suggested that each of them told part of the story; Leo could start and when their uncle nodded, Dickon would take over, 'without any arguing!'

This system worked well until they reached the point where they launched themselves from the window into the moat. 'Dickon can't possibly tell you what it was like—he had his eyes shut!' This was undeniable, and a reluctant Dickon gave Leo the floor. 'I saw the water coming towards us and had to let go of Dickon once we hit it.'

'It's still my turn. I remember what happened next,' and he continued with the tale until Pom decided Leo should take his turn. It took a little while for the events to unfold but the audience were captivated by this story of adventure and courage, although most of them had actually heard it before— several times. The two boys were gratified at the attentive silence with which they were heard and at the end there was a round of applause and 'Well done!' 'What bravery!'

Then Pom asked, 'And did you learn anything from this adventure, boys?'

There was a silence, then Dickon said, 'Possibly not to go poking our noses into places we shouldn't!' And there was a burst of laughter.

'I think we learned that there's always a way out of trouble if you think hard enough about it,' said Leo.

'That's my boy!' muttered Tony, who was as proud of his offspring as he could be. Although he had never overstated it to them, he was astounded at their initiative and courage. True, they were a handful at times, Leo especially wilful, but underneath the spasmodic ill-discipline, he had a good and brave heart. *All he needs is some decent structured training, and that's what I intend to get him.*

The Pickle ladies were next and Gisella introduced it as "The tale of a bull". 'This sounds interesting, Gisella,' said Jack encouragingly, although he had heard it before.

'You may say that, Jack, but it was terrifying at the time.'

'We're all attention; let's hear about the bull,' said Monty, who had also heard the story many times from the original.

'We went to the market in Cheapside, especially to buy lamb. It was a Thursday and we found there were many farmers bringing their beasts for slaughter. There seemed to be more than usual, and it was a mixture of animals, wasn't it girls?' And she turned to her daughters.

Shyly Isolde said, 'Yes, a great many pigs and sheep.'

'We had to push past them to get to the market,' said young Gisella.

'It was all so tightly packed; people were elbowing each other through the mass of animals. Suddenly there was—' and Isolde sat forward on her seat, pink-cheeked, '—there was a herd of cows coming towards us and, in front a farmer was leading a bull by a rope which was threaded through the ring in its nose.'

'That's right, Isolde,' said her mother. 'He seemed to have control of the beast, although it was a large bull; it had very big shoulders, didn't it girls?' They nodded and Gisella continued, 'I think it smelled the blood of the shambles. There was a lot of slaughtering going on; all the animals were nervous.'

'The sheep were bleating, the pigs snorting,' said Isolde.

'Oink, oink!' said Leo, with a grin. Tony cuffed him, and suitably chastened he retreated into his seat.

'Well, the bull was coming straight towards us and someone's dog started barking and snapping at the bull's hooves. You can guess what happened next.'

'No, Gisella, you must tell us!' laughed Tony.

'The bull strained on the rope and the farmer couldn't hold him. He let go and the bull was loose.'

'Mother saw what happened and grabbed us both and we tried to run through the crowd, but everyone was rushing to get away as the bull came closer.'

'Was it making a noise, Isolde?' asked Dickon, excited at the thought of this giant beast in a small street crushing everything in its path.

She nodded, and her mother said, 'Yes, Dickon, it began to bellow and paw at the ground as though it would charge. I really thought we might be crushed by him.'

There was a silence and the girls could see they had their audience's full attention.

'Mother was very brave,' young Gisella said. 'Instead of rushing about she kept her head and, even though the bull was nearly on top of us, she pulled us to one side and into a shop.'

'We saw the bull pass us and several people were trampled under his hooves,' Isolde was now very involved, wanting to give full weight to the story. It may not have had the dash and adventure of Leo and Dickon's tale, but it had been a very frightening experience.

'One person was killed, and about five injured,' Gisella said.

'What happened to the bull, Gisella?' asked Jack.

'A man shot it with a cross-bow, fortunately through its head and it dropped to the ground immediately.'

'We didn't see that,' explained Isolde. 'Mother kept us in the shop until the crowd had gone. The shopkeeper was very kind and gave us a drink—'

'—For the shock,' explained her sister.

'That's a pity—the killing, not the drink,' sighed Tom Pickle. 'I'd have liked to have seen him brought down!'

'Hmm!' muttered Monty, *bloodthirsty little beast*! he thought, although he did not say it.

'I suppose the farmer was in trouble—for letting go in the first place,' observed Pom.

'You could say it was the dog's owner who was to blame. If he'd kept the animal quiet, it wouldn't have frightened the bull.'

'That's how things happen, isn't it?' murmured Tony, philosophically. 'Chains of events.'

Maria, who had been listening quietly said, 'Well, I think you were very brave, Gisella. To have been faced with a charging animal and remain quick-thinking enough to dodge into a shop was very cool-headed. I don't know if I could have done it.'

Monty, having heard the story when it happened, was equally impressed with his wife's actions. 'You did well, my dear. I still shiver when I think what might have happened.'

'What happened to the farmer?' asked Jack.

'Well, we heard he did well out of it. Not only did he claim compensation from the man who shot his bull, he then received cash from the butcher—it was a very fine beast.'

'What about the person who died—did the family receive anything?'

Isolde, spoke up, 'The crowd were very angry with the farmer, and gathered round him shouting that he should give the widow some money.'

'Isolde's right—it began to get nasty and I wanted to take the girls away and back home. We heard later that the farmer gave the widow and those injured some cash and it never came to court.'

Pom nodded, 'An interesting story, ladies, and well-told. Is there a moral you can find from this tale?'

'Don't go to market when bulls are brought for killing!' And young Gisella smiled and went pink, relieved the ordeal was over. Leo was looking particularly hard at her and suddenly smiled back, which made her blush even more.

\*\*\*\*\*\*

They were away early the next morning, although it took some of Pom's best organisational skills to get them all together on the road. The weather was dry and bright and they made good time towards Leatherhead where they would join the South Downs, turning west towards Winchester. Their second night would be spent at Dorking, sixteen miles from Kingston.

Pom and Tony rode ahead, setting a gentle pace, aware of the variety of skills of horsemanship in their party. Anxious to hear more of Tony's recent battle experience, he began to probe a little into the events in Leicestershire. 'Where exactly did the battle take place, Tony?'

'Close to a place called Atherstone.'

'Atherstone! Why, that's only about twelve miles from Appleby Magna—my birthplace. Do you remember the exact name of the place?'

'It was close to some villages I don't know the names of. All I remember was that it was in wide-open fields and very marshy conditions, which made it slow going on horseback. The two armies were stretched out over a mile.'

'We've heard something of what happened, Tony, and that you distinguished yourself.'

'I don't know about that. As usual after a battle when one reflects on things, I was glad I wasn't a casualty; it was bad luck if you were because there were very few considering the numbers—three hundred or so dead out of about ten thousand.'

'Richard of Gloucester and The Duke of Norfolk being two of them! But I'm sure you'll be telling us tonight what actually happened.'

'If that's what the others would like to hear.'

'I know they would. The trouble is, you've led such an adventurous life, it puts anything we tell into the shade! I've nothing to say to set the juices going.'

'That's not true, Pom. All those exploits with Sir Tom.'

'Everyone's heard those stories over and over. Even your boys come and tell them back to me, as though they were there. They have them off by heart!'

'Just as well. It was the story of your escape from William Mountford's manor house that gave Dickon the idea for their dramatic leap.'

'Having heard what happened, I rather wish I'd never told them. It was a risky thing young Leo did; we jumped into a narrow moat; they went into a fast-running sea.'

'It was that or having their throats cut.'

'Do you think Percy would have done that?'

'Costello would.'

'What happened to them? You've not mentioned them since you were back.'

'We hanged Costello; he had a proper trial, quick but lawful, and was convicted of abduction and demanding money by ransom of civilians. Percy was useful to us because he had contacts in Spain and we were able to use them to buy arms and bring them in via Biscay. He's still in the jail in the Château de Suscinio. Duke Francis said he'll consider what to do with him "at some future date".'

'Knowing Percy's history, it's likely he'll turn up again sometime and somewhere least expected.'

'I'd have had him hanged with Costello; they're both cutthroats. But Francis felt Percy had cooperated to our advantage and should be shown some leniency; he doesn't know the man like we do.'

'Have you told Jack about Percy? Jack hated the man because years ago he and Costello frightened the wits out of him—and his apprentice. Put Jack's hand in the vice and threatened to cripple him.'

'I will do when there's time. There are others you might be interested in, besides Percy. Robert Stillington for example. By the way, what happened to Peter Crosby?'

'We can save that for later. But now I suggest we hang back and wait for our party to catch up. We've trotted on too fast—our conversation was too absorbing!'

******

They reached their next stopping point well before dusk. The streets of Dorking were still busy with tradesmen, shoppers, drovers and market traders. Pom, Monty and Jack had agreed they should use the same inns and taverns they'd stayed at previously, so Pom halted the party outside the *Boar Tavern* inn, a hostelry busy with customers moving in and out.

'Is this the place that the caitiff Peter Crosby tried to burn you all in your beds?' asked Wynkyn de Worde, who was very familiar with all the stories of the manuscript and its peregrinations. 'Well-remembered, Inkin',' said Jack. 'It was in that room up there,' and he pointed to windows on the first floor in the front overlooking the main street. 'If it hadn't been for Monty's quick thinking, he would have stolen the manuscript while we were distracted.'

'What happened to Crosby?' asked Meg.

'We'll tell you all about that later, Meg. First let's see if our host has enough rooms for us. If not, we'll have to divide the party and find some accommodation elsewhere.'

'That would be a pity—I was looking forward to our story-telling this evening!' said Maria.

'Perhaps it won't come to that. Monty, come with me and we'll see what can be arranged.'

When told of the size of the party, the hostess was at first somewhat disconcerted. But thirteen, plus servants and grooms, was good business. Not only accommodation, but food, drink and stabling. It would be worth disappointing some of her regulars.

'I think we can squeeze you all in; we're quieter in this season. Now, let me see. We have the main room which will

424

sleep six if I move another small bed in. Four can share the main bed and two can top and tail in the other. As for the ladies, I have two small rooms—a bed in each which can be shared three apiece. There are two closet beds which will suit the boys—two of them can share.'

Pom and Monty returned to the party and discussed sleeping arrangements. The only complaints came from Leo, who objected to sleeping in close quarters with his brother. 'Dickon snores, father!' He was, however, silenced by a look from Tony. Young Tom was relieved he would have a closet to himself. It might be small but, since their return from France he found the Tanner boys somewhat daunting as a pair. Dickon was all right—a kind boy, but in thrall to his brother. 'Leo is now so—so—', and he searched in his mind for the word, '—so brash, so confident,' he told his father. Monty reminded him that Leo had years more experience of the world. 'He's travelled; been in the courts of dukes and kings. I think you'll find he is an honest boy and would be a true friend to anyone. This journey will be an opportunity for you to really get to know one another. Remember, you're not a bad horseman and probably as good a swordsman as he is. Those years of training with Uncle Pom must count for something.'

'Are you saying I should offer to fight Leo, father?'

'Of course not. Just have more faith in yourself!' Monty felt somewhat of a hypocrite. *I spent the first half of my life telling myself the same thing*!' he thought. *It took me the experiences of Sir Thomas Malory's education, travel and the love of a good woman before I achieved it*!

When everyone had squeezed themselves into their various rooms, changed their garments and refreshed themselves with bowls of hot water, they met downstairs in a large parlour which the hostess had set aside for them. It was a tight fit, but she managed to find enough tables to put together, round which they arranged themselves. The meal was "passable", according to the ladies—good thick pottage, pigeon-pies and cheese. As usual, Pom oversaw the wine and ale. The children drank small beer and watered wine and were none the worse for it.

When the tables had been cleared, the jugs refilled, Tony said, 'Whose turn is it? I'm looking forward to this!'

'You know very well it's your turn, Anthony!' Meg always called her husband by his full name when she was scolding him.

'Yes, Tony, and I don't think you have a choice in what you tell us. We all want to hear what happened when Richard III lost his crown and Henry VII put it on his own head!'

'I'm sure I have more inter—'

'—No, you haven't!' burst in Pom. 'For sure, you have a host of exciting tales—more than any of us, but this is important. None of us know what's been going on. The news of the battle only reached London a couple days after it was over. We've heard no details and you were there! You owe it to us to give a full account.'

'Very well, but I'll make it as short as possible—don't forget, on a battlefield you're only aware of what's happening where you're standing. It all becomes very confused, especially when it's hand-to-hand.'

'Was there much of that Uncle Tony?' asked Tom Pickle.

'It always comes down to that, Tom,' said Tony.

Monty leaned forward, 'So, tell us what happened. We know you killed the Duke of Norfolk—tell us about that.'

Tony proceeded to give a full account of the early stages of the "Field of Sandeford" as he knew it, going on to tell them how Richard had made his fateful ill-considered charge at Henry Richmond.

'No one's sure what he was about, but it was a foolish stratagem—trying to strike off the head of the opposition. Henry fought well, for a novice in battle. He's not short of courage. After Richard died, as you must have heard, Oxford found the battle coronet in a bush and Lord Stanley presented it to Henry who was declared king there and then.'

'What happened to King Richard,' asked Gisella.

'Richard of Gloucester's body was taken to the monks of Greyfriars' in Leicester and they were arranging a simple burial for him, almost immediately I think.'

'And you, Sir Anthony, what did you do then?' asked Maria, who obeying the protocols of good manners, addressed him formally since they had been so shortly acquainted.

'Maria, please call me Tony—even Six-toed Tanner would be nice!'

'I suppose there must be a story in that too, Tony!' she laughed.

'That's for another time Maria. But, as for "what happened next?" we're still adjusting to having a new king. The next stage is his coronation at the end of the month, to which Meg and I are invited.'

'Anyway, Tony's a baron now!' said Monty. 'By the way—how do we address a baron?'

'My lord,' and Tony grinned. There was silence as his friends absorbed this news. It was difficult to apply this noble title to a man who they knew had such a colourful past. A rogue, an opportunist thief, a spy; but above all a man of courage and daring. Monty had always wondered how on earth his friend had come by a knighthood, but he knew it had been awarded by a grateful Earl of Warwick, "for brave and loyal service". As Tony had once told him, 'Anyone can get a knighthood if they can stump up £40 and show they have that much as an annual income. There are plenty of men who've tried to avoid the rank since it requires obligations of time, money and service. I've never found it a burden, since my livelihood involves military service to a lord—any lord who'll pay me.'

'Are you saying you're a mercenary?'

'No more so than any man, Monty. God's blood!— begging your pardons, ladies. You know we all work for one thing—money to put food in our bellies and the mouths of our children. A soldier is a professional and I've been lucky enough to serve honest masters. Warwick was always known for his plain dealing; Edward IV was not so reliable, but never let me down when it came to payment.'

Now, Tony having revealed his new title, Pom asked him, 'Lord of where, or what?'

'At the moment, just Lord—and Lady—Tanner,' and he waved his arm at Meg, who blushed a little, knowing full well what Monty, Jack and Gisella were thinking. But she was doing them a disservice if she thought they were appalled at the thought of Malory's ex-whorelet becoming a titled lady. They were more than a little impressed that she should have come so far but, as they knew, it was not unusual for a commoner to reach the dizzy heights of knighthood and grant a noble title to his wife. As far as her friends were concerned, Meg was a beautiful, kind and exceptionally bright woman—

and an excellent mother, even if her boys were regarded by Gisella as "something of a handful".

Maria Worms had not been informed of Meg's story, and Gisella did not consider it was her place to do so. Meg had not long returned from Paris, and there had been much to do in preparation for this journey. Monty and Jack discussed what should be done, and both agreed it was up to Meg to take her new friend into her confidence. Jack said, 'I'll talk to Tony who can then discuss what he and Meg should do. Maria is not an over-modest woman. She runs a business and has lived all her life in the city. She knows what goes on. She'll judge Meg on her own terms; so far, she has nothing but praise for Tony's wife.'

Tony and Meg decided it would be best if they were frank with Maria and told her the whole story—for her early life was bound up with Sir Thomas Malory and the Newgate Fellowship. Had it not been for her involvement with them all she would never have married Tony and certainly never become a baron's wife. Later the next afternoon Meg took Maria Worms to one side and briefly told her of her past. As Jack had foreseen, his wife was more impressed than shocked. As she told him afterwards, 'Any woman who can recover from such a start and make her way in the world as Meg has done, deserves our admiration, not our scorn!'

Tony, having brought the party up to date with the current state of weighty national affairs, left the floor to Jack and Maria who had a simple tale to tell of how they met.

Jack began, 'It was at Master Caxton's house and, for the first time I came face to face with Mistress Caxton without her veil. It was a shock and went someway to explaining why the lady confines herself to her rooms and only appears heavily veiled. She has a severely disfigured face.'

'Is from the small-pox?' asked Gisella.

'No, it's from a burn—an accident years ago; it covers the whole of the left side.' There was a silence as they absorbed this image. Everyone connected to Caxton's print-works had often speculated on the reclusive nature of his wife. It had been put down variously to shyness, haughtiness, unhappiness; also the possibility she was pox-scarred, although Caxton never mentioned it. In fact, he rarely mentioned his wife and she never appeared in the shop. Their daughter Elizabeth, a young girl of about fourteen, stayed within doors with her mother and did not mix with neighbours' children, or those of Caxton's employees.

Wynkyn de Worde was a shocked as them all at this revelation. 'The poor woman! Shocked she must have been when she was aware unveiled you had seen her.'

Maria continued the tale, 'I had lost the instructions as to how to get to the house and called into Jack's shop to ask for directions.' She smiled at him, 'He insisted he showed me the way and we knocked on the door. We must have caught her unawares, for when I told the servant I was expected, he showed me straight into her parlour. Jack followed—'

'I wasn't going to let up a chance of a peek into Caxton's house and meeting his wife, who has been a source of mystery to us all for years,' and he looked around for agreement. Monty nodded and said, 'I for one have found it very strange that she has never introduced herself to any of us. I think I've seen Elizabeth once or twice, but she scurries away as though she's frightened of people.'

430

Jack continued, 'As we entered she was sitting with her back to us. The servant told her of Maria's arrival, but it was evident that she had not expected her to be shown into the parlour before she had veiled herself; she was certainly not expecting a man to be present. She stood up, pulling at the veil, but it was too late, we had both seen what she had long-since desired to be kept hidden.'

'So, what happened? What did she do?' asked Meg, with concern in her voice.

'We were all taken by surprise. Jack and I by the unfortunate scar, Maud Caxton by the sight of Jack staring at her. She gave a little scream, grabbed at the veil and pulled it down, then she slumped into her chair. I told Jack to wait outside and tried to comfort her, but she accused me of bringing spies into the house and making a mockery of her misfortune. 'Master Caxton is the only man to see my face, apart from my physician. I will not have his employees staring at me and talking about me in the print-shop!'

'I tried hard to assure her that would never be the case, and suggested we sit and take our ease for a while. I began to lay out my samples on her table, all the time talking about the new fashions, and how different colours were now favoured over others—the usual sales talk. After a few minutes, she began to peer over my shoulder, attracted by the bright silks, doeskin gloves and other articles I brought with me. I don't know of any woman who, confronted with an array of pretty objects, would not become immediately entranced by them.'

'We know that, Maria, from the state of our purses!' laughed Tony. 'I remember a certain wench who begged for a pair of Spanish leather boots,' and he winked at Meg, who retorted, 'They were a pledge for my brave service to the cause of the Newgate Fellowship! But what happened next, Maria?'

'Not very much. Mistress Caxton was sufficiently taken with my samples that she ordered two pairs of gloves and some trimmings for a new gown. I told her I would return very soon, but without a companion. She nodded and rang for the servant who then showed us out.'

'Why did we not know of this—Wynkyn and I?' asked Monty. 'I had no idea this was the reason she's so reclusive.'

'When we found out, we were not sure what to do and decided we should keep it to ourselves,' explained Jack. 'But Maud Caxton herself had spoken to her husband and commended Maria particularly, for her discretion. When Caxton realised his wife's deformity was known to one of his employees, he made it clear that it was not something he was ashamed of but had kept it to himself for his wife's sake. "We live with it and that's all that can be said. As for others knowing, my wife would rather it was kept between our intimate acquaintances, which include Mister Pickle and Master de Worde. We have no objection to them knowing, but we would prefer it not to be bandied abroad." It was a key moment in our story, so we have included it, knowing you will all respect Master Caxton's wishes.'

'Of course we will! I suppose the most interesting part of the story is that Jack fell in love with you on the spot! At least, that's what he told me,' claimed Monty.

Tom, Leo and Dickon began to squirm in their chairs at this observation of the romantic affairs of the elderly and wished they could hear more of the disfiguring burn. How red was it? Did it cover the whole of her face? Did it have a peculiar shape? Did it itch at all? But of course they remained mute, only wishing the tale could be over soon.

Fortunately for them it was. 'This was how we met, courtesy of Mistress Caxton and a shared experience. There's no moral in the tale, except to quote Sir Tom's favourite maxim, *carpe diem* and believe me—I did, as you all know,' and Jack sat back in his chair looking very smug.

'We like a happy ending, don't we?' And Pom sat beaming at his friends. 'So far we've had tales of courage, martial skills and now romance. I hope you have something equally as interesting Tom?'

The young man went pink—a habit he had acquired from his father. All he could think to say was, 'I'll do my best!' but with Leo looking on doubtfully, he cleared his throat and started rather hesitantly.

******

It was not such an ordeal as he had imagined, although he had spent the previous night anxiously wondering what story he could possibly tell everyone. Finally, after much tossing and turning he decided he would relate the tale of his being threatened by villains on the road to the Mote in Maidstone and how he had to pretend to be deaf and dumb. Dickon was very impressed, but Leo probed for more details. 'Did they put a knife to your throat, like they did us?'

'No, but they pulled me from my horse and I think might have killed me, but father persuaded them we were on their side—they were going to fight against King Richard. But I had to stay completely silent and pretend not to hear, which was very difficult; you should try it!'

'Yes, Leo, that is a sound idea!' laughed Tony. 'It wouldn't do you any harm and I suppose it's much harder to keep it up than you would think. It took some courage, young Tom, well done!' This approbation from their father caused Leo to look with more respect at the lad and he wondered what Tom would be like in a fight. *He's only a few months older than me and not as tall, and I don't think he's had much experience. I wonder if he's done any training.* In truth Leo had hardly ever been in a proper fight, only rough and tumble with other boys he'd met on his travels. He'd not always come out on top, and once was soundly thrashed by a muscular French bully of his own age, who nearly broke his leg and left him with two black eyes. Tony had been less than sympathetic. 'You must try harder, lad!' was his only comment when his boy came limping home.

'There's no moral to your story, Tom,' observed Jack.

'I don't know,' said Monty. 'You could use that line in the poem.'

'What line—what poem?'

'An old one, I can't remember where it came from. It goes something like: "Who sayeth little he is wise, and few words soon amend".'

'I suppose it's as good as anything, Monty,' agreed Pom. 'Now, three stories are enough; I think we should all retire to our rooms and closets. Tomorrow, God willing, we'll begin our ride towards Farnham which is our half-way point. This time, instead of riding directly to that town we can stop the night at Guildford; it's about twelve miles away.'

Tony said, 'We could ride through Guildford and stay at Farnham tomorrow night, weather permitting.'

Pom shook his head, 'My instincts are to stick to the plan and head for Guildford. After all, there's no real hurry. It's nearly twenty-eight miles to Farnham from Dorking; too far and it means us travelling at speeds some of us are not used to. It's unnecessary; but I'll listen to what anyone else thinks? What do we think?' And Pom looked hopefully at his companions for guidance.

Sensing how Pom's mind was working, Gisella looked at Maria and Meg. 'You're thinking we women are not up to it, Pom!' she said accusingly.

'It never entered my head, Gisella!' he lied. 'But I was thinking of myself as much as anyone else. I'm not getting any younger and this old body's not up to sitting in the saddle for hours on end—it doesn't do my piles—'

'Yes, Pom, we understand!' said Monty swiftly.

Gisella smiled, 'Well, if you're sure that's the only reason. But have no worries on that score. We're all perfectly capable of keeping up!'

Pom nodded, 'Of course you are. Good, that's settled. We'll spend the night in Guildford, then ride onto Farnham; find somewhere to stay between there and Winchester. That makes three more nights on the road, and we have four more tales to be told—myself, Meg, Inkin' and lastly Monty.'

'As I remember we stayed a night at a poxy little inn in Alton after Farnham—there was barely room to swing a mouse, let alone a cat. They wouldn't be able to accommodate us.'

'We'll find somewhere Jack! But for now let's get to bed and up early ready to ride to Guildford.'

\*\*\*\*\*\*

435

'Is it a town you know, Tony?' Monty asked as they picked their way along the track which was badly rutted and pitted with potholes.

'Never been there in my life. Like you, Meg and I skirted round it when we were chasing after you; we didn't have time to stop and take it in.'

'Pom says it's a well-known market town and bound to have plenty of accommodation.'

'Good castle there, that's all I know of the place!' And Tony kicked his horse into a fast trot, turning the gelding's head to the direction of the town marked by a fingerpost.

They stayed at *The Stag* which was the largest of all the hostelries in the main street. The host came out into the yard to greet them. 'You're lucky, sirs, we've had a rush on, but might have just enough rooms to accommodate you.'

*This is a man who senses a business opportunity*, was Pom's immediate thought, *and this is where the price goes up considerably! But I'm prepared to haggle.*

The travellers had planned a budget of five shillings a night for beds for them all, plus servants; then three shillings for food, ale and wine and one shilling and six pence for stabling. With tips, it amounted to just under ten shillings a day, plus food at mid-day. The overall budget for five nights on the road and lodgings in Winchester for three days had been calculated as £4. At first, Pom had insisted he would bear the cost, but such was the indignation of the others that he agreed he would pay half and they could divide the rest in whatever way they felt was fair.

Mine host at *The Stag* was asking a staggering eight shillings for accommodation only. Admittedly, when he showed Pom the rooms, they were of a very superior quality to anywhere they'd stayed on this route. While beds would be shared, as was customary in any case, the rooms were spacious with closets for baggage. The three boys had small truckle beds each in one room; the ladies shared a large chamber overlooking the back of the inn towards the castle walls. Monty, Jack, Wynkyn and Tony were to share two beds in the front chamber on the high street.

'It's somewhat noisy at night with the town dogs loose, but the beds are feather-down and there will be a good fire in all the rooms.' The landlord looked expectantly at Pom and said, 'I have another party interested in the rooms, sir.'

*Another business contrivance*! thought Pom. 'Six shillings—in advance!' he said abruptly.

'Seven and six,' said the landlord.

'Seven, and that's my last offer.' The landlord hesitated, but money in advance was always preferable to waiting to see if guests could pay their bills. 'Done!' And they shook on it and Pom handed over the money. To show there was mutual respect from one businessman to another, Pom said, 'The rooms are very good. I hope the food matches it!'

\*\*\*\*\*\*

'I hope I can match the stories you've heard already!' said Pom and sat back in his chair, replete from an excellent meal of mutton stew, dumplings and a crisp apple tart and fresh cream. As if this wasn't good enough the wine was superb, and Pom determined he would seek out the landlord and enquire the source. The man was clearly knowledgeable and perhaps there was a business opportunity for Pom here too.

There would be time enough in the morning to enquire how the land lay in that regard.

But now he held the floor and the party were looking at him expectantly.

'The thing is, you've all heard my stories so many times—well, most of you,' and he looked at Maria. 'Some of those concerning Sir Tom are not really fit for ladies' ears; and you all know of my days as a soldier in the service of the Earl of Warwick. Perhaps it would be best if I tell you about my dealings with the Muscovites and their furs, who I first was in contact with in Bruges—you will remember, Monty and Jack?'

'Of course we do. Beautiful silver fox furs, Maria—wolf and bearskin, as well as beaver. You would have loved them.'

'We all would have loved them, Jack!' said Meg with vigour, 'and loved to have owned a silver fox fur hat. Perhaps now we are in favour with the new king, we could think about our wardrobes, Tony!' And she smiled, and Maria thought she saw a wink, but couldn't believe her eyes.

Tony wriggled in his chair and laughed nervously, 'Whatever you say, Magpie. One day!'

'You always say, "one day", and it never happens. Mother deserves some furs, father,' protested Dickon, who attended carefully when these conversations took place between his parents; he was a boy with a canny appreciation of the subtle undercurrent.

Tony laughed even more nervously while frowning at his boy, 'Indeed she does, Dickon, but let's hear Uncle Pom's story.

\*\*\*\*\*\*

438

'This is not my story but was told to me by one of my Muscovy traders. It concerns the Golden Wolf of Novgorod.'

'Where's Novgorod Uncle Pom?' asked Tom.

'A very far away place in the north; a land of ice and snow all the year round. The men from Novgorod are very tough and hardy. I've met some of them; they're all hunters and bring their furs to sell to us "soft southerners" as they think of us! Anyway, this story is about a wolf that was above all others; a huge beast as big as a bear. But what made it special was its coat, which had golden streaks in it and made it glow in the sunshine. The hunters realised it would be worth a fortune if they could catch it. Many men tried, but all were killed and found later with their throats torn out.' The boys leaned forward in anticipation of a gory story; young Gisella and Isolde shuffled closer to their father and he put a protective arm around them.

Pom continued, 'Now, one hunter in Novgorod who was recognised as the best for many miles made a pledge that he would spend a season hunting the beast. He had a small hut in the forest, where he lived with his wife and children and from where he made his sorties each day trying to track it down. Winter is a good time to hunt wolves, for their tracks can be clearly seen and followed. Day after day, for several weeks, he went out searching. Of course he was hunting and trapping other creatures also, for he must put food on the table for his family. But his main hope was to find the Golden Wolf of Novgorod.' Pom paused, took a long pull at his wine and looked round at his audience, which was silent and fully attentive.

'One day he was far away from his hut, as far away as it was safe to be, when he heard a howl such as he had never heard before; loud and commanding, drifting over the silent landscape. He followed the sound for at least three miles, coming closer with every step. The cry was eerie and almost deafening when he finally stepped into a clearing and he saw—'

'—I know, Uncle Pom—it was the golden wolf!' cried Dickon, completely breaking the spell.

Pom nodded and smiled, 'You're quite right, young Dickon, he came face to face with the beast.'

'What did he do then, Uncle?' asked Leo, glaring at his brother for interrupting.

'For a moment, he froze. The wolf was standing within ten yards, and in easy range of his crossbow and spear. He positioned a bolt and raised his bow, but something stopped him. The animal looked at him with its large golden eyes— stared into his face as though commanding him to stop. There was no doubt of three things; firstly the hunter had a clear and easy shot; secondly, the wolf had an injured front paw or leg, for it was standing holding it off the ground; and thirdly, and most important according to the man who told me the story, the wolf was magnificent, "the most beautiful beast" as the hunter told him. There was something in its gaze and its demeanour which made the man first hesitate, then lower his bow and bow to the wolf and say aloud, "Go, for I cannot shoot such a fine creature".'

Leo was intensely disappointed, 'So he let it go and that was the end of the story. Did anyone every catch it?'

'It was not the end of the story, impatient boy!' said Pom looking severely at Leo. 'The hunter never admitted to anyone that he'd spared the Golden Wolf's life. He felt he'd be thought of as weak—diminished in the eyes of his fellow hunters. But then the strangest thing happened. Two years later he was hunting in the forest, again in deep snow. He was at least two miles from his hut and, in a moment of carelessness, tripped and fell down a bank of snow, hitting his head badly on the trunk of a tree. He lay unconscious for a while until he woke and was aware he was being dragged. Something had him by the collar of his thick fur coat and was pulling him through the snow. At first, he wasn't sure who or what it was, but soon the sharp and familiar smell of wolf came into his nostrils. To his horror he realised he was being dragged by a large animal; he put his hand out and felt the thick fur. Immediately he started to struggle, thinking he was being pulled to a lair to be made a meal of. But however hard he fought the animal clamped his jaws even tighter and pulled harder. The man was already weak and cold from exposure and hunger, and slowly lost all desire to struggle, accepting the inevitable.' Pom paused and looked around. The boys were staring wide-eyed. 'Was it the Golden Wolf of Novgorod?' asked Tom.

'It was indeed.'

'And did it eat him?' asked Dickon, with relish.

'How could he have told the story if that had been the case, foolish boy? No, this was the wonderful thing about it. The wolf dragged the man two miles back to his hut and left him at the door, first howling loudly to alert the wife. She came to see what the noise was about just as the animal was disappearing into the trees.'

'So the wolf saved the man because the man had let it go free and didn't killed it?' Jack looked sceptical and Monty thought he'd heard the story before, but with different characters.

'Isn't this a similar story to the one in Aesop?' he asked. 'Androcles and the lion where Androcles pulls the thorn from the lion's paw and then the lion doesn't eat him when he's captured and forced for fight him in the Colosseum in Rome? I believe the moral was "One good turn deserves another"; isn't that right?'

'There are similarities I'll grant you,' nodded Pom. 'But there's a twist to this tale.'

'What do you mean "a twist", Uncle Pom? asked Dickon.

'Something unexpected.'

'And what was it?' asked Tony, privately agreeing with Monty: this was a well-worn story easily adapted to different conditions in the world.

'The hunter's wife opened the door and saw her husband lying in the snow, clear tracks showing how he'd been dragged out of the forest. She pulled him into the hut and laid him in front of the fire. He soon came to and she asked him, "How did you manage to get yourself here, husband? When I found you, you were unconscious at the door."

"I was dragged by a wolf, wife; a giant wolf which had me in his jaws, yet he made no attempt to kill me. Instead he brought me home."

"That's madness! How can that be, husband? You are mistaken. Can you stand? Come with me and I'll show you why." He rose to his feet and followed his wife to the door. Opening it wide she pointed outside to the snow-covered ground. "See, here are the tracks your body made as you dragged yourself to the door; but where are the tracks of the wolf? There are no signs of it. As I said, you were dreaming and in a frenzied state. It is something you imagined."

The man was silent, then he said, "But I was unconscious when you found me. How could I have brought myself home—over two miles—without knowing it? I know what I know, wife. It was no dream," and he went back to his chair by the fire and thought long and hard. "Wife, I tell you, this was the Golden Wolf of Novgorod and he has saved my life. He leaves no tracks because he is an eternal spirit of the forest. He'll never be caught but remain a presence here for ever."

'This was the story the Muscovite told me, and he seemed to believe every word of it.'

'So the Golden Wolf was a ghost, Uncle,' said Tom, who had been captivated by the story.

'Did anyone else ever see it again?' asked Leo.

'People said they did. Every so often someone would come back from a hunting trip claiming to have seen it "just out of range". I for one hope no one ever hunts it down and kills it.'

'If it really exists!' laughed Tony.'

'You're an old sceptic, Six-toed!' smiled Jack.

'What's a sceptic, Uncle?' asked Dickon.

'Someone who doubts everything.'

*Always eager for information, just like his father*, thought Meg, who had also been absorbed by the story and glad of the happy outcome. It was going to be her turn next and she was rather concerned as to what to tell her friends. Her life-stories were very interesting indeed, but most of them not fit for mixed company and certainly not in front of the children. In the end, she told the story of how she had been held for ransom by a wicked Frenchman but had been rescued by her knight errant husband, Sir Anthony. She carefully omitted any reference to an attempted seduction in the forest by said

443

Frenchman, an incident she had successfully kept to herself, although it had all ended perfectly innocently since the chevalier had behaved as he should, like a gentleman. Her two sons thought it very amusing that their mother had rolled up her sleeves and insisted to Robert, the grumpy French cook, that she herself would clean the filthy accommodation from top to bottom before she would deign to eat anything.

\*\*\*\*\*\*

Later that evening, two stories told and the ladies and children having retired, Tony, Monty, Jack and Pom sat by a good fire in a quiet area of the parlour which the landlord had set aside for their use. 'You gentlemen will be comfortable here I think.' The party had already boosted his profits considerably and he could sense a good tip at the end. 'It's not often we have such a group of polite and lucrative customers wife!' he commented. 'Let's hope they put the word around that *The Stag* is the place to stay in Guildford.'

Leaning back in the settle, his long legs stretched out in front of the fire, Tony suddenly remarked, 'While I was with the English exiles in Brittany I spent several evenings entertaining Lord Richmond with tales of Sir Tom's life. I told him all about *Le Morte D'Arthur*, at least the gist of it and snippets from the stories I could remember. He was captivated by the Knights of the Round Table and said he would really like to own a copy when it was ever found and printed. I had told him the story of how the manuscript was stolen and how you were still looking for it, for of course I was out of the country when you finally tracked it down. I mentioned Peter Crosby and Lord Stillington as possibly involved in the crime;

which he found very interesting. Afterwards he said, "You, know, Sir Anthony, when I have my first son—notice the 'when,' my friends—would-be kings are always so sure of themselves! When I have my first son, I'll call him Arthur—Prince Arthur. Your stories have inspired me.".'

'But what King Arthur will he become sir, first or second,' I asked him—rather mischievously, although that passed him by.

'Why, Arthur II of course.'

'But sir, are we sure the first King Arthur really existed?' I asked, still rather provocatively I thought.

'For sure! Everyone knows he was King of the Britains. When we return to England, I shall be seeking to show how my lineage stretches back to that noble king, and even further beyond to Brutus of Troy, the founder of Britain. Proving it must help my cause, since I'm aware many say my claim to the throne is weak. But what does Sir Thomas Malory have to say about Arthur?' That I couldn't answer. As far as I knew Sir Tom never said whether Arthur really existed. What do you think Monty—Jack?'

'I know he believed it, and, although he never actually said it, assumed his readers would too,' Monty said. 'Caxton has confirmed it—in his preface. He goes to great lengths to show how Arthur was a real king, despite the doubters. He talks about the artefacts connected to the man which are scattered around the country, and various documents which mention him. You know, Tony, we could go and see Sir Gawain's skull in Winchester.'

'Can we be certain it's his?' asked Pom.

Monty laughed, 'As certain as we can be of thumb nails and scraps of Jesus's foreskin claimed as holy relics. It really

445

come down to believing what you want to believe, if there's no hard evidence to prove otherwise!'

'That's true of many things Monty!' sighed Tony.

'Well, if the king does christen his first-born son Arthur I think it'll be a tribute to Sir Tom and his hard work in bringing Arthur to life again. Caxton will be pleased, and glad to hear Henry wants a copy. I'm sure you can do a splendid job on a binding—make it fit for a king, Jack!'

'I'm sure I can, Monty,' and Jack grinned. 'The question is will Henry read it cover to cover? My money says he won't!'

'I mentioned Stillington earlier,' said Tony. 'You'll be as pleased to hear as I was that he's back in prison. One of the first orders Henry gave as our new king was to have Lord Robert arrested and thrown in the Tower. Henry is incensed that Stillington was responsible for spreading the rumour that his father-in-law Edward IV was already betrothed to another woman when he married Queen Elizabeth, making all his children illegitimate, including Princess Elizabeth. This would have made Henry's proposal to marry her a nonsense. The king's ambition is to unite the two House of Lancaster and York, so Stillington has paid the price for spreading false information.'

'Well, I can't say I'm sorry,' said Monty who, whenever that caitiff's name was mentioned nursed the stump of the little finger of his left hand—the absent digit a casualty of a vindictive Lord Chancellor when Monty fell into his clutches. 'How long will he stay there—in the Tower?'

'Who knows. But obviously King Henry is making it a priority to sort out who are his friends and enemies. He wants to be magnanimous to many who opposed him, but unfortunately, after the battle in Leicestershire several Yorkists escaped and fled abroad, probably to Burgundy. We know there were among them some senior names: John de la Pole Earl of Lincoln, Francis Lovell and the two Stafford brothers, Humphrey and Thomas of Grafton in Worcestershire. Let's hope they don't live to make further trouble.'

'Indeed,' murmured Jack, 'and you mentioned Peter Crosby. Well, we have news of him, don't we Monty?'

'We do, and recent news. A few weeks ago we received a manuscript, specially delivered and from Essex. Of course, we realised as soon as we opened it that it was from Crosby. It was a manuscript of execrable verse! The cheek of the man to send it to Caxton's Press thinking he would be interested! In fairness, when I took it to Master Caxton I didn't say who it was from—for he knows the whole story of the man's deviousness—but left it to be judged on its own merits, or otherwise. As I expected, Caxton threw it aside, as "complete gibberish", not a word I'm familiar with, but I'm assured it's in the vernacular! Anyway, he told me to write to Crosby and say "thanks, but no thanks", which I did with the greatest pleasure.'

'I should think that gave you a deal of satisfaction, Monty,' laughed Tony. 'Did you hear from the caitiff again?'

'We certainly did! He wrote and demanded we send the manuscript back—at our expense—and said he might have known a new-fangled printer would have no appreciation of modern verse.'

'And what did Caxton say to that?'

'He asked me to reply and sign the letter myself, so Crosby would know who he was dealing with. I politely told the man we didn't consider the work to be of a suitably high standard for our printing works, which serves royalty and those with a discerning intellect. You've no idea how much pleasure that letter gave me, Tony!'

'Did he send money for the manuscript to be returned?'

Finally he did, and I wrapped it myself and sent it back with "my compliments".

'So Crosby had his nose put out of joint well and truly,' said Jack with relish. 'I don't think we'll be hearing from him again, stuck out on the Essex marshes with a peevish sister. Now his old employer is in jail, he has no hopes of reviving his position as Stillington's secretary. But of course, in these uncertain times I suppose we can't be sure of anything.'

'Enough of the trickster Crosby; how have you thrived in all this uncertainty, Tony?' asked Monty. 'I must say, you and Meg still look extremely happy.'

'Meg—ah, my Magpie! What can I say? She's been a stalwart. I couldn't have done anything without her and she's put up with more than any woman should. Above all she's been a great mother to my boys. But there is something I can tell you, something she doesn't yet know and probably won't like. So, if I tell you it remains a secret until she knows of it from me. I mean to tell her while we're journeying together. I hope her reaction will be restrained in the presence of company!'

'That sounds—er—alarming,' said Jack, who knew Lady Margaret Tanner's reputation for robust reactions. 'Go on,' he said, now very curious.

'I told you how I wore the Earl of Oxford's golden mullet during the battle. We fought together and took on Richard of York's infantrymen. It was then I went hand to hand with the

Duke of Norfolk. Anyway, I was present later in the day at the mêlée when Richard was finally bested, and Henry took the crown—I did my fair share of fighting at that time. When we were back in London, de Vere called me to his lodgings in Westminster and asked if I would agree to be his retainer—carrying on working as I do as an agent for himself and the king. He told me the king had proposed to elevate me to a baronetcy and that I will eventually have a parcel of land to either live in or rent out and take an income from it. Of course, I accepted the offer as that will give me a further income, as well as an annuity in the future. This last fact Meg does know about and is very happy, thinking I'll settle down to run my new estate.'

'Congratulations, Tony!' said Jack warmly, 'do you know where the estate will be?'

'I might have some choice and, if so, will ask that it's as close to London as possible, perhaps somewhere in Hampshire or Surrey. Hampshire would be useful, being nearer the coast if I'm to spend time abroad. This is one of the things Meg doesn't know. I'm to work as a confidential agent for King Henry in France and Burgundy and will therefore be away for weeks on end.'

'But she's used to that Tony,' Pom pointed out.

'Yes, but I rather promised her I'd pull back on my travelling, once everything has settled down. But the most serious thing she doesn't know is—' and he lowered his voice as though his wife might appear around the door at any moment.

\*\*\*\*\*\*

'Are Meg and Tony all right, Jack? I don't know them very well, but there seems to be a certain chilliness between them.' Maria and her husband were trotting quietly side by side on the way to Farnham from Guildford. It was mid-day and Pom proposed they make a brief stop to rest the horses and enjoy some food. Their route had taken them for some miles along the elevated Hog's Back from which they had good views of the surrounding countryside and they dismounted close to the highest spot where there was grass aplenty for the horses, and a place they could spread themselves, rest and enjoy each other's company, which was not always easy from the back of a horse.

That was everyone except Tony and Meg who, as Maria observed, "were very chilly" towards each other, withdrawing a little way off. Leo and Dickon were oblivious to this condition of their parents and, with Tom, went off to explore the local possibilities for adventure. The couple sat on the grass without speaking, Tony looking very sour and Meg showed evidence of tearstains.

*Whatever is the matter with them*, thought Gisella. She knew Meg quite well, they had been friends for years, despite long absences between meetings. *Should I ask her what's wrong, or would that be an intrusion*? She was torn between sorrow that her friend appeared to be so unhappy, and a natural reticence about involvement in what was obviously a marital disagreement. In the end, she casually wandered across to the couple, sat down and said, 'We've been friends long enough; there is clearly something wrong between you. Can I do anything?'

Meg smiled wanly, 'Thank you for asking, Gisella, but there's nothing to be done. Anthony has given me some news which I find very disagreeable.'

Ignoring Gisella, Tony said, 'Meg, this is the opportunity of a lifetime for our boys. It's just what they need; some discipline and training. You've spoiled them.'

'—I won't be blamed because they're a little unruly at times. If you were at home more often to—'

'—So, it's my fault is it? My fault that they go off and you have no idea where they are or what they're doing? My fault they come home having been involved in fights?'

'Well, since you say so, yes. They need a father who's at home, at least more than you are. And now you tell me you are to continue to be an agent, not only for Lord de Vere, but also the king. Away in France and who knows where else!'

'It's my living, Magpie—'

'—Don't call me Magpie!'

Gisella thought it might be a good time to ask what exactly the problem was, as the argument was getting nowhere. 'You said something about it being "an opportunity of a life-time for Leo and Dickon", Tony. What did you mean?'

Tony looked at her and shrugged, 'I think that, for an earl to offer to take on our two boys, raise them as soldiers, train and educate them and for free would be an excellent start for them. Who knows what will come of it. But Meg doesn't want to undo the apron strings and let them go.'

'That's not true, Tony and you know it. My objection is that you've already agreed they should go—without even talking to me about it—and that you propose to continue your travels as a king's agent—which means I'll be left on my own

451

without my two boys—my husband galloping around the continent at continual risk!'

'Well, I had to make a decision. You don't tell an earl, "I'm sorry, I'll have to ask my wife!" He made the offer and I accepted it. He's very taken with our lads. When he heard the story of their escape from the tower in Sarzeau, of course it resonated with him since he did the same thing himself—jumping out of the tower window of Hammes Castle. "By the bones of Christ! Sir Anthony", he said, "I want those boys in my service!" And the matter was finalised there and then. I've taken this time to tell you, because I was trying to find the right moment—I knew you'd be upset.'

Gisella saw that they both had a point. Tony had little choice but to accept the generous offer from the Earl of Oxford, but Meg should have been told about it as soon as Tony had returned to collect her in Paris. Attempting to mediate, gently she pointed this out. Meg sighed, 'Tony, it's not that I'm against the idea of them leaving home and living under the guidance of Lord de Vere, it's the fact that I'll be living in some manor somewhere among strangers, when I'm—I'm.'

'—You're what?' asked Tony.

'I'm probably going to have a baby.'

There was a stunned silence.

'Say that again, Magpie!'

'I think I'm going to have another child—we're going to have another child.'

Tony's face was a picture—pleasure, confusion, guilt and pride passed across it, until it settled into a look of happiness. He pulled his wife to her feet and put his arms around her. Then, cupping her face in his hands, he kissed her gently on the lips, 'Well, Magpie! This is most unexpected! I would never have guessed it.'

'That's strange when you were there when it happened!' And at last Meg gave him one of her sunny smiles. Gisella was ready to withdraw, feeling she was an intruder in this very private moment. Meg turned to her and said, 'Thank you for making us see how much we still love each other—despite our differences.'

'Yes, indeed, Gisella. You're a good friend.' He turned to Meg, 'This does alter things considerably, Meg. Of course you can't be left alone in a strange place without your friends around you. You must remain in London, close to Gisella and now Maria, both of whom will be of great comfort to you at this time—much more than I could be.'

Gisella knew when she could hear a responsibility being avoided, *Typical menfolk!* She thought but, of course, did not say it. Instead she said, 'Of course we'll look out for you Meg; I insist you have your lying-in with us.'

Tony sighed with relief, 'We'll be able to afford to continue to rent the Cornhill house, even though we won't need all the rooms. Will staying in London go some way to making up for the loss of the two boys?—Jesus! The two boys! What are they going to think about having a little brother—'

'—Or sister!' said Meg robustly. 'I hope we have a daughter.'

'If we do, we must call her Margaret—after her beautiful mother. She will be beautiful too.' Tony looked lovingly at his wife and Gisella felt she could safely withdraw and leave them to enjoy the moment.

***\*\*\****

    The Tanner boys were at first shocked at the very idea of their mother producing a baby, and immediately wondered when and where it had occurred. That night at the *Ewe Tavern* in Farnham, as they lay in their bed topping and tailing with Thomas Pickle, the conversation ranged from the most outlandish speculation about the female body and how it could accommodate a full-grown baby; curious opinions as to how the baby got there in the first place, and even more grotesque ideas as to how it could get out.

    'Kissing!' That's how it's done!' said Leo with authority.

    'How what's done?' asked his ever-curious brother.

    'Making babies. The man kisses the woman and passes something from his mouth to hers; she swallows it and it grows into a baby in her belly.'

    'What does he pass?'

    Leo hesitated, and then had to admit he wasn't sure. 'Maybe it's a very tiny infant,' he speculated.

    'I kiss my mother every morning and every night; nothing like that has happened—not since my twin sisters were born anyway,' Tom pointed out, equally anxious to be enlightened of the mechanics of the business, but also concerned he might inadvertently be the means of producing another mouth for his father to feed.

    'You have to be a man to do it, grow a beard and everything,' Leo explained. 'Also that's why men kiss only the hands of ladies who aren't their wives—it stops them having their babies.'

    Tom Pickle was very relieved to hear that his boyish daily gestures of affection would not result in any undesirable outcomes. But he was determined to pursue things. 'What happens then?' he asked.

Leo hesitated again. In truth, his knowledge came from a very unreliable source. While supposedly pike fishing down by the Seine, he had idled with a couple of French boys, slightly older but, to young Leo, the experienced revealers of all mysteries concerning women's bodies.

"Of course, babies come out of their arses!" they told him when their lecture on women's anatomy reached that portentous point.

Leo now passed this significant piece of information on. 'The baby grows and then has to come out.'

'Out of where?' asked Dickon, frowning heavily.

'Where do you think? There's only one place it can come out, dolthead!'

'You mean—?'

'Yes, their arse! Where else? It can't come out of the mouth, obviously!'

His audience was silent while unwanted mental images crowded into their heads. 'You mean I was squeezed out of my mother's arse like—like—?' And Tom Pickle's voice faded away in horror.

'—Like a turd, yes!'

Again shocked silence as this appalling detail was absorbed. Then Dickon, trying to dismiss it from his mind quickly moved on to another aspect of the business entirely. 'Leo, why don't men have babies?'

'That's easy! How could a man go into battle with a belly swollen the size of a pillow? And if he wasn't a soldier, how could he do any work for the same reason; think of a blacksmith, or a wheelwright. How could they swing a hammer with a great fat lump in front of them?'

Dickon opened his mouth to point out that there were plenty of very fat blacksmiths and wheelwrights who seemed to manage perfectly well; but felt that arguing with his brother would gain him nothing. Since neither he nor Tom could provide a satisfactory answer they stayed silent. More questions might result in some unsavoury responses and now, just before they closed their eyes to sleep, was not a suitable time for more unwanted images. But all three boys knew they would look on their mothers with a different eye in the morning and should Mister Pickle inadvertently give Mistress Pickle a "good morning" kiss on the lips, as he was wont to do, Tom wondered if he should shout a warning of the possible outcome. On reflection, he decided that it was most likely his father had matters in hand and knew what he was doing.

'Best not to let them know I know!' was his last thought as he drifted off to struggle with some very strange dreams.

\*\*\*\*\*\*

The tavern in the mains street of Farnham was fortunately as comfortable and spacious as the inn in Guildford. They were met with similar attentiveness by mine host and his wife, an extremely thin and rickets-riddled woman who stooped, although she was not so old that it would be expected. Isolde and Gisella discussed her appearance and thought she must be a witch, for besides her long face and fingers, she had a large hooked nose and some hairs on her chin. The poor woman became an object of study for the two girls who viewed her with a mixture of fear and fascination whenever she came into sight. In the end, Gisella took them to one side and pointed out that they were being "very rude". But the girls were spellbound and wondered whether "the witch-woman", as they named her, kept a cat or any other devilish creature on the premises. After searching around for evidence, all they could find was a friendly tabby who exhibited no diabolical properties, rather spending his time rubbing and arching his back against their dresses.

After what Pom called, "a reasonable repast!" it was Master Wynkyn de Worde's turn for a story. Like Tom Pickle, he had worried about this task when it was proposed by Mister Appleby at the beginning of the journey. Although he could make himself understood by his friends and workmates, he had still not mastered the subtleties of vernacular English, and his Low German syntax caused some amusement to his listeners. To be asked to deliver an entertaining story would require fluency to keep his audience attentive; this was a skill he had even now not yet acquired. He had half-a-mind to ask to be excused this duty, but then argued with himself, in his own idiosyncratic English, *Wynkyn, you are of this party; invited by friends, your duty it is to be companionable and "grasp the nettle"—one of those queer sayings with which the English are so fond of littering their speech.*

When it came to it he decided to take "a leaf out of Pom's book", another inexplicable English saying whose context remained opaque in his mind. He would tell a good German folk tale also set deep in a forest; not in Novgorod but his home in the Rhineland. The main characters of loving father, dutiful son and daughter, wicked step-mother and evil witch were laid out to a very receptive audience, particularly the

457

children. Even Leo and Tom, who thought of themselves as above being told fairy stories, were captivated when the two unfortunate abandoned children were shut up in the witch's cage to be fattened up for roasting in her oven.

Isolde and Gisella were equally engrossed; at the same time they were terrified. The witch woman of their acquaintance seemed to have much in common with Meister de Worde's German old hag, who apparently spent much time in her kitchen. Likewise the hostess of the *Ewe Tavern* was rarely seen out of hers. Could there be a connection? Did she have two captive children hanging from the ceiling in a cage, feeding them copious amounts of food prior to bundling them into a hot oven? They listened attentively, and with relief, to the happy ending and how the witch had been cleverly thwarted. Unlike the three boys who were sharing a bed, Isolde and Gisella were sleeping in a very large bed with their mother, Meg and Maria. It was no place for an intense discussion as to the best ways of avoiding capture, and worse, by a sorceress. The next day, on the road to Winchester, they managed to exchange views. 'I swear she was a witch!' determined Gisella.

'But were there any children in her kitchen?' asked her twin.

'We'll never know, but we'll know what to do if we're captured by one.'

'We must hope she'll be half-blind like Master de Worde's witch, and therefore not recognise the feather. That was a clever trick, making her think the boy hadn't put on enough weight to be cooked!'

'Isolde—'

'Yes?'

'You do realise we'll have to stay there again on the way home?'

'Yes, Gisella. I think we should keep very close to father and mother all the time and far away from the kitchen. Also we should collect some feathers, just in case.'

'You know what I think?'

'Tell me, Gisella.'

'It's a good thing we're small and slender.'

\*\*\*\*\*\*

They were within twenty-five miles of Winchester when Pom proposed they stop at the small village of Alton. 'It's too far to travel directly to the city from Farnham—just under thirty miles. Alton is the largest village on this section of our route; We'll be passing through very small hamlets so there'll be nowhere else to stay.'

'My memory tells me it was a shabby, badly-run place,' muttered Jack. 'We were crammed into a tiny closet bedroom after a disgusting supper. Let's hope it's improved!'

'That was fourteen years ago, Jack!' said Monty. 'My only concern is that it will be too small to accommodate us all and we'll have to split up.'

'That would be a pity,' commented Tony. 'We should spend our last night together before we reach Winchester.' Buoyed by the news that he was to have an addition to his family, he was pleased the boys had taken it quite well, although they had given Meg and himself some strange looks when they appeared for breakfast that morning.

*The Tup Inn* had changed out of all recognition. The flea-ridden pothouse had been extended and cleaned up; new owners had worked wonders with the place. It was not as large as the hostelries at Guildford or Farnham, but with imaginative organisation everyone was accommodated. The most useful change was that the eating and bar area was sufficiently large for the party to gather round a single table, mine host metaphorically rubbing his hands at the profits to be made and consequently helpful to the point of unctuousness.

'If he asks me again if everything is "in order", I'll hit him!' growled Pom.'

'He's a big improvement on the woman who was here before,' Monty observed.

'She did make some good porridge, as I remember; perhaps she's handed on the trick to the new owner!'

'Well he's said he has a haunch of venison—courtesy of the local lord who owns the place.'

'That's an unusual gift; lords of the manor are not generally known to give away the fruits of their chase,' observed Tony. 'What's he going to do with it?'

'Pom rubbed his hands. I've already explored the possibilities with him. He says he's going to broil it and serve it with a pepper sauce.'

'That sounds very acceptable. Will there be enough for us all?' asked Monty.

'Oh yes. But he's charging us, believe me; sixpence a head—no concessions for the children.'

'Ouch!' said Jack. 'I hope that includes wine.'

Pom nodded, 'It does, but only after I haggled with him. I also told him I was a prominent wine-merchant in London and would know immediately if he was trying to pass off inferior stuff.'

'Well,' laughed Tony, 'as they say, or not, "the proof of the venison is in the eating thereof". I can't wait.'

It was a merry party which sat together on their last night before Winchester. It had been decided at the outset that, when the manuscript had been safely delivered to its final resting place the group would disband and go their own ways, journeying back to London in their own time. Monty had long had an urge to take his wife and children to meet the remnants of his family who lived a few miles across the border into Wiltshire. 'I can't be in the area and not attempt to see them, Gisella. I very much want my sisters to see how I have made something of myself in the world. They always told me I'd be a failure—" the runt of the litter" as they called me!'

'I'm not so sure I want to meet them, Monty. They may be your kin, but they sound appalling!'

'Well, it would satisfy me to try—even if I never see them again. I know where the eldest is—somewhere near Whiteparish, about thirty miles from Winchester.'

'It seems a very long way; we'll need an overnight stay, which means we won't return to London for at least another week. Can you be sure they'll be hospitable and put us up. They may not like you arriving unannounced.'

'We'll have to risk it, Gisella. If they don't, we'll turn on our heels and that will be the end of it.' Reluctantly his wife agreed that they would attempt to mend the family breach, for that was what it was, she was sure.

Tony, Meg, Leo and Dickon planned to make all haste to London since Baron Anthony Tanner was required to attend the coronation of the new king. 'But we won't be riding at full tilt, Magpie. We must consider your condition.'

Meg, with full understanding of the demands of pregnancy, knew she need not be treated like a piece of Pom's best porcelain china, but decided to take full advantage of her husband's concern. *I shall enjoy the cossetting while it lasts!* she determined. Nodding she said, 'I think that's very wise, Tony!'

The remainder of the group, Pom, Jack, Maria and Inkin' would travel at a more leisurely pace, staying at the same inns and perhaps deviating to take in some shrines or other places of interest. Pom was not sure about the shrines, but Maria seemed keen and he was in no real hurry, except the new vintages from France and Burgundy were expected later in the month.

'As long as we're away no longer than two weeks, I agree we may take our time. Meister de Worde has never been outside London as I understand. It is good for him to see the English countryside and perhaps spend a couple of nights in the beautiful city of Winchester.'

Now, sitting with his friends at the large table, replete from what he admitted was an excellent and well-cooked supper, he looked around and beamed. 'Monty—it's your turn to delight us with a story. Last but by no means least!'

Monty cleared his throat and nodded. 'My friends, it's not a story I have to tell—'

'But father, we've all had to do it!' protested Tom.

'It's not that I don't want to tell a story, but I'd rather take the opportunity for us to remember all the events of the last fifteen years which have led us to this point. Not that there's enough time to discuss every single one, but to share our experiences of the manuscript and its history. Tomorrow, God willing, we'll arrive in Winchester, at Sir Thomas Malory's

Camelot and leave his precious work in safe and permanent hands. The book is now printed, the stories are available for everyone, and it's time to put the original to rest according to his wishes. But, as I say, the events which have led us here are undoubtedly special and interesting. I would be delighted if each one of you shared what were your favourite moments, and how *Le Morte D'Arthur* has impacted on your lives. I for one would not have met and married my beautiful wife, if I hadn't first been introduced to Sir Tom and persuaded to work with him. Thus there are so many links in the chain of events which, as I said, have led us to this precise moment. I think they are worth sharing—don't you?'

There was a silence for a moment, then Tony spoke up, 'I think that is a very good idea, Monty. Like you, and I imagine Jack here, I would never have met my darling Meg if it hadn't been for Sir Tom.' Meg flashed him a warning look as though to remind him that her distant past was not a subject for discussion in front of their boys. Catching her thoughts, he said, 'One of my favourite stories was our sea voyage from Southampton to Honfleur—the pirates—'

'I hope you're not going to tell yet again how you pushed me into a barrel full of maggots, Anthony!' Meg said severely. 'We've all heard that tale too many times; neither is it something I wish to be reminded of!'

'But you did end up with some fine Spanish leather boots, Magpie!' her husband laughed.

'Hmm! many months later, as I remember.'

Recognising that this might develop into an unwanted domestic argument, Pom intervened. 'Tell me Monty, do you still have it in mind to write down Sir Tom's life story. I know you told me you've managed to keep many of the notes you took from me. I've kept my own record safely, both remarkable feats considering how much we've travelled over the years. I would like the world to know of Sir Tom's history.'

'I'm not sure whether the world is ready for some of it, Pom,' Monty said doubtfully.

'Why isn't the world ready for it Uncle Monty?' asked Dickon, who, with the other youngsters had been sitting very quiet and still. This was not necessarily out of obedience to the well-known requirement that "children should be seen and not heard", but more subtly because it was always useful to listen to adults talking when they forgot their children were there. "It's surprising what you can pick up when they don't think we're listening", had been Leo's wise observation.

Monty was thrown by this question. 'Well, Dickon, Sir Tom was a very—very—um—'

'As well as a writer he was a soldier and a spy—like your father, Dickon,' said Jack helpfully. 'Some of his adventures are too confidential to be spoken of.'

'What does "confidential" mean, Uncle Jack?' asked Isolde who, like her father, enjoyed the sound and feel of difficult words.

'It means, private—secret. Sir Tom had a lot of secrets and many exploits. But I think it would be possible for your father to write them up in some clever way. They are very interesting. Leo and Dickon, of course know all about his escape with Uncle Pom from the manor house in Warwickshire. If it hadn't been for that story, they might not have made their own leap to safety. So you see, Sir Tom's adventures are worth the telling.'

This statement led to a lively discussion of the more savoury of Sir Tom's exploits, as well as many of the events concerning the loss and retrieval of *Le Morte D'Arthur*. The children were allowed to stay up—indeed it was necessary, as all the males of the group were confined in one room with two beds as, in another, were the females. Although they had heard many of the stories before, there were still twists and slants on them which were new. When they finally lay top to tail on lumpy palliasses, their young heads were still full of exciting images: pirates, rogue knights who held women for ransom; counterfeit doctors who stole important documents.

In the morning, they rose early for the final ride to Winchester. Pom was disappointed, "'The porridge is different and not good!" was his verdict.

'At least the beds were flea-less, unlike last time we stayed here,' laughed Jack. 'I must say, Maria, I'll be very glad to get home to the comfort of our own bed,' and there was not one word of dissent.

******

Winchester, 7th October 1485. The city was a fine sight as it lay in front of them. Standing proud above all other buildings was the cathedral, and close by the Priory of St Swithun. It was a cool, dull day with a keen north-easterly wind; not the day to be wandering the city looking at the sights and the travellers decided to head straight for the priory.

'The Benedictine order is well-known for its duty of hospitality. According to their rule, all pilgrims and travellers are welcome into its precincts. I suggest we call in that commitment and spend the night in the priory. It'll be worth

465

a mass or two!' And Pom crossed himself. 'Then we can search out the officer dealing with their library and scriptorium.'

It was as easy as he made it sound. Within the hour, they had been admitted to the grey-stone building and the men and women allocated small separate dormitories, the girls with their mothers and the boys with their fathers. 'It's only for a night, Leo,' Meg told him when he complained that his legs were too long for the bed. 'Your father has a bed of the same size and he's much taller than you. He's not complaining, even though he'll be sleeping doubled up!' Her only complaint was that the priory was excessively cold; there seemed to be no fires anywhere. 'I suppose the monks become inured to it,' she said to Gisella in their dormitory.

Maria said, 'We have sufficient blankets, and it's not as though it's the middle of winter. I'm more worried we might have to rise before dawn to perform the first Office of the Day. Do you think we will, Gisella?'

'No, I'm sure we won't. Certainly not us women! We just attend a mass at some time. It'll do us good. None of us have seen the inside of a church for a week! Will they do confessions here, do you think?'

'If you request it, I suppose they will. I prefer to wait until I'm back with my own father confessor,' and Maria, having finished making up her bed, stepped back and sighed, 'I'm hungry. What do you think the food will be like?'

\*\*\*\*\*\*

'May we congratulate you on a fine dinner, Prior Hinton,' and Pom sat back well satisfied in his chair in Thomas

Hinton's chamber. They had all fed well and Pom, Jack, Tony, Wynkyn and Monty were now cloistered with the prior ready to discuss the important matter of the placing of the manuscript.

'I received your letter at least a week ago, Mister Pickle and now understand why Sir Tom chose Winchester as the resting place for his *Magnum Opus*. We, of course, are well-acquainted with the stories of King Arthur and no doubt before you leave our great city you will take the opportunity to look at the Winchester Round Table hanging in the castle. It is a fine sight.'

'We have every intention of doing so, Prior Hinton,' said Monty. He picked up his leather satchel from the floor. 'No doubt you would like to see the manuscript?'

'Indeed I would, Mister Pickle,' and Monty withdrew the large oil skin-wrapped document from the bag and placed it on the table. 'My,' said the prior, 'it certainly lives up to the description *Magnum Opus*! However long did it take Sir Thomas to write it?'

Monty explained a little of the circumstances under which Sir Tom had collated the stories and finally put them together. 'I'm impressed. But you say the manuscript has been copied and is now in printed form?'

'Yes, as I explained, our master, William Caxton, owns the manuscript, but wishes it to be delivered here as Sir Thomas requested. As he says, "We must always do the author justice".'

'I agree. This development of what is now called "printing" has worried us here, and in all religious houses. Part of our income is derived from work done in our scriptoria—copying great religious works. What will become of that if printing takes hold?'

Monty and the others fell silent. It was the question Mister Pickle had asked himself when Malory had first told him of the process and its possibilities. The thought that it would put himself, and others who relied on their quills for their livelihoods, out of work had worried him significantly. He, Jack and Wynkyn de Worde were now part of this great impetus to develop a new process which must surely spread rapidly when people became acquainted with its results. But it was not his place to explain that to Prior Hinton. Instead he unwrapped the oil skin and took out the manuscript. Its cover was much thumbed and very knocked about, but the interior pages were still in good order. He pushed it towards the elderly prior, who touched it gently with his long fingers. 'We'll take great care of it, Mister Pickle. I've not heard all the vicissitudes this manuscript has suffered, but I'm sure it could tell as interesting a tale as the stories inside. It will be catalogued and placed in our cloister library. Are you aware that we have three libraries here?'

'We know the Benedictines are famous for their scriptoria and love of books. I'm sure that was one of the reasons Sir Thomas wanted the manuscript to rest here—as well as the city's proximity to the Arthurian past.'

'Come with me and I'll show you our collections. We are justly proud of them. Bring the manuscript and we'll find it a home.'

\*\*\*\*\*\*

'How do you feel, Monty?' asked Jack, as they walked towards the priory stables.

'It's like a burden's been lifted, Jack. Even when the manuscript wasn't in my possession, I still felt responsible for it and had many sleepless nights wondering whether it still existed. Now I've seen it safely bestowed in the priory library, I think I can rest easy.'

'What will the monks do with it, do you think?'

'Read it—copy it. I really have no idea. All I know is that Sir Tom's work is safe because it is in print and between your excellent bindings. Copies can be made as they are requested, which means *Le Morte D'Arthur* will be read by many more people than would have been the case had it remained as a hand-written manuscript. But in my eyes the original is priceless, and I'm confident the monks will take great care of it, as a work of great imagination and scholarship. Now, we'll find the others and make one final journey; let's to the castle and look at this famous Winchester Round Table.'

In fact, some of the party were rather disappointed, particularly the younger members.

'It's just an old wooden board with names written on it— no decorations and it's not even painted!' complained Tom.

'I thought it might have some blood on it at least—from all those jousts people have been talking about. I haven't heard of half the names that were written on it.'

'Well,' said Dickon, 'I saw Sir Galahad, Sir Lancelot, Sir Kay and Sir Percival. How many were there all together?'

'I counted twenty-four, and King Arthur placed over them,' said Leo.

'Do we know who put it in the great hall?' asked Tom.

'Nobody said anything about that,' said Leo. 'They were going on a lot about it being made for a special tournament, but I don't think they really knew much.'

'Which of the knights would you like to be?' asked Dickon of his brother.

'I think Sir Lancelot—'

'I'd like to be Sir Galahad!' said Tom firmly.

'Then you'd be my son!' And Leo grinned.

Tom was not so certain of the desirability of that situation and frowned. Then he shrugged and said, 'That would be all right. Sir Galahad was one of the bravest knights and did as many great deeds as his father.'

'My father is a knight and I shall be one too when I'm old enough. I chose Sir Lancelot because he escaped out of a tower. Who will you be, Dickon?'

'Sir Kay, I think. It's short enough for me to remember!'

'That's a silly reason to choose it, brother!' And the usual argument ensued, which on this occasion, because they were in a great company, did not end in a scuffle.

\*\*\*\*\*\*

What did end was the Fellowship of the *Le Morte D'Arthur.* The Quest achieved, and the Grail safely bestowed, the party began to break up in the manner which had already been agreed. Having decided to stay for a few days and explore the city, Pom, Jack, Maria and Inkin' went off to find a decent hostelry. Tony, Meg and their boys turned their horses' heads back to Alton, reversing the route they had followed over the last six days. Monty and Gisella waved their companions farewell and looked west towards the town of

Whiteparish and the home of Monty's relations. 'I don't know what we'll find when we arrive, Gisella; it may be a warm welcome, it may be a frozen one. We must take our chances.'

'The last adventure, Monty, before we settle into old age!' And Gisella smiled and patted his hand.

\*\*\*\*\*\*

Back in the cloister library, old Prior Hinton sat at a table with *Le Morte D'Arthur* in front of him. Turning to the first page he looked at the neat script and appreciated it had been executed by a "good" hand. 'Steady clean work,' he said to himself with pleasure. 'Now, let's see what all the fuss has been about,' and he began to read aloud:

*It befell in the days of Uther Pendragon, when he was king of all England and so reigned, that there was a mighty duke in Cornwall that held warrant against him a long time, and the duke was called the duke of Tintagel.*

'Hmm! All stories should begin with a sentence which engages the reader—just like Genesis in The Old Testament. Sir Thomas Malory's certainly does! I'll read on.'

# Epilogue

'There's good news and there's bad news, Sir Thomas.' The young man bustled in, full of his own self-importance. 'Which do you want first?'

'The good news,' and Sir Thomas Malory waved a hand that was as limp as all the other vital parts of his body. 'Tell me something that will cheer me up!'

Naked, he was lying on his back on a black silk sheet which covered a large, well-upholstered and very comfortable bed. The air of the richly furnished chamber was suffused with a melange of fruit and floral scents which gave Sir Tom a perpetual headache and set off occasional heavy bouts of sneezing.

'Well, the good news is that your manuscript—you remember, *Le Morte D'Arthur*—has not only been printed by Master Caxton—as you already knew—but is finally safely deposited with the monks of Winchester Priory, just as you wished.'

'Ah, Mister Pickle's managed it—in the end. It took him long enough. And the bad?'

'Well, the manuscript won't see the light of day for almost five hundred years and when it does no one will know you wrote it.'

Malory raised himself on his elbows, 'By the loins of Lord Lucifer! How can that be?'

'Please, Sir Tom, no profanities—you know the rules. They won't know because you didn't explain exactly who you were—just this vague reference in the text to some "knight-prisoner" by the name of Thomas Malory. What you overlooked was that there were a few other Thomas Malorys around at the same time. It's going to take some heavy research before anyone determines it was yourself—and then they'll issue a disclaimer saying: "We're not absolutely sure", as university scholars always do.'

'Fuck me!'

'That's what I'm here for, Sir Tom,' said the young man cheerfully. 'Would you like to turn over?'

'Not now, you fool. I was just using a figure of speech.'

'You shouldn't use that one so freely around here, Sir Tom; we're inclined to take people at their word.'

'I'm simply expressing my displeasure. Is there nothing we can do? Can our Master not send an emissary to one of these researchers and explain—somehow?'

'Retrospective changes are not in our gift, Sir Tom. Things passed must always stay as they were; anyway, that's what I've been told,' and the young man sniffed somewhat petulantly.

'How frustrating. It was my greatest wish to be famous and have a plaque in Westminster Abbey, like that dullard civil servant Geoffrey Chaucer.'

'I'm sorry for your disappointment, Sir Tom.'

Malory sighed and lay back on the bed. 'Who are you anyway? I haven't seen you before.'

'Giovanni Boccaccio.'

'Not the Italian writer? Surely you were much older when you died?'

'Of course I'm not! I'm his bastard son. I took his name, for that was all he would give me. But don't try and discuss his works with me; I've no talent for poetry. My skills lie elsewhere; that's why I'm here, and it's a long story. I was sent here over one hundred and fifty years ago. Anyway, the management has decided to refresh things by changing personnel around somewhat. As from this morning I am your designated catamite.'

'Oh, I see. Look, young Boccaccio—or is it more appropriate to call you Ganymede? I'm too tired to be entertained today. To be truthful, I'm too tired at any time after all these years. This Second Circle of Hell—I mean "The Other Place"—is not somewhere I would have expressed interest in had I known the demands it would make of me.'

'Well, what did you expect—the purpose of the Lust Area is exactly as it is described.'

'Yes, but I thought I would be tenderly ministered to by soft-handed girls or gentle young men who would understand my needs.'

'I'm afraid the soft-handed girls and gentle young men are not sent here. They get through the Celestial Gates: the girls become angels, and the young men are kitted out as cherubs. They are designated to please the nobility and clergy. It's only the sinful sexually robust, those with the stamina to maintain their libido under pressure who circulate in the Lust Area of Hell. Forget all this nonsense about not being judgemental,' the young man snorted derisively. '—I ask you—" The Other Place", how ridiculous! Anyway, you haven't done so badly, Sir Tom!'

474

'Let me stop you there Giovanni. May I call you that?'

'Certainly, Sir Tom.'

'This word libido—Latin root meaning inordinate desire, sexual passion?'

'As far as I understand it.'

'I've not heard it used in the vernacular before.'

'That's because it hasn't yet come into common parlance.'

'How is it you're using it?'

'I was browsing in the Library—in the Saucy Etymology section—and came across it in a box marked: "For use only after 1892". But I rather liked it and thought, *What the Hell! Words are meant to be used where appropriate.*'

'I agree! Giovanni, you may be Boccaccio's untutored bastard, but you've picked up his appreciation of words. I used to be the same—before—'

'Before you came here?'

'Indeed. I seem to have lost all pleasure in anything. I tell you, Giovanni, I'm fucked, and when I say fucked I mean fucked!'

'Well, I hope so; as I said, that's what we're here for.'

'But there's no enjoyment any more. I can't raise—raise—'

'—Any enthusiasm?' suggested Giovanni helpfully.

'Yes, that and other things,' replied Sir Tom lamely.

'As always, we can help you there, Sir Tom. I've brought someone with me to liven you up; she's waiting outside.'

His languidness deserting him, Thomas Malory sat bolt upright and said suspiciously, 'Who is it? Who are you proposing?'

'Well, Sir Tom, there's really only one person who can do it for you.'

'You don't mean—'

'Yes, I do. And you're very lucky she's available. It's the Lady Messalina!'

'Great Blistering Beelzebub!—'

'Sir Tom!' protested Giovanni. 'Language—please.'

'Sorry, but please, not Messalina! Anyone but her. I can't manage her today, or any time soon.'

'She's been allocated to you for the whole day. The fiends are concerned you're losing your urges and she has the great arts to revive them! I'll call her in,' and he rang a small exquisitely crafted silver bell. The door opened and in walked Lady Messalina; not in alluring Roman garb as might be expected, but wearing a sable collar, severe-looking black thigh-length leather boots and nothing in between.

Malory groaned, 'Not the boots! Please, not the boots!'

'Sir Tom,' and grim-faced, Messalina spoke in a tone to match her footwear. 'I've been ordered here because you have been reported as committing one of the four Cardinal Sins.'

'Oh? Please remind me what they are.'

'Fiddling, Fannying, Faffing and Flagging. You have been guilty of the latter on numerous occasions, despite the multitude of pleasures available. You must be punished and then revived.'

Giovanni Boccaccio stood watching with interest but, regarding the expression on Sir Tom's face, felt it would be polite to withdraw and turned to leave. Messalina snapped at him, 'Stay where you are young man; consider this a training session.'

She carried a short leather whip and stroked its sturdy stubby handle in a meaningful way. Then raising the implement she cracked the thong hard on a green marble tabletop. 'Now Sir Tom, turn over. You've been a very naughty knight!'

# Postword

The books in the *Malory Trilogy*: *Rogue Malory*, *Malory's Quest* and *Malory's Grail*, although following the real historical events of the time, are entirely works of fiction. They imagine how the original manuscript of *Le Morte D'Arthur* might have been researched, completed and then lost for fourteen years before it was first circulated as a printed work by William Caxton in 1485.

Subsequently, what has been claimed as Sir Thomas Malory's possible original manuscript of *Le Morte D'Arthur* remained hidden for almost five hundred years until 1934, when it was discovered in the Fellows' Library of Winchester College by Mr W.F. Oakshott, a school master and academic. A full text of the manuscript became available thirteen years later when an edited version by the literary scholar Eugène Vinaver appeared as *The Works of Sir Thomas Malory*.

# Who's Who

While most of the main characters are fictitious, others are historical figures from the period.

The following are the chief historical personnel who appear in the *Rogue Malory Trilogy*.

### SIR THOMAS MALORY (c1416–1471)

Much scholarship has been undertaken to pinpoint exactly who wrote *Le Morte D'Arthur*. There were several Thomas Malorys alive in 1469/71 but, given the evidence: "No-one but Sir Thomas Malory of Newbold Revel could have written the *Morte D'Arthur*".[2] Accepting that this is the man, all the escapades, crimes, misdemeanours described in *Rogue Malory* are well attested in existing indictments and court papers.

---

[2] P.J.C. Field *The Life and Times of Sir Thomas Malory*, (D.S. Brewer, Cambridge, 1993), p.35.

## JOHN APPLEBY (c1414–?)

John (Pom) appears with Sir Thomas Malory in several indictments and it is clear he was a confederate in many of the crimes laid at Malory's door during the period January 1450 to 1455. He was described at the time as Sir Tom's "steward".

## ROGER CLYFFORD

Keeper of Newgate prison (1469–93), Roger Clyfford was accountable to the Sheriffs of London and had full control of every aspect of prison life. He was responsible, at his own expense, for preserving the fabric of the building, as well as overseeing the welfare of the prisoners. Keepers could be fined for escapes, removed from office or even imprisoned.

## HENRY VI (1421–71)

The only child of Henry V, Henry of Lancaster became king as a nine-month old baby in 1422. He oversaw the loss of all the English possessions won by his father in France. His reign was under constant threat from the Yorkist faction, first under Richard Duke of York and then his son Edward Plantagenet, until he finally lost his English throne to Edward. For some years an exile in Scotland, he was eventually captured by Edward IV in 1465 and held in the Tower of London, until his brief return to the throne in 1470. When the Lancastrians were finally defeated in 1471, he was returned to the Tower and secretly executed.

## MARGARET OF ANJOU (1430–82)

The French wife of Henry VI, she led the Lancastrians in their fight against the Yorkists for the throne. A strong woman, she fought in several battles during the civil wars.[3] but was finally captured at the Battle of Tewksbury (1471) after her abortive attempt to keep the throne for her husband. She lived the rest of her life in exile in France.

## EDWARD LANCASTER (1453–71)

Only son and heir of Henry VI and Queen Margaret, shortly after his birth he was invested as Prince of Wales. Edward was killed at the Battle of Tewksbury where he was fighting alongside his mother.

## EDWARD IV (1442–83)

Eldest son of Richard Duke of York and a leader, with his three brothers, of the Yorkist faction fighting to take the throne from the Lancastrian Henry VI. After victories in various battles, Edward declared himself king in 1461. He secretly married a widow, Lady Elizabeth Grey who, although having noble relations, was landless. When this marriage was announced, it disappointed the expectations of some of his supporters, including his brother George, and his friend and mentor, the Earl of Warwick. The course was then set for a

---

[3] I have been careful to use the term "civil wars" for the conflicts in this period. The description "Wars of the Roses" was first coined by Sir Walter Scott in his novel Anne of Geierstein in 1829.

continuance of the civil war. In 1471, after finally defeating all possibilities of a Lancastrian revival, Edward ruled for a further twelve years and died in his bed.

## GEORGE DUKE OF CLARENCE (1449–78)

Third surviving son of Richard Duke of York. He fell out with his brother Edward and briefly changed sides, joining the Earl of Warwick and Margaret of Anjou in an attempt to return Henry VI to the throne (1470-1). Reconciled with his brother the king, he was later accused of treason and died mysteriously in the Tower of London.

## RICHARD DUKE OF GLOUCESTER (1452–85)

Twelfth of thirteen children of Richard Duke of York and Duchess Cicely. Richard of Gloucester was a stalwart supporter of his brother Edward and fought bravely for the Yorkist cause throughout the later wars. Immediately after his brother's death he took the throne as Richard III, but under questionable circumstances involving the deaths of his two nephews, the eldest being the legitimate heir Edward V.

## RICHARD NEVILLE (1428–71)

Earl of Warwick and Salisbury, he was one of the prime movers of the Lancastrian/Yorkist wars. It was many years after his death that the title "Kingmaker" first found its way into print (1521). For eight years, Warwick supported Edward IV against various attempts by the Lancastrians to topple him from the throne, but he finally fell out with the king and threw in his lot with the Lancastrians, supporting their attempt to return Henry VI as king. For a few months, they were successful, until Richard Neville was killed at the Battle of Barnet.

## BARON JOHN WENLOCK (c1400/04–71)

English soldier, diplomat, courtier, politician, Lord Wenlock fought in six battles during the struggle for the throne, mostly on the side of the Yorkists, although allegedly he changed sides on occasion. He held numerous offices, most notably Lieutenant of Calais. In 1470 he switched from Edward IV to support Warwick and the Lancastrians; he escorted Margaret of Anjou from France back to England. He was another casualty of the Battle of Tewksbury.

## LORD ROBERT STILLINGTON (1420–91)

Bishop of Bath and Wells, and Dean of St Martin le Grande. He was Lord Chancellor on two occasions: 1467-70, losing the role when Henry VI briefly regained the throne, and then in 1471, on Edward IV's return, reappointed, only to be dismissed from office in 1473. Later in 1478 he was imprisoned for a few weeks as a result of his association with George Duke of Clarence. When Henry VII defeated Richard III at Bosworth in 1485, Stillington was immediately arrested and imprisoned for a while. In 1487, he was involved in the Yorkist plot to place the imposter Lambert Simnel on the throne and sent to prison again, where he died four years later.

## ANTHONY WOODVILLE 2nd EARL RIVERS (1440-83)

Brother-in-Law of King Edward IV, he was recognised as a bibliophile and religious zealot. He was an early patron of William Caxton and his translation into English of the *Dicts or Sayings of the Philosophers* was one of Caxton's earliest printed works (1477). Uncle and protector of the two princes in the Tower, he was captured by Richard of Gloucester and beheaded in Pontefract Castle in 1483 when Gloucester made his bid for the crown.

## MASTER ANDREW DYMMOCK

Anthony Woodville's attorney and administrator. He was one of the several executors of Earl River's will and a close companion, being described in the earl's letters as "a well-beloved friend". Dymmock was evidently trusted with many of Woodville's affairs.

## WILLIAM CAXTON (c1422–c1491)

Born in Kent and considered as the father of English printing, he was originally a mercer and a diplomat while living in Bruges, a great centre of trade and artistic endeavour in the fifteenth century. Printing techniques had been practised in the German lands since Meister Gutenberg (1400-68) created a mould which allowed the manufacture of any quantity of type, uniform in all respects (c1438). Excited by its possibilities Caxton visited Cologne (1471) and brought back a press to Bruges (1473) where he printed his first book, his own *Game of Chess*. He brought the art of printing to England in 1476 and set up his print shop in Westminster. Between 1473 and 1490 he produced many famous works, including his own *History of Troy* (1473) and *Le Morte D'Arthur* (1485).

## WYNKYN DE WORDE (d1534)

A master printer born in Alsace he possibly came across to England with Caxton in 1476. He is credited with not only improving the quality of Caxton's printing techniques but also moving away from the patronage of noblemen. He achieved this by creating many less expensive books on an increased range of topics for a wider circulation. He published more than four hundred books, including some for children.

## MARGARET DUCHESS OF BURGUNDY (1446–1503)

Sixth child and third daughter of Richard Duke of York and sister of King Edward IV, Margaret of York married Charles the Bold of Burgundy in 1468. She was a patroness of the arts, and greatly encouraged William Caxton, both as a writer and printer. During protracted quarrels between France, England and Burgundy, she remained a staunch supporter of the House of York.

## HENRY RICHMOND 1457–1509

Son of Margaret Beaufort and Edmund Tudor, he was a descendant of Edward III's son John of Gaunt and had a slim claim to the English throne through the Lancastrian line. He spent thirteen years in exile in Brittany. In 1485, aided by the French and unopposed, he landed with an army in Milford Haven and went on to defeat Richard III on Bosworth Field. After his coronation, Henry VII married Elizabeth of York, daughter of Edward IV and the warring Houses of Lancaster and York emerged as the House of Tudor.

### JEAN DE WAURIN (c1398–c1474)

A Burgundian nobleman, politician, soldier and chronicler, his extended title was lord of Le Forestier of the family of Artois. He was present at the Battle of Agincourt (1415) and was a trusted ambassador in Philip the Good's court. Waurin visited England in 1467 where he became acquainted with Richard Neville. He had already commenced his major literary work: Recueil des croniques et anchiennes istories de la Grant Bretaigne, a large collection of stories of Great Britain from 688-1471. Four volumes of his first version appeared around 1444. The final manuscript occupies six volumes and remains in manuscript form

### DUKE FRANCIS II OF BRITTANY (1433–88)

He spent most of his reign in conflict with France while seeking to maintain Brittany's independence. Between 1471–84 he became involved in England's civil wars when, for thirteen years he sheltered the Lancastrian exile Henry Richmond in his chateau at Suscinio. In 1484 he supported Richmond with money and ships to make the earl's first, but unsuccessful invasion of England in a bid for the crown.

### PIERRE LANDOIS (1430–1485)

A powerful politician in the Breton court of Francis II, Landois did his best to thwart Henry Richmond's invasion of England in the earl's bid for the crown (1485). Landois agreed to capture

Richmond and return him as a prisoner to England in return for Richard III's support for Brittany against Charles VIII, King of France. Recognised as tyrannical, during his life Landois made many enemies and was finally captured by the French. Under torture he confessed to his crimes and was hanged.

## JOHN DE VERE 13th EARL OF OXFORD (1442–1513)

A soldier and commander of forces on the Lancastrian side during the English civil wars. He allegedly was the cause of the Earl of Warwick's defeat at Barnet from where he fled to Scotland. For the next ten years, along with piracy in the Channel, he began to mount several abortive campaigns against King Edward IV. He was eventually caught and imprisoned in Hammes Castle, Calais, from where he tried to make a spectacular escape by jumping from a tower window into the moat. Eventually escaping, in 1484, he made his way to join Henry Richmond and supported the earl's invasion of England. He fought bravely at Bosworth and became one of the most important men in Henry VII's court.

## LADY MARGARET BEAUFORT (c1441–1509)

The daughter and heiress of John Beaufort, Duke of Somerset and mother of Henry Richmond. In 1455, she married Edmund Tudor, Earl of Richmond and half-brother of Henry VI. Throughout her life she was a powerful advocate for her son and was instrumental in his successful bid for the crown, his marriage to Elizabeth of York and the eventual establishment of the House of Tudor. She was also a patroness of the arts and commissioned an early work of French romance from William Caxton, *Blanchardin et Eglantine* (1483).

# References

There are many excellent books on the period covering England's civil wars in general and those specifically concerning individual historical figures. Much has been written about the main protagonist in *Rogue Malory* and for the clearest demonstration of the "real" Malory, Peter Field's *The Life and Times of Sir Thomas Malory* (D.S. Brewer, Cambridge, 1993) provides a focussed and detailed view of this opaque individual. Also helpful was T.J. Lustig's *Knight Prisoner: Thomas Malory Then and Now* (Sussex Academic Press, 2013). For Caxton's printed version of *Le Morte D'Arthur*, I used the Penguin Classic edition: Sir Thomas Malory, *Le Morte D'Arthur*, 2 vols (1969; repr.1986) with modernised spelling and punctuation.